PRAI̧

LATE BLOOMER

"Eddings's latest romance is evidence of the author's own blossoming, as she uses Opal's and Pepper's individual struggles and stark personality differences to explore important discussions about mental health and neurodivergence that don't feel out of place . . . An endearing, emotional love story."

—*Kirkus Reviews* (starred review)

"Mazey Eddings's writing is authentic, emotional, and intensely romantic! To me, it's like a Taylor Swift song in book form."

—Ali Hazelwood, *New York Times* bestselling author

TILLY IN TECHNICOLOR

"A wildly fun travel adventure, poignant celebration of neurodiversity, and swoon-worthy romance all at once, *Tilly in Technicolor* is an unforgettable YA debut. It will leave you laughing, making heart-eyes, and running to add anything Mazey Eddings writes to your shelf. I loved every bright, colorful minute with Tilly and Ollie!"

—Kaitlyn Hill, author of *Love from Scratch*

"So freaking cute. *Tilly in Technicolor* will have you aching with love for these characters while swooning at their awkward adorableness together. I want to hug this book to my chest."

—Chloe Gong, #1 *New York Times* bestselling author of *These Violent Delights*

THE PLUS ONE

"I don't know how she does it, but somehow every book Mazey Eddings writes becomes my new favorite. It's impossible not to fall in love with Jude and Indira, both individually and as a couple. *The Plus One* is deliciously tropey but also raw, honest, psychologically rich—and scorchingly hot."

—Ava Wilder, author of *How to Fake It in Hollywood*

"This is a must-read for fans of Eddings, filled with moments of comedic relief and steamy, intimate scenes."

—*Library Journal*

LIZZIE BLAKE'S BEST MISTAKE

"Steamy scenes and smart writing will keep you wanting more."

—*USA Today*

"Joyful, voicey, sex-positive."

—*BuzzFeed*

"Eddings's second novel is an unconventional and messy love story brimming with steamy scenes between the instantly attracted duo, and has a raw wit that will leave readers cackling."

—*Booklist*

A BRUSH WITH LOVE

"Eddings's debut is equal parts hilarious and heart-wrenching . . . A poignant debut that will put a smile on your face."

—*Kirkus Reviews*

"Eddings's prose will hook you from page one."

—*Paste*

Well, Actually

A NOVEL

MAZEY EDDINGS

ST. MARTIN'S
GRIFFIN
NEW YORK

First published in the United States by St. Martin's Griffin, an imprint of St. Martin's Publishing Group

EU Representative: Macmillan Publishers Ireland Ltd, 1st Floor, The Liffey Trust Centre, 117–126 Sheriff Street Upper, Dublin 1, DO1 YC43

www.stmartins.com

Library of Congress Cataloging-in-Publication Data

Names: Eddings, Mazey, author.
Title: Well, actually : a novel / Mazey Eddings.
Description: First edition. | New York : St. Martin's Griffin, 2025.
Identifiers: LCCN 2025006225 | ISBN 9781250333315 (trade
  paperback) | ISBN 9781250397348 (hardcover) |
  ISBN 9781250333322 (ebook)
Subjects: LCGFT: Romance fiction. | Novels.
Classification: LCC PS3605.D35 W45 2025 | DDC 813/.6—dc23/
  eng/20250317
LC record available at https://lccn.loc.gov/2025006225

Our books may be purchased in bulk for specialty retail/wholesale, literacy, corporate/premium, educational, and subscription box use. Please contact MacmillanSpecialMarkets@macmillan.com.

First Edition: 2025

10 9 8 7 6 5 4 3 2 1

Hot Girl /hAHt gurl/ *n.* **1.** a state of being irrelevant of appearance, gender identity, or age **2.** a mindset found at the intersection of empowerment, enthusiasm, anger, freedom, excitement, defiance, and happiness

(from the personal dictionary of Mazey Eddings)

To all the Hot Girls, especially those that rise to the occasion when men need to be taken down a notch.

And to Megan and Serena, the hottest Hot Girls I know.

Content Notes

Hello, dearest reader,

We meet again! Unless, of course, this is your first time with one of my books, in which case, welcome! While this romance is rompy, goofy, and fairly irreverent, please be aware that the following are present/discussed in the novel:

- Internalized biphobia
- Workplace abuse
- Toxic masculinity and internalized misogyny
- Grief after loss of a loved one

As always, I've done my best to handle these topics with nuance and compassion. Please take care of yourself while reading.

All my love,
Mazey

Well, Actually

Chapter 1

I ALWAYS EXPECTED MY CAREER WOULD REVOLVE LESS around wieners than it does.

I assumed there would be *some* wieners, of course (more euphemistically, less the ingested type), but as I finish my fourth hot dog of the day, sliding it down my gullet along with any dignity and self-respect I may have had, say, a year ago, I'm reminded that assumptions don't pay the bills and when your hard-hitting journalism career (read: clickbait-centric joke of a job) asks you to eat hot dogs with B- to D-list celebrities for social media videos, you don't ask *Why?* just *How many?*

"Do you have a favorite cheese?" I ask Harry O'Connell, an Irish keyboardist of an up-and-coming band called Tea Time Tantrum.

"I feel like it's rather basic, but I'd have to say cheddar." He flashes a cheeky smile, his eyes so blue they make me blush.

Which also makes me feel old because he's only twenty-one and I'm a haggard twenty-seven navigating life without health insurance or a clue.

"Would you also say you're a Kraft Single ready to mingle?" I volley back in my deadpan, dead-soul voice that got me this job of "acting" miserable on the internet while talking to beautiful people.

Unfortunately, my stupid joke doesn't land. Not even in a way that we can turn into a "Hot celeb stares in disbelief and confusion at Eva Kitt's ridiculous question" that garners us shareable moments. Instead, Harry looks at me with an expression that's equal measures pained, confused, and blank, and I'm left wondering if I should take up a religion that believes in confession and repentance just so I can be absolved of how fucking pathetic this all is.

After a reset and replaced hot dogs we have to eat half of for continuity purposes, I hit him with, "We'd be Gouda together, don't you think?"

Prepared for the final joke, Harry doesn't give a truly honest reaction, but he's a good sport, shock and humor playing out in spades across his handsome face. It's a performance convincing enough that when he looks me in the eyes and says, "Don't toy with me if you aren't serious. You might just break my heart if this is a joke," I know viewers will eat it up and spread wildfire gossip about us.

"That's a wrap," Aida, my producer/guardian angel/best friend, calls after I take the last bite of my room-temperature weenie.

This is the extent of my love life: lukewarm hot dogs under

glaring studio lights, some contrived flirty banter with a guy too young for me, and us hugging briefly at the end as we lie about how much fun we had chatting, then parting ways forever . . . Or until his career stagnates and he's scheduled with me again to respark rumors around our flirtatious interview.

How shocking that I walk home alone.

Well, not fully alone. Aida keeps me company for the shared blocks of our commutes, her to Hell's Kitchen, me to the Lower East Side.

"That went really well, I think," she says, more to herself than me, as she furiously types an email on her phone, responds to a text, and somehow manages to post a flawless selfie to her story, finding the only slice of sunshine on this dreary October day, the rays highlighting her light-brown skin and the smattering of freckles across her nose so she looks like some sort of ethereal creature. The woman is the blueprint of the hustle, and that includes knowing her angles. "He was a great guest. We'll push this one hard on socials. I think there were a lot of meme-able moments in there."

"Yeah, some real disruptive journalistic investigation." My voice is as dark as the questionable puddle I accidently splash through while crossing the street. "Can't wait for my Pulitzer."

Aida rolls her eyes. "Your dedication to groundbreaking news and truth telling was cute when you had student loans to live off, but maybe tone down the angst. We're getting paid to create this fluff. Relatively decently, I might add."

I scoff but let it go. My paycheck would be objectively

comfortable in a small Midwestern town, but in New York, it makes splurging on silly little treats—which, granted, is a daily self-care measure in the form of Diet Cokes and lattes—come with a splash of financial panic. Just enough to keep things spicy.

We both chugged through college and grad school with the naive idealism afforded to students, but real life kicked us in the teeth as soon as we got a glimpse of our debt-repayment plans. She's handled it with a much stiffer upper lip than I have.

My listlessness must be palpable to Aida, because she grabs me by the shoulders at her subway stop, giving me a little rattle before smooshing my cheeks between her palms and placing a rough kiss to my forehead.

"Everything's okay," she says, making me hold her gaze as she gives me another shake. "Satirically interviewing low-level celebrities over hot dogs wasn't your dream career . . . so what? You're at least in the field you want to work in, even if it's a different beat."

I go to argue, but she cuts me off.

"You don't have to have it all settled and perfect. Life marches forward regardless of your plans, babe. Soundbites is a decent media outlet, one you could work your way up in to start covering topics you actually care about. Plus you have your column thingy. That's growing, right?"

I nod, deciding to spare her the bleak reality of my latest creative endeavor. I started posting a recurring column on a platform called Babble after reading about some frenetic twenty-year-old whose writing career took off on the site from her pieces about living with ADHD. The app basically gave blogging a Gen Z facelift, merging the best parts of Pinterest, Reddit, and Twitter (in its golden age). The content runs the gamut from aesthetic pics to current events, with plenty of shitposts in between.

I put out my column, "Unlikeable," weekly with updates in digestible segments on women's issues ranging from legislation to pop culture with a fair amount of international analysis too. While most news impacting women ranges from bleak to downright disgraceful of late, I try to end every piece with a touch of optimism—glimmers of humor and hope wherever I can.

It did well at first, gaining about four hundred subscribers in the first few weeks—admittedly modest by many standards, but I was shocked—and I stupidly started fantasizing about what it could become: maybe adding an audio component where I interview authors and activists. Have comedians write special guest posts until I top the engagement charts. Earn sponsorships and monetization deals while having my choice of freelance gigs for all my dream publications.

But it stagnated and is now on a downward trend. Any engagement I get, especially from screenshotted snippets I cross-post to other social media platforms, is filled with men familiar with my role on *Sausage Talk* taking to the comments and asking me to deepthroat a myriad of phallic-shaped foods.

"Stop acting like all your dreams need to be manifested before you've even had a chance to strive for them," Aida scolds.

"Stop being so reasonable, it's killing my vibe."

She smiles, giving my cheek a light smack. "Eva Kitt, you're the next Anderson Cooper, I can feel it. You're already halfway there with your hair." She fluffs my platinum-bleached tresses.

I roll my eyes, face twisting into a sour grin. I'm delusional, but not *that* delusional. "Whatever you say."

"That's the dispassionate spirit! See you later, dickhead." She jogs down the stairs to catch her train.

Ducking my chin against a sharp autumn breeze, I trudge the remaining blocks to my building. I huff up the five flights to my matchbox-sized apartment, stripping off my scarf and coat and dropping them to the floor as I flick on all the lights.

My place, which at one time felt significant and special to early-twenties-me, is sad and pitiful in the tepid October evening light. The popcorn walls are stale gray, a color that artfully reflects my sense of self, and my hand-me-down furniture isn't as quaint as it once was. When you're *nearing* thirty, without the automatic confidence boost of fully *being* and *embracing* and *loving* thirty, your thrifted, cigarette-and-vanilla-scented velvet green couch isn't the hipster, art-nouveau centerpiece you thought it was.

I've technically lived alone in my cramped one-bedroom since college, but it's only within the past year or so that I've actually felt *lonely*. Those first few years after graduating were filled with a restless hope shared among my friends, a stream of them crashing on my couch for months at a time as they waded from one situation to another until they found their footing.

I didn't even pretend to be annoyed at having squatters. I loved coming home to Donna stretched out on my carpet, crystals and tarot cards flung around her as she'd excitedly tell me about an energy shift or new reading for the day. Or Ray with a drama-filled Grindr incident he'd relay over mouthfuls of takeout. Even Aida had a not-so-put-together phase of unemployment before Soundbites where she'd alternate between manically cleaning my tiny apartment and moping on my couch. Despite her cloud of restlessness, every night ended up having a giddy, slumber-party feel for the six months she stayed with me.

But Donna migrated upstate where the energy was clearer, and Ray truly found The Ones and moved to Queens with his throuple and some sourdough starters, and Aida worked her way up to media producer, eventually getting me a writing gig for the celebrities and entertainment section—which was supposed to be temporary—that somehow morphed into me shoving dick-esque foods in my mouth and outwardly displaying my misery for laughs.

But even as my friends stepped into adulthood without me, it felt okay. I always had a relationship, or at least a situationship, to fill my apartment with noise and company.

Lana, who I started seeing around the time Aida got her own place, was great. The love of my alternate-universe life. She wasn't a believer in monogamy, and while I tried my best to be chill for the eight months we dated, my ugly jealous streak didn't play well with an open relationship. We dragged out our breakup for months of emotionally charged hookups, but she eventually moved out west, leaving my heart a bit bruised and my booty call-less.

Cal was next, a finance bro who I wasted over a year on. But still, even an annoying talking head in my apartment droning on about crypto and his AI "art" felt more comfortable than being alone with my thoughts for more than a few hours.

Then there was sad-boy Dom, and musician Tyler, and fashion designer Lisa, all burning bright for the first few months of dates and texting, then fizzling out as the newness withered and the reality of my sarcasm and emotional detachment became far less charming and much more draining.

Now, my friends are outpacing me in adulthood with their fulfilling careers and relationships while my love life is as dry as burnt toast. I don't even have a cat to blunt my loneliness. Marinating in my patheticness, I change into my sweatpants, burrow into a nest of blankets, and pour a glass of prosecco.

And another.

Oops, and a third because in this economy I can't afford to waste leftover bubbly, and I have far too much class to mix the flat leftovers with orange juice tomorrow morning.

Nothing pairs as well with a tipsy Friday night in as much as a social media doomscroll. Lab rats probably have greater resistance to stimulus than me at this point. The algorithm, which usually shows me unhinged shit posts and soup recipes, has pivoted to videos of men talking about how to be a supportive partner and offering practical examples.

While I don't, by principle, enjoy seeing men inflate their egos further (or talk in general), these content creators seem to offer genuinely helpful advice and action items to support a significant other, so I don't feel disdain quite so acutely as I usually would.

And then, I get the jump scare of all jump scares.

Him.

Dark, wavy hair. Piercing gray eyes and offensively thick lashes framed by tortoiseshell glasses. A jawline that could tempt a nun to sin and a rumbly voice you can't help but imagine between your thighs.

Gorgeous and he damn well knows it.

Rylie fucking Cooper.

I've worked hard over the years to train my algorithms not to show me this asshole despite his prevalence and ever-growing fanbase, but the universe is a messy bitch that loves disrupting my peace of mind.

Rylie Cooper has built a platform on the fallacy that he's the prophetic one to guide men out of toxic masculinity. This successful long con has earned him a heavily sponsored and well-listened-to podcast and over one million followers worshiping his hollow gospel.

The hypocrisy is unmatched.

I've always been the type of person to poke a bruise, press my tongue to a cavity, just to see how much I can make it hurt, and obsessively watching his videos over and over again when they pop up is no different, the rage growing hotter with each caress of his deep voice. This time, like most times, he's talking about what makes a man a good partner, particularly in bed. As if this discarded foreskin of a person has any clue.

"If this describes your man," Cooper starts in his low, sensual voice, holding a teeny-tiny bedazzled mic up to his perfectly formed lips, "he's not the man for you."

He launches into a spiel of poignant—if not obvious to actively dating women everywhere—reasons to be wary of

certain behaviors, a floating notes app list greenscreened behind him. My blood starts to boil at the final three points.

"If he's dedicated to a frat to the point that he refers to
other men not biologically or familially related to him as his
blood brothers, run." He levels a devastating look at the camera, humor glinting in his eyes. "And if you've had the unfor-
tunate experience of being in said frat house, run to a clinic
that can immediately test you for communicable diseases."

He pauses for half a second with perfect (fucking gag me)
comedic timing. "If you try to tell him before sex or during
foreplay what you really want, and he waves you off like he
knows all that, then is six inches to the left, he's not the man for
you. Do not return to his bed." There's an almost-imperceptible
cocky tilt to his lips, like this is a problem he's never created.

"And if you have real feelings for him or he says he has
real feelings for you, then he ghosts you, he is, most definitely,
not the one for you. Protect your peace, delete his number."
This one is delivered with raw sincerity, a stunning good guy
acknowledging the plight of so many women.

What a crock of horse shit.

This is coming from the man whom I dated for about two
months in college, an experience so awful, he scarred my love
life for eternity. He is the archetype of a dirtbag and it makes
me sick to my silly little stomach that he's seduced the world
into thinking he's the patron saint of nice guys.

My drunken fingers take over, and I'm hitting "stitch" before I can even worry about the fact that I've never used the
feature before.

Cooper's video cuts off as he advises viewers to not return

to a fumbling man's bed, and my skeptical reflection stares back at me, lip curled and one dark eyebrow raised, my blond hair as icy as my attitude as I hit record. I keep it together for point-two seconds before bursting out laughing.

"I'm sorry," I say through a snort. "But that video is pretty hilarious coming from the biggest fuckboy I've ever met." I cackle again, then let out a steadying breath through pursed lips. "Either Rylie Cooper is dabbling in extremely personalized satire, or he knows his pretty privilege will allow him to get away with lying to you all." I laugh again. "To fuck around is human, to find out is divine, so allow me to shed some light on the truth of who he is."

I'm unreasonably happy that my deep red lipstick I put on for shooting earlier today survived my drinking, because I am fucking *feeling* myself as I cock a dangerous smile at the camera.

"This guy"—I make a mental note to edit in a picture of Cooper at this spot—"took me on a handful of dates in college, filled with at least half a dozen red flags, mind you. Our relationship"—I throw in some aggressive air quotes with my free hand, my long, almond-shaped nails painted a dark green, adding extra drama to the movement—"culminated on the night he told me he had feelings for me, then made me watch him play hours of shirtless beer pong at his frat's party. This three-pump chump then led me to his room with a mattress on the floor—nary a fitted sheet or pillowcase in sight, I might add—then finished up what might be some of the most artless intercourse known to human history in about twelve seconds. What an amazing first time for me, one for the diary, for sure. He ended this fairy tale by telling me he'd call me, only to ghost me like the cliché he is."

A swell of vindication bubbles through me as I pause, ready to deliver the final blow. I mold my words into an arrow and take aim.

"Worst of all," I say, staring into the camera like I'm holding his arrogant gaze, "he didn't make me come. Not even fucking *close*. In fact, he might be the laziest person in bed I've ever had the displeasure of sharing unfitted sheets with."

I smile, a winning, dazzling smile, as I close it all out. "So, while his warnings may ring true, Rylie Cooper is *also* not the man for you."

I stop recording, check the captions for the audio, and insert a few stickers and his picture to the video, thoroughly enjoying myself as spite makes me drunker than the alcohol. I add the song "Sweet Home Alabama" in the background to really seal the deal. And because in my heart of hearts I am nothing more than a troll, I tag it #TheCancellationOfRylie Cooper.

With a proud snort, I toss my phone to the side. No one is going to see the video and I don't even care. I average about two-hundred views anytime I post.

It bothered me for a bit that no one is interested in what I have to say if I don't have a wiener in my mouth, but after wading through some of the fucked-up comments on my *Sausage Talk* videos, it's almost nice to have a nonexistent audience on my personal accounts . . . At least, that's what I tell myself whenever I'm feeling surly and defeated at my plateaued career.

With another proud sip of prosecco, I turn on my TV and flick through some streaming apps before deciding on *The X-Files*. The noise lulls me into a drowsiness that's hard to find in silence, and I drift off, letting the TV lie to me that I'm not alone.

Chapter 2

I WAKE UP WITH A POUNDING SUGAR HEADACHE AND MY phone buzzing itself off my nightstand. Bleary-eyed, I drape my arm over the side of my bed and bat for my cell on the floor for a few moments before finally scooping it up. It's still vibrating with a stream of notifications, and a hum of anxiety that something isn't right wakes up my system. I blink a few times, my eyebrows notching in a frown as my screen fills with social media alert banners, many of them listing new followers.

I don't have a lot of followers on social media . . . at least I *didn't* nine hours ago, but my measly count has plumped up to a number that makes my eyes bulge, and there are—

Jesus Christ.

I jolt upright so fast my neck pops. I bring my phone an inch from my nose, then hold it at arm's length. My post from last night has seven hundred fifty *thousand* views and . . . oh damn, a really decent ratio of likes to go along with it?

My video starts playing on a loop, and a profound level of humiliation sinks into my bones that so many people now know I was railed to dissatisfaction on a frat-room floor-mattress. With shaky fingers, I click on the comments, eyes a bit unfocused as I scroll, afraid of what I might see.

The comments range from hilarious—this woman's evil cackle just cleared my skin, watered my crops, and blessed my autumnal harvest—to horny—Mother, I am kindly asking you to sit on my face—to laughably cruel—like not even kidding ur a fucking joke. women r so vindictive and emotional it's embarrassing fr.

But most of them, to my utmost horror, tag Rylie Cooper.

My pulse pounds in my palms as my thumb hovers over his name.

Has he made a comment? Posted a video response?

With a queasiness like I'm cresting a hill of a roller coaster, I click to his profile, letting out a long sigh of relief when I see that he hasn't posted any new videos. I scan a few of the thumbnails, frown deepening as I scroll. It is truly a crime that someone so abysmally cliché is also so good-looking. His crooked smile moves along a spectrum from goofy to downright wolfish depending on the post, gray eyes hooking you in and pulling you under. But the one thing that's consistent, even through a screen, is that the man seems to radiate a genuine type of joy and pleasure in what he creates.

I click on a thumbnail featuring him and a woman laughing . . . accidentally. Not out of any sense of obsessive curiosity and instant jealousy. I watch for a few seconds, wondering if this beautiful woman is his girlfriend when his low, rough voice cuts through.

"As a very huge thank-you for eight hundred thousand followers," he says, a glint of mischief in his eyes, "I've invited my little sister, Katie, to roast the hell out of me. Katie, take it away."

I see the resemblance immediately. She's younger than him, probably only eighteen or nineteen, but she shares his raven hair and enviable lashes. Her lips are fuller, though, and she wears them in an earnest grin as she says through suppressed giggles, "You were a breech birth and it shows. Even from the start you've done everything ass-backward."

Cooper tries to keep a straight face as she continues with a few more jabs—"*Euphoria* and *Succession* are your comfort shows, and your teeth look like they belong on an American Girl doll . . . You are basically a billboard of a psychopath."

He bursts with laughter, his glasses askew as he reaches under them to wipe his shining eyes. I feel my own lips quirk at the corners at the sound.

Oh no. Absolutely not. I slam my mouth back down into a scowl as I flick out of the video, scrolling back to the top of his page. I will not find goddamn . . . *merriment* from his content.

I'm about to tap out of his profile completely when I notice something that makes my stomach bottom out and little black dots float in my vision.

Rylie Cooper now follows me.

Fuck.

Okay. Well. That was definitely not the case last night. I'm a vain, obsessive creature and I would have noticed if someone with a blue checkmark was following me. No, this is new. And this means he's definitely aware of my video.

My phone buzzes with a call, and I shriek, tossing it like Cooper himself just caught me stalking his page.

Taking a few deep breaths, I process that it's from Aida, which is a huge red flag in its own right. Aida usually texts me like a normal person, or FaceTimes when it's something important like her cat taking a nap or when she's drunk and sappy. We email and GChat for anything *Sausage Talk* related.

A phone call only comes when it's work related and it's bad, bad news.

Shit. Okay. This is okay. I'm sure this is not at all related to the video. She's probably . . . wanting to get brunch. Or . . . or . . .

Fuck. This is definitely about the video.

I consider letting it go to voicemail, but I wouldn't put it past her to hop on the train and bang down my door if she gets the sense that I'm avoiding her. With a deep breath and my drollest voice, I answer, "Hey, bitch. What's up?"

"Don't you dare *what's up* me," Aida snaps. "Did you tell the world last night that you fucked Rylie Cooper?"

"Okay, that was *definitely* not the point of my story."

"And you're *definitely* missing the point of what I'm asking."

I try to think of something to say, but all that comes out is a tiny, pitiful whimper as my hungover brain tries to organize the past few minutes.

"Eva . . ." Aida hisses. "What the hell is happening?"

"I don't know," I whine, nibbling my thumbnail. The tip

cracks between my teeth, and I grip my hand into a tight fist. "Everything is happening so fast. I—"

"Okay, first things first: Did what you said actually happen or does Soundbites need to loop in legal for a potential slander case?"

"Legal?" Anxiety drenches my spine. "I did it on my personal account."

"Covering my PR bases here, babe," Aida says, her tone lacking patience. "Is it true?"

"I mean . . . yeah?"

"All of it?"

I throw up my hand as I scoff. "Well, I think he lasted more than three pumps. No more than six, though. The essential point still stands."

Aida doesn't even give me a courtesy snicker. "Eva, this isn't a joke. *Landry* is requesting we all hop on a call ASAP." She says our boss's name on a breath of fear. Panic curdles in my gut.

"About this?" I squeak.

"No, about the weather. Yes, this!"

Landry Doughright, Soundbites' founder and CEO, is brilliant and poised and everything I aspire to be. A well-respected journalist of her day, she's now lauded as making news and media more accessible and digestible to younger generations. I have a massive career-crush on her, and have been secretly praying for a meeting where I can wow her with my drive and convince her to give me a chance at more serious topics. Having to explain to her my drunken internet ramblings about a guy I dated six years ago does not top the list of topics I want to speak to her about.

"There must be some sort of employee protection against talking to your boss about your sexual history," I say, throwing off my sheets and pacing the limited floor space of my bedroom.

"I think it probably has more to do with you being a recognizable face of Soundbites and sparking a massive amount of controversy with a beloved social media personality and less about the fact that you're still bitter about not getting off six years ago." She makes it sound so rudimentary when she phrases it like that. "In fact, I am begging you to not mention your sex life at all on this call. No more four-hump-dump talk."

"Three-pump chump."

"Eva!"

"Fine! Sorry for speaking the truth!"

"I'm emailing you the link to the GMeet," she responds, her keyboard clacking in the background for emphasis. "Please, whatever you do, do not make this worse."

"You really know how to make a girl feel better in a crisis."

"Sorry I'm prioritizing my job and ability to financially sustain myself over your feelings. It must be hard not to be the center of everyone's universe. You can cry about it later."

"I really appreciate the apology, it's a good start," I say with as much false sincerity as I can muster.

Aida is so caught off guard that she actually does let out a surprised laugh that turns into a groan. "You're a dumbass. See you in a few minutes." The line goes dead.

Women supporting women, am I right?

I resume my pacing, my phone continuing to erupt with

notifications, a tiny bomb in the palm of my hand . . . Then again, I'm the one who blew up my life last night.

With a mortified moan, I drop to the floor, back pressed to the edge of my bed and head cradled in my hands as I try to untangle this mess. The reality of my history with Cooper trickles in, memories I haven't looked at closely in years.

We both went to Breslin University, a small liberal-arts college in upstate New York that produces a new class of pretentious forward thinkers each year who inevitably move to the city, making Manhattan the world's busiest small town.

It all started simple enough. Cooper was a year ahead of me, but we met in a humanities lecture his final semester. It wasn't a full class, but the professor was chill enough to not make us cluster at the front of the auditorium, and everyone spread out.

I claimed a seat near the back, next to a wall to lean on as I took notes. I was absorbed in the presentation on the history of botanical symbolism in feminist art of the ancient world when the auditorium door opened behind me, closing with a loud click and a whispered curse. The tardy student shuffled to the row behind me, and I rolled my eyes as he conspicuously rifled through his backpack, cursing again. A few seconds later, his chair squeaked as he leaned toward me, and I pursed my lips into a scowl in anticipation of the next disturbance.

"I get the vibe that you already hate me," he whispered, close enough that my deep breath was filled with the scent of him, peppermint and January wind. "But is there any chance I can borrow a pen and some paper?"

I turned my grimace on him, ready to make him cower

away with the force of it, but something about those earnest
gray eyes trapped me like a snare, blanking my brain as I
took him in. Cooper didn't wear glasses back then, and I
was hit by the full force of his looks, nothing softening the
blow. There was a lazy mischievousness in his slouch, hands
loosely resting on the back of the seat next to me, forearms
coated in a fine dusting of hair and a map of veins and lean
muscle.

His lips curled at the edges as he stared back, openly ad-
miring me, glower and all. Silently, I held out my paper and
pen to him. His gaze flicked to my offering, then back to my
eyes, a glint sparking in his like flint on steel. I'm sure he knew
then and there he had me.

It was only after he slipped the items from my grip that I
realized I was handing over my notes and only tool for taking them. At the end of the lecture, I gathered my backpack
in a rushed fog, needing to get some fresh air to unhaze my
brain. He stopped me, of course, gently touching my elbow as
I moved to walk down the aisle.

"I'm sorry if this is way too forward," Cooper said, that
glimmer of humor still in his smile, "but would you like to get
a mall massage with me?"

I gaped at him. "A . . . a massage?"

He gave me a loose shrug, smile growing. "I couldn't help
but notice that your shoulders looked very tense during the
lecture."

I was silent for a moment. "You want me to get a massage
at the mall with you?" I repeated incredulously.

That shrug again. "We'd need plane tickets to get an air-
port one, though I do agree they're of a higher caliber."

"You're weird," I blurted out. My face heated at calling such an objectively hot guy weird, but facts were facts.

He laughed as I scuttled away, calling out, "Maybe next week, then?" as I darted out the door.

It took three weeks of coaxing before I finally gave in to Rylie Cooper's bizarre form of charm.

I can still remember the creak of his lecture hall seat as he'd lean forward during presentations, the warmth that would flood me when he'd drape his arms on the back of my empty row, a smile in his voice and his breath on my cheek as he'd make some sarcastic remark or unhinged joke that would have laughter bursting out of my throat that I'd try to disguise as a cough when heads would turn.

Of course I gave him my number, and texting him was a similarly outlandish and addicting experience. It wasn't long before I was waking up to a good morning message and off-beat date invite that I'd decline, using the excuse of classes and also not wanting to set myself up to be featured on a *Dateline* special for fraternizing with him. I didn't have a lot of game back then, but even young and naive me could tell how much Cooper loved the chase, and I loved the thrill of being in the center of his crosshairs.

We quickly became friends. Granted, the kind of friends who primarily wanted to fuck each other, but I still liked the asshole. Started looking forward to his texts. Enjoyed spending time with him, eventually relenting and getting coffee after class, going grocery shopping with him at midnight.

But as fun and strange as he was, and as dazzled as I became by his attention, he was also moody, going radio silent for days, leaving me on read, being as cold as a marble statue behind me in a lecture while I waited with bated breath for him to whisper something in my ear. By March, he was missing classes frequently, and I'd spend the hour poised like a hopeful tripwire for the sound of him coming in late or sending me a message to explain his absence.

The more he pulled away, the faster I fell head over heels for him in that way that feels as natural as breathing when you're twenty-one and untaught and it's the first time anyone shows interest in you, then snatches it away. In a panic that I'd lost his attraction, I cornered him after a class he'd spent ignoring me.

"I'll go on a date with you," I'd said, trying to keep my tone even and bored despite the pounding of my pulse in every joint of my body.

I watched his solemn, pinched expression melt into that vibrant smile that made butterflies erupt in my stomach.

"You won't regret it," he'd said, shooting me a wink and sauntering out, my chest feeling like it would burst open from the wild, happy rhythm of my heart.

I sigh, tapping the corner of my phone against my forehead as I remember how banal the rest of our story is: the handful of truly terrible dates, the bullshit, the needy feelings I still admitted, the immediate ghosting that carried him to graduation.

What a fucking joke.

Another text pops through from Aida: LOG ON TO THIS CALL RIGHT NOW OR I WILL MURDER YOU IN THE MOST GRUESOME WAY POSSIBLE.

My pulse spikes, nerves tripping up and down my skin . . . But I still manage to text her back: That's such a sweet offer, thank you <3.

Rifling through my closet, I grab a sweater to throw on over my braless form and clip my hair back into what I hope is a chic, messy updo and not a ratty, greasy mess. As I wake up my computer and launch the meeting, my camera tells me I'm definitely in the latter category.

My shitty internet finally connects, and my thumbnail pops up with the others, Aida on the upper left, Landry on the right, and the disinterested expression of some white man I don't know next to me. I wonder if he's from HR . . . Oh fuck, am I about to be fired?

"Good of you to join us, Eva," Landry says, the slightest purse to her perfectly polished lips. I shift in my seat, pushing at my tangle of hair as I scan Landry's sleek and smooth black bob.

"Sorry for the delay," I say, steadying my voice, taking on the slightly deeper pitch I use for *Sausage Talk* segments. I don't want a powerful woman like Landry to smell my fear. "I was trying to get as firm a grasp of, uh, what's happening on social media as possible before we talked."

Aida cringes, but Landry surprises me, her perfect, icy pout pulling into a smile, not a wrinkle creasing her flawless skin. "Ah, yes. You seem to have had a fun time on the internet last night."

"A forgiving way to phrase it," the random man mumbles, disdain dripping from every word.

I let out an involuntary *meep* of embarrassment, scrambling for something professional and crisis-mitigating to respond with. I end up just choking on my spit.

"Eva, this is my son, William Doughright. He's been overseeing our European operation for the past several years, and is now integrating into North American operations."

"Nice to meet you," I say, not sure I mean it. He's handsome in a brutal type of way—closely cropped hair, harshly carved cheekbones, eyes the color of coal, and a sardonic curve to his brows. He's young, probably mid-thirties, but there's nothing youthful about the taut set of his shoulders and firm line of his mouth.

He continues to stare at me coolly. "Congrats on the, uh, integration," I say, needing to fill the awkward pause. The silence stretches so long, my skin prickles with it. I glance at Aida, but she's pinching the bridge of her nose.

"Eva," Landry says, voice soft but commanding, a knife wrapped in velvet. "Would you like to explain what's happening or would you rather we all continue to waste our time staring at each other?"

Right. Fuck. That's my cue. "I, uh, I'm sure you've seen the video by now since we're having this meeting—"

"A not-insignificant percentage of the population has seen your little video accusing one of social media's favorite personalities of being horrible at sex and hurting your feelings," William interrupts.

I flinch. "Yes. Unfortunately. I, er, I didn't intend for this to go so . . . so viral."

"And yet, here we are," Landry responds. My shoulders hunch, my feeble attempt at confidence shriveling into shame.

Aida's video snags my attention, and I glance at her. Slowly, almost imperceptibly, she sits up in her seat, letting out a calm, controlled breath, her eyes meeting mine. It's like a virtual hug, a slap upside the head, a reminder to get my shit together and fake all the poise I don't feel.

"I'm sorry that this video has inadvertently become associated with *Sausage Talk* and Soundbites as a whole," I say, voice firmer. "That was never my intention. Honestly, I had no intention behind this video besides an impulsive, drunken therapy session that I truly believed no one would notice."

"They've noticed," William says in that cold, flat voice of his.

"No kidding," I say back, catching us both off guard. He tilts his head, one eyebrow arching just a millimeter, encouraging me to continue like my snapping intrigues him. Something about that silent nudge of respect spurs me on.

"Everything I said was true," I continue. "I mean, as true as a person's completely subjective feelings about something that happened years ago can be. But we did go on some dates, we did hook up, it was terrible, he did ghost me. I know there's some concern about slander, but I didn't lie. And that's the long and short of it. I didn't plan this out, I didn't mean for it to blow up like this, and I definitely didn't mean for my employer to somehow be dragged into the mix of it. Again, I didn't really think anyone would see my video or care."

Everyone is quiet again, Landry's eyes boring into me with a calculating heat I can feel through the computer screen, while her son's cool expression sends a chill down my spine.

"Your intentions with the video don't signify," she says at last. "What matters is you've created a spotlight of attention on yourself, one that illuminates your segment as well. Our organization as a whole."

I hang my head. She's going to fire me for being a dumbass on the internet. Why does this end not feel more shocking?

"And we're thrilled to capitalize on it."

My head snaps up so hard my teeth rattle.

"*What?*" Aida and I crow in unison. My gaze flicks to hers, and she looks as bewildered as I feel.

"Which word did you not understand, dear?" Landry asks calmly, looking off to the side like she's reading an email, bored with our ineptitude.

"I mean, I have a working definition of all of them separately," I say. "But strung together in this context has me a little . . ."

"Shocked," Aida finishes, voice cracking.

"Shocked?" William's cool facade cracks for a moment like the word offends him. His gaze pivots to Aida, and even I start sweating from the intensity of it. "I would expect the talent to lack foresight, but I'd hope one of our head media producers would have better instincts than to be *shocked*."

Aida's expression shifts from bewilderment to defiance. "Excuse me—"

"I guess I'm hung up on the word *thrilled*," I interrupt, scared of the bloodbath that would happen if she finishes that sentence regardless of William being our new boss. Aida's favorite ranting topics are nepo babies and men, and William checks all her boxes. "I thought you were going to fire me."

"Fire you?" Now it's Landry's turn to look shocked. "My dear, we would be fools to do anything but utilize this excellent opportunity you've created for us."

My blank, balking stare doesn't earn me any further respect from Landry, and she tuts in annoyance.

"Eva, you are the face of a satirical celebrity interview segment," she says slowly like she's talking to an exceptionally dense child. (Me. I'm the dense child.) "That segment does fine but it is not a household name. It does not have steady subscribers. It is fun, fluffy filler on that little tab at the top of our website that says *Pop Culture*. Are you following me?"

I manage to close my gaping mouth and nod.

"Your guests are decreasing in status and value as a result of *Sausage Talk* being filler, thus perpetuating a stagnation that doesn't condemn your segment but certainly doesn't lend itself to much growth. The value of your videos is based on viewership," William adds, picking up the condescending cadence of his mother. How precious.

"Overnight," Landry continues, "you not only put your personal account front and center of said viewership—having them foaming at the mouth at this tasty little story that completely destroys the persona of a highly popular social media personality—but also, by association, *Sausage Talk*. Our engagement has spiked since this took off. We are going to use that spike for all that it's worth. Because that, my dear, is what we in business call an opportunity."

"Use it how?" My cheeks are on fire, spine crushed to dust.

William offers me a gleaming smile, all teeth, like his happiness expands as I grow more and more embarrassed. "As we speak, our people are reaching out to Rylie Cooper's."

"What the fuck for?" I cry, immediately slapping a hand over my mouth as I realize what I said to my boss. Aida makes a choked noise from her corner of the screen. "I'm sorry. So sorry," I rush out. "But . . . but *why?*"

William's glee is full force. "Because you're going to do an interview. A live, in-person interview . . ."

No. Please god *no*.

"With Rylie Cooper."

Chapter 3

I THINK I'M HAVING AN ANEURYSM. OR HALLUCINATING. OR was hit by a biker walking home yesterday and this is some deep, dank circle of hell because there is no way they're serious.

"We're serious," Landry says, like she can read my thoughts. Or maybe I spoke out loud. Hard to tell since I've lost all sense of mind, body, and spirit.

"But why?" I echo, stuck on that pesky little question.

William rolls his eyes but Landry laughs, a light, tinkling sound. "Because it will make great content, and that makes us money, my dear."

"Landry, are you . . . are you sure that's a good idea?" Aida asks, voice quiet. I could kiss her for that small kindness of challenging this terrible idea.

"Positive." Landry's black bob sways with her nod. "It was William's idea. He's been looking for new ways to invigorate our viewership. Then this perfect nugget fell right into our laps. We'll do the whole schtick. The hot dogs, bitchy Eva, Rylie can bring his bedazzled mic for all I care. What matters is we get them in the same room and we move quickly while we have our audience in a chokehold. There will be drama and banter while these two dig at this paltry hookup. Viewers will eat it up."

William looks so smug my gut lurches.

"Isn't this kind of—" I slam my mouth shut, scared to challenge this smart, accomplished woman whom I've always admired.

"Kind of what?" William says, something sharp and predatory in his eyes.

"Trashy?" I say the word softly, part of me hoping they don't hear me. Their silence indicates they definitely did, and I press on, trying to do some damage control. "I mean, I know Soundbites is hip and has that perfect balance between trendy topics and hard-hitting news, and I just don't want to distract from the latter."

William moves to speak, but Landry cuts him off.

"Miss Kitt," she says, delicate voice barbed at the edges, indicating she's only going to say this once so I better listen the fuck up. "News outlets do not exist without revenue. Revenue, in the age of internet real estate, does not exist without advertisers and consumers seeing those advertisements. You went on social media and got a huge segment of our target demographic's attention, and now they're salivating like hungry little dogs for more. I would be the world's worst businesswoman to think *anything* trumps the capitalization on that, whether it's earth-shattering reporting or some tawdry sex story. Beggars can't be choosers if they want to hit that bottom line."

My head spins as everything slips further out of control.

"I have the shareholder meeting to prep for," William says. "Are you okay wrapping this up solo, Mom?"

"Of course."

With a terse nod, William exits the call, leaving us to stare at each other.

"Let me guess," Landry says after a moment, tilting her head to the side as she studies me. "As a little girl, you dreamed of growing up and becoming a journalist. One of those *real* journalists with boots on the ground in conflict zones and delivering exposés on corporate greed and senators abusing the system. You watched *Gilmore Girls* and resonated with Rory and subsequently learned who Christiane Amanpour is and also made her your role model so you could be smart and clever whenever an adult asked you what you wanted to be when you grew up. You went to some prestigious college and got your expensive degree and expected the pieces to fall into place—the jobs and the beats and the exposure to outlets that would broadcast your voice far and wide as you brought truth to people."

I go very still, shame cracking my skin as she paints me by the numbers.

"You didn't grow up thinking your big break would be eating hot dogs and interviewing whatever mid-list celebrity is desperate enough for some coverage, and now you want to dig in your heels because you're too good for this."

"Perhaps we should . . ." Aida's protest is weak, and Landry makes a cooing sound like she understands the sting of her words but knows they're necessary. Maybe they are. Maybe I need a reminder of how pathetic my situation actually is.

"What I'm getting at, Eva," she continues, a genuine look of care on her flawless face, "is that the world is not kind to your hopes and dreams, especially those of women. The universe does not give a damn about your plans and your aspirations and any of the grueling work you put in to reach them. The universe is random and harsh and throws whatever it wants at you, and all you can do is make the best of whatever shitty hand that is."

Landry leans forward with a look so intense it feels like she's in the room with me, peering into my skull, plucking out every withered dream by the roots as she tells me the truth. "And sometimes, when you play what you think are your piss-poor cards, a miracle happens. A different force in the universe sees your effort, sees how hard you're working and, maybe, *just maybe*, that force conspires to throw you a bone at the end of the deal. Do you understand what I'm saying, Eva? Do you understand what might be at the end of playing this out?"

My lips part, thoughts swirling and tangling with ideas that seem too good to be true. "Are you saying—"

"I'm speaking in metaphors, dear, that's all." Landry lifts her dainty hands, palms out. "Oh, sorry to change topics, but before I forget—Aida?"

Aida sits up in attention, jaw clenched and eyes lined with worry. "Yes?"

"Did you hear that Howards in the investigative group is leaving next month? Apparently he got a job at CNN."

Aida's mouth opens and closes a few times. "I . . . uh. No. I hadn't heard."

Landry nods primly, eyes off the screen again and fingers dancing across her keyboard. "We'll need to find his replacement soon. Not that it has much to do with you, I'm just making myself a note. Didn't want to forget to spread the word to the production team. Lots of transitions being made as William gets situated behind the wheel; deserving employees moving up while we cull the deadweight. You know how these things go. Anyway."

Landry's eyes are back on me, steady and focused and glinting while blood roars in my ears. She nods, almost imperceptibly, confirming the existence of the tiny carrot she's dangling in front of me. "Soundbites is a family, a family that takes care of each other."

While there are few traits more toxic than a corporation referring to its culture as family-like, I tamp down my revulsion, holding her gaze, thoughts spinning and teeth gritting with a sudden hunger for that hinted-at opportunity.

"And families are made up of team players," Landry continues. "Are you a team player, Eva?"

I let out a choked grunt that hopefully sounds like agreement. Now doesn't seem like the best time to point out that *teams* are actually the ones made up of team players, and *families*, in the nuclear sense, are made up of genetically connected, emotionally scarred people doing their best not to strangle each other at any given time. . . .

I manage to give her a calm, cool nod. "I am."

Landry's smile is dazzling, teeth as perfectly white as the pearls roped around her neck. "Good. Then we'll see you at the interview."

Chapter 4

DEPENDING ON THE DAY AND THE INTERVIEWEE, A TYPICAL *Sausage Talk* recording requires me to eat anywhere from two to five hot dogs that usually sit like a brick in my stomach, my fingers smelling like ketchup and wiener water by the time the day is through. It all generally helps feed into my miserable persona for the segment.

But as I walk into the office for today's shoot with Cooper, there's a very real chance that I won't be able to stomach a single bite with the combination of nerves and bitterness that's been fermenting in me the past three days. But hey, if I puke on him during a live stream, it'll probably be great for views, which is all I'm good for at this point.

While all of this is coming together with miraculous speed, the last few days have been a sick and slow type of torture, each hour hitting a new milestone of views and comments on my video. The post left its ideal audience of righteously indignant women and started picking up steam with trolls and incels. While it genuinely makes me laugh that any of these men (and some women) think they can hurt my precious feelings with a predictable and derivatively scathing comment, I never anticipated being called various forms of *bitch* at such a rapid frequency.

But, for every horrible thing someone tries to say about me, there are five other strangers hopping in with clever responses and digs in my defense that take a troll down a peg or nine.

Cooper, for his part, has been surprisingly silent on the whole thing. The guy I knew six years ago severely lacked impulse control or any type of filter, so I have no doubt this tight-lipped response is because some ludicrously expensive publicity firm has fitted him with a muzzle while his public adoration and accompanying brand deals teeter in the wind.

I've seen speculation posts about a few sponsors cutting ties with his brand, which makes his agreement to do this absurd sham of a live "interview" fairly obvious. This is a publicity stunt on his part, plain and simple.

Swiping through the security gates of the building, I take the elevator to the basement where the *Sausage Talk* set is housed. When the segment first gained some online attention, there was talk of shooting at an actual hot dog shop or one of New York's countless corner stands, but the powers that be decided it was more cost-effective to give me a dank corner of a storage area perpetually dressed up like a 1950s soda shop where they could microwave us cheap weenies on demand. The glamor is staggering.

I throw my purse on (at) the rickety IKEA side table I use for hair and makeup, plopping in the foldable chair as I take in my dismal reflection.

The bags under my eyes are almost as dark as my brown irises, declaring loudly and proudly how little sleep and how much doomscrolling I've done lately. My mouth is pinched in a perpetual frown, and a lovely cluster of stress zits on my temple complement the grim look.

This just won't do.

I pull out my makeup bag, getting to work on concealer and foundation with the focus of an artist at her canvas, flicking on my cat-eye liner like an executioner sharpening her blade. I tousle my hair and paint my lips and groom my eyebrows until the woman in the mirror reflects the woman I want to feel like on the inside—cool, unflappable, a bit imperious.

All in all, hot as fuck.

I'm a lot of things—coarse, sarcastic, anxious, aggravating, aggravated, emotionally stunted—but vain tops the list and I'll own that sin with pride, wear it like a scarlet letter to match with my perfect red pout.

This wasn't always the case. Vanity is a vice I've worked toward and cultivated the past few years. As the depressingly average middle child with five high-achieving siblings, I spent most of my adolescence blending into the wallpaper. My dad remarried when I was nine, and my stepmom, Laura, already had three teenage boys from her first marriage who instantly became the sons my dad always wanted, their penchant for sports and the promise of scholarships to D1 schools absorbing all his attention and adoration. By the time I was eleven, my dad and Laura had moved on to having kids together—

twin girls who were perfect from their first breath—and I was deemed self-sufficient enough to manage my level of mediocracy while they cultivated the girls' beauty and brilliance.

It became standard practice, pushing me to the side. How could my mandatory chorus recitals or school-sanctioned art shows compete with Derek's track meets or the twins' pageants or Chris and John's tennis matches? I couldn't even be sad that my dad and Laura didn't show when it would have been far more painful for them to see me in my lackluster misery.

I went through college with a similar dullness, keeping my head down and praying that one day my ideas and thoughts would shine bright enough to earn me the recognition and worth that my siblings grasped so easily.

It wasn't until Cooper talked to me in that lecture of my junior year that I'd ever felt any type of attention, and some greedy part of me became an instant addict to the warmth of another person's interest.

But even after that short fling went to shit, I spent my early twenties dimming myself down, making myself as palatable as possible for the people I was dating in the hopes that they'd tolerate me enough to stick around.

They left me anyway.

I eventually realized—with a tremendous amount of consistent and exuberant hyping up from Aida and Ray—that Hot Girl isn't something someone is born as. Hot Girl is an armor you put on. An impenetrable fortress of makeup or dyed hair or fake nails or killer clothes or expensive perfume or any other bodily adornment that makes you feel fucking *good*. Powerful.

Hot Girl isn't a look or a style, it's a commitment to doing whatever makes you feel unstoppable in the face of life's fuckery. And I'll be damned if I am anything but my hottest possible self on today of all days.

The problem is (to my total mortification) I'm spiraling out with nerves about seeing Cooper again after so many years. Not only was my post-sex expression of feelings to Cooper the most morbidly embarrassing thing I've ever done—the past few days excluded—but I also did *not* take well to being ghosted.

It would be fair to say that I leaned deeply into the scorned-woman trope with some of the more, uh, colorful texts and voicemails I left him—ranging from pitifully vulnerable to unhinged rage. All I can hope is that he blocked me early and never received them.

But if that one-sided melodrama of a situationship wasn't bad enough, here I am, six years later, drunkenly dragging him on the internet and now having to soberly confront him like I've been carrying a torch this entire time. Not very Hot Girl of me, I'll be the first to admit.

"Well, fuck me, don't you look amazing," Aida says, punctuating her greeting with a wolf whistle as she comes up behind me. I give a humble little bow, locking eyes with her in the mirror. "We'll have to put a not-safe-for-work tag on the video with an outfit like that." Her hands fuss around my boobs and I bat her away, readjusting my admittedly low neckline.

I've layered an oversized red linen shirt over a black lacy bustier top that does wonders for my virtually nonexistent cleavage, bringing the upper half all together with a stack of delicate gold necklaces that force attention to my chest, and finishing the look with high-waisted, wide-legged trousers for an overall coastal-grandma-meets-slutty-vampire vibe.

"You're going for blood with this one, aren't you?" Aida's eyes are wary as she watches my Cheshire smile.

"Landry and William want views, and I'm nothing if not a dedicated team family fuckhead whatever," I say sweetly, leaning forward to clean the edge of my lip line with my fingertip.

"Beautifully put," Aida says with a frown. "I'll have HR add that to our onboarding pamphlet."

My smile grows more devious.

"Are you worried about your nipples?" she asks after a beat, making me blink.

"My nipples? What about my nipples?"

"That they'll pop out and bounce everywhere on a live stream."

My eyes ricochet between Aida's concerned expression and my tits. "I wasn't even slightly concerned about my nipples until you brought them up, thanks." I place a protective clutch on my boobs, like that'll save me.

Aida offers a skeptical shrug. Her phone dings, and her frown grows as she scans the message. "Rylie's on his way down," she says with a sigh, then levels a look at me. "I know Landry and William want drama, but I'm begging you to do that in the most drama-free way possible."

"I have no idea what you mean," I say, studying my nails. I painted them black to match the lace of my bra.

Aida ducks her head, forcing me to meet her stern expression. "You know exactly what that means, you little shit-stirrer. This is not a public execution or WWE smackdown. You're representing Soundbites here and he's trying to save his own sponsored ass, so keep it funny but civil, get the job done, and, for the love of god, stick to the script."

The "script" is a loose outline of a mutually-agreed-upon flow for the conversation. A few opening quips from me, banter, banter, hot dogs, banter, wrap it up on a high note with just enough zing and a hint of hope to keep tongues wagging and begging for another episode . . . which I refuse to even consider, but I'll cross that minefield when I get to it.

It's sterile and whittled down in a way that theoretically will not make this man cry using only my words and an artfully arched eyebrow on a live stream, but I'm not making any promises.

I open my mouth to say something sarcastic and not at all reassuring when the double doors behind Aida swing open.

And in walks Rylie fucking Cooper.

My heart lurches as my focus hooks on him—the loose, goofy confidence he exudes as he scans the room, absorbing all the energy and radiating it back like he's the goddamn sun. He smiles and nods at the people milling about, then his gray eyes lock with mine, something sparking in them as our gazes hold, his lopsided smile creasing his cheeks to reveal a single dimple.

To my absolute horror, my eyes take on a mind of their own, skimming down his body, bouncing first to the ground and then slowly making their way up. He's wearing dark jeans that are clearly infatuated with his ass and thighs, which have developed defined muscles over the years, and a navy crewneck sweatshirt that reads YALE GRANDMA. The hem of it lifts as he raises a hand to his hair—raking his fingers through the perfectly mussed locks—revealing a sliver of skin above his waistband, a faint line of hair centered between the ridges of his hip bones.

My breath catches, a sudden, frustrating heat sparking across my skin. It's only when his smile grows that I realize my damn mouth is hanging open. I slam it shut so hard I give myself a headache.

No. Absolutely not. I will *not* be undone by an ironic sweatshirt and an endearing smile. I fix my face into a brutal scowl.

He walks toward me with the confidence of a man who . . . Honestly, a metaphor is kind of superfluous. He walks forward with the confidence of a man, parking himself in front of me, hands shoved in his pockets and smile fading into a look that's nearly bashful as he searches my face. I pray my cheeks aren't as red as they feel.

"Hi," he says. His voice is softer than it is in his videos, still low and rough, but lacking the sharp edge. "I can't believe this is happening."

"Cooper," I respond with a brisk nod, laying brick after brick of coldness in front of me until there's a sturdy wall of ice. "Wish I could say it's good to see you, but . . ." I gesture vaguely.

The corner of his mouth twitches up toward a smile, but my glare scolds it back into a straight line.

He clears his throat, pushing his glasses up the bridge of his nose before ducking his head and dragging a hand across the back of his neck. "The feeling might not be mutual"—his gray eyes flick back to mine, a reckless spark glinting there that makes me furious—"but I genuinely am glad to see *you.*" He rocks back on his heels, letting his tripwire grin win out.

My heart stutters, then kicks into overdrive. It must be the rage that's making my pulse pound and heat lick along my skin. I make a show of looking over my shoulders, then lift out of my seat to glance over his before fixing him with a bland expression. "Don't think any cameras are rolling yet, Cooper. You can cut the simp act."

He laughs—a big, bold sound that vibrates through me, and my fingers grip the edge of my chair like I'll float away without something to hang on to.

"You're not going to make this easy on me, are you?" he says, humor roaming free across his face.

"Not for a second."

"Let's get a move on," William says with a raised voice, entering the room with effortless authority. He claps his hands, and the already bustling crew picks up the pace.

Cooper's expression shifts, jaw working like he has something important to say to me and he needs to taste different words before deciding which are right. I look away, attention landing on Aida, my safe spot.

"Let's get to places and setup," she says, ushering us over to the shiny chrome table.

I pull out one of the chairs, its hairpin legs creating a shrill sound along the tile that makes Cooper flinch. Satisfied at catching a whiff of weakness from him, I settle into the tufted vinyl seat, crossing my legs and situating myself on the sparkly green cushion.

Aida goes through a quick run of show, and I diligently ignore Cooper despite feeling his eyes on me. When an assistant sets down the hot dogs, I accidentally spare him a glance, and the intensity of his gaze makes my breath scrape my throat. I purse my lips, looking away again with an air of boredom that's the complete opposite of the swelling nerves popping in my chest.

"Any questions, Rylie?" Aida asks. "Do you feel all set? I'm sure you've done interviews like this before, so it's probably second nature."

I make a mental note to call her a traitor later for speaking to him with a voice of kindness and respect.

"I'm great, thank you so much," he replies, flashing that dimple. It prods at something feral in me, making me want to scratch it off his face.

"Great. Places, everyone," Aida calls.

"Glad the princess is settled. I'm all good too, thanks for asking," I grumble. Aida at least rolls her eyes instead of ignoring me. I'm surprised by the bark of laughter from across the table.

"Did you just call me *princess*?" Cooper asks, his grin lazy and dangerous.

"Yes. Does that offend you?" I ask, a hopeful lift to my voice. "Or would you prefer baby girl?"

He laughs again, eyes crinkling. "Princess will do just fine."

My lips curl but I force them into an acrid smile. "Whatever you say, baby girl."

Aida starts the countdown to our live, and Cooper shakes himself, slipping on the cool mask he wears in most of his videos. When Aida gets to three, she stops talking, ticking the seconds off on her fingers before pointing to me. I slip on my own facade, an apathetic expression not far off from my real self, and look at the camera like it's a tedious younger sibling.

"I'm Eva Kitt," I say without feeling or energy, my trademark vibe. "And welcome to *Sausage Talk*, where fun in the bun is guaranteed. We have a semi-special guest for today's meat and greet, and his name is . . ." The neon MEAT & GREET sign is lowered into frame, and I ignore it, making a show of checking my notes, thumbing through a few pages and running my finger across some lines. "Rylie Cooper. And he . . . he . . ." Slowly and with a thoroughly disenchanted energy, I rifle through more papers, letting the silence linger.

"I host a podcast about deconstructing toxic masculinity and post stupid videos on the internet," Cooper says, voice low, a smile in it. I drag my heavy gaze up to him. He adjusts his glasses, then plants his elbows on the table, resting his chin in the cradle of his hands. "You know a few things about the latter, right, Eva?"

My lips part, unprepared for the poke, but I recover quickly, scrunching up my face. "A podcast? Hmm. You host it, you said?"

"I do, yeah," he replies, eyes glinting. He leans back in his seat like he's settling in for some fun. Okay, asshole. Let's play.

"And people actually listen to it?" I'm in dangerous territory here with my own piss-poor number of subscribers to my creative endeavors outside of this stupid show, but I'm committing to the kill.

"They do." His smile grows, an air of challenge in his relaxed posture,

I sniff, raising my eyebrows and looking off. "Huh. I would never willingly listen to a man speak in my spare time, but that's just me."

Cooper guffaws, then laughs, but Aida gets in my line of sight off camera, William right behind her, both glaring at me. A substantial portion of our viewers are men, and I'd guess a huge chunk of Cooper's audience are women interested in what he has to say, so I'm undoubtedly not helping the engagement goal.

"Anyway." I glance back at my notes as if I don't have every word memorized . . . to use against him, of course. "It says here your social media presence has been described as a safe space for men too afraid to be on Pinterest. Was that always your goal?"

His lips quirk like I'm moderately amusing. I find myself having to look away from the catch of his stare, something scrambling in my stomach at the warmth I see there. "Well, actually, I don't think anyone's ever described my social media presence like that."

"I just did," I say, a heavy dullness in my voice, boredom in my eyes.

"Yes. Creating content that is somehow Pinterest adjacent for boys was always my life goal. If Maslow were alive, he'd write a case study on my self-actualization. Was yours to interrogate C-list social media personalities over hot dogs but treat it like the correspondents' dinner?"

"I've had some B-listers on here," I say, facade cracking as I jump to defense.

"Oh, I stand corrected. Barbara Walters is *shaking* with career envy from beyond the grave."

Blood rushes in my ears with a fresh wave of rage that he's so easily needling under my skin and he damn well knows it. This is my domain, my turf. I can't let him get the upper hand and control this conversation.

He reaches for his hot dog, lifting it for his first bite. My arm snakes out, and I grip his wrist, halting him with his mouth hanging open, eyes equally round with horror. I ignore the singe of heat from where my skin touches his . . . probably the same cosmic reaction of holy water burning a demon.

"Are you sure you should eat that?" I ask, holding his pewter gaze.

His eyes flick between me and the hot dog, and he clears his throat, a genuine thread of worry in his voice as he asks, "Why? Did you poison it?"

"No. Higher-ups told me I wasn't allowed." I frown. "But I just wanted to double-check you *can* eat it."

He lifts an eyebrow in question.

"You look like someone with a lot of food intolerances."

He makes a choking sound as I drop my hand from his arm.

He recovers, then takes an aggressively large bite of the wiener with a look that says *Ha! This'll show you!* But after a few chews and an attempt at a swallow, he starts coughing, little bits of bun sprinkling his plate. Avoiding the impulse to recoil at this meaty shower, I reach out and thump his back a few times, hard enough that his glasses skitter to the tip of his nose.

"Oh no, was the ketchup too spicy for you? I told them they should give you mayo."

He bats my arm away, face red as he sucks in a deep, unsteady breath. He rights his glasses and we stare at each other for a moment, his eyes narrowed, expression taut. And then he . . . starts laughing?

Why the hell is he laughing? The man should be crying.

"While the ketchup is definitely testing my delicate palate's bravery, the spiciest thing here is undoubtedly you, Kitten."

"Don't call me that." The words are out way too fast, way too intense, the stupid nickname from college rankling me in a way I don't want to analyze.

In common sense according to Rylie Cooper's warped brain, Eva Kitt transformed quickly to Kit-Kat, then Evil Kitten, and eventually just Kitten. I'd never had a nickname before—always plain Eva to a family trying to keep track of so many kids, and something about the way it playfully and endearingly rolled off Cooper's tongue used to make my stomach swoop and cheeks heat. Hearing it now, with six years and a dump truck of animosity between us, makes my skin prickle and jaw clench.

"Why not?" he asks with a pout.

"Because I don't play well with dogs."

"Ah, and we circle back to the sentiment that got us here," Cooper says, casually tilting his chair on its back legs and waving his half-eaten hot dog around the studio. "Are we finally going to address the elephant in the room?"

A drip of worry starts in my stomach, and my eyes flick to the camera for half a second, then back to Cooper. He isn't supposed to be this direct about it. We're supposed to coyly dance around the video and our lackluster history, make a few bland but quotable statements of no ill-will, then part ways without a backward glance.

But the man has the subtlety of a freight-train on a good day, so I tamp down my concern. This is just how he wants to play it, and I'll be damned if he sees me sweat.

"The elephant being . . ."

"Your glowing review of twenty-two-year-old me," Cooper says, a cheeky grin making his dimple pop. I scowl at it.

"Not sure I'd amend much for twenty-eight-year-old you," I say, giving him a chilly appraisal. "Except maybe add in the receding hairline."

To my utter delight, his hand darts toward his perfectly intact and outrageously full head of hair. My grin must be vicious, because he narrows his eyes before giving me a flicker of a smile and an almost imperceptible nod acknowledging my arrow hit its target.

"Well, that's what I want to change," he says.

"Change?" He's going off script. He's not supposed to go off script. He's absolutely *not* supposed to be leaning closer to me like that, talking in a low voice with a private smile like I'm the only one he wants to hear what he's going to say next.

"You said in your video you could think of half a dozen other red flags besides me—"

"Being selfish in bed."

He snorts, biting on his bottom lip as he stares into my eyes. "I was going to say being in a frat, but if you want to talk through a play-by-play of my performance I'm more than happy to. I'd love your constructive criticism and suggestions for future reference."

Heat sears through me but I roll my eyes. "In your dreams."

"I've certainly seen you there a time or two," he purrs, eyes making a quick and heated flick over me. The hunger in his words shocks me speechless, and his satisfied smirk tells me that's exactly what he was hoping for. "I want a do-over," he says, louder now, that unabashed grin back in place.

"A-a . . . *do-over*?" My face twists like I sniffed sour milk. Unfortunately, all I actually smell is whatever absurdly sexy cologne he's wearing. Something clean and tempting. Sunshine and sin. I grab my hot dog, aggressively ripping into a bite so the smell of ketchup replaces him.

"I want a chance to win you over. Win back your good graces," he says smoothly, gaze fixed on my mouth as he watches me chew. I make sure to add a few open-mouthed chomps.

"To win them back you'd need to have had them at some point," I growl through a mouthful, a thick piece of bun clogging my suddenly dry throat.

He laughs again, and the sound unlatches memories in me, those flirtatious moments in college where it felt like I won a prize every time I'd pull the sound from him. I hate that his laugh is genuine—nothing like the shallow chuckles I use in interviews, barely convincing anyone that I'm amused. *All* his laughs seem to be genuine, though. He's incapable of faking good humor.

What a fucker.

"Okay. Fine." His eyes crinkle as he continues to smile at me. "I want the chance to prove to you that despite all your evidence to the contrary, I'm actually not a bad guy."

I blink at him. "And I want to live solely off fun-shaped noodles and forget vegetables exist. Are we going to continue trading fruitless wishes?"

He searches my face. "I have a proposition for you," he says carefully.

I can't help my terrified glance to the cameras before landing on Aida behind them, who looks equally confused.

Get HR, I mouth to her. She snaps back into work mode, glaring at me as she jerks her hand in a signal for me to focus on Cooper.

"I'm asking for your time. That's all," Cooper continues, his voice a rough pull to my attention. My lips part as I stare at him, the intensity of his look, the tiny furrow between his eyebrows, the sincerity of his smile. All of it creates a building pressure in my chest. "A chance for me to prove I'm not the asshole you remember. Give me six dates to make it up to you."

"Fuck yourself." The words burst out of me in a laugh so sudden and violent I clamp a hand to my throat.

Cooper's eyes twinkle. "Stop being so charming or I might fall in love with you."

"Fuck yourself," I repeat, enunciating the words carefully this time. I keep forgetting we're live. There's no way I won't be fired after this. "I'm not going on six dates with you. I'm not going on *any* dates with you."

"Five dates," he counters, crossing his arms over his chest and leaning back in his chair again.

"None," I retort, mirroring his pose.

"Why?" Hurt flickers across his features. "Let me make it up to you. I honestly do feel terrible about how I treated you and I want to rectify it."

"If you're such a good guy like you claim, why do you need so many chances to do that?" I arch an eyebrow in a way that usually makes men shrink.

Instead, he leans closer, planting both palms on the table as he looks at me, mouth curling up in that uneven grin of his.

"That's how many dates we went on before. It's only fair I have an equal chance."

"We went on four dates," I say automatically, then steel myself against a cringe at how earnest and fucking factual I sound. His delight is indecent.

"Someone was keeping count. Core memories?"

"Only because I've had to outsource them to my therapist."

He tilts his head to the side, the skin around his eyes and mouth creasing with a bitten-back laugh. It's with a sharp jolt that I realize how close we are, that my chest is leaning across the table, my clenched jaw and pursed red lips only a few inches from his terribly nice smile.

"Fine," he says, gaze tracing my face, resting for a beat on my mouth before skimming back up to lock eyes. "The truth is, I want all the dates you'll give me because I'm terrified of you, Eva Kitt. And I know I'll need as many opportunities as I can get to shake off the nerves and show you a good time."

Despite my resistance, this pulls a smile from me, sharp and fast, a warmth searing through my stomach. I quickly school my features so the flash of my teeth portrays resentment instead of misplaced glee. "And what do I get?"

"Are seven dates of guaranteed fun not enough?"

"You guarantee disappointment and that's about all," I mumble, lurching away from him and collapsing back against my chair, crossing my arms to emphasize my surly pout. Somehow his smile only grows.

"Maybe so," he says, lifting his palms in surrender. "And you'll have every right to blast me for it. In fact, we can even debrief on my show after each one. Worst case, you get eight dates to analyze, rip apart, and very publicly explain how much I suck with up-to-date examples. I'm handing you material."

"What a gentleman."

He bows his head in false deference. When he looks back up at me, his eyes are sparkling. "But best case, you spend nine dates with someone dedicated to showing you an amazing time. And food."

"Good food?"

"Whatever food you want." He gestures broadly like a game-show host. "Your ten dates will be filled with it."

"Stop counting up," I snap. "You said six dates."

"Six dates. You've got yourself a deal." He grabs my hand, pumping it in agreement. I laugh, more from shock than anything, slipping out of his grip and smacking his arm away.

"And what if I just genuinely don't like you?" I say, watching as he slowly drags the fingertips of his left hand over the knuckles of his right. Something about the hint of control in the movement has my mouth going dry. "I don't like most people."

His eyes flash. "I love a challenge."

I glance again at Aida, and am horrified that William's joined her, staring at me with commanding force. He nods once, slowly and with authority, an exact mirror of his mom's during our video call. The barest hint of a promise.

Fuck. I want that job. Need it. If this is what it takes to get it . . .

But, god, Cooper's such a shithead—one who isn't hard to look at, I'll admit, but a shithead nonetheless. And just the idea of being forced to spend time with him has me wanting to rip out my hair. And his.

He must sense my weakening resolve, because his voice drops to a coaxing rumble. "Come on, Eva. What have you got to lose?"

"My dignity and self-respect." My gaze flicks to William and Aida once more, but Cooper's laugh calls me back.

"Give me six dates to try and turn those red flags green."

"A man acting halfway decent for a handful of dates isn't the triumph you're trying to paint it as," I reply carefully, trying to find a loophole, an escape route as he backs me further into the corner.

"It isn't," he says, face turning serious. "And I won't pretend it is. But I also don't do anything halfway anymore." He says it like a vow, and my heart kicks in response. "So use me, Eva. Make an example of me. Help me show people what it's like to work for it."

There isn't a trace of double meaning or lewdness in his face, but his words send a shiver down my spine, heat curling low in my belly, a dark promise that washes over me and sends my brain spinning in a very wrong direction.

"And if you don't succeed?" I whisper.

"Well, I imagine you'll have a very fun time roasting the hell out of me for living down to your expectations." His smile is slow like honey, and I'm a fly.

For a moment, the world fades, no William or Aida or cameras or live viewers. All that's left is the trap of Cooper's gaze. I refuse to be prey.

He wants to play with fire? He'll get an explosion instead.

He'll get the worst of me. I'll get exposure. I'll get a new job. I'll get material for my Babble platform and articulate what a run-of-the-mill asshole Rylie Cooper is to his own listeners on his own show, adopt a few loyal followers along the way.

I'll bring this man to his goddamn knees.

It's a long game for revenge, but I can be as brutally patient as it takes.

"Six dates," I say slowly, a challenge in my voice. I lean toward him again, and he meets me across the table. "You've got a deal."

"You won't regret this," he says, voice confident and steady. His smile is incandescent, but my glare is stormy enough to block out his light.

I let out a clipped laugh. "Oh, baby girl, I already do."

As if following a silent cue, a *click* travels through the room, everything stilling for a moment. I scramble to get my bearings, to remember that all this is for an audience, to figure out what's happening now. What I just agreed to.

Then William's clear voice calls out, "Well . . . that's a wrap."

The crew jumps into action, and I think I hear Aida say something along the lines of *what the fuck* over the noise.

Cooper's attention turns to the hustle around us, but a need for answers pierces through me. My hand darts out, and I grip a fistful of his stupid crewneck sweatshirt. His gaze flashes back to mine, eyes widening with a hint of fear. I smile a hunter's smile.

"Why?" I ask, twisting the fabric tighter.

"Why what?" His gaze bounces between my hand and what I'm sure is my unhinged expression.

"Why are you doing this?" I hiss, needing an honest answer before he's pulled away by his people or William or we're back under the eyes of viewers.

"Didn't we already cover that part?" His fingers circle my wrist, hovering just over my skin like it'll burn if he touches me. I see his throat work as he swallows, then the heat of his palm lands on my hand. He doesn't tug it away, just rests it there, his thumb pressed lightly against my clanging pulse.

"Seriously, why put in this much work?" I drop his shirt and pull out of his too-gentle grip. My stare is hard and cold, demanding he cut the nonsense.

He glances away, something sheepish clouding his features. "Haven't you ever wanted a second chance to right a wrong?"

I chew on this, flashes of all my exes flickering through my mind like thumbed pages of a magazine, all the nights I stayed up late wondering why I'm so easy to leave, making an endless list of all the things I'd do differently given half the chance.

"No," I answer back, tilting my head to the side with a cold smile. "I'm thoroughly pleased with all the wrongs I've committed."

Cooper stares at me for a moment, then laughs, dragging a hand down his face. "You're impossible." He stands, and I bolt up too, putting myself between him and the door.

"And you're hiding an ulterior motive." I study him closely, trying to piece it all together. I glance at the crew packing up around us. "You must be losing more sponsors and clout than I thought. Need some huge PR stunt to really forge a comeback."

Cooper throws his arms up, rolling his eyes. "Sure, Eva. Is that what you need to hear? I *desperately* need you, the single most obstinate person I've ever met, to go along with this elaborate scheme for social media clout. My life and livelihood cannot possibly survive without your cooperation here. Want me to get down on my hands and knees begging you?"

An image burns bright like a flare, Cooper kneeling, head bowed between my . . .

I shudder the thought away. Despite my evidence damning his capabilities, I've never been able to shake my sharp attraction to him, but I'd rather chew on rusty nails than let those traitorous, horny thoughts win. I search his face as I scour through his statement. His tone is sarcastic, but I'm having trouble spotting the lie. It's pretty hard to have a conversation nowadays without an undercurrent of irony anyway.

"Well," I say with a sour tinge to my voice, "as long as we have a firmly established power dynamic, fine. But I refuse to enjoy myself."

"I'll make you eat those words." There's a sinful promise in his look that has heat rushing through me.

"Let's make one thing clear," I say, face twisting as I go toe to toe with him. We're about the same height, and I offer a silent thanks to whatever entity made it so I don't have to look up at him. "Under no circumstances will I be taking your Mini Cooper for a joy ride." I give his chest a rough poke in emphasis.

He tilts his head, feigning innocence. "I drive a PT Cruiser. I'll pick you up in it for our first date."

"Oh my *god*. This literally could not get more embarrassing for me." I poke him one more time, then step away. He rubs his palm against his sternum like he's trying to embed my touch there. Or erase it.

For his sake, it'd better be the latter.

I feel Aida and William's eyes on me, and I know I have a lot to sort out if I'm going to use this shitshow as career advancement.

"Don't contact me, I'll contact you," I say over my shoulder in goodbye, striding away from him.

"Lovely catching up," he calls.

I flip him off without looking, and I hate the way his resulting laugh echoes through me.

Chapter 5

HELL EXISTS ON EARTH, AND IT HAS LAID ITS FOUNDATION in my phone.

I've always taken a disgraceful amount of pride in keeping my home screen organized and notifications in check. Pictures are delegated into concise folders, apps categorized to perfection, texts promptly answered.

But since the live stream yesterday, my phone has become an endless, buzzing beast lobbing calls and texts and tags and emails at me, every app glowing with a red circle of notifications in the upper-right corner.

The internet, apparently, is really fucking excited to see the worst thing to ever happen to me play out publicly.

A frenzy has erupted on social media, and I can no longer keep up with the tags. I've spent the entire day rotting in my bed as I refresh apps and watch the view count tick up, up, up. People are fixated on chopping up our interview, making video edits of Cooper saying *Stop being so charming or I might fall in love with you* over trending songs, screenshots of stolen glances flashing after like watching some stupid-ass love montage in a movie. I'm horrified that so many managed to catch a smile I did not mean to offer, always flashing to Cooper's own dimpled grin.

Cooper is feeding the fire and my personal rage by liking so many of these videos. I glare at my screen as I scroll through the comments on one of the latest:

> They're definitely gonna fuck
>
>> Reply: are you delulu? They already fucking
>>
>> Reply: please let it also be live streamed
>
> I'd be on my knees for this man idgaf
>
>> Reply: same
>>
>> Reply: same
>>
>> Reply: god SAME
>
> I love that she looks like she's gonna strangle him and he's just like 😳 😳 😳
>
>> Reply: The best way for her to suffocate him would be to sit on that pretty face . . . just sayin

That last comment goes off like a flashbulb in my mind, jolting through my nervous system as if it's a memory and not a suggestion.

The problem is, the way he looks at me in those edits, I could actually believe some of this is genuine. Or, at least, that he genuinely wants to fuck me. And some addled part of my brain is fixating on that, dulling the hard-won souvenir of what being with Cooper is like with a sparkling, heated image of what it could be.

If he didn't suck so much on a cellular level. Obviously.

I exit out of the app, tapping in to my texts again. For the umpteenth time, I start a draft message to him. The Soundbites PR team sent me an outline of how his podcast episodes will be cross-posted on the company's socials, and William sent an oh-so-subtle email that the first date better happen sooner rather than later. The team included Cooper's contact info, but, because I'm pathetic, I didn't need it. I never deleted his number from college. I didn't even change his name in my phone to something hilarious and mean like any self-respecting woman should.

Stop liking peoples' thirst traps of us, I type, then delete. Can't let him know how aware I am of the excitement around all this. I chew on my lip for a second. Let's get this stupid-ass charade over with and get the date scheduled, I try. No, way too eager.

I sit up, looking out my thumbnail of a bedroom window at the dark fall evening. City lights wink at me, and I frown at their loveliness, my sour face coming into focus in the pane's reflection. I stare at myself for a moment, my pinched expression and furrowed brows. The curl to my shoulders. My messy bedsheets.

I've never had attention like this, but all of it feels fogged, directed at a shell of me—a facade that people are latching onto and fabricating entertainment from. It's overwhelming and confusing and more unpleasant than I would have anticipated. Something dull and hollow pangs in my chest. It takes me a moment to realize it's . . . loneliness.

I glance back at my phone, leg jiggling as the feeling takes root and starts to bloom into a sharper ache. With a small huff I type: why didn't you ever call me back?

Seeing the words there, addressed to Rylie Cooper, are cold water to my deplorable self-loathing, and I straighten my shoulders as I erase it, letting out a brittle laugh at that pitiful second-long version of me. She's not someone I want to get too comfortable in this tough skin I've worked so hard to grow.

As I exit out of Cooper's name entirely, another FaceTime call from Ray pops up on my screen, his fifth in the past two hours. I decline it. His follow-up text is instantaneous.

So you aren't going to explain what the hell is happening on social media rn, huh?

I let out a long breath through pursed lips. Ray is one of my best friends, but he's notoriously bad at checking in with people, and he and his partners have been having some sort of pet turtle crisis as of late that has been absorbing all his attention, so I didn't bother to fill him in on the Cooper drama when it was starting. Apparently, he doesn't live under as thick a rock as I had hoped and has seen the interview circulating. I text him a reply.

What is there to explain that hasn't been summed up in countless videos already?

Maybe the fact that you fucked a celebrity and never shared it with your bestie??

He is NOT a celebrity. I grind my teeth as I type, feeling so keyed up I scramble out of bed and start to pace.

I'm sick of thinking about Cooper. Sick of his stupid face popping up in my stupid head and stupid thoughts. A pressure builds in my stomach, up my throat, and I stomp across my apartment and turn on the shower, cranking the heat so I can wash away whatever grime being around him embedded in my skin.

Because this is New York, my shower is in my kitchen, barely bigger than the sink across from it, and I lean against the counter as I wait for it to warm up. Another text from Ray comes through.

He's social media famous and that pretty much counts double nowadays

No it doesn't

Fuck off yes it does and you know it.

I drop my phone on the windowsill at the end of my shower, then step under the steaming spray. It calms me for a moment— the fog dulling the garish mental images of Cooper's smile, the scorching water smoothing the sharp edges of my nerves, the echoing sound of droplets splashing against the porcelain tub drowning out my intrusive thoughts. My shoulders lower from my ears. My jaw unclenches. The building pressure in my body sighs in relief. Here is peace. Here is a place without reminders of Rylie fucking Cooper.

Then my phone buzzes again.

And, like the well-trained technology zombie I am, my eyes flash open and I follow the tug from my phone, water sluicing down my nose and fingers and plonking on the screen as I read Ray's latest message.

I know this is probably breaking friend code but I gotta know . . . was it really that bad? I feel like he's packing.

I roll my eyes so hard I feel the force of it in the center of my brain. Another message from Ray immediately follows.

I also feel like he's curved to the left for some reason. Just gut in-stinct. He has that energy.

This at least makes me snort. But the humor is short-lived, a long-buried memory resurfacing with heat along my skin like a fever breaking.

Cooper had walked me home after our shitty second date, the sharp spring night cutting at my cheeks and through the thin dress I'd worn to impress him. He didn't offer me his coat like I'd come to fruitlessly hope for from movies and books. He'd been distant all night, his thoughts a thousand miles away, and nothing I said was witty or charming enough to pull him back. Growing up, I'd become accustomed to this feeling, my voice not strong enough, my thoughts not interesting enough, to pull the split attention of my parents. Of anyone.

"What are you thinking about?" I'd asked as we ap-proached my building, his head bent low and stare fixed on the pavement.

He startled like he'd forgotten I was there, eyes taking a second to focus as we stopped in front of my dorm. I pressed my back against the rough brick wall, studying him closely. It was odd to see him frown, and I let out a sigh of relief at the slow, sensual smile that traced across his mouth as he came back to me. But that smile didn't reach his eyes, something tangled and heavy sitting at the corners.

"Just trying to figure out my ren faire costume, Kitten," he'd said, taking a step closer. "It's never too early to start planning."

I snorted. "Court jester is the obvious choice."

This pulled a genuine laugh from him, and I felt the rough

heat of it caress my skin. "God, you're right. I've been over-thinking it."

"Don't hurt yourself."

Another rumbling chuckle. Another step closer, his toes touching mine, his eyes on my face, stilling at my mouth. "You'll be a bar wench, I assume?"

I rolled my eyes, but my smile won out, a blush heating my cheeks. "I think I'd need a bit more going on to fill out the costumes." I made a deprecating gesture toward my flat chest.

Cooper's eyes dipped for a moment, then hooked back on mine, the most present he'd been all night. He slowly raised his hand, catching a wayward lock of my hair battling the wind and brushing it behind my ear. His palm went to my cheek, then down to my throat, cupping it gently as his thumb pressed to my erratic pulse.

"Well," he said, eyes still stuck on mine. "*I* think you're pretty close to perfect."

A puff of white steam between us emphasized my startled breath, and Cooper caught it.

"You're cold," he said, frown back in place as he looked at the pink tip of my nose, then glanced up at the sky like he was just noticing the weather and was personally offended at its chill.

"A little, yeah." A shiver ran through me that had nothing to do with the temperature, a gentle heat already starting low in my belly and tracing through my limbs.

He fixed his attention back on me, and I watched him clock my every movement. The rise and fall of my chest. The trace of my swallow. The way he felt it against his hand still at my throat. His hungry look all but ruined me.

"Let me warm you up," he murmured.

He kissed me then, avoiding pressing me harder into the bricks by turning us—one hand on my hip, the other cradling the back of my head—so his shoulders were against the wall and all I felt was him as my body molded against his. The warmth of his arms around me, the soft raggedness of his breath. The playful coaxing of his mouth against mine and the smooth glide of his tongue as he traced the seam of my lips. He made a hungry noise in the back of his throat when my tongue touched his.

Cooper deepened the pressure, swallowing my moan of pleasure. My limbs became languid and heavy, head light and spinning. He caught my lower lip between his teeth, nibbling gently, desire threading through me until it was the only thing holding me together. After a few minutes, he grew hard between our flush hips, and I pressed even closer, dragging my fingers through his hair and then grabbing it by the fistful, holding on for dear life.

Eventually, we came up for air. I was delirious. Starving. About to ask him up to my room. But as he stared at me, cheeks flushed, his jaw tightened, a muscle ticking.

I watched him fade again, all the fire in me still not enough to keep him in the moment. He brushed his knuckles along my cheek, then cupped my shoulders, turning me toward my door, telling me he had a nice night as he walked away.

I didn't embarrass myself further by telling him that was my first kiss.

I didn't hear from him for five days.

I snuff out the ember of the memory before it sparks a forest fire. Being young and tenderhearted was such a fucking curse.

I look at Ray's message again, more water dripping down my body. I leave my phone on the windowsill and step back under the stream, grabbing my shampoo and lathering up my hair.

A well-adjusted, emotionally evolved person would ignore the bait, wouldn't engage in further conversation.

I am not that person.

If there is an opportunity to talk shit, I will be talking shit. Similarly, if there is an opportunity to gossip my ass off, I will be spilling as much piping-hot tea as I can provide. It's one of my most honed skills, and I've considered putting it on my résumé.

"Hey, Siri, send a text to"—a glob of shampoo drips into my mouth, and I start to choke—"Ra—" I cough so hard I gag. *"Really?"* I wheeze out. "I can't have one moment of peace?"

"What do you want it to say?" Siri's robotic voice replies.

"Rylie"—*cough, gasp, heave*—"is the antichrist—period." *Hack, retch.* "He does have a huge dick for what it's worth. No distinct curves but I agree he gives off that vibe."

There's a moment's pause, and I see the purple-blue circle twirl on my phone screen through the drops of water in my vision. Siri's voice rings out, echoing off the walls: "Sent to Rylie: *Antichrist. He does have a huge dick for what it's worth no distinct curves but I agree he gives off that vibe.*"

Wait . . .

No.

. . . No.

Fuck. No!

"Siri, unsend! Siri, no send! Hey, Siri, unsend!" I scream as I lunge forward. My feet slide on the wet tub, moving like a cartoon character's under me before completely giving out and slipping away. My body crashes forward, my chin clipping the edge of the windowsill and hip catching the majority of my fall as I land.

"Okay, resent," Siri's serene voice calls.

I instinctively try to curl into the fetal position, but my tub is too small, so I lie there scrunched like an accordion, chin blood coasting down my body and mixing with the overhead spray. I wonder how long I need to lie here in order to drown. Maybe I could reach my toaster from here.

I'm contemplating the likelihood that the brown water stain on my ceiling will finally give way and all the upper floors will collapse on top of me when my phone vibrates on the windowsill with a text.

I reach my arm up and slap around for it. I finally palm it and bring it to me, water spraying into my eyes and across my phone. For the first time, I find it extremely annoying that Apple made phones waterproof, because an old-school model would have died long before this type of incident. Maybe mine is faulty and will malfunction. One can only hope.

But the screen lights up like normal, proudly displaying a text from Rylie fucking Cooper.

Wow. When you said you'd contact me, this wasn't what I was expecting as the initial message. Another one comes through in rapid succession. You really want me to know about the antichrist's dick. A third message pings. Is all of this info firsthand? Did you fuck the antichrist? When did you fuck the antichrist?

I switch to defense. You would know, you were there, I type like each tap of my fingers is going directly for his pretty gray eyes. He goes low, I go lower.

Three taunting dots bounce in the bottom-left corner for a breath, then his reply pops up: Glad you think my dick is huge 😵

Shit. I can't let him take that as a compliment.

Don't take that as a compliment.

I'm running on adrenaline here, I can't be expected to come up with something clever. Then, as a follow-up: isn't your whole schtick to detoxify masculinity? Should've guessed you'd be that shallow

Just because I can't let virtual silence linger for even half a second, I add: and regardless, size is no indication you know how to put it to use.

I know how to put it to use

Well . . . fuck. My entire body flushes hot. In anger, obviously.

I sit up, slapping the knob to turn the water off and gracelessly dragging my body out of the tub. I spare myself half a glance in the mirror over my kitchen sink, ignoring the feverish look in my eyes, focusing instead on the small cut on my chin. I press a wad of tissues to it, although the bleeding has mostly stopped.

That wasn't the case when I knew you, I shoot back in a message, still dripping wet and naked in the middle of my kitchen. But I can't let too many seconds pass and let him think he got to me.

I roughly dry off, trying to ignore how sensitive my skin feels, how the drag of my pajamas over my still-damp body sends a shiver through me that doubles in intensity at my imagining of Cooper whispering *I know how to put it to use* in my ear.

Clearly I scrambled my brain with my fall.

I crawl into bed, my head pounding with annoyance, a frustrated scream building in my throat.

His response comes through: Believe it or not, I've learned a thing or twelve in the six years since I've known you.

I reposition myself, trying to alleviate a sudden, annoying pressure between my thighs. Probably a prelude to . . . menstrual cramps.

I'm not bullshitting when I say how vital communication is between partners, he adds. Because he's really trying to prove a point and waste my time, he sends a third message: you're my only complaint, actually.

Indignation flares. I know, instinctively, he didn't say that to cut me. Cooper isn't one to go for the jugular like yours truly. Even in college, he was good-natured to a fault, always seeing the best in people and vocalizing as much if they ever came up in a roundtable of gossip. It was one of the things that always drew me to him back then. Even the light stalking I've done on his videos lately shows that he doesn't come from a mean-spirited place as far as I can tell.

But his text makes me feel wrong all the same. Broken. Pokes at that hidden, festering wound that the problem in relationships is me, I'm the reason I can't get off with another person. No one can figure my body out because I'm too damn difficult.

Your right hand doesn't count as a partner, I text, shooing the self-doubt far from my head.

I'm left-handed

I hate that I am collecting facts about this man against my will. I should have guessed, you have that vibe

REGARDLESS of how you want to paint me, I do listen to my partner and actually take great care in making sure they leave every encounter fully satisfied

Heat erupts across my cheeks. The dickhead is rubbing my nose in it. Guess you returned the calls from those willing to teach you, I type. Shame I wasn't one of the chosen ones to worship at the Cooper cock of fame

Again, I'm sorry for the way I treated you. I truly do mean that and regret how things ended. I didn't mean to hurt you, Eva.

Lick my butthole, Cooper

I will if you ask nicely ;)

Oh, this fucker. I throw my phone to the side as my pulse pounds, sinuous warmth unfurling through my body. No. Absolutely *not*. I refuse to be aroused by that Neanderthal.

He's an asshole, I tell myself as I drag my palms over my stiff nipples, the sharp lines of his jaw flashing in my head. *A total fucking prick*, I scream internally as I fumble through my bedside drawer, then shove my vibrator below the elastic of my pajama bottoms, picturing those heavy-lidded eyes looking up at me as his mouth dips between my legs. *I hate him so much*, I chant over and over as I touch myself, imagining his shoulders pushing my thighs further apart, his stupid, gorgeous, annoying face as he licks me to completion. *He won't get the best of me*, I promise through the shaking waves of pleasure, seeing his dark eyelashes kissing the tops of his cheeks as he savors every minute of my taste. *And what I just did will* never *happen again,* I swear to myself through the aftershocks.

My phone harmonizes with my vibrator, and I reluctantly glance at the screen. First date on Saturday? Cooper asks. I'd be more demanding and tell you to block out the morning but I don't think that'd win me any favors.

Maybe you aren't as clueless as I thought, I respond, a shiver tracing down my spine.

He sends me a series of disco dancer emojis in response. Then adds, see you at 7:30am on Saturday, Evil Kitten. Have fun with the Antichrist in the meantime <3

I read the text over and over, red bleeding into my vision.

Who in their right fucking mind schedules a date for that early in the morning and doesn't anticipate violence?

Chapter 6

"YOU HIRED A CHAUFFEUR?" I SAY, SQUINTING AT THE shiny black SUV Cooper's leaning against in front of my apartment. I make out the silhouette of a driver in the front seat as the early (way too damn early) Saturday sun glints off the chrome trim in sharp slices. "Are you fucking joking?"

He shoves his hands in the pockets of his (over-the-top and tragically stunning) suit pants, lazily shrugging as his dimple flashes. Thank god I'd rather shave my head before showing up anywhere in an outfit that could be deemed casual, because clearly Cooper has some plans that require more than a kitschy crewneck, not that he bothered to give me a heads-up on the dress code.

Doing a quick assessment, I determine that my black, ass-worshiping pants and silk-lace top under my oversized peacoat still have me looking better than him, but the margin is closer than I'd care to admit.

Not that I dressed nice for him or anything like that . . .

"Believe it or not, Eva, I picked up on a few subtle hints that maybe you weren't impressed with my PT Cruiser." Cooper taps the side of his nose. "I'm extremely perceptive."

I shift my frown from his beautiful suit to the large car behind him. "The only way this could be more obnoxious is if you showed up on a pubcycle."

"I love a pubcycle," he says, smile star bright.

"Jesus fucking Christ." I march forward, and Cooper opens the car door with a flourish. I flash him a glare before ducking in. Two rows of seats face each other, a glass partition separating us from the driver up front. A massive bouquet of lilies is plopped on the smooth leather across from where I sit. The floral scent is so pungent my eyes instantly water.

"For you," Cooper says, following me in and shutting the door behind him. He picks up the bundle of flowers and holds them out to me.

His expression is so damn earnest and warm—his glasses slipping down his nose, cheeks glowing with a soft pink—that I suddenly don't have the heart to tell him I'm allergic to the lilies he's holding right under my nose. Instead, a series of body-wracking sneezes arrest me. I endure about seven of them before I lean back, lifting the toe of my stiletto-capped foot to push against his wrist and create some distance between me and the bouquet.

With a crestfallen expression, Cooper takes the hint. Fumbling, he finds a hidden button and lowers the partition. "I'll leave these up there, then," he mumbles, tossing the flowers through the open window to the front passenger seat. "We're ready," he adds to the driver, who nods.

Cooper raises the dark sheet of glass, our equally horrified eyes meeting in the reflection in a taut moment of silence. He turns to me as the car rumbles to life and pulls into traffic.

We carefully avoid each other's gazes for a few seconds, and I wonder if I'm the only one realizing that this is the first time we've been alone together since six years ago when we were. . . . *together.* Then he blinks, good humor flooding his features.

"Mimosa?" Cooper asks, digging around a darkened corner of the car before holding up a chilled bottle of sparkling wine and a small jug of orange juice.

I balk, eyes flicking between the sweating, dark bottle and his radiant smile. I open my mouth to tell him that while, generally, I'm a slut for champagne, it's also seven thirty in the morning and all I really care about is locating the nearest reservoir of coffee, but he doesn't wait for my response.

Instead, Cooper thumbs the top of the bottle, the loud *pop* erupting through the car. The noise in the small space slows down time, allowing me to take in everything in fine detail.

The cork whizzes like a bullet in my direction, colliding into the window before ricocheting off the glass with a bang. It changes course, hitting me with startling force in the throat. The direct hit scares me so badly I throw my arms up in delayed defense, subsequently punching my fists against the roof. The noise of fear that retches out of me isn't a cute little yelp or squeak. It's a prolonged, full, bloody-murder scream of terror.

The car jerks as the driver slams on the brakes, my seat belt digging into my chest and gut, turning my scream into a wheeze.

The world is still for half a second—my body slumped forward like a rag doll, my pulse pounding from the hefty dose of adrenaline from almost being slain by a stray cork—then another car bashes into us from behind, my head bouncing around my neck like a bobblehead. In the chaos, my eyes somehow catch Cooper's alarmed gaze, his glasses askew and mouth gaping.

He sums the past twenty seconds up pretty succinctly with a whispered, "Oh fuck."

Everything picks up speed after that. The driver's side door opens, then slams; people on the street start arguing with raised voices; Cooper opens the back door and scrambles out, ducking back in and awkwardly gathering me in his arms like I'm an overstuffed laundry basket.

"Get off me," I grumble as the cold morning air slaps my cheeks. I push away from his chest, then wobble on my heels for a moment when he drops me like a hot coal.

Commotion surrounds us—a sleek Audi's nose is crunched into the SUV's bumper, the owner and our driver only a few centimeters apart as they yell at each other in the street. Cooper and I watch in silence for a few moments, and I keep looking around, waiting for a bona fide grown-up to step in and handle the mess. It's with a sinking heart that I realize that won't be happening.

Someone threatens to call the cops and another person calls them a pussy-ass tattletale. I glance at Cooper, wondering if he'll insert himself and get this sorted, but he looks at his watch, his face falling.

"We've gotta go," he says, straightening up and grabbing my elbow. He tugs me down the sidewalk like a man possessed.

"We can't just . . . leave? Can we?" I pull out of his grasp, looking back at the mess over my shoulder.

"Believe it or not, this is my first hired-car car-crash," Cooper says, mouth pressed into a frown. "They have my info. My credit card. I'm sure I'll be the one charged for the damages when it's all said and done, but we have a date we have to get to."

He takes my hand and starts marching us down the block again.

"Um, excuse me, what are you doing?" I dig in my heels, wrenching so hard on the hand he's holding that his arm jerks in its socket.

"I'm walking us to the date," he says, rounding on me, his eyes frantically sweeping up and down the street.

"Where is it?"

"I can't tell you. That will ruin the surprise."

I fix him with a pointed look, jaw set in defiance. "We've had enough surprises in the twenty minutes we've spent together. And hi, hello." I wave down at my knife-blade heels. "I'm not walking anywhere far in these."

"Eva, we have a reservation we have to get to."

"Cooper, I don't really care," I reply, dropping my voice in an imitation of his. "Three blocks and I'll feel my pulse in the tip of every toe. It's also highly likely that I'm concussed from the literal car crash you caused and I think you damaged my windpipe with that stray cork."

"I don't think you'd be talking back this much if your windpipe was damaged."

"Let me toss a quick blow at your throat and we'll see how you manage."

"I don't have time to fight with you, we have a timetable to stick to!" he says, his voice pitching up.

"Oh, buddy! Big feelings!" I match his volume, planting my feet more firmly on the pavement.

"You're so patronizing." He tugs at my hand again like an impatient toddler.

"Glad you're keeping up, kiddo. You weren't lying about being perceptive earlier." I fix him with a dark look. "But the point still stands, I'm not walking an undefined distance at the snap of your fingers."

His jaw works as he stares at me, and I cross my arms over my chest, lifting my chin. With a resigned shake of his head, he mumbles "Fuck this" as he steps toward the curb. He raises his hand, hailing a taxi. A few zoom past, and I feel a petty thrill that he's having to work for it.

Finally, one pulls up, and Cooper quickly opens the door.

"Your chariot, princess," he says through gritted teeth.

"Thanks, baby girl." I lightly smack his cheek as I duck into the back seat. I hear his lengthy sigh before he stoops down to follow me. I don't immediately move over for him, but the look Cooper pins me with has me scooting to the side to make room.

"Where to, boss?" the taxi driver asks.

I stare at Cooper, a smile of victory on my lips. His glare could cut diamonds as he says, "The Met."

"You got it." The driver turns on his blinker and pulls out.

"The Met isn't open this early," I argue, a tiny hiccup of excitement releasing in my chest. I smother it down. I love the Met. I love art, period. But I also know it doesn't open until ten in the morning.

"Shut up, Eva."

Cooper collapses against the seat, his glasses sliding up toward his hairline as he digs the heels of his hands against his eyes. My lips part, but, to my horror, I obey the command.

Manhattan passes us in a blur as we make our way uptown, that kernel of excitement sprouting roots and digging into my chest.

It's the kind of startlingly perfect fall day that reminds me how head-over-heels in love I am with this city—the streaks of gray pavement disrupted with fiery leaves and a morning sky so blue it makes you question reality. New York's energy flows at different beats and frequencies depending on the day and time of year, but today's is a hopeful hum, a radiant goodbye to the life of summer and a promise to care for the island through the colder months to come. I'm so lost in the hallways of my thoughts that it takes me a moment to realize the taxi has stopped, the grandeur of the museum rising like a beacon through Cooper's window.

He lifts his hips and fishes his wallet from his back pocket, pulling out some bills and handing them to the cabbie. "Keep the change," he says as he unfolds his limbs from the back seat and steps out. He ducks back down, holding out a hand for me.

I stare at his outstretched palm, adrenaline thudding in my chest as my gaze traces up his arm to his face. His expression is still strained, but the curl of his smile is pulling through. "I won't bite," he murmurs. "Unless you say *please*." The fucker winks.

"Pig," I scoff, recategorizing the delirious warmth in my chest to the fire of indignation as I take his hand. I also successfully ignore the spark that shoots up my arm from where we touch. I mean . . . not that there was a spark at all. There's no spark. There's only my skin crawling from touching an extraterrestrial life form.

"Add it to the list to go over on the podcast," he says grimly. "I'm sure it's already a mile long."

"You're the gift that keeps on giving when it comes to grievances." I step out of the car and drop his hand as quickly as possible, making a show of wiping my palm off on my pants.

Cooper watches the movement, his eyes taking their time to climb my body before fixing me with a sly smile. "Ever the charmer, Kitten."

"Call me that again and I'll let you find out how these heels taste," I reply sweetly, walking past him and up the Met's steps.

Cooper's laugh is low and close to my ear as he follows. "Aren't you going to ask me what we're doing here?"

I'd never give him the satisfaction. "I've used a few context clues to narrow it down to an art heist or waiting in the cold for two hours for it to open," I say, working way too hard to keep my voice even and wheeze-free as I climb the final steps.

"Boo, you're no fun." Cooper pouts, and the look is

alarmingly adorable, waves of dark hair tumbling across his forehead, gray eyes wide and doe-like behind his glasses.

We're at a stalemate, my jaw clenched insolently, Cooper's expression turning downright endearing. I roll my eyes and scoff when he juts his lower lip out, but I give in. Out of boredom.

I clasp my hands in front of my chest, fixing my features into a mask of desperation. "Oh, Rylie Cooper, pretty please tell me what we'll be doing at the ass-crack of dawn on this date you've all but used brute force to get me on for social media clout. I'm just *dying* to know."

He laughs again, a dubious puff of breath. He steps toward me, tilting his head so his forehead almost touches mine.

"Happy to ease your pain." His words shouldn't have heat flooding through me, but they do, and I step back, clearing my throat and looking away, praying the wind takes credit for any color on my cheeks. Cooper stares at me for a prolonged moment with a fiendish smile like he can see the warmth licking through my veins. "The Met has a new exhibit—'Emotions Through Rodin'—showing off some of his best sculptures. And I got us a private tour. Before opening hours."

"P-private tour?"

He bites his lower lip as he nods. "The place all to ourselves."

My knees almost buckle, and my hand darts out, grabbing his arm, my lips parting as I try to process what he's saying. Cooper's heavy gaze moving from my face to where I touch him breaks me out of my trance. I release him with an exaggerated flex of my hand.

What is this, a fucking swoon? Good god, I need to get a

grip. And not one on Cooper's surprisingly solid bicep. The
boy is wiry, but apparently strong ropes of muscle are hidden
under those stupid-ass sweatshirts. And well-tailored suits.

Christ.

"Let's go," Cooper says, nodding toward the entrance. His
hand falls with a whisper of pressure to my back as we walk,
and I aggressively reach behind me to remove it as the doors
are opened for us. Cooper flashes the tickets on his phone as
we walk in.

The museum is beautifully, hauntingly quiet as we're led
through the great hall by our tour guide, who introduces
herself as Anya. Our footsteps echo off the tall ceilings in a
cadence that matches my heartbeat as we weave through reli-
gious works of the Byzantine Empire and medieval times. The
guide patiently waits as I hover over various displays, offering
some historical tidbits on specific works that catch my eye. I've
seen all this before, a hundred times at least, but it never stops
amazing me, pulling the breath from my chest and making
my head swim at the beauty.

"Here we are," Anya says with barely contained excitement
as she stops us in front of the door leading to the special exhibit. "Auguste Rodin is considered by many to be the father
of modern sculpture."

"I'd certainly call him daddy." Cooper and I speak in unison. My jaw crashes open as my eyes lock with his, our dumb,
harmonized joke sitting between us. He blinks a few times,
then his smile turns impossibly bright, a cascade of giggles
tumbling from us both.

I duck my head, trying to choke down my laughter that

feels sacrilegious in such a beautiful place, and Cooper's hand returns to my back, tracing a soothing circle as he similarly shakes in a fruitless effort for control. His touch feels so comfortably welcome, it jolts sobriety through me, and I straighten, stepping away. I can't let one shared, immature joke crack my resolve to have a miserable time.

After a deep breath, I look back at Anya, flashing her a strained smile in apology. She presses her own lips together in a battle between amusement and horror.

"Right . . ." she says, letting out an uncomfortable chuckle. "Rodin was a passionate believer that art should be a true reflection of nature, and his collection of work explores the expression of emotions and the human psyche in extreme physical states displayed in his sculptures." She opens the door, gesturing us inside as she continues her oral history of Rodin. A room has been cleared for the special exhibit, and it feels like stepping into a holy space, my spine tingling as my overeager eyes dance from sculpture to sculpture.

The guide gently leads us through the exhibit. We start with *Eve (after the fall)*, the guide speaking to her devastation, her desperation for self-protection. We move along to *The Thinker*. *Despair*. The writhing, sensual arch of *Torso of Adele*. The agony of *The Cry*. Anya gives us the history with hushed reverence, her voice filled with wonder and pride as she points out minute details—creases around the eyes, a posture poised with symbolism, the choice of bronze over marble. All of it creates a lump in my throat, Cooper seeming equally awed.

Our eyes lock in the space between the curve of two hands reaching for each other with need. I stare at him for a moment, absorbing the soft curl of his smile, the shallow way he's breathing like he's as scared as I am of disrupting the magic.

"I'll give you two time to explore on your own," Anya says, backing toward the exit. "I'll return in an hour to walk you back to the entrance."

I nod in gratitude, eyes still fixed on Cooper and head spinning as I try to map out all that I want to revisit, how many moments I can spare at the altar of each statue without missing anything.

Breaking my gaze from his feels like the snap of a rubber band, and I shake myself as I look around. I start at *The Kiss*, a marble rendering of a man and woman embracing.

It's devastating, the seductive grip of the man's hands on her bare hip, the tips of his marble fingertips dimpling her smooth flesh, her arm thrown around his neck as she begs him closer, the deep pockmarks in the base of the foundation of the piece emphasizing the carnal humanity of art and beauty.

I slip my heels off and hook the straps around my crooked finger, standing on my bare feet as the grandeur of the sculpture expands and expands and expands, my thoughts quieting as I process the reality that something this beautiful exists.

Cooper walks up next to me, and I wonder if he's holding his breath too, if he's feeling the alteration in his body from seeing something so wonderfully made.

He ducks low, his breath brushing my cheek as he says, "I'm sorry, but we have to go."

I turn to him, moving so abruptly that my nose crashes into his, both of us wincing.

"What do you mean?" I say, pinching the bridge of my nose as I look at him. "She said we have an hour."

Cooper's expression is pained, but he steps toward the exit. "I know, and I really am sorry, I can see how much you're loving this, but we have . . . well, we have another reservation we have to get to."

I gape at him. "Are you joking?" My gaze darts around the room and its magnificent contents. "What could be more important than this?"

"I . . . I'm sorry. We can't miss the next thing."

"No."

"No?"

"I don't want to leave," I say like an insolent child, gesturing at the sculpture next to me.

Cooper's shoulders droop, his expression turning desperate. "Eva, we have a timetable we have to stick to."

"Oh my god, don't get hysterical."

"I'm not hysterical!" he cries hysterically. "We just . . . we have to get to the next thing."

Cooper grips my elbow, leading me toward the exit. With pure disbelief, I shoot one more hungry look over my shoulder. He ushers me out of the museum, offering a brief thanks to our tour guide as I consider begging her to save me and let me live here forever.

The cold pavement hits my toes when we step outside, and Cooper spares me a second to slip my heels back on before he drags me down the steps and back to the street.

He leads me by the hand across a few blocks, my heart

breaking the further we get from the museum, the jarring hustle of the real world feeling like a thousand cuts on my skin.

"You really will love this," Cooper says like he's trying to convince himself.

Eventually, he pushes through the doors of a high-rise building, marching us straight to the elevator bank.

"I'm sorry I cut that short," he says as we wait in front of the golden doors, my solemn expression reflected back at me. "But this will be even better. I promise."

I stare at him, unable to conjure the energy to glare. The elevator dings, and we step on. With a sinking stomach and a painful squirt of adrenaline, I watch Cooper hit the button for the sixty-ninth floor, the highest in the building. My heart is beating so hard in my throat that I don't even have the where-withal to say a mental *noice*.

My pulse pounds in my palms and the arches of my feet as we climb higher and higher, a shrill ringing starting some-where in the back of my skull.

"W-what . . . Where are we going?" I ask through a dry throat.

"It's going to be amazing," Cooper replies, completely oblivious to the prickling panic locking up my joints, the sweat beading at my upper lip. The walls of the space tilt toward me, trapping me in a golden cage racing toward the sky. After an eternity and all too soon, the elevator jolts to a stop, the doors sliding open, my warped reflection disappearing in a wave.

The floor is empty, only a few doors on either side of us, most of the space taken up by a short staircase and an ominous-looking door at its peak.

Every instinct in my body tells me to curl into a ball and lie on the floor, but Cooper grabs my limp, clammy hand, smiling and talking as he leads us up the stairs; I don't hear a word, my ears filled with a buzzing panic that makes it hard to put one foot in front of the other.

Becoming the human embodiment of my most terrifying nightmares, Cooper does the worst thing he ever could to me: he opens the door at the top of the stairs and tugs me through.

Out onto the roof.

The wind grips my shoulders and neck, threatening to yank me to the edge of this dangerously tall building. My watering eyes scan my sky-high surroundings, taking in a large, glossy, bug-like machine in the center of the roof. It takes me a few seconds to realize through the fuzz of sticky panic that it's a helicopter.

"Ready for the best view of the city?" Cooper says enthusiastically, still gripping my wrist and drawing me toward the deathtrap with propellers.

Oh my god, this is how I'm going to die.

"Absolutely fucking not," I choke out, a mortifying crack in my voice as tears blur my vision. I rip my arm from him, wrapping it around my middle and tucking into myself, crouching down and balancing on my toes in an attempt to lower my chances of falling from these horrifying heights to the concrete below.

"Are you . . . are you messing with me?" Cooper's question comes to me over the wind, the words distorted through my panic.

I manage to shake my head, a surge of dizziness lurching my stomach as more fear floods my body.

"Eva, are you okay?" Cooper says, voice softer. The wind quiets, a sudden sturdy presence blocking out the harshly close sun. I peek over my arm to see him squatting next to me, face taut and lined with confusion and worry. "What's wrong, sweetheart?"

I rub my head against my kneecaps, taking deep, rattling breaths as tears burn my cheeks. "H-heights," I splutter. "Can't."

With a determined grip, I feel Cooper's arms go around me. I let out a shocked gasp as he gathers me to his body, lifting us to standing. I sway for a moment, hands clawing into his suit jacket, head tucking under his chin and nose pressing against his chest. I breathe in the scent of him, and I make a mental note to be furious about how good he smells and how nice he feels later when I'm safe on normal ground.

Still holding me, he guides us back toward the door. Hearing the click of the lock and feeling my feet back on the landing of the staircase creates a whoosh of relief through my muscles that threatens to lay me to the floor. The panic stains my veins, tattooing my skin, and a tiny, choked whimper pulls from my throat.

"I'm sorry. So sorry," Cooper coos, too much tenderness in his voice. "Please don't cry, Eva. We won't go." His hands cup my jaw, thumbs brushing away the tears tracking down my cheeks.

"Get off me," I say, pushing him away. I find a surge of fortitude fueled by embarrassment. I trip down the steps on wobbly legs, falling and hitting my ass on the edge of a few of them. I let out a stream of curses as Cooper pounds down the staircase behind me. He steps around me to the bottom, gripping my shoulders and hauling me up.

"Calm down, Eva. It's okay. I'm so sorry."

"Don't tell me to calm down," I grit out, indignation flaring. It's the only feeling that can take a deeper root than my fear. "Telling someone to calm down literally has never had the intended effect."

"You seem to be feeling better," he says, a kind laugh in his voice as his gaze traces my face, hand brushing back my wind-ruined hair. I choose to resent that kindness.

I pull away from him, darting for the elevators. I slap the button a few hundred times before the doors finally open. Cooper slips in right as they're closing. We ride down in silence, our chests heaving through jagged breaths like we sprinted a mile.

When the doors slide open, I bolt toward the exit, but Cooper's right on my heels. I'm too disoriented to figure out where the closest subway station is, so I stop at the curb to flag down a stray cab. This man is going to cost me an arm and a leg just to escape him.

"I'm sorry," Cooper repeats, defeat in his voice and etched in his face. "I had no idea you were afraid of heights."

I shake my head, face twisting in acidic humor. "Yeah, because you don't know anything about me." A taxi pulls over, and I wrench open the door, sliding in. "I thought our first round of dates were bad with you ignoring my existence and just trying to get into my pants, but this took it to a new level of awful." I grip the handle, moving to slam the door shut.

Cooper catches it, jaw set in defiance as he holds it open. "I'm going to make it up to you, Eva. I promise."

With a deep breath, I smooth my frazzled features into

an icy stare. "You keep saying that, but the bar's been on the ground, and you keep showing up with a shovel."

I give the door another yank and it slips from his hand, slamming away the image of his wrecked expression, the last thing I see as the cab speeds off.

Chapter 7

I KNOW IT MAY BE HARD TO BELIEVE, WHAT WITH MY CALM, cool demeanor and mature responses to life's biggest curveballs, but I do sometimes overreact. Rarely, but it happens.

And as I make my way to Cooper's house for our first debrief, I wonder if maybe I overreacted just the teeniest-tiniest bit at the end of our date two days ago. It's juvenile, but I really hate heights. And Rylie Cooper. The latter goes without saying.

Even the barest of heights have always induced a wooziness in me, but I lost my ability to gulp down the fear around the age of ten. My three stepbrothers lured me into climbing up to the roof of our garage one random day that summer, convincing me that it was the best way to scope out the ice cream truck making its rounds. I bit back my shaky hesitation at their coaxing smiles, wanting so desperately to be one of them, weave into their tightknit siblinghood, learn what made my dad prefer their company over mine.

The boys stuck together like glue, the youngest of them still five years older than me, and the disconnect between us didn't give me much hope for the even-larger gap that would exist between me and the twins who were on the way.

I existed in the shadow of the boys' shine, but that day they acted like they wanted me to join them in the light. I was so thrilled to be included in a small summer adventure, I was determined to swallow down my fear.

The boys sent me up the ladder first, claiming it was for my safety and they'd catch me if I fell or slipped. The garage wasn't tall, probably no more than ten feet off the ground, but I might as well have been scaling the Empire State Building for how badly I was trembling as I climbed each rung. After what felt like an eternity, I hoisted myself over the gutters and onto the hot shingles, lying flat on my belly and straining my neck to peek over the edge. My stepbrothers' grins greeted me from below, but it created a sinking feeling in me instead of one of comfort.

The world sprawled below me was too big, the patch of roof too small, my heart beating too hard, and my head spinning too fast.

"I need to come down!" I screamed, tucking into a ball as my vision tunneled. "Help me get down!"

They laughed in response, and the shriek of the metal ladder being lowered pierced through my haze of fear.

"No! No! No!" I scrambled closer to the edge, bile rising in my throat as my stomach pitched from the sudden movement. My stepbrothers continued to cackle as they walked away.

"Enjoy the view, Eva!" one of them called.

I screamed my head off, slicing my voice to ribbons as I begged someone, anyone, to save me. I dug my fingers so hard into the shingles of the roof that my nails cracked to the quick. My ten-year-old mind was fully convinced I would die up there, alone and afraid and suffocating from fear. I don't know how long I was up there—it felt like hours but was probably only a matter of minutes—but eventually my dad came out of the house, propped the ladder to the side of the garage, and climbed up until his shoulders surfaced over the edge of the roof.

"Eva, come here," he'd said gruffly as he stuck out his hand. I continued to wail, unable to do anything else. With a few mumbled curses, he reached out, looping his strong arm around my middle and dragging me to him. The shingles scraped against my skin, burning my bare arms and the tip of my chin. I was so inconsolably afraid that I threw off his balance on the ladder, making us sway. I clung to him in a white-knuckle grip as he worked to steady us.

Somehow, he got us safely down, depositing me without ceremony in the grass. I reached for him again, wanting to bury my face into his huge frame and hold on to his sturdiness, but he held me at arm's length, mouth pressed into a firm line, brow furrowed in frustration.

"Stop crying," he commanded, shaking my shoulders. "There's no reason to be crying."

I tried to choke back my tears, but they were pouring out

of me with such force that I started gagging on the tangle of emotions. He shook me again.

"You can't be afraid of heights," he said, fixing me with his harsh look. "Do you hear me? It's a stupid thing to be afraid of. Understand?"

He stared at me so hard, I realized he was waiting for an answer, and I managed to nod, my body still vibrating with fear. He shook his head in disappointment, sparing me a final, skeptical glance before releasing his grip. "Only the tough survive, Eva," he said, not bothering to look back at me over his shoulder as he marched toward the house. "One day you'll have to get that."

I stayed rooted to the spot until the sun went down.

But Cooper doesn't know this story. He doesn't know the dreams I have of falling or the way looking out windows on certain floors of buildings makes my knees buckle and palms sweat. Cooper doesn't know anything about me, so I can't really fault him for planning a date that revolved around my worst fear. Except I'm nothing if not spiteful, and he roped me into this, so fault is what I cling to as I get off the train in Brooklyn and drag my feet to his brownstone in Park Slope, his silver PT Cruiser with wood paneling marking the spot on the street in front of his house.

Of course this shithead nabbed a prewar building. I bet he also has a washer and dryer hookup and crown molding and a kitchen that doesn't triple as a shower and living space. Stoking the coals of my resentment, I climb the stoop and aggressively ring his doorbell six times. He opens the door with a brilliant smile.

"Hey," he says, voice laced with warmth. "I honestly didn't think you'd show. I'm glad you're here." His eyes skim over me like I'm some precious piece of pottery that just crossed an ocean and he's checking for scuffs and damage. Where does he get off looking so . . . *caring*?

"Believe me, if my job wasn't riding on my participation in this disaster, your doorstep is not where I'd be right now."

"Ah, really?" His face falls into a look so devastated my breath catches. "And here I thought I'd won you over by involving you in a car crash and inducing a panic attack over the course of a single morning. I'm not sure where I misread things . . ."

A genuine bark of laughter erupts from me, startling us both. Cooper seems to catch the sound, absorbing it as he blinks, that smile returning as his hand absently rubs against his sternum.

"Come in," he says after a moment, stepping aside and gesturing me through the door.

I hesitate, a jangle of nerves and something close to— Excitement? Animosity?—curling through me. In college, the only glimpse I got of Cooper's domestic world was the infamous frat house. And even then, I was starved to see more, wanting to collect endless snapshots of him in his simplest, most mundane moments so I could piece them together on a reel and study him over and over.

There's something so jarringly intimate about the ease of how he's welcoming me into his space now when this was all I wanted then; not a whisper of the hesitation and distance that would wedge between us when I would even hint at hanging out at his place. That old craving in me licks its chops.

But I'm being ridiculous and idealistic. This is for work—his need to save face on the internet and my need to grab at any flotsam that might keep my career afloat. With a steadying breath, I step inside.

I only have a second to take in the foyer that leads into an open-concept living space (frosted with crown molding, called it) when two people zip down the stairs to my left, staring at me with very different vibes but equal intensity.

One is a tall and burly white guy, with a body like a linebacker and a strikingly full beard to round off the look. His size would be intimidating if he weren't bouncing up and down on his (ginormous) toes with a puppy-dog eagerness, eyes glinting as they flash between me and Cooper.

"She's real," he hisses to Cooper, his smile wide.

This is the first time I've ever seen Cooper embarrassed, and he fixes the man with a stony gaze. "Eva, uh, these are my roommates," he says slowly, like he's scared of setting off a bomb. "I was under the impression they wouldn't be here while we recorded."

"We wouldn't miss this," the bearded guy says, throwing an arm around the Latina woman next to him. Her expression stays steady and cool. As tall and jolly as he is, she's compact and reserved, midnight-black hair falling in perfect layers around her golden-brown skin and intricately winged eyeliner accentuating her delicate features. There's something vaguely familiar about her face, and I work to place her.

"Nice to meet you," I say, holding out my hand to her first. "I feel like I recognize you from somewhere . . . Did you go to Breslin?"

"Yup. We had freshmen stats together, I believe," she says,

taking my hand for a quick shake. "With Dr. Shornen? I went by Liam back then."

"Oh my god, hi!" I say, slapping a palm to my forehead as the class and the woman in front of me resurface in my memory. We'd also known each other from the campus Pride organization, and she'd shared her early stages of transitioning at the meeting toward the end of my senior year.

"My name is Lilith," she says, some of her iciness thawing as she smiles at me. "After the first she-demon."

"And I'm Steve. After my grandpa Steve," the gentle giant adds, raising his arm in a way that I could either take for a hug or opt to shake his hand. There's something so damn jovial about him that I shock myself and take the quick embrace. I'm a sucker for a himbo and this man exudes that energy in the best way.

I feel Cooper's eyes on me, and I blush at the moment of softness, backing away from Steve and tucking my hair behind my ears as I roughly clear my throat.

"I didn't realize you two were friends in college," I say, gesturing between Lilith and Cooper.

"We weren't," Lilith says sharply, waving her hands. I cackle that the suggestion seems so genuinely horrifying to her. "We didn't get to know each other until a couple of years ago. I got hooked up with an interview on Rylie's podcast. I founded and run an advocacy group and shelter for queer youth in the city. It's called Euphoric Identity."

My jaw drops as the final pieces of her familiarity click into place. "Wait, wait, wait, you're *Lilith Flores*? Holy shit, you've done some amazing work. I'm a huge fan of yours." I read a profile on Lilith in *New York* magazine about a year ago, the article covering five of the most influential and in-spiring young activists in the city. Over the past five years she's created a network of resources and programming that's transformed the landscape for queer young people to feel safe and loved. She's also responsible for a huge grassroots effort advocating for Black and brown kids in the community.

Lilith's lips curl in satisfaction, but she waves me off.

"No, seriously." I know I'm tiptoeing into level-five fangirl status, but I can't help it. I've had an altruism-crush on this woman since I learned about her accomplishments. "I can't even tell you how much I admire all that you do. I'd love to talk to you about your work. I've had this fantasy of interview-ing you for like, ever."

"You mean on the hot dog thing?" she asks, her nose scrunching in dismay. She quickly wipes the expression, but I'm already flooded with embarrassment.

"Oh. Um. No. I mean, yeah. I do that . . . hot dog thing. But I, uh, I have a . . ." I gesture vaguely, the term *blog* sounding so damn juvenile and dinky that my skin itches. But throwing out the term *platform* would make me sound like a self-important asshole and a huge exaggeration of my reach outside of phallic-shaped foods.

"She writes these really great think pieces on Babble. They're amazing, Lil. You'd love them."

It takes me a moment to realize that the endorsement came from Cooper. I spin around, frowning at him. His gray eyes meet mine with a docile stare.

"You . . . you've read my stuff?" I ask, voice tight and cracking in earnestness, my face erupting in heat.

"Course," he says, lifting one shoulder, then letting it drop.

His smile is gentle and lopsided, and I can't pull my eyes from the curve of it.

I blink a few more times, my lips parting. I feel oddly jarred by his confession. Which is silly. So what if he's read them? Or he could be lying. Or if he's not lying and actually has read them, it was for some weird form of research to find my soft spots and use them against me in this bizarre game he's playing.

He leans toward me like he's going to tell me a secret. "Don't swoon on me, Kitten," he whispers, shooting me a cheeky wink. The spell is broken, and I let out a deep breath, fixing my mouth back into a frown.

"I just didn't know you could read," I reply sweetly. "Lea Michele is shaking."

Lilith's snort fills me with an absurd amount of satisfaction, and she and I share a look.

"I like her," Lilith announces.

"Me too!" Steve chirps. "Don't fuck this up," he adds in a cheery tone, smacking Cooper on the back.

"Only his career on the line as he pays for past sins." I shrug. "No pressure."

"Okay, so this went about as obnoxiously as I expected," Cooper mumbles. "So, uh, bye. Thanks." He makes a shooing motion with his hands, and Lilith rolls her eyes, traipsing down the hallway toward the kitchen. After one more beatific smile, Steve follows her.

"Sorry about that." Cooper rubs his jaw as he grimaces after them. "I asked them to make themselves scarce when you got here so it wouldn't be so . . . energetic, but they don't really believe in boundaries."

"I could talk to them for hours," I say, waving away his concern.

"But you're stuck with me."

"I suppose so," I reply bleakly. His gaze flicks back down the hall, a flare of emotion crossing his features before he smooths them and smiles. If I didn't know better, I'd call that look . . . jealousy.

"Come on. We'll record in my studio." He leads me up the stairs, pointing out the rooms as we pass. "Steve's room. Our bathroom. Lilith's room—she gets her own bathroom and I'm not jealous at all and living in a chronic state of horror over Steve's bathroom habits—"

"She puts up with living with you, the girl deserves a monument, not just a private place to shower."

He narrows his eyes in a half-hearted attempt at a frown. "Fair point. My room . . ." He distractedly waves at a door to our right, and I'm alarmed by my impulse to kick the wood off its hinges and scour adult Cooper's room like a spy gathering crucial intelligence.

I shake myself. As if there'd be anything worth seeing. I'm sure it smells like a mix of weed and dirty laundry and has a bare mattress in the corner. Old habits and all that.

"And this," Cooper says with a flourish, opening the door at the end of the hall and revealing a short staircase that leads up to an attic, "is where the magic happens . . . Outside of my bedroom, I mean." He shoots me a goofy, exaggerated wink.

"You're the human equivalent of Comic Sans," I respond, working to check my own twitching lips as they try to mirror his.

Cooper's grin only grows. "I'm so glad you've picked up

that words of affirmation are my love language. You make me feel so good about myself." Against my will, a honk of laughter bursts out of me. His eyes glint like he was just handed the winning numbers for the lottery.

"After you," he says, gesturing up the stairs.

I click my tongue against my teeth, planting my hands on my hips. "Yeah, right. I've seen this horror movie. You probably keep severed limbs up there. I'm not going to willingly *lead* the way into your creepy attic."

Cooper pouts. "But how else will I get an ideal view of your ass?"

My eyebrows lift, warmth splashing my cheeks as I let out a goddamn *giggle* of surprise. I wipe my features into a grimace. "Well, I can at least respect your honesty. I do have a great ass."

"Always been one of my favorite things about you." Cooper agrees with a gentlemanly nod.

Oh my god, I am horrified at how much pleasure shoots through me. I hustle up the steps, trying to shake off whatever new form of madness I've acquired since setting foot in this alarmingly charming home.

The attic, to my shock, is not creepy nor does it have any dismembered limbs. It's actually rather . . . cozy. A large skylight slants golden sunshine into the space, striking a grand bookshelf overflowing with novels and vibrant green plants. A small bar cart is parked near it, housing an electric kettle and compact coffee maker, a hodgepodge of well-loved mugs arranged on the lower shelf. A plush yellow rug fills up most of the floor, a comfy-looking couch in one corner, two uphol- stered chairs surrounding a round table opposite.

The mics are set up on the table with water bottles next to

them, various other recording and filming equipment tucked neatly into the room. I turn in a slow circle as I take it in, and the sun strikes hanging stained glass, refracting on the walls so it feels like I'm in the center of a kaleidoscope.

My rotation stops on Cooper, attention latching onto his sheepish smile, the way he fiddles with his glasses, pushing them up his nose.

"What do you think?" he asks.

I swallow. I'm probably in competition with Belle on who's more shocked and impressed by their beast's secret room of books and beauty. Wait. No. Belle falls in love with Beast. I despise the vulnerable-looking man before me.

"It's nice," I say with a shrug. I point at one of the chairs. "Should I . . . ?"

"Yeah. Yes. Please, sit." He waves me forward and plops into the opposite spot.

We're silent for a moment, and I keep my eyes far from Cooper's. For some reason, I feel like if I meet his gaze, something humiliating and dangerously tender might play across my face.

"Want some coffee? Tea?" he asks, bouncing up from his seat like the quiet is a physical pressure and he's a spring fighting against it.

"Uh, sure," I say, my voice a bit hoarse. "Tea would be great."

"Peppermint, right?"

My attention snaps to where he stands by the kettle, an unwrapped box of peppermint tea held in his hand. My brows pinch, eyes bouncing between the box and his cautious look. "How did you . . ."

"Come on, Eva." He lets out a rough breath of a laugh. "You drank a giant thermos of it every class. The smell of peppermint and you became practically Pavlovian for me." His smile is timid but automatic, and I have to look away, a painful rasp of emotion scoring down my throat. I let my hair cover my burning cheeks as I fiddle with one of the wires in front of me.

"Tea would be great, thanks," I repeat when I can trust my voice to be cool and unaffected. The crinkling of plastic wrap as he opens the box and prepares my cup sends my brain into a flurry wondering if he bought that specifically for . . . *me*.

No. *No*. I'm delusional. Ridiculous. Of course he didn't buy it for me. It's common knowledge peppermint is good for voice work. I'm positive he keeps it on hand for himself and podcast guests. It's purely coincidence. Coincidence and one decent memory of me.

But a tiny, rapidly beating chamber of my heart keeps echoing the thought, *Unless* . . .

Cooper gently puts a mug in front of me, and I watch with way too much focus at the way his fingers uncurl from the red handle, the thick veins and dusting of dark hair that trace up his exposed forearms. My gaze travels up his arm to land on his face, my stomach tightening when I find him looking at me.

"Thanks," I say, horrified at how breathy I sound. I clear my throat, reaching for the mug and taking a scalding gulp. Why are my hands shaking?

Cooper parks himself across from me again, fingertips framing the base of his mic as he rotates it a millimeter to the left. I toy with the tag hanging from the teabag, avoiding eye contact again.

"All right, Eva. Hit me. What are your rules?"

The question catches me off guard, and my gaze snaps to his. "M-my rules?"

He leans forward, gesturing at the mic setup. "Yes. Your rules. As you like to say, I trapped you into this scheme and already monumentally fucked up one of the dates. I'm trying to avoid screwing anything else up by asking you a pretty simple question. What are your rules?"

Jesus, why . . . why am I suddenly so *hot*? It feels like a heater kicked on, like my face is flushed with a fever. Probably some sort of low-grade allergic reaction to his proximity. I'll likely break out in hives next.

But damn, when did his voice get so low? It's always been rumbly, but something about the quiet timbre and the way his eyes stay hooked with mine makes this conversation feel like he asked me my hard limits in the bedroom and to name my safe word.

I take another boiling sip of tea, sufficiently burning off the roof of my mouth. I frown at the brownish water. Cooper must have poisoned me. *That's* why my body is going through some sort of goddamn riot.

"Well, obviously, I don't want to spend hours of my life sitting here and listening to you mansplain your behavior," I say, already imagining the litany of excuses men seem so ready to deliver. "That's a waste of my time."

"Agreed."

"And I would hope it goes without saying, but don't give away any like, super-private info about me. I don't want hot dog fanatics showing up at my apartment at two A.M. dressed like giant wieners."

"Of course," Cooper says, nodding. "And I'm making a note to change your birthday gift, but I'll worry about that later."

I snort with laughter, then disguise it as a cough, snuffing out the tiny ember of enjoyment glowing in my chest. I look at him, sizing up if I dare hand over the vulnerable thought pacing around my skull. His face is open and inviting, eyes twinkling. What a shithead.

"I guess the other thing is . . ." I let out a deep breath. "I know I totally overreacted to the end of our date and was irrational and ridiculous with the whole . . ." I wave a hand, hoping he'll spare me from having to admit my childish fear.

"Heights situation," Cooper says evenly, expression serious but gentle.

I look away, my leg bouncing so rapidly the table trembles. "Yeah. That. It was silly of me to flip out like that over heights, but, obviously, I'm not a fan and I kind of . . . yeah, lost my cool. And I do recognize that the date ending on such a sour note is partially on me and I'll own that, but I guess what I'm trying to say is . . . um . . ."

"I would never make fun of you for your fears, Eva." Cooper's voice is edged like a knife, eyebrows furrowed as he frowns at me, like even the suggestion he'd poke at that is personally offensive to him.

I open my mouth—to say what, I don't know. Probably to argue, downplay the seriousness of his tone, wipe away the heavy cloud of tension between us with a barb of my own. Anything to toughen up all these soft spots I'm showing. But instead, I nod, letting out a quiet "Thank you" that's more breath than voice.

A few beats of silence pass between us, and I look anywhere but at his face, slotting my bricks of coolness back into place.

"What are *your* rules?" I eventually counter, leaning back and fixing him with an appraising look, trying to regain the upper hand here while I feel like I'm drowning.

Cooper searches my face, a private smile revealing his dimple. He looks at me like he knows I'm all bluster. "Well, I'm not bullshitting you when I say I want you to be honest." He worries his bottom lip between his teeth. "The whole point of this is an airing of the grievances that got us here, yeah?"

"And you trying to make up for them," I point out. I meant it to have a little bite to it, but it comes out delicate.

Cooper's laugh is self-deprecating, and he shakes his head. "*Trying* being the operative word, it seems."

I don't know what to say—probably something witty and cutting and emotionally distant—but he looks so sincere, I suddenly don't have the heart. I shrug.

"So, I guess my rule would be unconditional honesty between both of us," he continues, holding my gaze.

My throat is dry, tongue thick. "I can do that."

His resulting smile is so brilliant, the sky must study his sunniness.

After a moment, he slips back into seriousness, clearing his throat. "I think the only other thing—and I promise I'm not saying this as some sort of dig or scolding for the texting, er, incident . . ." Mortification is a quick flame, my blood gasoline. "But I do try to avoid language and conversations on here that place value or judgment on genital sizes and shapes, if you know what I mean. Lilith has really drawn my attention to how common that ends up being when discussing sex and intimacy and just like, gender in general, and I'm trying to be more aware of it. I don't ever want to make a listener feel, you know, badly for something I flippantly say about dick size or vulva types or whatever. I'm, uh, yeah, just trying to be more intentional about harm avoidance. And whatever." Cooper lets out a whoosh of a breath, pink staining his cheeks and ears.

I stare at him, shame trickling through me. "I'm sorry," I whisper, teeth gritted and hands clenching into tight balls on the table. "You're right. And I'm sorry if I . . . if the texts made you uncomfortable. That wasn't cool of me. I wasn't even thinking. . . . I . . . I'm—"

"Hey, stop." Cooper reaches out, closing his hand over the top of mine, his palm warm and broad and enveloping my curled fist completely. His thumb brushes gently against the jagged pulse at my wrist, and my fingers unfurl at the sudden comfort. "I really meant it when I said I wasn't bringing it up as some sort of scolding. God knows I'd be up on the highest horse for policing how other people talk. I just . . . I'm trying on here, you know?" He waves at the mics. "Trying to learn and grow, at least. I know you were joking around and . . . Well, I get the feeling that message wasn't exactly meant for me."

I snort, my cheeks on fire. The embarrassment is hot and thick, quicksand in my gut. I know he's right, and I know better. Ray and I are petty and run the gamut of bitchy talk between the two of us, but I hate that Cooper thinks I'm the type of person who might publicly shame people's bodies.

"Eva." His voice is low and clear and pins my attention through my flurry of worries. "Me saying this isn't personal. This is a conversation I have with every guest on here. Our timing was just off because of your latest rendezvous with the antichrist and his massive schlong."

I let out a wet laugh, shaking my head, then biting my lip hard.

"But in the name of unconditional honesty," he says softly, "I wanted to bring it up with you."

Holy fuck. Is Rylie Cooper . . . actually showing consideration for other people?

"I get it," I croak. "And you're totally right. Thank you for bringing it up."

Cooper continues to look at me, each moment measured by the heavy thud of my heartbeat. I swallow, looking away and pulling my hand from his. "Should we get started?"

"Are you asking me if I'm ready for my public slaughtering?" he asks, face grim. Then he smiles. "Hell yeah. Let's do it."

He snaps into motion, getting up to adjust the camera on its tripod. He posts the full recordings on YouTube and puts snippets on other social media platforms, and he's agreed to give Soundbites access to the footage for similar promotion and use on their channels.

I take a steadying breath, remembering why we're here, why this matters. If I do this, play into this game, show what a good little soldier I am to Landry and, by extension, William, I'll get that promotion. I'll gobble down my last hot dog and flip the bird to *Sausage Talk*, covering real stories instead. I can do this.

After a quick sound check and Cooper giving me the rundown of his intro, he cues up the recording and launches in. He mentions two sponsors, and I try to weed out if he sounds particularly desperate during that part, remembering he has some skin in this game too. He then gives a brief recap on the outrageous events of the past week-plus, even offering me a particularly kind bio: "While you may know Eva Kitt as the host of *Sausage Talk*, she also writes incredible pieces on her Babble platform. Seriously, I encourage everyone to check her stuff out."

I try to cool the golden ball of satisfaction in my chest from his praise. I don't need a man to hype me up.

Finally, Cooper lets out a deep breath, pretending to be winded. ". . . Which brings us . . ."

"Here," I say, a snarky curl to my smile as I gesture around.

"I'm tempted to imitate the Paul-Rudd-on-Hot-Ones meme," Cooper says, grinning at me.

"How original."

His smile doesn't waver. "That's what I love about you, Eva, you're just so easy to please."

"You're really setting me up nicely to talk about the disaster of our *date*," I say, using air quotes around the last word.

"Why delay the inevitable?" His voice and body language drip with easy confidence. Fuck. Why is he being so chill about this? "Do you want to start or should I?"

"That's a dangerous door you're leaving open for me," I say with an amoral smile. "But I'll go in if you're ready."

He waves me on, a delightful mix of fear and enjoyment playing across his face.

"Well, dear listeners," I begin, pressing close to the mic

and lowering my voice in a parody of his. "The date started with a car crash."

"It didn't *start* with the car crash," Cooper says, leaning toward me.

"Fine, it started with you showing up with a giant hired SUV like we aren't in the midst of a climate crisis and then five minutes later the car crash happened. Is that a more accurate timeline for your liking?"

There's a weighted pause.

"Yes," he reluctantly mumbles.

I paint the picture of the seven A.M. champagne cork to the jugular and the near death-by-stilettos walk of shame (because I was walking in a public place next to him). "I will at least give you credit that the art museum was amazing."

"I knew you'd like that," Cooper says, absolutely glowing. I hold up my hand to silence him, but he's so hyped up he reaches across the table and gives me a high five. I jerk away from him.

"Absolutely not," I say, wiping my hand on my skirt with a grimace. "You don't get a high five for that."

His face falls. "Why not?"

"Because it was extraordinary but you rushed us through it! You almost pulled my arm out of the socket dragging me to the next harebrained thing on the itinerary—a damn helicopter ride, no less—when we had entire hour to ourselves in that amazing exhibit."

Cooper lets out a sigh, shoulders curling as he deflates. "I know. I was just trying to create this really amazing day for you. Us. I wanted it to be special. Start this redemption tour with a bang so you didn't regret agreeing to this."

"I will always regret agreeing to this, so don't trouble yourself with impossible endeavors," I taunt. But my voice is softer than usual, a thread of gentleness knitting through it and into my small smile.

Cooper catches it, his eyes brightening.

"But that's the issue," I continue, firming up my too-soft thoughts as I get back on track. "You were more concerned about *creating* an itinerary that on paper looked great but inevitably set us up for unrealistic expectations. You were so focused on the timetable and details that we hardly had a second to breathe, let alone enjoy what we were doing."

"I get that," Cooper says quietly. He drags his hand along his jaw as he looks at me.

"And a helicopter, dude? Really? Don't you think that's a bit *Fifty Shades*–level extreme for a first date?"

"Huh . . ." He drums his fingers against the tabletop. "Are you saying I can't pull off love bombing as successfully as Jamie Dornan?"

I laugh despite myself. "The differences between you and Jamie Dornan don't begin and end there, baby girl."

He sways toward me, grin magnetic, and I feel myself lean in to the pull.

"I . . . I see what you were trying to do," I admit, horrified to be throwing this man a bone. "And I fully recognize that it was a recipe for a really amazing date, but probably for people who actually know each other better than we do."

"So you're saying you want to get to know me?" The spark of hope in his eyes is so sweet I have to bite back a smile while something in my chest melts.

"*No.* No, no. You misunderstand. I was trying to be generous and allow you to get to know *me.* I'm a goddamn delight."

The radiance in his expression softens to a shimmer, his head tilting to the side as he looks at me. "Well, I already knew that."

Heat rushes up my neck, curls across my cheeks. I look away, becoming aware again of the camera, the microphones, the fact that this is all for show. For both of our jobs. I'm here to challenge him, not be endeared by his smile.

"Piss off. I'm a bitch and you know it." I flick my hair behind my ear, letting out an unbothered chuckle. "I wear it with pride; you don't have to lie to your listeners."

"Okay, calm down, Meredith Brooks," he says, mouth twisting. "You may have quite the bite, but that's what makes it all so fun."

I shake my head, annoyance bubbling through me, but my expression stays calm for the cameras. "You don't get to say stuff like that."

"Why not?"

"Uh, maybe because we haven't talked in six years?" My cool facade cracks, voice pitching and eyebrows furrowing. "Maybe because you ghosted me after I showed you an ounce of emotional vulnerability? Maybe because you don't know me, so how can you act like you enjoy being around me?"

Cooper's eyes make a thorough circuit of my face, his forehead lined and jaw working. He licks his lips. "You keep saying I don't know you, but I know *some* things, Eva."

Challenge is a lightning strike on my tongue. "Oh yeah? Like what?"

He huffs, pushing his glasses further up his nose before planting his forearms on the table. "I know your middle name is Mary and your favorite color is red."

I roll my eyes. "Wow. Congrats on your Google search and learning your colors," I say, waving at my red silk blouse and coordinating skirt. "Do the slutty little glasses you wear now help with that? Is that why you couldn't see all the red flags you were waving in college?"

"You think my glasses are slutty?" he says, smile huge and voice hopeful.

"We both know your glasses are slutty," I say, narrowing my eyes. "Men don't pick tortoiseshell frames like that without being a little bit of a ho."

It takes him a few moments to tamp down his smile, but he fixes me with that serious look again. "I know you studied journalism in college. Got your master's in it too. I know your favorite course, at least up through junior year, was art history. You liked it so much you were thinking of adding it on as a minor."

I shift in my seat, eyes darting away. So maybe the date wasn't as randomly planned as I thought. "Wouldn't put it past you to have called Breslin and bribed the registrar for that info."

"I know your favorite type of food is Thai and you order it at a level-five spice, then don't even break a sweat."

A memory flashes to the one time we'd gone out to a restaurant all those years ago. I'd offhandedly told him how much I loved Thai food during a lecture, and it had surprised me speechless that he remembered when no one in my family had ever bothered to retain the fact. Cooper took me to my favorite place near campus for our third date. He'd tried to match me on getting the dish extra spicy, and spent the rest of the dinner choking and sweating. But also smiling as I gently teased him about it. I remember how charming I'd found him, how goddamn endearing he was. It's funny to think that only a few weeks after that, he spent the remaining handful of our shared lectures in a different seat, ignoring my existence completely.

"I know you're the middle child of six kids and you grew up in a suburb outside of Philly." He pauses, tilts his head as his gaze softens, turning thoughtful as he searches my face. "I know you write some of the most thoughtful pieces about current issues and poignant critiques of media and pop culture that I've read recently."

My lip snarls, and I want to snap at him to stop. I want to tell him not to bring my writing into this artificial bullshit. I'm 99 percent sarcasm and flagrant irreverence, but I actually *care* about my writing. I don't want him tarnishing that in this ridiculous nice-guy parade.

"Maybe I don't know everything about you, Eva," Cooper says, leaning forward. "But I know some things, and all those things make me want to know more. If you'll let me."

The way he says it scrapes the bone, the sincerity seeming so raw and real. I hate my stupid, overeager heart for leaping at the idea. Someone wanting to know me. Someone seeing my sharp, prickly edges and gleefully asking for more. But that's not how it works, not for people like me. It's fun and games and an exercise in sparring until it becomes too much work, too many minefields to navigate the second things get a little bit real.

Rylie Cooper was the origin story for the trend that's plagued my entire dating life, and I'd be a fool to fall into the same trap again.

"That's enough for today," I say, ripping the headphones from my ears and tossing them on the table before fumbling with the mic's off switch.

"Eva—"

"I'll see you for our next sham of a date," I cut him off, scurrying for the door and not looking back.

"Hold on," Cooper says, chasing after me down the stairs. "Why are you so mad?"

"Why am I so mad? Are you serious?" I spit, barreling down the second-floor hallway. "Aren't you supposed to be some psychic master problem-solver of people's feelings?" I despise the way my voice cracks, feelings damming up my throat and building pressure behind my eyes. Being an angry crier is the world's greatest curse.

But even if I could speak, I'm not sure I'd be able to artic-ulate exactly why I'm so mad, and that fuels my rage all the more. I make it to the ground level and flounder with the front door's lock, finally wrenching it open. Cooper's palm lands on the wood, shutting it again. I stare at the gold handle, unable to look at him.

"Damnit, Eva, will you talk to me?" There's fire in his voice, making the threatening tears in my eyes burn even more. "Tell me what's going on. Tell me what you're thinking."

I grit my teeth and pinch my thigh to regain control over these pesky and pathetic feelings. I force my features into a glare as sharp as a dagger, looking up and pinning him with it. I hope it slices him to ribbons. "No."

"No?"

I shake my head, offering a cruel smile. "No. I'm not going to tell you what I'm thinking. You want a gold star for remembering a region of food I like and a color that I wear all the time? Good for you, I'm sure your fans will be weeping at how goddamn sentimental and caring you are. But none of this is real. You don't *get* to know me. You don't get to back me into a corner and demand I tell you things about myself so you can feel better about being a fuckup in college, then use it against me in a stupid podcast recording to prove you're some sort of nice guy and deserve the frenzy of adoration you've somehow tricked people into. Now move your fucking hand."

Cooper's face is ashen, lips parted as he stares at me. His palm slides from the door, landing with a heavy slap at his side.

"Wow, you *are* a good listener," I say with a sneer, then walk out the door.

Chapter 8

EVERY PLANET MUST BE OUT OF ORDER WITH NEPTUNE double-penetrating Uranus because something unbelievable is happening: I'm actually having a good time at work.

It's taken me almost a week to recover from the sour taste the podcast recording left in my mouth, but my current *Sausage Talk* guest is doing some serious heavy lifting on my mood.

"And then you squirt just the tiniest bit of mayo as a classy touch to bring it all together," Lizzie Blake, a Philadelphia-based erotic baker turned internet sensation, says as she places a dollop of mayonnaise at the tip of the bun and steps back to evaluate her gloriously vulgar work. "There you have it, wiener à la titties," she says with a booming laugh.

I stare at her with hearts in my eyes. While we usually try to get actors and musicians on the show, this isn't a huge stretch. After going viral multiple times for her shocking work, Lizzie has built a small but mighty vulva-shaped empire . . . The power of the entrepreneurial spirit and what have you.

After begging (exploiting) a favor from Aida for going along with all the Cooper stuff, she let me mix things up with Lizzie.

"Where do you come up with these ideas?" I say, my usual deadpan mask slipping as I smile between Lizzie's freckled face and the homemade pretzel buns she's fashioned into boobs with halved olives as the nipples, a hot dog artfully carved with a very detailed head and veins sitting in the doughy cleavage. The whole, er, package is completed with a dribble of mayo jizz and a side of shredded lettuce with tomatoes to look like bush and balls.

It's so crass. I love it beyond measure.

"Anything phallic I model after my partner," she says with a wave behind her shoulder.

My eyes widen as I look from the foot-long hot dog on the table to the tall man in the corner whose furious blush I can see from here. He's so absurdly handsome that Lizzie's swollen, pregnant belly that she's currently rubbing makes a whole lot of sense to me.

She cackles as she takes in my face. "I'm kidding. Kind of. More than anything I just never evolved beyond my perverted twelve-year-old-maturity-level brain and found a way to channel it for good. If we have to work, we might as well have fun with it, right?"

I blink, a sudden surge of envy cinching my throat. Well . . . damn. She pretty much summed up all my withered hopes and jaded dreams. I shake off my sudden storm cloud, volleying some banter for a few more minutes, then wrap up the shooting.

"This might have been one of my favorite interviews ever," I say, turning to Lizzie.

She beams. "I was about to say the same thing. Honestly, I was super nervous about this because you're just so damn . . ." She waves her arms at me wildly. "Cool. And I have zero chill, but this was awesome."

"Do you want to be friends?" I blurt out. A blush claws at my cheeks, but I don't take back the question. It's an indisputable fact that I will develop the most intense (parasocial if need be) connection to any woman who is both hilarious and by some miracle finds me cool.

Lizzie looks me dead in the eyes. "We already are. All that's left is the formality of a blood oath."

"I'll grab the knives."

Lizzie's still laughing as her partner approaches. "This is Rake, my baby-daddy and muse," she says by way of introduction. "Rake, this is my new best friend, Eva."

I shake his hand and he offers me a warm smile. I know I shouldn't push my luck and embarrass myself even further by being so overeager, but a sparkly connection like this in your midtwenties is a hell of a drug. "Since we've already established that I'm moderately obsessed with you, would you two like to join me and my friend Aida for brunch? She's the producer of the show." I point to the side where she's hunched over an iPad with her assistant producer.

Lizzie follows my finger and lets out a longing groan, leaning against Rake. "Me of six months ago would jump on that, but current me feels like I'm about to be cracked in half by this giant thing"—she rubs her bump—"thanks to this giant thing"—she gestures to Rake—"and I need to get my feet up and body down as soon as humanly possible or Rake will suffer the consequences of my meltdown." He smiles at her, smoothing back her hair before planting a kiss to the crown of her head so tenderly my teeth ache.

"Is this your first?" I ask.

"Christ, no," Rake says hoarsely. I almost start panting at the sound of his Australian accent. Damn, good for Lizzie. "We already have two girls at home."

"These are little ladies three and four," Lizzie says, patting her rotund stomach.

"Good god, twins?" I say because, honestly, in this economy, how?

"I know," Lizzie says with glee. "My little red-headed army. Unfortunately, we'll have to have at least one more after this. I hate even numbers, so four girls just won't do."

Rake's face drains of color, his eyes popping out of his head.

"Ready to go, Eva?" Aida asks, sparing us all from whatever might come next.

Lizzie and I say our goodbyes, exchanging numbers, Rake still looking shell-shocked as he ushers her out the door.

"Well, she was a goddamn delight," Aida says, leading us out of the studio to the elevators.

"I want to be her when I grow up." I punch the up button a few times with a sigh.

"I don't think she ever grew up," Aida says kindly. "That's probably the secret to it all."

I open my mouth to respond, but Aida holds up a finger, shooting me an apologetic look as she answers a call.

I mull over what she said, a surprisingly sharp ache growing in my chest as I realize how right she is. I fucking hate being a grown-up, if I can even claim the moniker. It's nothing but emotional politics and taxes and having your heart broken by every person you let in even a smidge. When I was a kid, all I wanted was to grow up, get out of my too-crowded house and away from my too-successful siblings, and be the main character in my own life. I never imagined I would become as tragically average an adult as I was a child, still as lonely as ever.

My mood sinks low, but Aida doesn't notice, fully engaged on her phone our entire walk to a brunch spot on St. Mark's Place, a former wig shop turned sex shop turned evening tapas bar with an unbeatable Thursday morning bottomless-brunch deal.

"It's a ninety-minute wait!" Ray whines by way of greeting at the hostess stand. Aida finally pockets her phone, sensing the crisis in his voice. "I offered to blow anyone and everyone to be bumped up the list, but it didn't do any good."

More than a few heads turn, taking in the beautiful tall Black man with zero filter and a bubblegum-pink buzz cut. I bury my face in Ray's chest as he pulls me in for a hug, laughing as I breathe in his familiar scent. "This town has gone to hell."

"In a handbasket," he agrees, nudging me away to give Aida a hug of her own. "And not to be a cog in the capitalistic machine, but I have to be at work by four. That doesn't give a lot of flexibility to my bottomless-champagne-indulgence-and-two-hours-to-sober-up-before-my-shift plan."

"What? No!" Aida pouts. "The whole point of getting

drunk on a Thursday midmorning was because you were supposed to be off."

"I got called in last minute, but it's okay. I'll quit."

I snort. Ray acts blasé about his job as a station chef in a
trendy Tribeca restaurant, but I know how deeply he cares.
He has big dreams of running his own kitchen someday, and
I know it will be the best damn restaurant on this island, but
at the moment he's doing his time and coming when called.

But I need this brunch. Desperately.

Both of my friends are impossible to pin down, and I've
been looking forward to this date—entered on both my Google *and* Apple calendars—for three goddamn months. I'm
not about to go another fiscal quarter without making this
happen.

"Maybe if they didn't make such asinine seating choices
we wouldn't have to wait this long," Aida says, craning her
neck to look around the dining room overflowing with six-top
tables seating groups of two or three.

"We could go somewhere else?"

Ray shakes his head. "I already tried some spots next
door and did some scanning for online waitlists. Everywhere
is packed. Some nerdy-ass pumpkin-carving convention is
starting today and anywhere close is a similar wait. We might
have to reschedule."

No.

The hostess clears her throat. "We had some spots open up
at our community seating," she says in a hushed voice, glancing
at the crowd of people hovering by her stand. "I think a pair
already took some of the seats but if you hurry you might be
able to snag something."

Ray moves faster than a bolt of lightning. Aida and I laugh as we follow him toward the back of the restaurant at a more reasonable pace. I try not to get my hopes up, but then Ray comes into view, arms spread wide and palms planted along one side of the banquet table to save three seats, scanning the room like an apex predator looking for movement.

He fixes us with his electric grin as we approach, and it raises my spirits to see him so excited. But as we get closer, I realize there's an undercurrent of wickedness in that smile. The hairs rise on the back of my neck as his eyes widen in a manic look.

"Eva," he says when I'm finally next to him, giving him a confused frown at the high pitch of his voice. "I believe you know our tablemates."

With horrible, sinking dread, I slowly drag my eyes away from Ray, praying to every Roman and Greek goddess I can remember that the person I'll see is some extremely hot celebrity and not the man I want to avoid for the rest of my life.

But the goddesses like to laugh at mere mortals like me because Rylie fucking Cooper smiles at me from across the table, Lilith seated next to him.

"Maybe we should cancel brunch," I blurt out. I feel the shocked looks of Aida and Ray, but all I can see is the horribly enchanting, crooked smile Cooper's trapped me with.

"Subtle," he replies with a wink. "But I would never ditch Lilith just so you could have me all to yourself, Kitten. I would hope you'd treat your friends with a similar level of decency." He gestures at Ray and Aida, and they melt at the beautiful roughness of his voice. Aida collapses in her seat with a contented sigh. Fucking traitor.

My face heats to the point of discomfort, and I grope for something witty to say back.

Nothing.

The shock of seeing him (and his peach-colored sweatshirt with a retro Santa Claus walking a dachshund with *Santa's Favorite Wiener* written in red cursive) has cleared my brain of all thoughts.

"Nice sweatshirt," I manage, my lip curling. I'm still looming over the table, something my height has me used to, but I'm also struck with an awareness that it puts my tits at about eye-level with the man I want to withhold all things pleasurable and good from. I plop into my seat.

"Thanks, I just got it yesterday," he says, pulling it taut and looking down at it. "It reminded me of you, actually."

I roll my eyes, and am horrified to hear Aida and Ray laugh.

"I love it, but it should be illegal to wear holiday gear in early October," Ray says. "Happy Hallo-Wiener is literally right there."

Cooper's jaw drops. "I'm ready to invest."

I grab the arm of the passing waitress. "Please bring me a pint glass for my mimosa and hold the orange juice." She spares me the time for a dirty look before traipsing away.

Ray, Aida, and Lilith introduce themselves, passing pleasantries back and forth while I wait for my quart-jug of champagne.

"So you're the infamous Rylie Cooper," Ray says, propping his chin in the palm of his hand and smiling at the object of my loathing. "You were a highlighted topic on our brunch agenda."

"Eva has endless kind things to say, I'm sure," he responds, mirroring Ray's pose. I hate how fucking adorable it is.

"I looked up how to create a bowel obstruction on an effigy doll," I mumble, only to wheeze as Aida and Ray elbow me.

"Are you as terrible as Eva makes you out to be?" Ray asks, ignoring my scowl.

"The me she knew definitely was." Cooper straightens his shoulders. His serious expression solicits a double look from all three of us, and he blushes from our attention, pushing his glasses up his nose and clearing his throat. "I mean, I like to think I did a modicum of growing up in the past six years."

"I would never dare trust a man who uses the word *modicum*," I reply, getting another elbowing from my friends. Damn, if they're so enamored with him, maybe they should be the ones forced to date him for the viewing pleasure of the internet.

"There's a sex joke in there somewhere," Lilith says, meeting my eyes and winking. I laugh, but the sound harmonizes with Cooper's, and I cut mine short.

Another thing I hate about Cooper is his laugh. It's so deep and rich, the afterglow from a shot of whiskey. He laughs with his whole body, shoulders shaking and face crinkling, his fingertips covering his mouth like he's half-heartedly trying to hold back his humor. I have the alarming urge to slap that hand away and scold him for attempting to keep that from the world. Clearly, I am extremely ill and in need of medical attention.

It isn't until a few seconds later that I realize the table has fallen silent, Cooper's eyes fixed on me, something gentle and tempting in the way he holds my gaze. Everyone else is staring at me staring at him, and I correct my face into a grimace, trying not to name whatever softer expression it's replacing.

"Is this weird for you two?" Lilith asks, flicking her finger between me and Cooper.

"Yes," I answer over Cooper's clueless "What?"

Lilith rolls her eyes at him. "This whole . . . whatever this is," she says, twirling her wrist. "This experimental dating, make-up thing. Seeing each other again after so many years."

"Well, *this*"—he gestures at the table—"isn't one of the dates, this is just glorious happenstance."

For some reason this delusional man looks at me for confirmation, and I tut like a disappointed grandmother. He turns his attention to Ray. "Eva makes no secret of her love of hanging out with me, so this probably just made her week. I'm going to change her ringtone to 'Obsessed' by Mariah Carey after this."

Ray's laugh is uninhibited, and he leans around me to look at Aida. "I'm sorry, but I kind of love him. He gives it right back to her."

"Be careful how you respond to that or I'm taking you both off my Spotify family plan."

"Don't let her bully you," Cooper says, pressing his lips into a line against his fighting smile.

"Because what you let her do to you on your own podcast this week was . . . ?" Aida nudges.

Cooper laughs again. "Touché."

"Should I leave?" I ask, getting dramatic. "Seems like I'm

not even needed in this conversation since you all want to talk about me like I'm not here."

Ray and Aida roll their eyes in unison, and I focus my attention on Lilith, returning to her original question. "Yes. It's all very weird and very annoying. It's like being in some psychological experiment without a governing body for ethical oversight."

"Gosh, you know how to stroke a fella's ego." Cooper flashes his dimple.

I ignore him. "So far it's just been an artificial and curated date that I then had to give a play-by-play recap for all of Pedro Pascal's internet to dissect and comment on. But at least I can say he's living down to my expectations. I'll always take satisfaction in being right."

"That last bit kind of sums up dating men in general," Aida says. The server lets out a tiny snort of amusement as she sets down a round of mimosas, and I'm mortified that Cooper and I flash her matching grins.

He gently touches her arm before she can leave and leans up to whisper something in her ear. Jesus, he might as well suck on the lobe for how close they are. I can't believe she's giggling at whatever he's saying instead of running away screaming. When he finally lets her go, she nods and winks at him, a blush fanning across her cheeks.

I grind my teeth and look away. Poor girl. I should probably warn her. Instead, I gulp down a hefty amount of my drink, letting the bubbles float to my head and trying to think of anything besides the way Cooper's lips ghosted near the server's skin. My lovely brain lands on how brutal everything's been since the first recording released.

I've turned off notifications on social media, overwhelmed by every person on every app wanting to give me their every opinion on this whole thing while calling me a raging bitch at a rate that isn't exactly surprising but doesn't make me laugh quite as much as I thought it would.

I know that's the point of it all, and William's thrilled (cold, humorless, straight-to-the-point) email yesterday telling me about the spike in *Sausage Talk* traffic and cross-promo stuff with Cooper's podcast has made the powers that be very happy. There was even another dangle of that promotional carrot at the end with encouragement to keep up the good work as the dutiful dancing monkey. Hell, even my Babble posts have seen a substantial hike in engagement. But the bitter, loud part of my brain is regularly reminding me that all of that attention is thanks to this asinine social media charade and not any actual journalistic talent on my part.

I want to ask Cooper if he sees the comments. I want to ask him what goes through his head when some kind soul calls me hot or hilarious. If he feels quietly justified when the majority of people call me mean and say he's too good for me. But, more than anything, I want to know what he *thinks*—about me, about this, about our past, about the fucking weather and what bodega has the best bacon, egg, and cheese—and I hate that damn curiosity that's only been growing since he reentered my life.

"Call me old-school," Ray interjects, saving me from my own spiraling thoughts, "but I prefer the thrill of seeing a date crash and burn in real time." We all look at him. "Don't get me wrong, your little podcast thing is hilarious and all"—I could kiss Ray for referring to Cooper's livelihood and career as a *little podcast thing*—"but there is no higher form of living art than witnessing a terrible first date or dramatic breakup in the flesh."

Lilith lets out a choked laugh, hiding her smile behind the rim of her champagne flute.

"Like, I don't mean to call attention—"

"You literally get out of bed each day for the sole purpose of calling attention," Aida interrupts.

"But the table over your right shoulder"—he nods toward Cooper—"is about two minutes away from full screaming breakdown."

With the subtlety of a wrecking ball, Cooper whips around to look right as a broken sob from the table in question echoes toward us. On instinct, I reach across the table, grabbing his face between my hands and pivoting his head to look back at me.

"Be chill for one minute, I'm begging you," I whisper, eyes locked on his. Cooper's pupils dilate, nearly eclipsing the silver of his irises, his glasses falling down the bridge of his nose.

I try not to notice his swallow or the weighted breath he lets out that tickles the sensitive skin of my wrists. I ignore the gentle shift of his cheeks under my palms as his mouth curls up in an inevitable smile. I have absolutely zero awareness of the trace of his tongue across his bottom lip, his low, nearly laughing voice as he says, "You better talk me through it, then."

My hands drop from him like he burned me, his words creating a deep flush from the tips of my fingers to the apples of my cheeks. If Cooper has any awareness of the innuendo he painted in my mind—his lips parted and lids heavy with lust, words like *good* and *yes* and *right there* panted out under twisted bedsheets—he doesn't show it. Instead, he quirks a questioning eyebrow, smiling innocently at me, then at the table, waiting for an update on the disaster unfolding behind him.

"He's shaking his head mournfully," Ray whispers, eyes fixed on the couple.

"She's clenching the sides of the table so hard her knuckles are white," Lilith adds, shifting in her seat so it looks like she's facing Cooper when really she's spying over his shoulder. "Leaning across the table now. Fringe from her infinity scarf just dipped into her egg yolks."

"Infinity scarf? Good god, what year is it?" Cooper mutters.

I laugh so hard a few heads turn, and I disguise it as a cough.

"He's shifting from pathetically contrite to righteous indignation," Aida relays without moving her lips.

"A terrible move," Cooper says, eyes widening, body vibrating with the urge to turn and stare. It isn't until he looks at me, gaze bouncing to my mouth and lingering there for a beat too long, that I realize how big I'm smiling at him. I fix my lips into a flat line.

"She's pointing her finger in his face now," Ray says breathlessly. "Man is beet red. He's looking around for an exit like a passenger on a crashing plane."

"Now he's templing his fingers and pressing them to his mouth. I repeat, his fingers are templed," I say, watching as the guy tries on the impassive look of a tech-bro posing for a magazine spread. The sweat running down the sides of his face makes his inner peace look less than convincing.

"Oh my god, she's—" Ray's voice is cut off as the woman

stands up from the table and raises her voice so loud that no one would blame Cooper for turning and looking.

"Yeah?" the woman bellows, sizing up her soon-to-be-ex-boyfriend from tip to toe. "Well, I fucked your cousin on Memorial Day so I guess we're even." With a soap opera actress's level of flair and precision, she picks up her champagne flute and splashes the contents in the man's face. "And just so you know, being with her was the first time I didn't have to fake it in over a year, you lazy prig."

My jaw crashes to the floor as I gasp. Cooper whips his head to me, his expression a mirror image of my own. We watch with a healthy mix of shock and admiration as the woman storms out, muttering something about giving the cousin a call. A full minute later, with an audible sigh and a ducked head, the man pulls out a few bills from his wallet, drops them on the table, then scuttles to the exit.

The entire restaurant holds its breath in a weighted silence, scared to disrupt the bubble of drama we just witnessed.

"Cheers to his cousin," Cooper stage-whispers, restarting time as our group breaks into nervous laughter. We raise our glasses, and Cooper's eyes meet mine over the rim.

"I've never seen something like that," Aida says, shaking her head, then taking a long sip.

"Brunch is truly the beginning and the end, the alpha and omega, of a relationship's lifespan," Ray says sagely, making me snort like a piglet.

I slap my hand over my nose, and I don't know why the first place I shyly look to is Cooper. His gunpowder eyes spark as they hold mine, crinkled at the corners as he smiles at me. Like he heard me. Like he loved the sound. Like he's calculating how *he* can make me laugh in such an unfiltered way.

A few slutty little curls tumble across his forehead as he studies me, and I have the disarming impulse to reach across the table and run my fingers through them, push his hair back and cup his cheek in a way motivated by far more tenderness than when I touched him a few minutes ago. My palms still burn with the memory of the contact.

Ray says something witty and biting, and the conversation tumbles in a million different directions with the electricity of the drama. I focus on the sweat of my water glass, watching the cool droplets roll to the table, trying not to think of anything else.

Everyone shares anecdotes of the wildest things we've seen in this bizarre city, and at some point, we order food and dig in.

"This burger will heal me," Lilith says, taking a giant luxurious bite. She lets out a happy moan, eyes closing. "Yup. All my problems have been solved."

"Poor Lil's been under a mountain of stress lately," Cooper says, patting her back as he takes a bite of his breakfast burrito. "I had to force her to come out with me."

"A tactic you use on everyone in your life, then?"

Cooper's eyes flick to me, and he winks. My cheeks flush, and I hide my misplaced smile with a sip of my drink.

"What's stressing you, Lilith?" Aida asks, ready to cortisol commiserate at any given moment.

Lilith slumps in her chair, pushing her hair back. "I'm

finalizing the details of this huge fundraiser my organization is hosting in a few weeks, and it's taken several years off my life."

"What's the fundraiser for?"

Even through her palpable exhaustion, she beams. "We're starting this new series at EI, getting a bunch of guest speakers and experts to come and talk to the kids about what healthy queer relationships look like, and the fundraiser will be the main source of financing for it. It's been a long time in the making, and it's wrung me dry, to be honest."

"I love it," Aida says, lifting her glass toward Lilith.

"I can't even tell you how much I could have used something like that," Ray adds, leaning toward her. "I mean, hell, I could *still* use something like that. There's so little out there representing happy, healthy romantic relationships for folx. You should be very proud of what you're doing. It's filling a huge need for queer youth."

"Thank you," Lilith says, bowing her head. "It was Rylie's idea, actually."

I shoot a skeptical glance at Cooper as he chokes on a sip of his drink. He frantically waves his hands. "Don't listen to her. She's giving me way too much credit."

"I'm *not . . .*"

"You *are*," Cooper says, fixing her with a stern look. After a beat, he turns to us, expression softening. "We were watching a movie and all I said was that I would love for there to be a sort of queer renaissance of Meg Ryan–esque rom-coms. That it'd probably be really impactful for younger people to grow up with a backlist like that."

"Right, but that was the seed for the whole idea!"

"Lil," he says, that frown back in place.

"You do give him way too much credit," Ray says in a gently teasing voice. Cooper points at him and nods. "But that's also a really lovely thought, Rylie."

I am truly perplexed to find myself nodding in agreement, eyes glued to him as my brain reorganizes itself, trying to fit this version of Rylie Cooper who has caring thoughts about queer kids and the representation they'll grow up with into the mold of the dude-bro Rylie Cooper from years ago that would use *gay* as a pejorative when joking with his frat. That old version starts to crack at the edges, time eating away its foundation.

"Well, regardless of if you want to take credit or not, I'm blaming your good idea on the truckload of stress I'm being crushed under."

"I'm much more comfortable being at fault for something. Can only go up from there." His eyes flick to me, and I ignore the surge of butterflies through my stomach.

"My biggest issue is that my caterer quit," Lilith says, rolling out her neck. "This is the third one, actually. For a city with some of the best chefs in the world, we're definitely short on reliable ones."

"I'll do it," Ray says without missing a beat, eyes wide and earnest. He checks himself, clearing his throat and trying to fix his features into something slightly less excited. "I mean, I'm a chef and I would love the opportunity, if you'd consider."

Lilith perks up. "What kind of food do you cook?"

Ray chuckles. "Babe, I can cook whatever kind of food you want for an opportunity like this."

"And you have a team?" Lilith asks, folding her hands on the table, full businesswoman.

"I'm not going to bullshit you because I actually respect you, unlike most people I interview for jobs with, but no. Not at the moment. That doesn't mean I can't get one together, though. A good one."

"How good?"

"The fucking best," Ray says with a winning smile.

Lilith eyes him for a few moments, then nods. "I'll give you my info and you can send me your portfolio. We'll set up a tasting."

Ray somehow manages not to squeal in excitement, and it takes all my willpower not to let one out on his behalf. This could be huge for him, and my bones vibrate with how badly I want it to work out.

My eyes accidentally flick to Cooper, and I'm startled to see such genuine enthusiasm in his expression when his gaze clicks with mine. He looks like a guy who truly cares that my friend and his friend might help each other out. With a sinking gut, I also realize that Ray working for Lilith would be one more thread knotting me to Cooper, and all of those will be snipped as soon as I get that promotion and out of this stupid scheme.

But Lilith's event is in just a few weeks. I'm sure our charade will fizzle out on a similar timeline. Maybe it will be the perfect parting gift from this huge headache. Yes. That's it. If I have to suffer Cooper's company, at least my friend can add a huge event to his list of impressive culinary experiences.

"I'm sorry to be a wet blanket, but we should probably get our checks," Aida says, looking around for our waitress. "Ray, you work at four, right?"

Ray's elated grin dims and he nods, searching for his wallet. My heart sinks down low with my gut. I don't want brunch to end . . . despite Cooper's presence.

"It's taken care of."

We all snap to attention, looking at Cooper.

"What?" Aida says, thick brows knitted together.

"Brunch was on me," he says with a shrug. We all continue to stare, and a blush creeps up his cheeks. He pushes his glasses up his nose, then drags his hand through his hair. "Eva has gifted me a rather profitable couple of weeks with our, er, notoriety and some sponsors . . . It's the least I can do."

My gape turns into a snarl as his words sink in.

Wow. Here I was thinking he was in this to win back lost sponsors that finally realized he was a clown. But no, apparently I've acted as a financial catalyst for my least-favorite person while I whimper like a kicked puppy for a promotion that gets me out of shoving hot dogs in my mouth for a paycheck. Cool.

"That's so nice of you. Thank you," Aida says, looking genuinely grateful.

"Seriously. That's so awesome. We'll get you next time," Ray adds, reaching across the table and giving Cooper's forearm a squeeze.

The only way there will be a next time is if I'm six feet under and they're coming together for my memorial, I swear to god.

Cooper's humble smile rankles, my blood boiling, and I push back from the table. "Bathroom," I mumble, trying not to break into a dead sprint for the toilets.

I lock myself in the small space, pressing my forehead to the surely disgusting and germ-riddled door as I try to catch my breath.

Oh, that fucker. That *fucker*. I thought this whole thing was hurting him, that he was losing sponsors and revenue streams. That we were on opposite but somewhat even footing. But of course he's already making dividends from this shit. I should have known it was more than just getting into the public's good graces.

With a rattling breath, I stumble to the sink, turning on the cold tap and reluctantly meeting my eyes in the mirror.

Get a grip, you horny, angry monster, I scream in my head, fixing my features into a look that could freeze hell over. *Stop seeing a good guy who isn't there.*

I wash my hands with icy-cold water to calm down. I need to get out of this thing as quickly as possible and with any scraps of dignity intact. I'll play the game and jump through the damn hoops and I *will* get that promotion at the end. And I'll eat Rylie Cooper alive along the way.

My reflection is more resolute while I dry my hands. I square my shoulders and lift my chin, adjusting the hang of my white silk blouse, undoing a button from the top on a whim, revealing more of the black lace bralette beneath. The silk creates a deep V to the cinched waist of my tight black skirt. Satisfied that I look confident even if I don't feel it, I exit the restroom.

And am met by Cooper's sultry smile as he leans against the wall directly across from me, hands in his pockets. He straightens up, and we stare at each other for a few silent seconds, his eyes making a quick circuit of my body. I force mine not to do the same to him.

"You look really nice today, Eva," he says. I tilt my head and lift an eyebrow. He clears his throat, color burning his ears. "I mean, you look nice every day. But I, uh, like your, um, shirt."

Eat him alive, Eva.

"This was fun," I say, cocking my hip and resting my shoulder on a stack of boxes lining the hall.

"It was." Cooper takes a timid step toward me. Moth to a fucking flame. "I had a really good time," he adds with a lazy smile. His eyes glint behind his glasses, sparking some tinder in my chest. I snuff it out but it leaves me with an idea.

"That sounds like a cliché someone uses at the end of a date," I reply in a low purr, leaning toward him a fraction of an inch, toying with the ends of my hair. Cooper catches the movement, watching my finger twist the strands before trailing to my necklace, following the gold chain to the pendant of a snake that sits right between my breasts among the black lace. I watch his Adam's apple bob as he swallows.

"I guess it kind of does." He sways toward me, almost imperceptibly, and I smile, his eyes tracing the curve, pupils dilating.

"Well," I murmur. Less than an inch separates us, and his nostrils flare, jaw going tight. I breathe in deeply, aware of the way my chest lifts, the neckline of my blouse parting and my bralette visible. Cooper's eyes predictably dip. "Guess that's date two on the books." I straighten my shoulders and raise my voice to a normal tone.

Cooper blinks a few times, cheeks flushed and lips parted as he stumbles back like the coolness in my voice was a gust of wind pushing him away. He clears his throat, but his voice is still strained. "Um. What?"

"Date two wasn't life-changing by any means, but one of your better performances thus far," I say, adjusting the cuffs of my top with businesslike jerks. "Glad we crossed that off the list."

It takes him a moment, but Cooper catches up, shaking himself. He moves forward, planting a hand on the wall behind me, leaning close again. "This doesn't count as one of the dates," he says, voice firmer than I'm used to. I fight back a shiver.

"It most certainly does." I lift my chin, refusing to budge a molecule of personal space. "For all I know this was some elaborate setup you created. Wouldn't put it past you to go way too big instead of just going home."

He scoffs. "Yes, Eva. You're right. I've planned every moment of my week around filling up this restaurant so you'd be forced to sit with me for brunch while our friends gawk at us. Couldn't think of better circumstances to win you over."

I let out a tinkly laugh, digging through my purse and pulling out my compact and red lipstick, my knuckles brushing his chest as I lift the makeup to eye-level. "It's cute that you said that sarcastically. Some self-awareness would do you good." I open my mirror and twist the tube, painting my lips with a practiced stroke. I pout, then stretch my mouth into my most alluring smile. "We'll debrief this weekend, yeah? Your place again?"

I *think* Cooper tries to speak, but all that comes out is a sort of choked sound.

My reflection glints back at me with deep satisfaction that I've regained the upper hand. I snap my compact shut, shooting him a wink followed by a swift pat to his cheek. "You're a trooper, Cooper. Try not to miss me too much in the meantime."

I float away, radiating satisfaction that I got in the last word. I'm almost out of the hall when his voice reaches me, both earnest and amused as he calls, "Too late. Miss you already."

Chapter 9

IT PHYSICALLY PAINS ME TO OGLE COOPER—I'D RATHER walk on hot nails than be attracted to this man—but it's impossible not to notice he has an impeccably bombastic ass as he leads me up the stairs to his recording studio a few days after brunch. It's a bit obscene and offensive for a man to be so caked up on a Sunday afternoon. I force my eyes to my feet.

Cooper is all good cheer and chatter as we set up, oblivious to my attempts to ice him out. He gushes about some amazing pasta dish Steve made for them all last night as he places a perfectly brewed cup of peppermint tea in front of me, and I deeply resent that he has the home life I crave like an orphaned Victorian child.

"Congrats on conning people into taking care of you, but can we get on with this?" I wave at the mics and camera setup.

Cooper blinks a few times, his smile slipping. I almost

feel bad, but then his grin fixes back into place and he says, "Right. Gotta give the people what they want." He laughs, and it's a harsh reminder that this is all a scheme to him, that I'm a pawn in his sponsorship ploy.

With little fanfare, Cooper starts recording, moving smoothly through his intro. "Well, let's recap," he says coyly. "Date one was a shit time with good intentions, but shitty nonetheless. Date two, you took the lead on and tried your damndest to woo me."

"I was not *trying* to woo you," I interject.

"Sorry. I should have known all that charm of yours comes effortlessly," Cooper says with a flirty wink.

I glare back, my annoyance compounded from the tattletale blush burnishing my cheeks. "I must have walked under a ton of ladders and shattered all the mirrors recently because bad luck would have it that I ran into you at brunch," I say into the mic, trying to navigate away from Cooper's insatiable flirting.

We go over the main points of the meal for listeners, then Cooper asks, "Where does the experience rank in my sparkling track record?"

While I'm not feeling generous by any stretch of the imagination, I shrug and decide to be honest. "You've done worse in a group setting."

Cooper's smile is radiant, eyebrows raised in excitement. "Does that mean I've made up for the infamous frat house night that haunts you still?"

"Oh god, nothing was worse than that frat house night. I'm not sure you made up for it, but you certainly did better than it."

"Come on, that night couldn't have been that bad!" Cooper splays his hands, leaning back in his seat. "Me and the boys always knew how to have a good time."

"You and the boys were toeing a fine line between a good time and a massive drunken orgy incorporating Solo cups and beer pong."

It all comes back to me as rancidly as if it happened last night. The heavy scent of weed and beer and Axe body spray. The pumping music and rowdy crowd. Cooper and his buddies all shirtless in jeans and cowboy hats, a sheen of sweat on their chests as they slapped each other's backs and loudly ogled the few women in attendance.

"Like I said, we knew how to have a good time," Cooper quips, but there's something deflated in his tone, his smile forlorn and not reaching his eyes.

"I have never seen a more homoerotic gathering of men than at your frat house and I've been attending NYC Pride for nearly a decade. There were numerous points during the night where you and 'the boys'"—I offer my most exaggerated air quotes for the video recording—"screamed 'No homo' before pantsing someone or sticking your tongues down each other's throats after successfully shotgunning a beer. All in the name of brotherhood, of course."

The memories feel like a smack on sunburn, a quiet, hot ache that lingers even after all these years. The humid, suffocating energy of Cooper and his friends, their toxic deployment of neutral words, the sinking feeling of disappointment I wasn't sure I was even entitled to.

I've been aware of liking people, not genders, since I was

old enough to register a crush, but growing up lonely in such a crowded house required all my energy be applied to getting by and taking care of myself. I didn't have the bandwidth to process a label for my sexuality until I found breathing room in college. But even twenty-one-year-old me tiptoeing around my pansexual identity—not sure if I was outwardly and actively queer enough to claim a spot in the community—felt uncomfortable at the way Cooper and his friends acted. I remember watching him, the cavalier way he paraded around as a stereotype of masculinity, the reeking perfume of it that I pretended to like as I curled into myself, annoyed that I felt annoyed.

I'm surprised to see remorse flash across Cooper's features now before he hangs his head. "I remember that. I think about it a lot, actually."

"One of your prouder moments?"

His head snaps up. "One that eats at me. So much about that time in my life haunts me."

My lips part, instinctually prepared to snap back with something inflammatory, but my throat hollows out at the serious expression on his face, the lines notched between his eyebrows in a frown instead of around his eyes in a smile. I bite my lip, then tilt my head, silently telling him to go on.

Cooper leans away from the mic and takes a deep breath. Then another. I hear the rattle of nerves with each exhale, and something in my chest shifts, my heart giving a sudden and surprising squeeze at his discomfort.

And it clicks. I sense what he's about to say, the defensive but proud set to his shoulders and jaw. My expression turns open and genuine for the first time in a long time with him, and I give the tiniest shake of my head, telling him it's okay. Telling him he doesn't have to go on.

He drags his hand down his face, then leans his cheek against it, partially covering his mouth from the cameras. *It's okay*, he mouths, then gives me a wink and a smile before dropping his hand back to his lap.

"I'm bi," he says at last, forming the words clearly and steadily as he hunches closer to the microphone. "This isn't my coming-out or some secret, I've alluded to it a few times on here before, but my sexuality still feels somewhat of a private topic to me so I don't talk about it often . . . Maybe that's just my internalized biphobia holding me back, though, who knows."

He lets out a rough, self-deprecating laugh, eyes meeting mine. His smile is slow, a little timid. I want to return it. I want to silently, softly, encourage him to keep going, but my breath is snarled in my mouth, and all I can do is stare.

His smile falters, and he clears his throat, bashfulness returning. "Regardless, I was *not* out in college. I was very, *very* deep in the closet, and acting out in a lot of ways that were toxic and perpetuated this idea of heteronormativity that I thought could save me, especially within frat life. I thought if I was masculine enough, aggressive enough, the one delivering the funniest jokes at the expense of a community I wasn't openly a member of, I could maybe earn my straight guy card. And that infamous night with you was one of my more extreme showings of that."

There's an extended pause, and I belatedly realize I'm supposed to fill it. Cooper is staring at me with a brave face, a tiny glint in his eyes that says he's ready for whatever jab I'm going to throw.

Instead, I shake my head, trying to clear the fog. "What . . . what changed?"

Cooper starts like I surprised him. His jaw works as he studies me, weighing how genuine my question is. And in his true, unguarded fashion, he slowly smiles again, eyes locking with mine like nothing makes him happier than opening up to me.

"Well . . . I hit rock bottom. And it was dark and shitty and I lived down there for a while. But, eventually, I realized I couldn't hate myself into someone I liked. So I decided to give accepting myself a try." His voice is low, almost a whisper, eyes fixed on me. "Extensive therapy did some heavy lifting too, I'll be honest."

From a distance, I remember we're recording all of this, that he's sharing this into a microphone, and part of me wonders if what he said was even picked up. But the greater, stronger, delirious part of me wants to shut down every microphone and camera and grab Rylie Cooper by the front of his sweatshirt and shake him, demand he tell me every last detail that has actually changed in him since I knew him. Beg him for more of this truth. Collect all these new pieces as I try to put his puzzle together. Make him tell me if I can trust this version of him or if I'm just adding layers to the man that's profiting off this whole ordeal.

But this moment isn't about me. None of this has ever been about me, and that's a new and hard truth I need to reconcile with.

Silence stretches again, and Cooper clears his throat. "So . . . yeah. I was a total dumbass that night—"

"Interesting you used past tense," I say, words sharp but mercy soft as I half-heartedly step back into my role. It seems to spark fresh energy in him, and he reaches across the table and gently chucks my chin.

"Fair. But I'm a dumbass in new and exciting ways now. Ones much less clichéd and damaging than being closeted and homophobic. And I'm very grateful you've given me a chance to explain myself. That's not an opportunity people get often."

It feels like my chair is pulled out from under me, my world tipping and temple hitting the floor, the impact rattling my brain and scrambling all the things I thought I knew about this guy.

He . . . he sounds genuine. Like he truly is grateful to be around my hateful ass, working to undermine every notion I have about him. The idea is candied, too sweet to tolerate, and my teeth ache as the idea melts through me.

The rest of our conversation passes in a blur. I must respond, because Cooper's eyes keep trailing to my mouth, his own curling in a smile or opening in a laugh every few minutes from something I say. I can only pray it's nothing as soft and dangerously tender as the pressure building in my chest.

Do I . . . Oh good god, do I actually *like* talking to Rylie Cooper? Have I not done anything to cure this terrible affliction in the past six years? I must be more mentally ill than I realized.

"Regardless, I'm sure I'll knock it out of the park with our third date," Cooper says in a way that signals a wrap-up to the episode, a smirk that's pure, hungry challenge.

"Not gonna hold my breath, baby girl."

"Want to give me a hint on what will win you over?" he says, leaning forward, his glasses slipping down the bridge of his sharp nose.

"And ruin all my fun? I'll pass."

Cooper laughs. "That's fine. I'll nail it without your help."

I go to make a low-hanging sex joke, but Cooper holds up his hand.

"Now I know what you're about to say, I'm sure it's the same thing our listeners must be thinking: *Rylie, you took a women's study elective in college, why would you need a hint? You must be an expert on women!*"

I roll my eyes so hard I see spots.

There's a laugh in Cooper's voice as he continues. "Well, I'm here to set the record straight by saying, yes. Yes I am. But you, Eva Kitt, are not just a woman. You have the devil in you. But don't worry, I'll win her over as well."

I roll my eyes again, but a giggle bursts out of me. "You're an idiot."

"Yeah, I'm that too," he says with a crooked grin.

Heat rushes through me, and I swipe my headphones off as Cooper closes out the episode. I take a deep breath to clear my head. Another. One more should do it . . .

It's no use. This is all so much, and the urge to flee shoots through my muscles.

The second he turns off the recording equipment, I jump out of my seat, grabbing my jacket and purse and taking a step toward the door.

"Wait." Cooper jerks to standing, knees hitting the edge of the table, microphone wobbling. The command, the whisper of desperation in his voice, locks me in place. He pushes his glasses up his nose, clears his throat a few times, then coughs.

"Ew, are you sick?" I ask, twisting my face into a look of dismay.

Cooper blinks for a moment, then shakes his head, laughing shakily. "No. Not with a cold, at least." He lets out a long breath, dragging a hand through his hair, the waves springing back against the smoothing gesture. "Will you get coffee with me?"

He asks in such a rush, I process it on a delay, but my shoulders stiffen in a defensive posture like he just asked me to gargle with cyanide. "You're in charge of making the dates," I say, forcing my voice to be as churlish as possible. "If you want the next one to be coffee, that's up to you."

Cooper shakes his head again. "Not as one of the dates." He holds up his hands, ready to block my protest. "I know. I know. You would never willingly spend time with me outside of this arrangement, you've made that very clear. But please, just this once, can you give me an hour over coffee where we pretend to be friends?"

His gaze is so intense, I have to look away, eyes sweeping around the room. I can't keep them occupied for long, my attention obstinately set on returning to him. His lean frame and hands shoved in his pockets, the slight curl of his shoulders toward his ears, the tips of which have turned bright pink.

I know I need to turn him down, come up with a quick excuse or a flat-out no. Too many egregious, confusing emotions are grappling for purchase in my stomach, and I need to remember that he's profiting from this, making strides in his career while I scramble to get away from hot dogs and non-

sense. My heart beats up into my throat, and I feel jittery—
exposed—like I was the one who was just brutally, beautifully
honest and not Cooper. I can't even imagine how raw he must
feel.

It's only when his eyes light up, face breaking into a smile
equal parts victory and disbelief that I realize I'm nodding. I
clear my throat, but my voice still comes out scratchy, "I can
pretend to be your friend for an hour. Just this once."

Somehow, his elation grows. "You won't regret it," he says,
grabbing his coat and shepherding me toward the door.

I let out a rusty laugh, and I hope it sounds disbelieving
instead of nervous. Because the way something soft shifts in
my chest—a warmth radiating from the center and growing
hotter along the back of my neck, like tendrils of energy are
needily reaching out arms for Cooper—I already know this is
something I'll regret.

Chapter 10

COOPER LEADS US A FEW BLOCKS TO WHAT HE'S TOLD ME
is his favorite coffee shop in his neighborhood, a cozy cafe in
a squat brick building with a million potted plants hanging in
the window.

"After you," he says, holding the door open for me.

Something about his smile hits me—how damn happy he
looks to be welcoming me to his favorite spot—and suddenly,
it feels like I'm walking on shifting sand, and I trip over the
threshold.

But Cooper's there, one hand at my elbow, the other at the
small of my back, steadying me. I straighten, and his hand falls
away from my arm, but the other stays gently pressed at the
base of my spine, the warmth of his palm making it feel like
I'm lying in the summer sun.

"You okay?" he asks, voice a low vibration near my cheek.

I shake my head, then jerk it into a nod. "Fine," I say, not feeling fine at all. He still doesn't move his hand. "Grab us a table." I nod at the only one open as I step away from his touch. "I'll order. What do you want?"

His eyes flick to the board as he bites his lower lip. The way the edge of his teeth push into the pillowy pinkness makes heat rush to my cheeks, and I dart my gaze away.

"I'll do an iced latte," he says, turning back to me. I make the mistake of looking at him again, his grin sunny and lopsided. God, I hate him.

I nod, pursing my lips and shooing him toward the table.

The line is long, the barista taking the time to actually chat with each customer in a way that's disarmingly personal. It makes sense why Cooper likes this place. The bright, mismatched decor, the staff that genuinely seems to give a shit, patrons greeting each other with knowing smiles . . . He's found Midwestern friendliness in this brutal city.

As much as I try to fix my attention to the chalkboard menu, it keeps slipping to Cooper. I can't help but study the way he absorbs the room and then reflects it back—a smile playing at his lips as he watches a little girl blow bubbles in her pink drink while her mom beams, his ears perking up as a trio of friends whoop with laughter over some joke, the subtle way his eyes melt as an elderly man reaches across the small table to brush his thumb at the corner of his companion's lips.

Finally, I put in our order and wait for the drinks at the

end of the bar. Cooper catches me looking at him and makes a big show of waving his arm like I lost him in a crowd. My cheeks heat and I look away, taking a scalding sip of my black coffee the second it's placed on the counter.

With a deep breath to calm my shaky center, I head to my demise . . . I mean, our table.

"Iced latte with oat milk, Polly Pocket," I say, sliding it to him.

"My hero." Cooper grins, tapping the wrapper off his straw, poking it in the drink, and taking a sip. "Why oat milk, though?"

My eyebrows dip low. "Aren't you lactose intolerant?"

"No?"

I blink a few times, studying him. "Oh . . . I thought for sure you were. You give off that energy."

"I give off lactose-intolerant energy?" Cooper says, leaning back, face fixed in a sour expression. "What does that even mean?"

"I . . . I just . . ." I swirl my hand at him. He glances down at his sweatshirt, which is embroidered with SILLY GOOSE ON THE LOOSE and an image of the animal fleeing from a pond. At least this one he's upgraded with a hood. "I feel like someone who can consume cheese without issue wouldn't compensate with a fit like that."

"This shows I'm a warrior," Cooper says, slapping a hand to his chest. It makes me think of a goose flapping its wings and I snort.

"I don't know, man, you just have the energy of someone who tweeted about being a tummy ache survivor long after it stopped being funny. Probably pinned it as your last one as that ship sank. It seems reasonable that milk could take you down."

Cooper is silent for a moment, jaw slack as he rapidly blinks. I shift, worried that somehow this was the jab that hit him too hard.

Then his face creases with a smile, his laugh infectious. "You're brutal."

I try to hide my own smile but it sneaks through. "So?" I mumble, taking another sip of my coffee.

His grin slips into something more pensive, head tipping to the side as he studies me. "It's alarming how much I like it."

I gulp down another sip right as he says that, and the hot liquid stabs down the wrong pipe as I involuntarily gasp. It takes everything in my power to choke it down instead of spitting it right in his face. Would serve him right if I did. Who does he think he is, saying something like that out of the blue?

"You good, Kitten?"

I wave him away, blinking back tears and holding in some rib-shattering coughs. "Fine," I wheeze. Cooper gives me a skeptical look, casually sipping his drink as I collect myself.

"As much as I love spending time with you and listening to all the creative ways you bully me, I did have a motive for asking you for coffee."

"You've decided to preserve the remainder of your dignity and call this whole thing off?" I'm speaking from a way higher horse than I deserve to be on as my eyes continue to water.

"Not a chance, sweetheart. I'm having way too much fun, and dignity is overrated." He winks at me. My grumpy reflexes aren't quick enough, and I flash a smile. He stares at my lips, gray eyes sparking, and it feels like he's trying to memorize the shape of them.

I clear my throat, and he comes back to himself, shifting in his seat. But he's still quiet, toying with his discarded straw wrapper. His face is clouded, and he twists the white paper around his finger so many times the tip starts to turn purple.

I don't register the decision, but my hand darts out, stilling his fidgeting. With a flick of a manicured nail, I slice the vise of paper, my palm settling over his knuckles.

We both stare at where I touch him, and, with a delayed reaction, I pull my hand away, toying with my rings as I mumble, "What's wrong with you?"

Cooper rakes his teeth over his bottom lip, watching— entranced—by *my* fidgeting now.

"There are things I need to tell you," he says at last, eyes dragging up from my hands to my face. "Things I need to tell you without an audience or the pressure of me trying to win you over. Things I spent six years sorting through and agonizing over that I finally have words for."

My throat is tight, but my face must display all the questions bouncing through my head that I can't manage to verbalize.

"I owe you an explanation, Eva," he says in a rush, his body deflating with the force of it. "Will you hear me out?"

A voice in my head breathlessly whispers, *Finally.* I

smother it down, scolding it with a scream that this is a trap, that getting my hopes up with Cooper—with *anyone*—is a parable I've repeated way too many times for it to be acceptable or cute. But, like the fool I am, I feel myself nodding in agreement.

Cooper looks at me—really looks, like he's seeing every alarm-bell fire in my brain, like he's wading through the swamp of my worry and dismay to find something to say that will satisfy me.

"I met you at one of the worst times in my life," he finally says.

I'm incapable of not taking things personally, and I feel my expression sour.

Cooper shakes his head, holding his palms up and giving me a pleading look. "Nothing to do with you, Kitten. You were a bright spot."

I shouldn't bask in the praise like it's sunlight on winter skin, but I do. "Please, continue telling me how great I was and how you screwed everything up," I deadpan, fixing my face back into an unimpressed mask. His smile is all-knowing like he can see his words glowing in me and his gray eyes linger for a moment longer before he sinks back into a steady seriousness.

"The spring of my junior year, my younger sister died in a car accident." He says it simply, voice crystalline and free of emotion, but pain flashes across his face, his entire body flinching like the words cut him just to say.

Sympathy slices through me, chilling my blood. I am, quite simply, the world's biggest dick, making jokes while he was getting ready to tell me something like that.

"Don't give me that look, Kitten," Cooper says, voice strained with an attempt at levity.

"What look?" I say, feeling tears well up in the corners of my eyes.

"That look that says you feel guilty for negging me two seconds ago."

I open my mouth to protest, but he shakes his head, offering me a strained smile as he reaches out and places his hand over mine. I let him keep it there.

"You didn't know, and I wouldn't want you to hold your tongue on my behalf." The world pauses, shrinking down to where it's just me and him, those gunpowder eyes of his seeing right through me. There's a pulse where our skin meets, and I can't tell if it's the jagged thump of my heartbeat or his. I'm not sure it matters.

With a slow movement, like I'm trying not to spook a skittish animal, I rotate my wrist until my palm rests against his, my fingers curling around his warm skin.

Cooper stares at our hands, teeth working against his lower lip. He clears his throat and then continues. "It was a Thursday night and she was hit by a drunk driver when she was heading home from practice. She was eighteen, a senior in high school, with a track scholarship to Columbia and a beautiful fucking life ahead of her." I watch his throat work as he swallows, jaw tight and lines of tension etched around his eyes.

His breath rattles, ripping the air from my lungs like a moment of my discomfort can do anything to match his years' worth.

"My world fell apart, Eva," he continues, voice grating like sandpaper. "It fell apart in a way that's hard to comprehend even now, let alone for a dumbass twenty-something-year-old who doesn't have a clue. Like I said, this was the year before I met you, but that year, I was a wreck."

Even feeling like an outsider with my step and half siblings, it would absolutely destroy me to lose one them. I couldn't imagine not seeing Serena's smile or never hearing Derek's laugh again. I grip Cooper's hand tighter, pulling his sad eyes up to mine. I'm not sure what my expression looks like right now—probably some paltry, useless show of sadness that will never be enough—but whatever he sees there has his shoulders relaxing, his hand holding mine back with gentle strength.

"I had another younger sister at home who I still couldn't talk to without breaking down or feeling anger over the sister I lost," he says, keeping his voice low. "My parents' marriage fell apart, and they were fighting nonstop. I was drinking and smoking a ton of weed and hating who I was and doing everything I could to dull myself into a husk. Someone who could tell a joke or throw a good party that didn't have to feel anything real."

His confession sits heavily between us, the air thick. I have the urge to look away, hide behind a veneer of competent but distant understanding instead of looking directly at the raw honesty he's handing me. Run away so I don't feel the urge to hand him something real in return.

"You met me at my worst, Eva," he reiterates, keeping a hold of my hand even though my grip has gone slack, palm sweating. "I was dumb and devastated and I can't take it back

but I want to give you the context as to why. You didn't deserve my mess, but I gave it to you anyway."

I stare at him, emotions a mangled, pulpy knot in my
throat. His cheeks turn red, eyes flicking down in sudden shyness.

"Do you . . . do you kind of see why I was the way I was?"
he asks, a touch of desperation in his voice as if he needs my
absolution. I'm not sure why he would. I was a blip in his timeline of tragedy. My feelings shouldn't matter . . . They didn't
matter then.

"I understand," I manage, voice rusty.

Cooper looks at me again, eyes roving over my face as he
checks for my sincerity. Whatever he finds there makes him
smile. "I really nailed this light and cheerful friendship hour,
huh?" he says at last, pulling his hand away and taking a sip
of his latte.

My fingers curl into a tight fist like they're trying to hold
on to the lingering heat of his skin, embed it into my own. I
make a conscious effort to release my grip.

"Yeah, you're really good at small talk." I allow a sly smile
to play across my face, no matter how fake it feels. "A damn
court jester."

Cooper laughs, the sound coursing through my chest like
voltage, and it takes a concerted effort not to rub my palm
over my heart. "Next friendship hour I'll make sure to do a
vibe check and let you choose between a wine-and-whine or
beer-and-queer so you have a better idea of what you're getting
yourself into."

"Don't forget the third option," I say, shooting him a playful look. One of his eyebrows arches up, enjoyment dancing

across his features. "Dessert-and-hurt where we trauma dump over cheesecake and espresso martinis."

Cooper laughs again, dimple highlighting his boyish grin. His hand darts across the table, grabbing mine and pumping our arms in an overzealous shake. "You, Eva Kitt, have got yourself a date."

Chapter 11

"I HATE THIS IDEA," I SAY TO AIDA OVER FACETIME AS I GET ready for the recording starting in half an hour.

"Thanks. I worked really hard on it."

I drag my attention from my mirror as I finish applying mascara, giving her a disbelieving look. "Really? It was *your* innovative and brilliant idea to recycle the worn-out trend of people reading mean comments about themselves? That's the kind of forward thinking they pay you the big producer bucks for?"

Aida rolls her eyes, twisting her curly hair into a bun on the top of her head. "Okay, obviously my first choice is not to replicate an idea that peaked in popularity in 2013, but I'm also not paid *big enough bucks* to contradict a directive sent from the top."

"This was *Landry's* idea?" My scowl is so severe my wet

lashes smear along the tops of my cheeks. "Award-winning journalist Landry Doughright is leading this derivative charge?"

"Technically, it came from Prince Nepo, but Landry replied to the email chain with endless praise. They think this will be a good way to generate more engagement. Encourage people to keep commenting if they think they can make it on one of your videos."

As much as I'd prayed all of this attention would snuff out, it's grown like a wildfire. I feel like I'm not far from choking on the smoke.

People have continued to make dramatic video edits of us from snippets of our recorded sessions, which is fine and expected, but still feels a bit weird to see the reality of what actually exists between me and Cooper warped into a false romantic narrative. But those videos are nothing compared to how creeped out I was to find that pictures of us walking to get coffee and saying goodbye outside of the cafe had been added to the usual mix. The invasion of privacy was instant and physical, like I could feel some watcher's hot, sour breath on my skin as I lay in bed and zoomed in on the shots, not believing my eyes.

I'd called Cooper at two A.M. in a panic I disguised as anger.

"Hey, Kitten. I was just dreaming of you," he'd said when he answered the phone, voice rough with sleep.

"A nightmare, I hope. Did you have something to do with these photos of us?"

There was a long pause, and I could hear the sheets rustling as Cooper repositioned himself in bed. For some reason, it had felt obscenely intimate, and I pulled the phone away from my heated cheek, putting it on speaker.

"What photos?" he'd asked, sounding slightly more awake.

Instead of answering, I texted him a slew of posts, a picture of us midstride in a crosswalk near his apartment as the thumbnail of one, his hand on my lower back as I'd walked into the cafe for another.

His breath caught, then turned deeper as he looked at the messages. "I didn't know about these," he said at last. "But I wouldn't worry about it, Eva."

"I shouldn't worry about some creep on the street taking my picture without me knowing and then posting it on the internet?" I could tell he was trying to soothe me, but I refused to be soothed.

"They probably thought you were Florence Pugh and wanted to capture a celebrity sighting. Figure out who her sexy new boyfriend is."

"You definitely have personal assistant vibes in that photo," I said, the fist of worry in my gut loosening a bit despite my better judgment.

"A workplace romance? How scandalous," Cooper teased, pulling a reluctant laugh from me. "I'm sure it was nothing, Kitten. Get some sleep."

Bizarrely, I did as he said, but my sleep wasn't at all restful. The rough lilt of him saying *romance* and *scandalous* looped through my head in a heated soundtrack, images of his lips dragging up my stomach, between my thighs, hands cupping my ass and lifting me onto a desk playing in fragmented and feverish clips as I tossed and turned.

I haven't slept well since.

"Rylie has to read mean comments too. It isn't just you," Aida says, knowing full well that won't placate me.

"Isn't the whole idea that *I* am the mean-comment generator and he reacts to what I say with nothing but charm and good humor?"

"We're taking the opportunity of bullying to the masses," Aida deadpans, clearly reading an email instead of focusing on my whining.

I frown, returning to the mirror and finishing my makeup. There's a ticking in my gut, a tiny scrape of possessiveness that says I'm supposed to be the only one who teases Cooper; that random people in the comments don't have a right to snarky remarks because they don't know him like I do.

But that's ridiculous.

I don't *actually* know Rylie Cooper. Sure, the fucknut has been stuck in my head for weeks, and I can't seem to have a thought without it relating to him, but that doesn't mean I *know* him. I guess I just feel territorial about my right to antagonize him.

"Are they really bad?" I ask, trying to hide the trepidation in my voice.

Aida shrugs. "I don't know, honestly. I haven't seen them. William, or one of his interns more likely, grabbed them. They'll auto-generate on the screen for shock value."

"Oh, good. Can't wait."

"All right, let's get on the call." Aida ends our FaceTime without fanfare. William requested a quick turnaround on this video to feed the ravenous algorithm, so we're recording remotely on our computers . . . Soundbites not wanting to pay a filming crew's measly wages to record in person probably also has something to do with it.

I flick on my ring light and log in to the video call, trying to ignore the giddy swoop of my stomach when Cooper's goofy grin is the first thing to greet me.

I haven't seen him since our coffee last week, and it bothers me that I'm still caught off guard by his looks—the way his lips are perpetually curved in an almost grin, ready to laugh at a second's notice, the deep creases around his eyes that are a shade lighter than the rest of his skin, like he's spent every sunny season smiling and the humor is tattooed there. No amount of exposure therapy seems to cure me.

And then there's his fucking personality.

Cooper has worn away my resistance to contact with his absolutely ridiculous texts. They come at random times a day— questions like in a jellyfish situation, would you rather pee on someone or be peed on? Or do you think bees let out a lil moan when they do their thing on a flower? Videos of puppy bellies being jiggled to a pop song's beat, or a meme of a sleepy kitten dressed in a bonnet with photoshopped flames behind it and the text HOW DARE YOU LOOK AT ME WITH THAT TONE WHEN IM FEELING CRANKY AND SENSITIVE over the top, with the accompanying message: got the sense you were thinking of me <3.

It made me furious that I had, in fact, been thinking of him. I made sure to tell him I hadn't. To my surprise, I also found myself arguing for peeing on, accusing him of being a weird bee voyeur, and telling him about how our golden retriever was my best friend when I was growing up.

And Cooper always responded. Promptly too. Seamlessly navigating us from the silly and trivial to coaxing out detailed answers about my day, what I was researching for my next Babble piece, what I thought about a book I was reading. And in this bizarre alternate universe I find myself living in, I was genuinely asking him about his day in return. Hungry for the answers.

It's all so different from how it originally was, and I keep waiting for him to go radio silent like he used to.

It takes me a beat to realize Cooper is waving his hand at me on the screen. I come back to myself with a shake, and his smile widens. "Oh, you *are* there. Thought your screen froze with you gazing longingly at me."

I give him a blank look. "You know how in baby books and pre-K they show children flashcards and diagrams of people's emotions? You must have gotten your wires crossed between abject disgust and mooning."

"So now you're saying you want to moon me?" Cooper's eyes shoot wide, and he makes a show of looking over both shoulders. "I mean, it's just us here so if you insist . . ."

Aida's login stops me mid-curse, and I'm horrified to see William's name join the screen. As if it isn't bad enough I have to read mean comments for internet engagement, now I have to do it in front of an entitled rich boy with the personality of a wet wipe.

"Rylie, Eva," he says by way of greeting.

I give a pathetic little wave, Cooper professing his love of William's silky gray pocket square instead of hello.

"Good to see you too," Aida says coolly, not taking well to being ignored. William's eyes slit to her in the barest degree of acknowledgment.

"Just a quick run of show," he says, glancing at a printout in front of him. "This should be fairly straightforward—all we need is for you each to read some preselected comments and give us a clip-worthy reaction. We'll be recording both of you during the readings so make sure to react to each other's as well."

I raise my hand like a shy kid in class, and William looks at me like he can smell my timidity through the screen and it's foul. "Can we see these comments before we start? Kind of, um, gear up for the tone?"

"No. We want this to be as authentic as possible."

My gaze slides to Aida, alarm bells going off in my head, but she has her professional mask on.

"Right. Yeah. Of course." I kick myself for being so soft and nervous. This is a job, *my* job. They aren't going to set me up for something that makes me look stupid . . . at least, not any stupider than shoving hot dogs down my throat.

William goes through a few more boring production details and editing plans, then leans back in his chair, the subtlest uptick at the corners of his mouth like an emperor about to watch a match at the Colosseum, raising the hairs on the back of my neck.

"Sounds like I'll probably cry. Can't wait," Cooper says, meeting my eyes and giving me a reassuring smile. I relax a fraction. If I'm going down, I'll be dragging him with me, that's for sure.

The countdown begins, and I quickly adjust my top, dragging my fingers at the edges of my lipstick before stilling my fidgeting. Aida gives us the signal to start, and we volley smoothly through introductions while a gnarl of suspense grows in my stomach.

"All right, I'm up first," Cooper says with a clap of his hands, rubbing his palms together as he grins at me. "But I personally doubt the comment sections have anything on you, Eva."

I flip my hair, shooting him a baleful smile.

Text pops up along the screen, and he leans forward, squinting as he reads it. "*No one tell Freud but I'd call him Daddy.*" His eyes light up and he looks straight at me. "Did you know that 'Spank me, Daddy' in Dutch is *'Geef me een klap, Papa'*? Can you imagine whipping that out in bed?"

It takes me a beat to process that. "Do you let every intrusive thought win?" I blurt. "And Freud was Austrian."

"Yes, of course," Cooper says, waving away my argument. "But can you imagine him working through that kink with a Dutch patient?"

I laugh, then disguise it as a cough, trying to hide my smile from the camera. The tension in my shoulders eases a bit. Maybe this won't be as brutal as I was thinking.

Cooper holds my gaze, a glint flashing in his eyes that says we're in this together, then he clears his throat and reads the next one. "*You know a man holds too much power when you crave being teabagged by him.* Oh my. Okay. Are these mean comments or unhinged thirst comments?"

"Jesus Christ, did you write these about yourself?" My face twists in annoyance.

His eyes shoot wide and he shakes his head. "Despite circulating rumors, I have never actually craved being teabagged by anyone."

"We'll bring in a polygraph for our next video."

"Aw, Kitten, you're always so eager to figure out the next time you'll see me. It's sweet."

My mouth falls open in a mix of surprise and indignation, but Cooper's laugh is a magnet, pulling me closer to the screen. With a start, I straighten my shoulders, chancing a quick glance at William's thumbnail, then back to Cooper. My stomach swoops when I realize William looked pleased.

"Okay, last one," Cooper says, wiping imaginary sweat from his forehead. "*I feel*—Oh god, this one is going right for my jugular."

"Read it, coward," I tease, returning his look that we have each other's backs in this.

Cooper wilts for the camera, but carries on. "*I feel like if Rylie Cooper had facial hair his mustache would never connect with his beard* . . . That one really does hurt. Not that I'm saying it's true or anything . . . but I can't say it isn't either."

"The only thing worse for a man than facial hair commentary is a hairline critique," I say with a solemn nod. "Rest in peace, friend."

Cooper's face lights up like a kid on his birthday. "Eva Kitt, am I your *friend*?"

I blink a few times, trying to connect his overjoyed expression with my statement, my mind tripping over itself in the process. "I—No. I mean . . . What? Stop." I try to wipe my features to neutral, leg bouncing under the table in an effort to dispel whatever silly demon has recently possessed me because, against my wishes, Rylie Cooper does feel a bit like a friend lately.

Which is utter nonsense.

"I'm your *friendddddddd*," Cooper croons like we're children on the playground and he's accusing me of French-kissing him. "Oh my god, Eva, you're so obsessed with me."

"Can we cut for a second?" I snap, eyes bouncing between Aida and William. She's smiling like she's watching a rom-com; he's smiling like a shark that sniffed blood.

William's face falls into a scowl and he unmutes himself. "Why are you cutting? That was great content."

"I just, uh, really need a second," I say, sweat trickling down my back at the scolding and the sudden surge of generally nice feelings toward Cooper.

William shakes his head, the disapproval of it gripping me by the throat. "This is journalism, Miss Kitt, and I'd appreciate some professionalism. You have to lean into a moment, expose its truth. Or are you not up for the task?"

I open my mouth, not sure how to respectfully express that I don't think a recorded Zoom call where we read social media comments actually counts as journalism, but his expression has me slamming my jaws shut and nodding in agreement.

"Right. Sorry. You're right. I just had a moment where I was too in my head. Sorry. I . . ."

"You're doing great," Cooper says, the low tenderness in his voice surprising me so thoroughly I flinch. I slant a look at him, and his expression is serious, fixed on me. "That was fun, but Eva's right, we should cut the friend stuff. It undermines our whole back-and-forth schtick."

"I'll make the editorial decisions on the content of the company I'm running, thank you," William says in a stony voice.

I catch Aida's eyebrows dipping, and I can tell she's wondering if that's true or if she'll have to work through the night to get everything edited and uploaded herself at the rate Soundbites demands.

Cooper holds up his palms, leaning back. "Not trying to overstep—"

"Your gait isn't long enough," I mumble.

He shoots me a good-natured eye roll. "But I did want to gently remind you my contract states I have a not-insignificant say in the final content put on the site," he continues. This is news to me, and my instinct is to be resentful that he has some level of protection and control in this thing while I'm floundering, but Cooper's jaw is set, muscles poised in false relaxation contradicted by the protective glint in his eyes that I realize is for . . . me.

Indignation and anger flash across William's face, but he smooths it into something placid, a hint of a patronizing smile on his lips. "Of course. And this is something that can be discussed over email instead of taking up significant filming time."

"Right," Cooper says with a genuine kindness, attention slipping from William back to me. "It's Eva's turn to get roasted, isn't it?"

There's a simmer to his voice, a hint of teasing that tickles down my spine. I tense my shoulders against it. "Taste of my own medicine, I'm sure you'd call it," I reply, getting back into my apathetic character.

"Only if I were clever enough." Cooper's grin is so crooked and goofy I almost laugh. Aida counts us down again to start.

"All right, let's see," I say as my first mean comment pops up. I rapidly skim it, trying to fight a frown. "*She seems like one of those girls that smell overwhelmingly like artificial vanilla,*" I read in a monotone voice. I offer a catlike smile to the camera. "I actually smell like expensive perfume and disdain, but thank you for thinking I'm that sweet."

"Your breath always smells like peppermint, so they aren't that far off," Cooper chimes in.

My head jerks back. "What are you talking about? Vanilla and peppermint are totally different scents. Also, don't smell my breath, you creep."

Cooper purses his lips and shrugs, fighting a flirty smile. He's such a scamp and I want to strangle the insufferable cuteness out of him.

I focus instead on the next comment. "*She's like a skunk always ready to spray. Girl chill you don't always need to go so hard* 🙄🙄🙄 ." I blink a few times, trying to tamp down the twist of pain in my gut, but I keep my cruel smile in place. "Right. Because the second a woman makes a retort or a sarcastic comment, she's overreacting and being too sensitive. Men pick fistfights at bars over less but I'm the one who needs to chill."

"For what it's worth, I like you piping hot, Eva," Cooper says, his voice more soothing than teasing. It irritates me all the more.

"Oh, good. You know how I live to please you."

Cooper's wounded expression has me wondering if maybe I am a skunk.

I read the next one quickly as a distraction. "*I'm praying for Eva. Not for anything good to happen to her but that she falls in a ditch.*" Wow. Okay. That's kind of . . . awful. Whatever. I can recover. Quick as light in a vacuum. "Wishing for that too, girl. Anything to escape this post-capitalist hellscape, am I right?"

Cooper's face is much more somber, and I don't know how to respond.

William calls cut. "I didn't love the latter part of your re-action. Let's try a fresh take with a different one."

"Uh, really?"

"I'm sure we can smooth it out in post," Aida argues weakly.

William doesn't visibly react. "Another one."

After a beat, Aida counts me down again. Gritting my teeth, I start to read. "*She looks like a*— No. I'm not saying that."

"Excuse me?"

"I'm not going to read something derogatory like that about sex workers. It'll need to be a different comment."

William stares at me, skin taut and jaw clenched. "Fine. But I do ask that you not be unnecessarily difficult about this. We all have other important things we need to get to and this recording is eating up more time than anticipated. My mother led me to believe you would be a professional about all of this and I'd hate to report otherwise."

I feel so abjectly mortified, I just sit there, praying my lower lip doesn't start quivering.

"Well? What's the holdup, Aida?" William snaps, gaze flicking to her. "Feed out another."

Aida jumps, hands darting to her keyboard. In her panic, she must hit some wrong buttons, and a series of comments start popping up on the screen.

Someone PLEASE get this girl a muzzle i cannot with her

She's literally so gross to me

Listening to her talk makes me believe women's suffrage was a mistake

It's such a shame and embarrassment that we give platforms to girls with nothing else going on besides being passably pretty.

They hover there for a few seconds, but it feels like I read them a thousand times, and they become an instant, awful mantra that etches into my bones.

"Shit. Sorry." Aida frantically clicks away the text bubbles.

"I . . ." I shake my head, squeezing my eyes shut. I feel so small, so laughably tiny. My insignificance is like a fresh slap to raw skin as my mind repeats people's worst opinions about me.

"I'm sorry, but I find this pretty fucked up."

It takes me a moment to process that Cooper spoke my thought out loud. I blink at him, emotions threatening to spill over. Silence stretches on the call, William's thumbnail so still I wonder if my internet froze.

"What did you say?" he grinds out in a tone that makes me *wish* the connection failed.

"These just aren't funny," Cooper states, crossing his arms over his chest and leaning back in his chair. "This is punching down, and invalidates the whole point of what we have going."

"And what exactly is it that you have going?" William says with a snide laugh.

Cooper's face twists in disbelief. "I mean . . . it's pretty obvious, no? The whole gist is that guys historically are able to get away with shitty, emotionally damaging behavior toward women, and Eva is calling me out on it. But having her read comments this harsh derides it all."

"I'm not emotionally damaged," I add weakly, kidding myself.

"Your precious speech is rather redundant considering you're *both* reading harsh comments about yourselves. Having a sense of humor about it is the point."

"One of Cooper's is about how badly someone wants him to teabag them while mine essentially say I'm a shallow bitch with questionable looks who's never had a real thought. I don't see how we're operating on the same level here," I snap on a sudden rush of boldness, then cower at William's returning stare.

He allows the silence to stretch, bending it into a needle that pokes and scratches my skin. "I'm sorry," he says slowly, sounding anything but. "I was under the impression you two were serious about your careers and creating high-quality content with the potential to really take off, but now I'm not so sure. There are hundreds of people who would take both of your spots in a heartbeat, and I'd much rather speak with them than waste my time here." He logs off before any of us can take a breath.

"Shit," Aida says after a moment.

"That was really messed up," I say, voice wobbly. "You told me it wouldn't be that bad."

"I said I didn't know what it would be like," she snaps, fear and worry etched across her features. "But William is not happy. I need to do some damage control here before we both lose our jobs."

"I don't give a shit about our stupid jobs right now," I yell. "And you shouldn't either after that bullshit."

"That *bullshit* is the thing that pays our bills. I don't have the luxury to say fuck it," Aida hisses. "I actually *care* about my career. And thanks to your temper tantrum, I now have to grovel to our new boss and his mommy for us to keep them."

She logs off, and I'm smacked with my own reflection—lips parted and eyes rimmed with tears threatening to spill over. Not care? Not fucking care? What a cheap shot and Aida damn well knows it.

I care so much about this career—about doing something, *anything*, worthwhile—that I'm carving myself hollow trying to get there. I'm humiliating myself day in and day out at the snap of William's fingers to chase the glimmer of a promise for something more.

And oh god, *Landry*. I should not have talked to her son like that. I admire the woman more than anyone, and it won't win me any favors to turn her successor against me. Anxiety seeps through me in a rotten cloud as my brain gleefully catastrophizes what will come next. I can't let this happen again, be this pathetic and reactive. From here on out, if William tells me to jump or sit or bark on command, I need to do that for him. It's the only way to keep scrambling up this landslide of a career trajectory.

With a shaky breath, I try to collect myself, suddenly very aware that Cooper is still on the call.

"You okay, Kitten?"

"Never better," I say back, voice breaking. I rub the heels of my hands against my eyes, cursing at the dark stains left on my skin from my smeared makeup.

Cooper catches my gaze and holds it. Something about his steadiness creates a shaky feeling in my chest, and I let out a slow, controlled breath through pursed lips. It doesn't help. I just feel like crying more.

"You don't have to pretend that was okay," he says softly. "You can admit it was unfairly brutal."

"No offense, but your shoulders aren't nearly broad enough to be ones I'd cry on."

Cooper laughs, rolling his eyes. "Or use humor to cope. That's fine too."

"Why do you put up with me?" I ask suddenly. I want to snatch back the vulnerable question, force the words back down my throat and slap my hand over my mouth for good measure.

Cooper swallows, and I trace the bob of his Adam's apple. He adjusts his glasses, drags a hand down his jaw. "Because I like you, Eva."

I suck in a breath. "You—"

"I like listening to you. I like never knowing what out-of-pocket thing you're going to say next. I like hearing about your ideas and your thoughts and then reading how you piece them together. I like that you're a little bit feral and that sometimes you let me get away with teasing you."

Each word is tapped into the blank page of my skin, inking deeper and deeper until I feel covered in his confession. "I like when you tease me," I whisper, my admission feeling both too intimate and too inadequate.

Cooper's grin is radiant, so warm I can feel it in my chest. "Well, that's good, because I can't seem to help myself when it comes to you."

"I just assumed it's a defense mechanism for my bullying," I respond in an attempt at levity, trying to snip the cord of tension wrapping around my chest, tugging me toward the screen.

Cooper presses his lips together in a crooked line, but it

can't hold back his next laugh. "Well, I suppose that's part of it too."

The way he's looking at me is far too tender, too kind. He's looking at me like he sees more than there is. I know he'll be disappointed if he looks any closer.

I cough and start fiddling with my mouse, figuring out the best excuse to escape. "Well, this was, uh, an awful time, but I better—"

He cuts me off. "What are you doing tomorrow at four?"

"Lighting my Rylie Cooper doll on fire."

His smile should be considered unholy for the flood of sensations it releases low in my belly. "I hate to interrupt something so important, but would you be willing to move things around to go on a date with me instead?"

I try to cage the butterflies erupting through me. "Can you promise the same amount of pyrotechnics will be involved?"

"Oh, Kitten, you know I always make sparks fly." He winks, and I smile in spite of myself.

"Yeah, I can do tomorrow. What do you have planned?"

"You'll love it. It's the most romantic thing in the world."

"You're going to play guitar at me while aggressively making eye contact and I have to bob my head along like I'm enjoying it?"

Cooper's mouth twists to the side. "Okay, the second most romantic thing in the world."

I laugh, trying to tame the wild giddiness pulsing through me. How does he do it? How does he perk me up when I'm so low? "Just tell me. You can't be trusted with surprises."

"I'm taking you . . ."

He draws out the moment, eyes glinting, my heart hammering.

". . . to couples therapy!"

My jaw crashes to my keyboard. *Couples therapy?*

"Cooper, what the fu—" He logs out of the meeting and leaves me staring at my own bewildered expression.

Chapter 12

"YOU KNOW WE AREN'T ACTUALLY A COUPLE, RIGHT?" I say in greeting as Cooper shuts his front door behind him and meets me on the sidewalk.

"What?" His face falls as he slaps a hand to his chest. "You mean none of this is for realsies? But I wrote *Rylie hearts Eva* in my diary sixty-nine times!"

I punch his shoulder. "Har-har."

Cooper scoops up my fist and swings our arms like a couple holding hands as he leads us to his hideous PT Cruiser, the wood paneling glinting in the sun.

"I just don't get the *point* of couples therapy," I continue as he opens my door. I look at him sideways and bump him out of the way with my hip as I climb in. I hear his chuckle through the closed door, and I grind my knuckles against my chest to calm down my rabbiting heart.

Cooper slides into the driver's side with a move far too suave for this tragic excuse of a car, slipping on a pair of sunglasses and pushing his hair back. He turns to me, mouth lifting in a slow smirk, and I realize I was gawking. I scowl in return, digging my nails into my palms. I refuse to feel anything in the realm of turned on in a PT Cruiser.

Because I'm nosy and nervous, I pop open his glove box and rifle through it to distract myself. I'm disappointed that there's nothing damning or embarrassing in there, just standard car paperwork and a ton of napkins. "Good god, how often do you eat at Arby's?"

He snatches my fistful of napkins and shoves them back into the compartment before snapping it shut.

"The point is," he says in a huff, circling back to my question, "I was a shit communicator at twenty-two. And, honestly, I'm sure I'm still pretty subpar at it. But, as you might have noticed if you weren't so fixated on my many flaws, I'm trying to do better. Trying to encourage others to do better too." Cooper's honest look makes my chest tighten, and I blink away, squirming in my seat.

"Damn, dude. Way to get super vulnerable and shit. You could have just lied."

His laugh is a rough mix of resignation and surprise, and he shakes his head. He starts the car and pulls into traffic. "I'm genuinely concerned for my therapist's emotional well-being after you're done with her."

"She's survived you, so she must be pretty resilient."

We drive in silence for a while, and my thoughts get too loud and circular. Aida is still annoyed at me for yesterday, responding to my obsessive string of texts last night that she understands why I got upset and she's sorry things played out the way they did, but she's having to do quite the groveling to pacify William and save our necks. A new round of layoffs is rumored to happen any day now as restructurings at Sound-bites kick off, and being on the bad side of the man in charge doesn't bode well for either of us. While I know I should be doing some groveling of my own to William, and smoothing things over with Aida, I don't have it in me to apologize. But I also can't stop ruminating on it all . . . Berating Cooper seems like the best distraction, though.

I scan the interior of his car with the hungry instinct to un-earth some hidden clues about him, turn over every stone so I can finally grasp the reality of this man I had so well defined in my head but don't seem to understand at all. I'm annoyed that his car is impeccably clean and not a pigsty I can pester him about.

"Is your therapist on Long Island or is this actually an abduction?" I ask as the drive drags on.

"Brighton Beach," he replies with a terseness I'm not used to. I glance at him out of the corner of my eye. His jaw is set with tension, knuckles white as he grips the steering wheel.

"Isn't that a pain to get to every week?" I ask more gently than I intended. Cooper clocks it, glancing at me in surprise, then back at the road.

"I usually don't mind it." He flicks on his turn signal and merges to the other lane. "It lets me clear my head before-hand. Process things after."

"But this week?" I poke, having the sinking feeling that Cooper is regretting bringing me. That he's finally come to his senses that I'm more of an annoyance than I'm worth.

He wouldn't be the first person, or the last, to come to that conclusion.

He spares me another look, his face shifting from stress to softness. "This week I feel nervous having you with me."

"Why?" I'm mortified at how my voice cracks.

Cooper swallows, eyes back on the road. "Because I'm supposed to be tapping into my feelings but all I can think about is that you look really good in that skirt."

My mouth falls open while Cooper's curls into a devilish grin. I bite my lip hard to try and fight my own traitorous smile, but when he looks at me again, it breaks free. I feel like a little kid jumping on a trampoline, pivoting midair and hoping something will catch me as I come down.

"You're ridiculous," I mumble, pressing my hot cheek to the window, fingers absently twisting the silky fabric of my skirt. Despite not having any sporty inclination, it's one of my many athletic skorts—short and flippy—this one vibrantly red.

"We agreed to unconditional honesty," he says defensively.

"Yeah, well, in the name of unconditional honesty you should probably cover your skanky forearms before we start the session." He's traded his tacky crewnecks for an olive-green linen shirt, the sleeves rolled to his elbows to accommodate the unseasonably warm fall day, the sun through the open window burnishing the fine dusting of hair along his arms.

"Jesus, Eva, put that female gaze away and stop undressing me with your eyes." He grips his open collar like he's clutching at pearls.

I shake my head and stare out the window, trying to collect myself. "I mean this with all the love, light, and peace in my heart: What the hell is wrong with you?"

"Today or generally speaking?" He turns in to a parking lot, a squat concrete building of medical suites lobbed in the center. I stare at the entrance, my giddy heart's rhythm keeping up the pace but adding in an anxious squeeze, the promise of more honesty awaiting behind those doors, making me want to bolt.

"Never mind," I say, opening the car door. "I'm sure whatever is about to happen in there will give me all the answers I need."

"I want to preface this appointment," Roberta, Cooper's therapist, starts, "by saying that, considering my long-standing relationship with Rylie, I am not able to come to this conversation as someone completely impartial and without at least one side of knowledge of your history."

She fixes me with a gentle smile, and I offer a tense one back, the urge to flee itching through my muscles. What has Cooper said about me? How did he frame it? Why would I even come up at all, though? Has he . . . has he thought about me that much over the years?

I shake myself. That's ridiculous. I'm sure it's just that the past few weeks have jarred him too, even if he's faring better financially and in the court of public opinion than I am.

I look away from Roberta's intense gaze and take in her office. It's a warm, welcoming space, the walls lined with shelves cradling equal amounts of worn books and pieces of art. Roberta sits across from us in a comfortable-looking velvet armchair, one leg slung over the other, hands resting on her stomach.

I squirm on the couch, burrowing as far as I can into the corner to put as much distance between my hip and Cooper's where he sits next to me.

"While this space is safe and being held for both of you to have this conversation," Roberta continues when my fidgeting stops, "I would be remiss not to reiterate that he is, first and foremost, my patient as an individual, not the pair of you as a unit. That being said, I'm not here to take sides or pass judgment or do anything outside of facilitating the conversation and helping everyone dig a bit deeper into their emotions."

"Why do I feel like this is a really nice way for you to imply you're about to be mean to me and call me on my bullshit?" I ask with unfounded confidence in my voice. Roberta's kind smile and penetrating gaze tell me she sees right through my false bravado.

"Oh, don't worry," Cooper chirps. "She'll do that to both of us indiscriminately."

"Calling Rylie on his bullshit is the majority of our sessions," Roberta adds, shooting him a conspiratorial wink.

An awkward silence drops through the room, Roberta smiling expectantly at us, Cooper's body angled toward me, and mine practically hanging over the arm of the couch as I try to escape the threads of expectant intimacy weaving between us all.

"Shouldn't therapy have a bit more talking?" I ask drolly, looking at my nails.

"It's nice when it does," Roberta replies. "What would you like to talk about?"

"Uh-uh. He dragged me here." I cock my thumb at Cooper. "He should be the one who has to start."

Cooper lets out a measured breath, sitting up straighter. "Of course. Yeah. Well . . ." He drags a hand through his hair, tilting his head back as he searches for words. "I guess what I was hoping for with this, uh, session was to dig a little deeper into our past, um, bullshit. Create an open forum to air grievances and work through everything that happened."

"So what I'm hearing," Roberta follows up, "is you're wanting to revisit your past relationship and come to a mutual understanding of what happened and perhaps why you both acted in the ways you did?"

"We weren't in a relationship," I say like an impertinent child. Both of them turn to me. I feel my cheeks heat, but I clear my throat. "It was like, four dates and a lousy hookup. I feel like all of this"—I wave my hand around the room—"is making too big a deal out of what it actually was."

"So you feel like the time you spent together didn't hold much significance in the grand scheme of things?"

I shrug. "I was hurt by how it played out, but it's kind of ancient history at this point. We all need to move on."

"And moving on includes blasting me on social media?" Cooper asks. There's an impish curl to his mouth, one brow quirked. He said it in a gently teasing way, but my hackles rise.

"We all say and do stupid shit on the internet when we're drunk and see our biggest mistake's face pop up in our feed."

"You feel as though your time with Rylie is your biggest mistake? That seems worth talking about, Eva."

My gaze whips to Roberta. "Jesus. I was hyperbolizing. I . . . It . . ." A small tornado of anxiety swirls up my arms and touches ground in my chest, sweat prickling at the back of my neck. I feel naked, exposed. I don't want them to see these hideously weak spots.

I take a deep, measured breath, leg jiggling, eyes burning a hole into the fabric of the couch. "My thing with Cooper was the first time I ever romantically pursued someone I liked. He was my first date. My first kiss. My first, uh, sexual partner. So, yeah, I didn't enjoy being ghosted by the person I handed all those firsts to and I harbored some resentment. But that doesn't mean the whole situation is something I think about anymore. I'm over it; there's no need to harp on it or make it into this giant *thing*."

Liar, a voice hisses in my ear. It sounds a bit like Cooper's.

"I didn't know that," Cooper says gently like he's trying to soothe a skittish animal. "That I was your first for all of those things. Why didn't you tell me?"

I scoff. "Would it have changed how you treated me?"

"It might have," Cooper says, face etched with earnestness.

My sneer is pure acid. "It shouldn't. Someone's experience or lack thereof with relationships and sex shouldn't be some metric to determine how shitty you can be to them."

"It still would have been nice to know."

"And it would have been nice for you to ask," I say in a patronizing tone, throwing up my hands. "No one likes to admit how inexperienced they are when they're young and trying to impress someone they like; it makes them feel . . . I don't know, like they're weird or sheltered or behind the curve. I always felt like I was on shaky ground with you anyway, I wasn't about to scare you off even more by being vulnerable and shit." I already felt like I was handing over way more of myself to him than he was returning; I needed some level of preservation. "So, I didn't tell you. I didn't confide in you about my history because history wasn't something we talked about. Did I attach a lot of unnecessary meaning and emotion to all of those firsts? Yes. Of course. I was a young girl desperate for male validation in any form I could find it. But you also weren't entitled to that information if you weren't willing to hand over any of your own."

"Eva." Roberta's voice is kind, its tenderness dragging my unwilling gaze to hers. "Before we continue, I do think it's important to correct one thing you just said. Your emotions and the meaning you attach to things that happen to you in your life are *never* unnecessary. Attaching meaning and emotion to events is the most necessary part of living. It's your story. It's your narrative to write and rewrite and revise as you see fit, but, at the end of it all, it's *yours*."

"That kind of misplaced vulnerability is one hundred percent unnecessary," I argue. "This entire ridiculous social media experiment we're doing is unnecessary."

"Then why are you doing it?"

Because I wanted vindication for my pathetic hurt feelings. Because every time I'm with Cooper he surprises me. Because I'm actually starting to like being around him.

"Because my job made me and I am nothing if not a meat puppet for the hands of capitalism," I reply, crossing my legs and bobbing my foot.

Roberta looks skeptical. "Rylie?" she says, directing the question at him but keeping her eyes on me. "Why are *you* doing this?"

"Because I carry around my guilt like an extra appendage and I wanted a chance to make things right between us."

My gaze snaps to his profile. He's said it before—over and over—and it terrifies me that some naive part of me is actually starting to believe it.

Cooper looks back at me, pushing his glasses up his nose as he clears his throat. "I get it. You don't trust me. But for once, I want us to have a conversation of radical honesty. No bullshit, no recordings, no confusion about if this is for our audience or for us. I want us to *talk*, Eva. I want to listen to you."

My throat tightens, nails digging into the arms of the sofa. I feel the sudden urge to cry. To run. To curl up in a ball on his lap and beg him to hold me tight. I want to whisper every thought I've locked up in my head since I was a little kid because I knew no one would care to hear it. But how am I supposed to trust it? Trust *him*? No one's ever shown up for me before—not my parents or my partners or even my employers. How am I all of a sudden supposed to believe Cooper is being authentic about wanting to listen to me?

I cough, trying to blink away the pinpricks of emotions behind my eyes. "In the spirit of honesty," I say when I think I can trust my voice. Big mistake, it's still hoarse and horrifically timid. "I feel kind of uncomfortable talking about my hurt and emotions around the whole situation now that I know about what happened to his sister during that time. It makes my feelings on it all seem extremely trivial."

Roberta nods, biting her lower lip for a moment. "I can understand feeling like that. It isn't easy to learn about some-one else's pain, then have to explain your own. It can feel like the trauma Olympics and everyone loses. But life doesn't exist in a vacuum, and neither do our actions, even if they result from our personal experiences. It's okay to acknowledge that Rylie was going through a tremendous loss and grieving process and offer him grace. But it also doesn't do you any good to swallow your feelings altogether. You were swept up in the storm of his grief and injured by the whiplash. It doesn't make you a bad person to admit that you were hurt by the actions of someone also hurting."

I'm silent, my heart ticking like a timer counting down an explosive.

"Is that something you feel like you can explore?" Roberta nudges when it's clear I'm not going to make this easy for her.

I look down at my hands, cracking each knuckle with my thumb, pushing back my cuticles. I ball my hands into fists, my nails digging into the fleshy pads of my palms. Cooper is giving me the courtesy of looking forward instead of at me, unlike Roberta, whose eyes feel like a physical weight. "Yeah, we can explore that," I finally mumble.

"Good," Roberta says softly. "But know we can stop at any time. You're in control here. You have the power to say whatever you need to, but also withhold if you don't feel comfortable."

I nod tersely, lifting my chin and tossing my hair back. "Right. Of course."

"Why do you feel your relationship didn't work in the past?" Roberta asks, ripping the Band-Aid right the fuck off and dumping some salt on the wound along with it.

I snort, leaning into petulance. "Like I said, there wasn't a relationship. There was me mooning over him for a few months, some sporadic dates when he could be bothered to give me the time of day, about four minutes of really shitty sex, and an extremely successful ghosting. Rather cliché."

"Now, I will admit that I am aware of the video you posted online about all of this," Roberta says, giving me an apologetic smile.

"I've been discussing everything going on during sessions," Cooper adds. I still can't look at him.

"Yes, thank you for clarifying," she says, nodding. "It's come up. It seems like that night, those four minutes of really shitty sex, as you phrased it, are actually quite a focal point for your hurt. That evening seemed to have a ripple that we're still seeing the effects of now. You brush over it with flippancy but I wonder what details have stuck with you, Eva."

I remember *all* the details. That's the problem.

I remember the night before too.

We'd gone to a crappy college bar that sold lukewarm watery beers for a dollar on Thursday nights and never bothered to card anyone. The evening ended before nine, Cooper shit-faced and glassy-eyed, talking about his ex at a volume that got louder by the second, heads turning and girls laughing at my red face and his weepy voice.

I ended up paying the tab—an alarming total for how cheaply we were being served—and convinced Cooper it was time to go home. With his arm slung heavily around my shoulders, we stumbled back toward his frat house. We made it about a hundred feet before he started crying in earnest, blubbering about how much he missed his ex, how much he wanted them back. How he really thought he loved them.

Being shameless and jealous and nosy to the point of self-destruction, I asked who she was, but Cooper wouldn't tell me, only shaking his head like a wet dog and crying harder. Even when he slumped onto the porch of his house, eyes closed and face flushed, I couldn't leave well enough alone, trying one more time for a name.

I wanted to look her up, stalk her on the internet, study every grainy, filtered picture I could find until she was burned in my retinas, only to spend months trying to morph myself into a girl like her—a girl who could make a guy that deeply obsessed. I wanted so badly to be the object of that much want, to cup it in my hands, dive headfirst into being needed. But Cooper passed out on the porch and I walked home alone, brain spinning on how I could get him. Keep him.

Sex seemed like the surest way. It wasn't by the heat of the moment I ended up on his twin mattress on the floor, bra pushed up over my boobs, Cooper's beer-stained breath on my cheek, and my body thoroughly unsatisfied as I told him I loved him.

So unbelievably mortifying.

"I don't know that there's much to say about that night," I lie, my voice cracking in betrayal. "He spent the party ignoring me until he was pushing his hand up my shirt and kissing me like he wanted me. Like I wanted him to want me. I wanted to have sex, Cooper wanted to have sex. We did it without talking about what it meant for either of us and I guess . . . I don't know, I guess I wasn't actually ready for it. I'd attached more meaning and significance to it than I think I realized at the time and I . . . I just felt so fucking naked. Not like, literally naked . . . A lot of clothes actually stayed on for both of us." Cooper coughs, and I squeeze my eyes shut. "But I guess I wanted to feel loved at that moment, and I . . . I blurted out that I loved *him*."

The room is as silent as it was all those years ago when I said that damning phrase, and my gut twists like a dirty dishrag in the relived embarrassment.

"And . . . yeah. He didn't say anything. We lay there in silence for what felt like an eternity until he fell asleep. I fixed my clothes, walked home alone, and didn't hear from him after. And it . . . well, it really fucked me up, I guess." I gesture vaguely at the mess I've made of everything. "That was the first time I was vulnerable with a guy—with anyone, really—and it went horribly. And I haven't opened up that way again. It was so singularly humiliating that I suppress any intimate feelings as much as I can. I haven't, um, told a partner I love them since."

"How long ago was this?" Roberta asks softly, tipping her head to the side.

I glance at Cooper, then away. "I guess a little over six years now?"

She nods. "That's quite a long time to carry these feelings."

"Yes," I agree emphatically. "It is. It really screwed me up and I'm angry that it did. I need to get over it. Get over myself."

"What have you done to address these feelings?"

The question is a record scratch. "I'm sorry?"

Roberta shifts in her seat. "You're saying this moment drastically altered the way that you interact with partners—that you withhold telling people you love them because you're so hurt by what happened—so what have you done to work on that?"

I make a series of choking, spluttering sounds.

"Because to me," Roberta continues, ignoring my crisis,

"it seems like you had this experience where you tried being vulnerable with somebody you cared about and it didn't go the way you wanted or planned or even objectively well. But it also sounds like you've used it as an excuse to stop opening up with other people. To stop searching for intimacy in relationships."

"I feel like you're a really mean therapist," I blurt out, back pressed so harshly against the couch I might weave myself into the fabric. "I didn't think therapists were supposed to be this brutally honest."

Roberta tries to hide her smile, then shrugs. "I just think you're strong enough to handle some tough love."

"Eva's as tough as they come," Cooper says, reminding me he's even here. I grind my molars together, a ripple of anger tracing down my arms.

Tough. *Tough.*

The word exerts an irritating pressure like a piece of meat stuck between teeth.

I *am* tough.

And I'm sick of having to be.

I'm sick of having to choke down my feelings, fend for myself. I'm sick of stepping into glass armor every day, waiting for whatever stones people on the internet chuck my way, whatever fractures the powers that be at my job chisel onto my surface. I'm sick of having to scrape my way to aloofness just so I'm not a nuisance to my friends. My family.

I deserve softness, goddammit. I deserve tender moments and gentle caresses and whispered sweet nothings. I deserve someone, somewhere, wanting to like me for me and not the hardened veneer I gloss my vulnerability with.

"You thinking that might be part of the problem," I say on

a shaky breath, finding the courage to look at Cooper. "Things hurt me like they hurt you. I'm just as human as you are." Apparently my body is really trying to prove the point, and a few hot teardrops roll down my cheeks. I furiously scrub them away before dropping my hands to the couch.

The room is silent, another moment where my too-big feelings have rendered everyone speechless and uncomfortable.

The warmth of skin on skin is sudden and jarring, a jolt of comfort and an instinct to recoil and compress myself into something small. I glance at where Cooper's fingers wrap gently around my wrist, just enough pressure to feel like a buoy as I sink in these feelings.

"You're right," he whispers. My eyes skip up to his face, but his focus is trained on where he touches me, his eyebrows furrowed. The pad of his thumb grazes a circle along the sensitive skin of my inner wrist, gentle as butterfly wings. "Just because you can take it doesn't mean you should have to. You shouldn't always have to be bouncing back."

I can't look away from him, and fear claws like a trapped animal in my chest as tenderness surges through my limbs.

"Thanks for saying that," I mumble, finally breaking eye contact and slipping my hand away from his. I brush my hair off my face. "And I appreciate the sentiment, but, as I've been trying to say, it's also not that big of a deal."

Roberta lets out a soft breath, and I decipher disappointment in the sound. She leaves the space for me to say more, but a minute passes and I don't take it.

"And Rylie?" she says, turning to him. "What are your thoughts on that evening?"

Cooper clears his throat, and I feel him adjust in his seat but I keep my eyes pinned on the carpet.

"I think about it a lot, actually. With regret," he adds quickly. "I can't say that what I felt for Eva at that time was love—"

"I wasn't actually in love with you," I cut in, embarrassment flooding me as I shoot a horrified look at Cooper. "It was just me being a dumb twenty-one-year-old with weepy post-sex emotions. I didn't love you." He flinches and I want to punch myself in the face for my harsh tone. Why can't I say anything right?

"With all due respect, Eva, you had your time to share," Roberta gently scolds. "And while I understand your desire to clarify the hindsight of your feelings and emotions—I promise I do—I think we already have a grasp that it was more of an infatuation than love. Now is Rylie's time to speak."

She nods at Cooper and he clears his throat. "Right. Well, uh, like I was saying, I don't know that what I felt could be defined as love for you, but I did feel something strong and real for you. I really liked you. I was so excited to be with you."

"Interesting way of showing it," I mumble. They both (rightfully) ignore me.

"But, for lack of better phrasing, I had a ton of shit going on at home, and I handled it all horribly."

I swallow, looking at my lap. Guilt churns in me so violently it could capsize a ship. "I am so sorry about your sister," I whisper, meaning it. Cooper makes a harsh, fractured sound in the back of his throat but doesn't say anything. I see his hand, still resting in the space between us, twitch. On instinct, I reach for him, curling my fingers through his and offering a reassuring squeeze, an echo of his comforting touch for me just minutes ago. He sucks in a breath, but doesn't pull his hand away.

Instead, he holds mine tighter.

"Losing Hailey was one of the worst things to ever happen to me," he continues. "My world was changed in an instant, my little sister just *gone*. Do you know how fucking weird it is to lose someone? To never be able to talk to them again? I couldn't comprehend how I could exist in a world where I didn't hear her voice. Where she didn't beg to borrow my car during the summers. Where I wouldn't see her smile and I couldn't ever make her laugh again." His voice cracks, and I look at him. His head is tilted back, eyes fixed on the ceiling.

"A piece of me died when she did—the version of me that had the privilege of loving her, the version of me that watched her grow up and be a far better person than I could ever hope to be."

The pain in his voice strikes me straight in the chest, the faces of my own siblings flicking through my head. An ache to hug each and every one of them grips me so hard, I have to bite the inside of my cheek not to whimper.

"There's no way you can ever be prepared for losing some-one that special," Cooper says. "But you also can't be prepared for the other things you lose too. My entire family fell apart. My youngest sister, Katie, stopped speaking. Stopped eating. She didn't leave her room for *months*. My parents stopped talking to each other. We all moved around like ghosts, like that's all we were allowed to be if that was all we had left of Hailey." His voice cracks again, and I watch tears roll down his cheeks. With his free hand, he pushes up his glasses, rubbing his eyes. His other hand stays locked tight around mine.

"And I felt so guilty about it," he says in a muffled tone, digging his knuckles against his sockets. "But by the time summer finished, I couldn't wait to get back to school. I wanted to get as far away from my family and our sadness that was rotting us from the inside out. I wanted to be around people who didn't know what it felt like to lose the best person in the world. I wanted to drink and get high and fuck my way across campus and not think about how much I missed my little sister. So that's what I did. I went back to Breslin and drank every night and partied all the time and ignored my future because I couldn't imagine one without Hailey."

Cooper grinds his teeth together as he blinks at the white tiles of the ceiling. With a slow movement, he drops his chin, turning to look at me. His silver eyes fix on mine, and, for a moment, I wonder how I'm ever supposed to look at anything else.

"It wasn't far into the fall semester when I started hooking up with one of my frat brothers," he says. "I was deep in the closet and so was he. Since we were freshmen rushing we'd been toeing that line, but never crossed it. Not until senior year. We'd hook up in stolen, shame-filled moments, usually drunk or high or both, pushing each other into dark corners or sneaking down the hall like our lives depended on the silence of the floorboards. He'd tell me how much he wanted me, how much he liked me, while we were doing it, then treat me like a piece of shit immediately afterward, like I was the most disgusting thing he'd ever seen. It fucked with my head.

Or maybe I was just fucked in the head. I guess both things can be true."

Out of the corner of my eye, I see Roberta nod. I feel a surge of anger at the reminder of her presence, like this moment is a gift that Cooper is giving me, and she's intruding on something sacred. Then I remember she's his therapist, his safe outlet. I'm the only one intruding.

"He got a girlfriend right before winter break," Cooper says, tone going flat. "I was supposed to go home with him and spend the holiday break there, but he was so freaked I would tell his family or his girlfriend about the things we'd done, he uninvited me. Pretended he hardly knew me. It was different, but it felt like a loss all over again, and I was devastated and hurt and angry. But I had nowhere to put those feelings. So I went home to my sad family and saw my sad dad drinking and my sad mom fading and my sad sister hollow-eyed and lost not only in the face of her own grief but the grief of the people who were supposed to take care of her.

"It was seeing Katie hurting so badly that finally woke me up, at least a little bit. She was only twelve—so young. Too young. And it made me want to change. It made me want to step into being human again just so I could be a real, stable person for her to rely on. I wanted to stop chasing after someone who made me feel like shit for liking them. I wanted to continue pretending I wasn't bi. I just . . . I just wanted to feel like a normal twenty-two-year-old who didn't have a gaping hole in his life."

Cooper swallows, the movement painful looking, his expression wrecked. I lean toward him. I want to reach out, hold his face between my palms, fold his body against mine, absorb his pain like heat through my skin. But I'm too scared, terrified, of doing the wrong thing. So I hold his gaze, squeeze his hand, scream in my head that I'm here and I see him.

"And I met you, Eva," he says in a low voice. "I met you and I liked you and I wasn't anywhere close to being okay enough to do anything about it, but you made me feel good at a time when all I felt was terrible. So I pretended to be okay. I pretended to be whole and normal and thought that was enough."

He takes a shuddering breath, and I feel the ripples through my chest.

"I really did like you, Eva," he says, eyes dropping from mine. The past tense doesn't escape me, but it shouldn't hurt like it does. "But I also felt guilty for feeling happy. I felt guilty enjoying my time with you when I knew that what remained of my family was breaking into pieces. I was hung up on a guy who made me feel like shit because feeling like shit was my new normal."

Cooper lets go of my fingers, rubbing the heels of his hands against his eyes and shifting in his seat until he's angled away from me. I don't know why I notice that.

"Eva," he says, looking in the general direction of Roberta. "I know how horrible it feels to tell someone your feelings and not have them say it back. Especially after sex. I know how embarrassing and crushing and consuming a moment like that is, and I am so, so sorry I did that to you. It wasn't because I didn't want you, I just didn't think I was allowed to have you."

There's a long, weighted silence, and I realize I'm holding my breath.

"And sometimes, I wonder," he whispers, still not looking at me, "if you would change anything. If you would take back meeting me. I know it's selfish, but I don't think I could ever take back meeting you."

Silence ticks, incessant like a fly buzzing in my ear, my head swimming and my heart beating so hard my teeth ache with the force.

Roberta clears her throat, the sound loud and awful like a skip in a CD, disrupting the natural flow of things. "I'm sorry," she says, the sentiment ringing true. "But that's all the time we have for today.

Chapter 13

WE WALK OUT OF ROBERTA'S OFFICE IN A DAZE, SILENCE lingering like thick perfume. The sun has disappeared behind some clouds, only a few weak rays breaking through. It still feels too bright, both of us too bare and exposed. Without looking at each other, we lean against the hood of his ugly car, staring at the asphalt, not ready to share a small, intimate space again.

Cooper's voice plays a hushed loop in my head. *I wonder if you would change anything.*

What a stupid question. I'd change everything and nothing. I'd pick a different college and pick that exact same seat in that lecture hall. I wouldn't give him my number and I'd trip head over heels all over again. Even with the hurt I've attached to the ending, I sometimes find it hard to regret how excited I felt to be with him.

Cooper's arm brushes against mine, and I startle, expecting

him to readjust. But he leaves his bicep gently pressed against me. I don't have enough fight left to lean away. After a pause, his hand inches toward mine, then covers it, giving my fingers a gentle squeeze where they rest on the dirty metal of his car.

"Will you get dinner with me?" he murmurs. I look at him, my expression a deranged twist of delight and horror. His eyes flick briefly down to my mouth, then back to my eyes, a slight twitch of satisfaction playing at the corner of his mouth.

My throat goes dry, pulse pounding and nerve endings rerouting to the feel of his skin on mine. "You're my ride, I'm kind of beholden to your wishes."

Cooper laughs, the sound rough and low. "This might be the only chance I'll ever get to experience that. I better make the most of it." He surprises me by releasing my hand and wrapping his arm around my shoulders, sliding me toward him. I let out a flustered yelp as he gathers me to his chest, tucking my head under his chin as he hugs me. I'm too surprised to move, to even breathe, the pounding of his heartbeat against my cheek matching my own anxious rhythm, encouraging me to run.

But he's too warm and smells too good and feels too safe, and I sigh, melting against him, my arms snaking around his waist and holding him back. We stay like that for a moment, Cooper gently rocking us, the autumn wind twirling fallen leaves at our feet.

Too soon, he pulls back, looking down at me with a smile, his glasses slipping a centimeter down his nose.

If he kissed me right now, I wouldn't push him away.

The thought is sudden and sharp, a flare in a midnight sky, red ink dropped in water. I shrug away from his touch and roughly push my hair behind my ears.

What *is* this? *Longing?* Why do I want to take up a permanent residence in that crease between his eyebrows? Why do I have the urge to huff the scent of his skin until I pass out? I'm disgusted with myself.

"Do you like pancakes? There's a great diner a few blocks from here," he says, pushing away from the hood of the car and looking down the street, oblivious to the absolute shit show of feelings erupting in my brain. "We could walk. Although the clouds do look a little ominous."

I shake myself, taking a deep, calming (hyperventilating-adjacent) breath, then step next to him, dropping into my most apathetic voice. "Why do you insist on wasting my time on questions with obvious answers?"

Cooper catches my chin between his thumb and forefinger, making me watch how hard he rolls his eyes. I pull back from his grip, pressing my lips tightly together to suppress a smile.

"You're just always so sweet, Kitten, wasn't sure how much added sugar you could handle."

"Ew. I think I just blew my back out from cringing." With a haughty sniff, I take a gamble and start down the sidewalk to the left.

"You actually aren't the first person to say that to me," Cooper says, letting me get all the way to the street corner before looping his arm through mine and turning me around, leading us in the opposite direction.

I swallow down my embarrassment, trying to listen to Cooper as he keeps up a steady stream of chatter instead of focusing on the feel of his arm still threaded with mine. He walks us toward the pier, pointing out an ice cream stand that apparently has the best butter pecan, a kitschy gift shop with the finest airbrushed tees, a gallery that once showcased his roommate Steve's ceramic collection.

"I feel like you'd buy art off cruise ships," I say when there's a lull and I realize he's expecting me to actually contribute to the conversation and not have a full-blown physical crisis because his elbow slit is pressed against my elbow slit.

"Oh," Coopers says, frowning. "Thanks?"

"I meant it in the most derogatory way possible."

"We're here," Cooper says with a sigh, holding open the door for me. "After you . . . you turd."

I stop in my tracks, jaw crashing open. Cooper giggles as he breezes past me. "Did you just call me a turd?" I hiss, following him to a booth. "No one's called me a turd since I was like, twelve."

"See, *that* I find genuinely surprising." He gives me a winning smile. I hate that mine matches his. "I'm gonna run to the bathroom. Try not to make anyone cry while I'm gone."

"No promises, baby girl," I call to his retreating back.

A beat later, our waitress appears. "What would you like to drink?" she asks, popping her gum as she places menus on the table.

I purse my lips as I scan the back of the laminated sheet. "I'll have an iced tea," I say. Inspiration strikes. "And he'll have a glass of skim milk." I gesture at Cooper's open seat.

The waitress's eyebrows quirk but she says nothing, jotting it down and then walking away. Cooper slides into the booth a minute later.

"Miss me?" I ask wryly.

His smile is a quick twitch, almost bashful, and he keeps his eyes fixed on the menu. I watch color creep across his cheeks, and I don't know why mine share an echoing warmth. He clears his throat and looks at me, opening his mouth to say something, but the waitress is back with our drinks.

"Iced tea," she says, setting it in front of me. "And, uh, skim milk." She places a full, creamy glass in front of Cooper garnished with a single ice cube and a striped bendy straw. His eyebrows furrow, mouth hanging open. "I'll give you another minute to look at the menu," she says before walking off again.

"*Skim milk?*" Cooper growls as he leans across the table. "Why the hell would you order me skim milk?"

"You made such a fuss about the oat milk!"

"So a tall glass of skim was the obvious solution?"

"I can't win with you." I shake my head, eyes fixed on my menu as I try to hide just how much fun I'm having. Cooper catches it.

"You might be the most conniving woman I've ever met."

"Thank you." I blow him a kiss. "Maybe you have more game than I've given you credit for."

"That wasn't a compliment," he murmurs. "You terrify me."

My heart does a little flip as if he just told me I'm the most beautiful girl in the world, but I keep my face neutral.

"What'll you have?" the waitress asks, rematerializing at the edge of our table.

"Stack of pancakes," Cooper says with a smile, tilting his menu toward her. "To complement the milk."

There's a substantial delay in how long it takes her to check her reaction. "And you?" she says, eyeing me.

"The same," I say with a resigned sigh. "Hold the glass of

skim, please." She walks off with a pained expression and I make a mental note to tip her double.

"You're something else," Cooper says, voice low. I glance at him, expecting to see sharpness in his face—annoyance, resignation, disdain, something similar to all the other people I've pushed just a step too far—but he's looking at me with a dopey expression. Almost thunderstruck.

"What the fuck is that supposed to mean?"

Cooper's face remains serene. "Tell me what you think it means."

"You aren't nearly as hot as Roberta. I'm not about to spill my guts to you." I tear my napkin into tiny pieces as he continues to stare at me.

Cooper rolls his eyes, but it somehow feels tender and intimate. "Can I tell you what I want you to think it means?"

"If I say no, will you stop talking?"

"Probably not."

I wave him on.

"In the six years since I've met you," he says, placing his hands on the table, only an inch from mine, "I've never met someone quite like you."

"Careful. You're tiptoeing very close to 'not like other girls' territory," I deadpan, moving my hands a millimeter back while they vibrate with the desire to move closer to his. "But, yeah, I am exceptionally witty and brilliant." The deprecation is a habit of self-preservation. I can't let him inflate me with false things when I know everyone opens the plug and lets out the air in the end.

His smile is indulgent, eyes fixed on my hands. "And no

one has ever challenged me like you do," he says, inching closer until the tips of his fingers barely touch mine. In a slow, steady movement like I'm a feral cat he's trying to coax out from the trash, he rotates his wrists until his palms face up.

"I mean . . . congrats on being a white man in America," I say, horrified to see myself broaching the minimal space between us, an electric hum moving through me as I lay my hands in his. What is *happening*?

It's because of the therapy. I feel too cracked open. Too raw. A fragile, pathetic creature that needs to be cuddled. My hands twitch as I try to will them back to my lap, but it's like invisible strings are binding us together,

"Can I ask you something?" His thumb traces the edge of my pinky.

I huff, but it sounds soft when I was aiming for snotty. "If you must."

"If . . . God, this feels so silly . . ." A blush creeps up his neck, across his cheeks. His glasses slip a notch, but he doesn't let go of my hands to fix them.

"That's never stopped you before," I say, leg bouncing so hard his glass of milk ripples. Cooper's eyes finally meet mine, and my heart gives a painful squeeze.

A look I can't read flits across his face, his jaw tightening and a muscle ticking in his cheek. "If I hadn't screwed up that night like I did, do you think—" He clears his throat. "Do you think we might have ended up together?"

The world stops, capturing us in a Polaroid moment staring at each other. The image shifts, and it's us from six years ago, faces young and cheeks aching with laughter. It morphs again—smiles loose and eyes glassy as we celebrate a birthday over drinks. And again—noses burnt on the Fourth of July, ugly sweaters at Christmas, a kiss at New Year's.

I see all of these precious snapshots of what could have been like I'm viewing a tenderly made scrapbook—the way our bodies curl toward each other, the easy intimacy, the sharp glint of playfulness in our eyes as we take for granted another giddy night at a cheap diner. The idea sears itself in my mind like a memory, blistering as I remind myself it's not.

It hurts too much to linger in flighty fantasies, cutting my fingers on the edges of all of those fake photos and blank pages.

"No," I say, shaking my head and pulling my hands away. Cooper's face falls, and I keep going, slipping into my most flippant mask, creating the distance everyone is so comfortable holding with me. He doesn't get to leave me and then come back and play a game of what-ifs over the tombstone of my hardened heart. "We're way too different. For example, your love language is physical touch. My love language is mac 'n' cheese. This would have never worked between us."

"Eva," he says on a breath that's half laugh, half frustration. "Come on."

"No," I repeat, anger rising. "You come on. Where do you get off asking me a question like that? Be serious for a fucking second, I beg you."

Cooper opens his mouth, but I cut him off. "I'm not some social experiment for you. You don't get to fuck off just long enough for things to heal only to resurface and reminisce about the past, tearing the cut wide open again."

This wasn't part of it. This was never supposed to feel real or honest or important. This was never supposed to unravel me, chip away at all my armor until I'm standing bare-boned in front of him.

"Eva. I'm sorry. I—"

"I'm out of here." With shaky hands, I dig through my wallet, throwing whatever cash is in there on the table before I bolt for the door. It takes me a good ten seconds of storming down the sidewalk to realize it's raining. Of course it is.

I look around, trying to get my bearings through the sheets of rain falling in every direction. I'm not super familiar with Brighton Beach, and I pull out my phone, trying to find the closest subway stop so I can take what I can only imagine will be a super-convenient two-hour train ride back to Manhattan.

"What the hell are you doing?" Cooper calls over the heavy wind. I jump when I realize how close he is, my phone slipping out of my hands into a puddle.

"Oh, real nice," I say, pushing my drenched hair out of my eyes and glaring at him. "Look what you did."

"Don't start," he says through clenched teeth, making me want to dig in and really fucking start.

He bends down to grab my phone, but I shoulder him aside, getting it myself. I don't need him playing hero. I randomly pick a direction and start marching, trying to get my screen to respond to me instead of the raindrops. I almost cry out in relief when I see the Q train is only three blocks away and I'm heading toward it.

"Where are you going?" Cooper says, chasing after me.

"I'm taking the train home," I say, ignoring the rain in my eyes as I keep my chin lifted, pace fast. But Cooper's faster. He grabs my arm, spinning me around.

"Don't be ridiculous. That'll take forever. I'll drive you home."

"I don't want to go anywhere with you," I say, ripping my arm from his grasp. I know I sound like a petulant child but I couldn't care less.

His look is thunderous, and he rakes his hands through his wet hair. "Would you just stop it, you ridiculous woman? Why can't you let me do anything for you?"

"Why didn't you ever call me?" I yell. It shocks us both.

Cooper blinks, water sluicing down his cheeks, the lenses of his glasses collecting raindrops and making it hard for me to read his expression.

"Why?" I repeat in a whisper, voice cracking. Embarrassment swamps me, but I continue to stand there, waiting for an answer. It's a pathetically old wound, but it's only festered with time. Gouged deeper and deeper as I've watched more and more people step into their lives without me, leaving me behind like a used doll they're tired of playing with.

"I already told you," Cooper says, his voice so low it's hard to hear over the rain. "I made a mistake. I regret it."

"But *why*?" I push, unable to leave well enough alone. "Why was that the choice you made? Why did you make me like you? Why did you chase me, if you knew how it would end?"

Why was I so easy to leave? What is it about me that's so simple to forget? Recitals and parent-teacher conferences and important dates and milestones where I'm left alone on the curb with my heart in my hand desperately wishing someone thought I was important enough to remember.

Cooper lets out a rough noise, scrubbing his hands over his

face. "Because I was a mess, Eva," he says, dropping his arms with a wet smacking sound against his jeans. "And I need you to listen to me when I say that because it's the goddamn truth." He stares at me, his expression harsh, jaw working. "I wasn't coping with the loss of my sister. I was about to graduate college with no job lined up. I was secretly hooking up with a guy who I had feelings for but both of us had too much internalized shit to ever tell the truth and it screwed me up. I was at rock fucking bottom. Then I met you and I messed that up too. I really liked you, and it scared me because I was too much of a disaster to even look at myself in the mirror, let alone start something with this cool, funny woman with her life figured out and these amazing dreams I had no doubt she'd reach with the snap of her fingers. It's pathetic but for a twenty-two-year-old idiot, that's a pretty intimidating picture to try and squeeze yourself into."

Cooper takes a step toward me, gripping my shoulders, forcing me to look at him.

"I can't change the past," he says, fingers tightening around me. "Do you have any idea, any fucking clue, how much I wish I could? How many nights the idea has kept me awake with frustration? I'd do it in a heartbeat. I'd go back in time and slap myself and tell that idiot version of me to get his shit together and not hurt the amazing girl who actually seems to care about his pathetic ass."

A shiver runs through me, emotions knotted in my throat. I can't tell if it's the rain on my cheeks or if tears have started slipping out.

"*I'd call you*, Eva," he says, giving me a tiny shake. "I'd tell you I liked you. I'd tell you I was a mess and ask you to be patient while I sort it out. But I can't. I'm not that guy and you aren't that girl anymore and I can't unhurt your feelings or push myself out of my own way. But right now? I'm trying, Eva. I'm fucking trying. Can you at least meet me halfway?"

I open and close my mouth, trying to say something. Anything.

No, that's not true; there are very specific things I need to say to him.

I need to tell him *no*. I need to tell him to get lost. I need to tell him that all of this is fake, *fake*, FAKE. My teeth clench, throat closing around the words I need to say to protect myself from another letdown.

Cooper's hands move from my shoulders, trace up my neck, cradle my jaw. The space between our bodies crackles, tendrils of electricity urging us together, sparks growing stronger against our final shreds of restraint. We sway closer, not strong enough to resist the pull.

"Please," he whispers, face creased in agony.

He strokes my skin, thumb brushing my lips. I part them, exhaling, and his nail gently scratches at my sensitive flesh. I try to find a floating rational thought, grip it with both hands and shove it into my mouth, say the words I need to say, instead of the ones I want to.

The fear is too real, too raw.

It sounds so lovely, what he's asking. So soft and gentle, a cloud I want to luxuriate on as I float toward the sky. But he'll hurt me again. Everyone always hurts me in the end.

Cooper leans toward me, our eyes locked, his body flush

against mine. He's so close, so warm. His lips right there, saying the things I wanted all those years ago.

"Say yes, Eva," he whispers, the words ghosting across my mouth, sending a shiver of want through me, my pulse pounding like a hammer against an anvil, the need to have every inch of him pressed against every inch of me so overwhelming, I get dizzy with it. The word bubbles up my throat, curls across my tongue. I open my mouth to say it, to give in.

A crack of thunder booms around us, rattling my bones, making us jump. The bubble is popped, the world—with its freezing rain and harsh wind—crashes back through. We're both breathing like we just ran a marathon, eyes wide and wild.

Cooper speaks first. "Eva—"

But I'm the one to move. As sudden as the thunder, I turn, sprinting away, working to outpace the feelings trying to drag me back to Cooper's arms.

Chapter 14

RAIN SPECKLES THE SUBWAY WINDOW, TURNING THE CITY into a gray funhouse mirror as I try to focus on the passing view instead of my clown of a reflection. If there wasn't a distinct grease smear on the glass, I'd bang my forehead against it in frustration.

Meet me halfway.

Cooper's voice is a litany in my head that not even the noise of the train can drown out.

Please.

A couple sits across from me on the otherwise empty train. They're giggly and punch-drunk, the woman's head resting on the man's chest, his arm wrapped around her shoulders as he plays with the ends of her short black hair, the display of affection doing little to ease the fist clenched around my heart, and I choke back a whimper.

"Why are you crying?" the woman asks suddenly in a lightly slurred voice, still nuzzled against her partner.

"Harper," the man murmurs sweetly, slightly less tipsy than her. He shoots me a kind but apologetic smile.

Harper sits up, eyes wide and fixed on him, her hand resting on his thigh like she can't stop herself from touching him. "What?" she whines. "This lovely woman is hurting. I want to make sure she's okay. You're so beautiful, by the way," she says, turning to me and imparting drunk-girl kindness usually only found in bar bathrooms. "Something about you. You're too soft to hurt this badly."

I flinch, lips falling open in surprise. No one's ever called me soft before in a way that wasn't meant to harm me.

Even in a cocktail haze, Harper's gaze is sharp as she scans my face, a loose smile curling her mouth like my surprise resonates deeply with her. "What's wrong?" she coaxes.

My eyes flick to her partner, but he's staring at her with a wonderstruck expression. I take a deep, shaky breath, the bricks in my walls shifting, edges crumbling. I have nothing to lose from pouring my misery out to this stranger.

"It's this guy . . ."

"It's always about love, isn't it?" Harper says with a knowing giggle, her gaze still on me but body tilting closer to her partner.

"I don't love him," I rush out.

"Of course you don't," she says with a level of conviction neither of us believe.

"I'm okay," I say, sniffling in a way that confirms I'm a dirty liar.

"You don't look okay."

I open my mouth to argue, then shrug. I'm soaking wet and miserable on the train; the facts aren't on my side here.

There's a contemplative silence as Harper takes me in, her partner looking between us.

"I almost let Dan here get away," she says at last, leaning back into the cradle of his arms. "But I chased him down." She pats his chest a few times, tilting her head up as they share an indulgent smile. "And now we're here celebrating our second wedding anniversary."

"I'm happy for you," I say through a thick throat, more tears chasing down my cheeks as I look at their easy intimacy, a closeness I'm not destined for. "Congratulations."

The train comes to a stop, my body lurching with the movement.

"Seventh Avenue–Park Slope Station," the automated voice crackles over the intercom.

Park Slope—Cooper's stop. My heart folds in on itself, eyes straining as I look out the darkened window like I'm not underground and can magically see his place four blocks away.

I'm trying, Eva.

"Sometimes you have to shove yourself out of the way and take a risk," Harper says as the two of them stand, leaning on each other as they stumble toward the door. "Happiness might not be the outcome but it's worth a chance."

I stare after them, the world slipping into slow motion. Her voice and Cooper's and my own that I've pushed way, way down echo through my skull, the words fuzzy at first but gaining volume as they tell me, *Go, you idiot, go!*

I bolt up to standing like my seat just electrocuted me, my heart thumping a bruise into my ribs. Time speeds up again, and my step toward the door feels too fast, too giant, but it brings me to the gap between the safety of this train and the unknown of the platform.

I don't know if seeing Cooper right now will make me happy. In fact, the pessimistic voice that guides most of my choices is telling me it will have the exact opposite effect. I scramble to rationalize what's happening, but my brain can't keep up with my feet hustling me off the train, not slowing as I'm almost sliced in half by the closing doors.

I pound up the station steps to the sidewalk, looking frantically around to get my bearings, ignoring the fresh chill of the rain on my already-soaked skin. Clocking a street sign, I dart across the intersection, soliciting a few honks. I give an unhinged wave, continuing my run. I make a left, then a right, wheezing by the time I get to his block.

I slow (more out of cardiovascular necessity than conscious choice) as I get to his place, climbing the steps to his door. I stand there for a moment, trying to catch my breath, put some order to my scribbled thoughts. But all I know is Rylie Cooper is on the other side of that door, and I want to see him.

I lift my fist to knock, but a crack of lightning illuminates the sky, thunder immediately following, the boom pausing my movement.

It's a threat. A scolding. A warning that I need to leave his doorstep, trudge back to the subway station and actually make it back to my lonely apartment, hole myself up in there until this painful knot in my chest eases and I can think straight again.

I lower my arm, heart pounding with warning and want.

I slowly turn, staring at the dark glistening street, trying to get my feet to walk the three steps off his stoop. But his voice ghosts through my mind.

I can't change the past. Do you have any idea how much I wish I could?

The hungry, desperate creature in me howls, then takes control. I whip around, cocking my fist and banging on his door like I can punch through it.

I can hear his quick footsteps on the other side but I don't stop pounding until he's wrenching the door open and I'm swaying toward him like a drunken sailor. Drunk is a good word for what I'm feeling—flushed and frantic and aware of my thoughts but completely out of control of them.

Silence hovers between us, and the weight of it opens my jaw, tugs on my vocal cords, has me whispering *"Rylie"* in a harsh, broken breath.

He stares at me, glasses slightly askew and hair a mess like he's been dragging his hands through it for hours. He's changed out of his wet clothes into a white T-shirt and gray sweatpants showing a rather impressive—

I jerk my eyes back up to his face because I have a single thread of self-control left and if I pay too much attention to how little those sweatpants are leaving to the imagination, I might start blowing him right here and now. And wouldn't *that* be pathetic.

"What are you doing here?" Rylie's tone is low, and I lean closer to hear it over the pounding rain.

"I don't know," I answer honestly.

He swallows, eyes skimming a quick circuit up and down my body. I watch, mesmerized as pink crawls across his cheeks.

He drags his knuckles against his lips, fixing me with a merciless look as his jaw tightens. Another bolt of lightning cracks through the sky.

"I don't think you should be here," he whispers in warning. The roughness of his voice slips into me, swirling up my spine, dancing between my ribs, taking up space in my chest.

"I *know* I shouldn't be here." It's my final fully formed thought before diving headfirst into the feelings.

I close the space between us, throwing my arms around his neck. I feel him suck in a breath right as I seal my mouth to his, kissing him hard.

Everything else dissolves. There's only the warmth of Rylie's mouth, the initial surprise and the instantaneous hunger. One large palm cradling my jaw, coaxing me to open for him, the silky heat of his tongue finding mine. The growl in the back of his throat as he pushes his body closer to mine. His free hand slides to my lower back, under my clinging wet shirt, hitching me against him.

I'm feral, fisting my hands in his hair, wrapping my thigh around his hip, threatening to push him down right on his stoop. Rylie has the audacity to laugh, a smug, delighted sound, and I almost manage to protest his enjoyment, but he's turning us, pulling me the rest of the way in, kicking his front door closed behind him. His touch is everywhere—lips at my throat, teeth at my collarbone, palm under my skirt and cupping my ass—and I gasp in a few fractured breaths, head spinning.

"What is this?" he says, more to himself than to me. His expression is dazed, eyes mapping a wild course down my body. He grips the hem of my T-shirt, pulling the soaked fabric up and over my head. "What's happening?"

"Bed," I pant against his mouth, only breaking apart to similarly remove his shirt. "Take me to your bed."

I have the briefest thought that I hope his roommates aren't home, or are at least sequestered in their rooms, but then Rylie's bare palms are at my waist, firmly guiding me toward the stairs, and I realize I don't much care who's home. His eyes are fever bright, color high on his cheeks and lips parted as he stares at me like he's a starving man. Like he wants to devour me.

"What *is* this?" he asks again, question steadier, but he continues to walk me up the steps, both of us clumsy and desperate, tripping more than progressing.

"One night," I gasp out as Rylie takes matters into his own hands and lifts me, wrapping my legs around his waist and carrying me up the final steps. I'm a tall girl, and I've often been denied the soft luxury of being made to feel dainty by a partner, but Rylie cradles me against his body like I'm something delicate he's so glad to hold.

"One night?" he echoes, letting me slide from his arms when we make it to his floor, using his hands to frame my face, kissing me harder.

"Just one," I emphasize, somehow getting the words out over the bubble of protest in my throat. "You better make it good."

We bounce our way down the hall, slamming against walls and skewing picture frames as we claw at each other, mouths and teeth and tongues never leaving the other's skin. We crash through his bedroom door and there's nothing but his hands in my hair, at my neck, my fingers tearing at his sweatpants, my shoes kicked toward his bed, the . . .

"What the fuck is on your bed?" I pant out, rearing away from him. My sudden movement throws Rylie off balance, and his face lands against my chest with a groan. He takes longer than necessary to lift his head, dragging his face side to side. I tug roughly at his hair. "You've got to be kidding me."

Even in the low light, Rylie's blush is luminous, and he straightens, righting his crooked glasses as he follows my look of horror to the . . . *thing* covering his bed.

"It's . . . it's a jomforter."

"A *what*?" I take a wary, but morbidly curious, step closer toward it. A giant navy . . . I guess you could call it a comforter is stretched across his mattress. I realize with a gasp of horror that it is in fact made of denim, a giant back pocket taking up the majority of the space, belt loops lining the top edge. It's stitched with gold thread.

"A jomforter," Rylie repeats, dragging a hand along the back of his neck. "A jean comforter."

"Why in god's name is it on your bed?"

"I . . . I think it's pretty hilarious, to be honest with you," he says, wrinkling his nose, his chest heaving. "I can see how maybe it's not the most, uh, alluring of bedding in this moment, though."

Jesus. I can't believe I'm about to have sex on a denim duvet.

"Do you curl up in the pocket?" I ask, unable to help myself.

Rylie's laugh is rough and bright. "Once, yeah."

I continue to stare at the hideous thing, wondering what has happened to me that I somehow find that so endearing it makes Rylie even more attractive.

"I wanted an obvious signal to visitors that I'm a freak in the jeets," he whispers, coming up behind me and dropping his hands to my waist and his smile to my neck.

"Stop fucking talking," I growl, turning in his arms and letting him back me up until my thighs hit the edge of his atrocious bed. "Never speak again, I'm begging you."

"You'll be begging for a lot of other things in a few minutes."

"I'm gonna hold you to that."

His eyes glint in challenge, fingers hooking into the elastic waistband of my skirt. He gives me a questioning look, and I nod, helping him shimmy it off my hips as he goes back to kissing me. He sucks in a sharp breath as his hands cup my bare ass. His eyes shoot open in surprise as he pulls his head back.

"It's, uh, one of those built-in underwear skirts," I explain, feeling overwhelmingly pleased with myself at his fevered look.

"The world's best fucking invention," he mumbles, kissing up my neck again, his hands gripping and kneading the curves of my ass.

With a roughness that shocks and excites me, Rylie pushes me onto the bed, staring at me for a heartbeat. I watch a small tremble move through him, and he shakes his head like he can't believe I'm actually there. With a swift movement, he rips off his glasses, tossing them to the side, then plants one knee on the mattress in the space between my legs, making my weight slide toward the dip.

Instinctually, I move, seeking friction against his thigh, but then I lock my muscles, forcing myself to be calm.

"Uh-uh," Rylie says, a dark wickedness to his voice. He leans over me, palms on either side of my head, caging me. My heart hammers as I take in the wild flush of his cheeks, his heated focus, the way he licks his lower lip like he's so hungry for me he can't stand it. I've never been so excited to be trapped. "Don't you dare stop yourself, Eva. Fucking use me."

Something in me untethers, his words a spark that starts a wildfire, my inhibitions burning away. I lift my head until my lips crash against his, my pelvis grinding against the rough cotton covering his thigh. I don't know what this is, this greedy, uncontrollable thing that has me so desperate to be close to him I might scream if I don't get more of his weight on top of me.

But Cooper's there, his hand cradling the back of my neck, tips of his fingers digging in with just the right amount of pressure. He kisses me like I hope he'll fuck me, deep and dirty and consuming. I feel his hardness pressed against my hip bone, the tautness of his muscles as I drag my nails down his chest and stomach.

Rylie groans. "God, Eva. You're so . . ." He doesn't let me hear the rest, burrowing his face against my chest, his words vibrating against my skin. We're still for a moment—well, as still as we can manage, our hips moving in small, desperate nudges, hands gripping and kneading. He breathes me in, a deep, shaky breath, like the scent of my skin is more vital to him than oxygen. He lifts his head again. "I can't believe this is happening."

Rylie readjusts us, looping one hand around my waist and lifting me farther up the bed. He settles fully on the mattress, kneeling between my spread legs. I'm in a haze, limbs heavy and pulsing with desire, letting him move my body wherever he wants it.

"Can I take this off?" he asks roughly, snapping one of the straps of my bra. The bite of it makes me jerk, a hot pulse of pleasure scorching through me.

"Fuck. Please."

His movements are smooth as he reaches under me to the clasp, but I feel a slight tremor in his fingers as he unhooks it, gently dragging the straps down my arms. It's so different from how it was all those years ago, the tenderness in his touch, the way he's savoring me instead of rushing to the finish. He pauses again, jaw set, staring at my exposed breasts, down my stomach, up to my flushed face.

He traces the tips of his fingers from my belly button up the center of my body, and it feels like something in me is unzipping, like I'm coming apart at the seams.

Rylie's hand returns to my neck, and he holds me there, palm at my nape and thumb at my throat with a pressure that's both reverence and demand, and for some absurd reason, I know I'd give him anything he asks of me right now.

"I'm going to make this so fucking good for you," he says, then dips his head, kissing me, this time unhurried. The ease with which he's touching me, like he has a lifetime to memorize every inch but he's not going to waste a second, has me squirming against him, desperate for more and wanting to hide all at the same time.

"This is . . . this is just part of it, right?" I pant into his mouth. His hips grind harder against mine.

"Part of what?" He groans as I take his lower lip between my teeth and bite. Hard.

"Part of the whole making-up-for-being-an-asshole thing?"

He pulls back, eyes suddenly serious through the haze of lust. "This can be whatever you want it to be."

I panic at the flash of a thought, that I want it to be

something. I kick the idea out of my head before it can put down roots, sprinting in the opposite direction. Even in the delirium, I manage to give him a slow, deviant smile. "I want you to fuck me like you're sorry for letting me down the first time."

He grunts, his mouth going to the column of my throat, sucking until I arch into him, then he bites the spot, making me gasp. "That was a given."

Rylie's hands trail down my torso, cupping my hips and notching me firmer against him. He moves me up and down, my pussy dragging against the hard ridge of his erection. "Tell me how you like it," he demands. Pleads.

My head tips back, eyes fluttering closed as I focus on the feeling of him. Pleasure rises through me, ankles, thighs, pelvis, chest, head, until I'll float away from it. But it's not enough. I squeeze my eyes more tightly, fighting the swell of embarrassment trying to tug me out of the moment.

"Since we only have this one time and I have nothing to lose," I rush out, hoping he thinks the fracture in my voice is from desire and not nerves. "I might as well let you know I'm on an SSRI so it can kind of take a long time or not happen at all and I know how frustrating that can be for the other person and I just don't want you to get annoyed or—"

One of Rylie's hands is back at the angle of my jaw, his thumb over my lips. My eyes flash open and lock with his. He drags his fingertips from my mouth, down my throat until he cups my neck with steadying pressure. "Eva, just this once, I demand you shut up."

I huff in outrage, rearing back to snap at him, but he keeps me in his gentle grip, his steely expression making my words die on my tongue.

"Annoyance doesn't fucking exist in this room, in what we're about to do," he says, voice low and jagged as a serrated knife's edge. "I will fuck you any way you want. Any speed, any position. I will go down on you all fucking night if that's what it takes to make you come, and I will do it with a goddamn smile on my face the entire time. Do you understand me?"

I don't say anything, lips parted and breath ragged. He gives me a gentle shake.

"I asked you a question."

I nod.

His smile is wicked, outrageously delighted. He licks his lips, eyes making a leisurely circuit of my body, then back up. "Good. Now tell me what you like."

You, some desperate, delusional part of me whispers. I shake the thought away. "I don't know," I say instead.

Rylie's eyebrows notch down with his frown. "What?"

His confusion is genuine, not judgmental, but I want to disappear all the same. I talk a big game in my posts about sex and the orgasm gap, but I'm nothing if not a timid hypocrite in my personal sex life. I'm all for people asking for what they want in bed, but I've always been so hung up on pleasing the other person, I don't really know what *I'd* ask for. I don't know what I need to get there with another person. I've never allowed myself to be vulnerable enough to explore that.

"I-I think I'd like it a little bit rough," I manage to say, staring at the bob of his Adam's apple as he swallows. His fingers flex into my thighs, breathing frayed.

"Rough how?" he asks in a low rumble before placing a quick, sharp bite to my breast.

"Like that," I gasp out.

"How else?" When I don't immediately speak, he bites me again, then soothes the area with a decadent lick of his tongue, ripping another gasp from me.

"I . . . I don't . . . I mean . . . This isn't . . . I haven't . . ." He drags his teeth to my nipple, gently nipping at the peak before sucking it deep into his mouth. My vision blurs.

"You haven't what, Kitten?" he whispers.

I groan in response, wriggling closer, holding his head to my chest and silently begging him to do it again.

Rylie pulls back instead, color flagging his cheeks, his mouth slack and wet. "Use your words or I'm stopping."

The sound I let out is so pathetically needy I want to melt into the mattress, but Rylie grins, dipping his head to my throat with a restrained laugh. I'd push him away to save some of my dignity if his weight didn't feel so damn good on top of me. I hold him closer instead.

"I haven't asked anybody for it rough before so I don't know what I like or how much," I say in a rush. I keep going, knowing if I stop I'll never fess up. "All the sex I've had is bland and boring and I'm so deep in my own head being worried about making it good for the other person that I've never bothered to ask for what I want instead."

Every relationship I've been in, my priority is always to please the other person any way I can, including sex. In my teens and early twenties I devoured every glossy magazine article I could find about what moves I could do to make a man feel good. My desperation to please someone enough to get them to stick around was my only tangible desire. Why would I bother figuring out my own needs when I was too tied-up figuring out how to make it good for the other person?

Rylie pulls against my grip like he wants to look at me, but I hold him tight against my body. This is easier to say to the ceiling than to his earnest, hungry eyes. "But if we only have tonight, I might as well make sure you don't fuck it up."

Rylie laughs, a tiny puff of hot air against my skin that sends a shiver rushing through me.

"Tell me more of what you think you want," he coaxes, turning his head so his cheek nuzzles against my breast, the sharp stubble making me arch against him. "I want to hear it all." His fingers trace a lazy path over my rib cage, across my stomach, down my thigh to the back of my knee, then reverses the movement. It's a soft touch, not desperate or overtly sexual, but it lights me on fire, my legs falling open a bit more.

"I want you to keep touching me," I choke out.

Rylie laughs again. "That's a given, sweetheart. You feel too good to stop."

A broken groan falls out of me, my body bucking beneath him, and I bite my lip.

Rylie pulls back, eyes roving over me until they glint with knowing, his dimple popping out as he smiles. "Do you like that, Eva? Do you like me telling you how fucking perfect you are?"

Another gasp betrays me, every cell in my body sparking to life under the coarse rumble of his words.

Rylie's grin is downright sinful, and my heart pounds in my chest as he leans to my ear, lips ghosting across my cheeks along the way. "You do. You like it. Now keep being a good girl and tell me how rough you want me to be with this beautiful fucking body of yours. I'll give you anything you want, you just have to ask." He bites the lobe and my back bows.

"Jesus fucking Christ, please just touch me," I nearly scream, grabbing his gentle, roving hand and thrusting it between my legs.

The pressure soothes me for a second, but only one, because Rylie snatches his touch away, gripping my hip instead. Quick like a bullet he's up on his knees, using them to force my legs wider as his other hand grabs my inner thigh then hooks behind my knee, spreading me for him.

He stares for a moment, then licks his lips, eyes tracing up my torso to lock with mine. "I'm starving, baby. Let me taste you instead."

I garble out something close to *please*, my head falling back. Rylie reaches past me, snatching a pillow from the top of the bed.

"Lift your hips, beautiful," he says gruffly, already raising them for me as he slides the pillow beneath. I find some semblance of strength in my rapidly spiraling body to prop myself up on my elbows, watching as he repositions himself between my legs.

"God, you're fucking pretty," he growls as he leans forward, draping both of my thighs over his shoulders in the process. "So fucking wet and needy and soft. I've dreamed about you for years, but none of my memories did you justice."

Before the thought can gain purchase, his mouth is on me, tongue making a dirty, desperate swipe up to my clit. I shudder, whimpering at the shockwave it sends through me, a sensation so intense my thighs try to close around him. My desperation doesn't faze him. He makes another leisurely swipe. Then another. Taking his time, tracing every inch of me, circling my entrance then dipping in, lavishing his way up to my clit.

"You taste even better than I imagined," he says against me, more vibrations than voice. His breathing is almost violent, the vault of his rib cage expanding against my thighs with every inhale. He focuses on my clit, eyes meeting mine over the planes of my body as he catalogs every reaction. What pressure makes me writhe and claw at the sheets, the suction that makes me cry out as my thighs tremble against his face, the merciless rhythm of his tongue that has me babbling out his name in desperate pleas, tears gathering at the corners of my eyes as sharp pleasure builds in my pelvis. Rylie pulls back for air, curling his fingers inside me in a way that makes me whimper.

"That's it. Look how fucking good you're taking it. So perfect." His words are muffled, my pussy grinding against him in my wrecked desperation. "Let me hear how badly you want it."

He puts his mouth back to me, dragging his head side to side so his stubble scratches along the sensitive skin of my inner thighs, and incoherent words pour out of me, voice a shout as need turns me inside out, mindless and desperate for release. Rylie makes a triumphant noise between my legs, rewarding me with more rhythmic curls of his fingers.

It's never been like this before. *I've* never been like this before—thrashing and crying and wild with the need to come, not a moment of thought if he's enjoying himself because I fucking *know* he is. He's grunting in pleasure as he tastes me, shoulder muscles bunched between my legs, hips thrusting against the mattress because he's so out of his mind with it too.

He builds me up higher and higher, my cries fractured, my thighs clamped tight against his head as he works me, entire body shaking so hard the headboard rattles against the wall as a feeling so intense that it's almost painful rushes through me.

"Fuck. Fuck. Don't stop. I'm coming. Don't stop."

He doesn't, keeping that perfect rhythm, that matching movement of his fingers, those delighted sounds of need as he takes me there. Wave after wave crashes through me, and I continue to tremble, tears slipping down my cheeks at the endless release of it.

I pull his hair when I become too sensitive to handle any more, and he pulls back, mouth slick, eyes glazed. He kisses my thighs like he can't keep his lips off me, and I whimper at the soft sensation.

My breathing gets only a degree below ragged when he speaks, eyes locking with mine over my belly. "Can you give me another one, beautiful?" he asks, voice coaxing, fingers demanding as he pumps them into me at an angle that's just fucking right.

My hips buck, a string of curse words pouring out of me at the sensation. "I'm not sure if I can," I pant, needing him to take mercy. Needing him to keep going.

"I am." His voice drips with confidence. It speaks volumes to how good that orgasm was that I don't suffocate him with my thighs right now out of annoyance.

But then he's making up for his cockiness—or, more like proving its merit—his tongue back on me, softer this time, almost gentle. Almost.

There's something so dirty and delicious about the way he devours me. He grunts praise between my thighs—*sweet* and *greedy* and *fucking perfect*—and it isn't long until I'm right at that edge again, sweating and swearing and begging Rylie to let me come against his mouth.

"*Holyfuckingshit*" is the only coherent thing I manage to garble out as Rylie kisses his way back up my body, my muscles still twitching with the aftershocks. "You didn't know how to do that last time."

He laughs as he stretches out next to me. I somehow find the strength to swivel my head to look at him. "I'm a big believer in character growth," he says, reaching out to tuck a damp lock of my hair behind my ear. "And despite your unnecessary warning earlier, you make it very easy to be very good to."

Something in my chest shifts, his words melting through me. I want to hide from the kindness of it, the tenderness in his eyes, so I kiss him instead, tasting myself on his tongue and loving the reminder of how much he enjoyed it. Enjoyed me.

Rylie wraps an arm around my waist, sliding me closer against him, our sweaty chests rubbing together. I'm dismayed to realize his sweatpants are still on, and my greedy hands dive to the waistband, trying to tug them off. Rylie laughs again, stilling my eager fingers.

"Not sure what could possibly be funny right now," I growl against his mouth, batting at his hands. He playfully swats

back, then grips my wrists, turning me so my back is on the
bed, hands held up near my ears as he looms over me.

"I'm not a piece of meat, Eva," he says, smile smug. I can't
believe I actually like seeing this man so happy. "I want you
to *tell* me what you want."

"I want to come with you inside me," I say, abandoning
any self-consciousness about demanding too much. If Rylie
wants to hear it, I'll fucking tell him. "I want you to fuck me
hard and deep and tell me again how pretty I look while you
do it. I want you to make me come again, and I'll do whatever
you tell me to make it happen."

He pauses for a moment, lips parted and eyes electric.
"God, you're so fucking lovely when you beg."

I wish I could play it cool, even for a second, but my smile
is radiant, body glowing from his praise. Before I can grap-
ple the word from my hazy brain, Rylie's reaching into his
side drawer, pulling out a condom. He sits back against the
headboard, kicking off his sweatpants and ripping open the
silver packet. He holds the base of his cock to position it, and I
grab the condom from him, overcome with the need to touch
him, feel him in my hands. I slide the rubber down his length,
eyes bouncing between his dazed expression as he watches
my movements, and the way he swells even more in my palm.

"Show me how much you want it," Rylie whispers, gripping my thigh and nudging me to straddle his hips.

I position myself over him, the head of his cock brushing
my slick entrance. My hips start rocking, just the tip of him
in me, and I clench hard, wanting him to fill me fully. Rylie
hisses through his teeth. I slide down his thick length slowly,

reveling in the stretch, the way every new inch is more delicious than the last. I watch his face as I tease him, the concentrated agony in the set of his jaw, the flare of his nostrils, pupils blown wide and black as he watches me.

When I can't take it anymore, I seat myself fully, flush to his pelvis. Rylie's groan of need is scraped from his throat, desperate and hungry and ready. His abs flex as he curls up, taking my nipple into his mouth with an insistent pressure, the movement pushing him even deeper so sensation slices through me and I cry out, fisting his hair in my hands and gripping him tighter to me. I may be on top but there's no doubt who's in control here.

Rylie collapses back against the sheets, and I plant my palms on his chest to keep my balance, nails biting into his flesh.

"Look at how perfectly you take me, Eva," he says, voice revenant, almost slurred, eyes hazed and locked on where we're joined. His hands frame my hips, fingertips digging into my ass as he grinds me back and forth, a barely there motion that emphasizes how full I am. I squeeze around him. "Fuck," Rylie grunts, expression shattered. "How are you so tight? I feel like I'm already gonna lose it, you feel so good."

I whimper with the need for friction, moments away from sobbing if I don't feel the slick glide of him soon.

"Move for me, beautiful," Rylie says, reading my mind and my body. "Give me everything."

I bite down hard on my lower lip as I gladly do as he asks. I flex my thighs and lift my hips up the thickness of him, already aching from the retreat, whining for him to fill me again. Rylie's hands tighten on my hips with a possessive grip when I reach the tip of his cock, and his lust-crazed eyes meet mine for a breathless, heavy moment. Then, he smiles, a piercing wicked thing, and I know I'm a goner.

He slams me down, thrusting up in counterpoint, hitting a spot deep inside me that has me seeing stars as I cry out. He does it again. And again. My nails dig harder into his chest, arms braced and back arched as he fucks me, voice coming to me in fractured pants as he drives us both toward the peak. *So good* and *tight* and *sweet fucking girl* all growled at me as he works, the praise winding through me and cinching tight into a pulsing knot of pleasure low in my belly.

"Touch yourself, Eva," he says, gripping one of my wrists and dragging it to my clit. Our fingers tangle for a moment as I shakily try to do as he says. He smiles as he watches me find a rhythm. "That's it. Show off for me, gorgeous."

My climax bursts through me quick as a flare, my body clenching around Rylie in frantic spasms as I try to suck in a breath. My hands slip from his chest, and I collapse on top of him, wave after wave still pulsing through me. I try to prop myself up but I don't have the strength, tiny sobs pouring out of my throat.

"I've got you, baby," Rylie says into my ear, still pumping into me from below. "You've done so fucking good."

I squeeze tightly around him again, and Rylie bites my shoulder against a shout, losing his rhythm, grabbing my hips and holding me tight to him as he comes. I can hear my heartbeat in my ears, feel it down to the tips of my toes and every inch in between. I feel Rylie's heartbeat too, fast and loud against my cheek, my body a boneless heap on top of his.

He doesn't seem to mind. And for a moment, while we work to catch our breath, chests clashing in unmatched tempos, I don't mind either.

Then Rylie goes and fucks it all up.

With the barest brush of his lips to the top of my head, he plants a kiss there. It's too tender. Too endearing. A cuddle and kiss on the forehead isn't how you end rough, one-night-only sex. I scramble off him, Rylie hissing when he unceremoniously slips out of me.

"You're going to kill me," he says, voice hazy.

An unhinged peal of laughter tumbles out of me, as harsh as breaking glass, and his eyes widen. Then he laughs too. The warmth in his face, the uninhibited enjoyment etching his features, sobers me up. Cooper notices—damn perceptive bastard, of course he does. I can see him trying to read my expression. I turn on my back, staring up at the ceiling. A moment later, I feel him shift as he follows suit.

"That was . . ." His unfinished thought floats there, and I know we're both playing a game of mental hangman to see what word will fit the blank space.

Amazing. Unexpected. Game-changing. Possibly the best sex of my life. A one-off . . . A mistake.

The last one makes something sharp hook in my chest, and I rush to fill the silence before I can feel the crushing blow of it from Cooper's mouth.

"Weird." Oh good god, I landed on *weird*?

Cooper turns his head slowly to face me, his eyes heavy-lidded but bland. "Weird," he echoes.

I open my mouth. Close it. Bite my bottom lip, then shrug. Everything about my time with Rylie Cooper is weird. One, because *he's* weird, but two because he rewires my brain in a way that has me totally off-kilter.

He turns on his side again to face me, propping himself up on his elbow and resting his head in his palm. "I just delivered what was arguably the best oral sex performance of my life and the peanut gallery calls it weird?"

"That part wasn't . . ."

"Weird?" he offers, nonplussed.

I nod. "That part was, er, really good." His smirk is so arrogant I have the urge to bite him.

"So the weirdness was when I—" He gestures toward his crotch with his free hand, and I grab his wrist.

"No," I growl, twisting his skin in opposite directions with both my hands to give him a rug burn. He easily slides out of my grip and swats me away. "That part was, uh, exceptional as well."

"Exceptional?" he squeals, the corner of his mouth twitching up with his quirked eyebrow.

"Acceptable," I correct through a dry throat, face heating.

"Exceptional," he agrees with a nod, snaking his arm out to wrap around my waist, tugging me to him. I burrow into the hair on his chest, feeling the warmth of his skin against mine. And it feels good and tender and safe and . . . *right*. A flare of panic erupts in my chest. Because that can't be. That's not how this is supposed to go.

This is one night, a private stop on his public redemption tour for hurting my precious feelings years ago. I'm not going to be that fool again. I'm not going to find emotions where there are none just because I feel raw and exposed after sex. Again. Fucking hell.

I wriggle out of his embrace, sitting up and pulling the sheet around my body. I make sure to kick his hideous comforter to the end of the bed.

"I guess I landed on *weird* because this whole thing is just that," I babble. "I mean, we go from not talking to doing public dates for social media attention to having a heated fight after fake couples therapy like any of it means anything at all to either of us when we both know it doesn't."

I can see Cooper out of the corner of my eye, and I watch him blink a few times, his face falling. I feel a twinge in my gut, and I want to take back the words. But what would be the point? I'm not going to lie to myself just because I'm high on post-sex hormones. I can feel the intensity of his stare, an expectant expression like he's waiting for me to laugh and say I was joking.

I don't. Instead, I pull my knees to my chest and rest my chin on them.

After a beat, Cooper sits up too, getting out of bed and handling the condom before grabbing his discarded sweatpants. I don't notice the thick tension in the muscles of his back or how absurdly perfect his ass is as he pulls them on.

"Bathroom," he mumbles in explanation as he heads to the door. "Back in a second."

I know I should wait my turn for the restroom, take a moment in there to pull myself together, and handle this like a grown-up. I should apologize for being so harsh, and make sure we're on the same page.

But the idea of hearing Cooper agree with me that this was a fun, one-time thing rips down my spine, and I get out of bed, frantically grabbing my clothes and pulling my skirt on backward, my bra inside out. Some deranged, scolding voice in the back of my head tells me a UTI would serve me right for the stunt I'm about to pull, but I've never prided myself on acting like an adult, so why start now?

I hear the flush of the toilet and water burbling from the sink, and my movements speed up double-time. I finally re-member my shirt is in his damn foyer, and, with one final look at the bathroom door, I sneak out of his room and bolt down the stairs, throwing on my shirt haphazardly before disap-pearing into the night.

Chapter 15

RAY IS FACETIMING ME INCESSANTLY THIS MORNING. AIDA too, which is a terrible sign, because I still haven't smoothed work things over with her.

But, because I'm *so* good at addressing problems head-on, I once again decline Ray's call. He takes it to the group chat.

> Ray: ummmm bitch you better fucking answer because you have some explaining to do

He attaches a link to a social media post. The thumbnail preview makes my stomach drop—a red skirt twisted at the waistband, disheveled white T-shirt, purse clutched in a fist like a weapon. I click through, one hand darting to my mouth in horror. It's a carousel of three pictures of me fleeing Cooper's place last night like I just committed a capital offense. I can't stop myself from reading the caption.

I live in the same neighborhood as Rylie Cooper and when I was taking my dog out last night Eva Kitt wasn't so much doing a walk of shame as she was a dead sprint of one

> Comment: the only person who should be ashamed is rylie's dick for going so much lower

>> Reply: I FUCKING KNEW THEY WERE HOOKING UP. YOU CAN'T FAKE CHEMISTRY LIKE THAT

>> Reply: kind of needing a video of her eating his hot dog ngl

>> Reply: the adage is true, men really do love bitches (or at least banging them)

I keep reading until my eyes blur, stunned and disoriented as I try to process what this means. The internet knows I hooked up with Cooper.

No, that's not true. They *think* that. They don't have proof. These blurry photos of me aren't *proof* . . . because the internet always places so much value on legitimate proof over gleeful conjecture . . .

Fuck.

It terrifies me that my first impulse, besides wanting to curl up into a ball and die, is to call Rylie, to seek shelter in his voice, the effortless way he can make me laugh even when I feel my worst. I feel so exposed, so irrevocably perceived, I want to crawl out of my skin.

Okay. Maybe this can be fixed. I look at the post again. It only has a few thousand views and far less likes. It hasn't taken off yet. I go through and report a few of the nastier comments, then the video itself, needing to do something to regain an ounce of control in my rapidly spiraling life.

My intercom rings, the sound grating down my nerves, and my sweat-slick palms almost send my phone flying across the room. The buzzer goes off again, someone hitting the button incessantly.

"Hello?" I hiss into the speaker, not playing at politeness for someone so damn impatient.

"It's me."

I know that voice. I hate how intimately I know that voice. Despite the hard edge of it, it sends a shiver down my spine as memories of that voice from last night swirl through me.

"Me who?" I squeak out, trying to buy some time as panic sets in that Cooper is at my door.

"It's Rylie," he says, making it clear he isn't looking to play my game. "Let me up."

"How do you know where I live, you creep?" I say into the intercom, butterflies erupting in my stomach.

"I picked you up here on our first date, you headstrong fruit loop. Now let me up." His voice is louder, and the rough frustration has me backing up a step. There's a pause, then a long sigh travels through the tinny speaker. "I've brought you food. Please let me up."

Food? What kind of food?

Like an animal sniffing the edges of a trap, I scurry over to my window that looks down to the entrance of my building. I crouch down, the top of my head peeking over the windowsill to try and see if he's being serious.

Rylie Cooper is staring straight at me from the street below, his mouth pressed in a frown. His gaze locks me there and, after a moment, he lifts up two large brown bags of what appear to be carry-out like he's making a crude hand gesture at me.

I go a bit weak in the knees.

I shouldn't let him up. The man is clearly a glutton for punishment, and he brings out the worst in me, every thorn sharpened. I look at my phone from where it sits on the floor, vibrating with another slew of notifications, and I feel a sudden stab of loneliness as I think about the mess that awaits me on there. The loneliness is so vast, so terrifyingly empty, panic spears through my chest and my gaze shoots back to Rylie out the window. As much as I hate to admit it, he's the only one I can relate to in this moment. With a defeated sigh, I drag myself to the door and buzz him up. A minute later, he knocks.

I crack the door open, and Rylie gives me a sardonic look through the sliver that says, *Really?*

"Open the damn door, Eva. Let me in." He nudges it with his shoulder, and I step back, not exactly welcoming him into my home but no longer having the fight in me to push him away.

"What are you doing here?" My lips feel numb, blood stinging through my veins.

"I saw the post." He steps around me and places the bags of food on my small kitchen table. His gaze makes a wide sweep of my place, lingering for extra beats at the art on my walls, the books on my coffee table, the giant and somewhat horrifying blobfish plushie on my couch. His lips twitch in amusement.

"So naturally you wanted to recreate the moment and give everyone more fodder by trying to bust down my door?" I say blandly, studying my nails.

"No." There's no softness in his voice. None of the usual good humor or playfulness.

I risk a quick glance at him, then do a double take. Rylie is looking at me like a man possessed. By anger, annoyance, need . . . I can't fully tell. Color sits high on his cheeks, his breathing shallow and fast. He takes a step toward me, and I have the instinct to back up, but I hold my ground.

"No," he repeats, taking another step. "See, Eva, I'm not recreating last night. Because I'm here. I'm showing up. You, on the other hand, left."

"So what?" I shoot back, acrid hostility burning through my veins, my hands shaking with the need to push him back, hold him close. "Are you looking for a congratulations on figuring out the subway system and wandering to my door-step? Or did you drive here in your hideous car?"

"Stop making fun of my car!"

"Then stop driving a car so easy to make fun of!"

Rylie stares at me so intensely I have to fight the urge to squirm. The energy shifts between us, becoming alive and crackling with tension. He takes another step toward me. "I'm here to check on you, you contrarian witch. I'm here to see if you're okay."

"I'm not okay!" I yell, storming to him, closing the space between us so we're nose to nose. "I haven't been okay since you waltzed back into my life with this ridiculous publicity stunt. I have not been okay for a damn second of this man-ufactured bullshit between us that we serve on the internet like a slab of meat to rabid dogs. I'm not okay because you're making me feel things and I fucking hate it! So stop. Stop pre-tending. Stop checking on me. Stop, stop, *stop* and let me get back to being generally miserable in peace."

Our chests clash as we breathe, ragged, sharp intakes that

border on panting. Rylie's eyes look wild, his glasses fogged at the edges from the agitation simmering between us. With considerable effort, he lets out a controlled exhale, and I want to bat away the steady coolness that tickles across my cheeks.

He reaches up his hands, and I can't tell if he's planning on cradling my cheeks or throttling me. At my look, he drops them heavily to his sides.

"Listen to me," he says, voice low and leaving no room for argument. "For once in your goddamn life, listen to me. This was never a stunt for me, Eva." His eyes flash with anger. "Never. *You* were never a stunt. Why can't you get it through your thick skull that I fucking *like* you? Not past tense. Present. I liked you then, and, despite the desperate pleading of my sanity and your every attempt to push me away, I like you now. All of this is because I want to know you, be around you. Because I fucked it up once and I saw a second chance. Because now I'm so deep in this I would crawl through hell on my hands and knees over a bed of broken glass before I let you go again."

My ears ring in the resulting silence, my head spinning as I try to decipher the bomb he's just dropped.

"So I'm here," he says slowly, keeping his eyes locked on mine, "to check on you. I'm here, despite being fucking furious at you for leaving like you did last night, because I was worried about you. I wanted to make sure you're okay. And if you're not, I wanted to see what I could do to make things better."

My body is a riot, my stomach lurching and heart yo-yoing while hot panic drips through me. But I stay still as a statue, wide-eyed and tight-lipped as I continue to stare at Rylie.

He stares back for another moment, then sighs, the tension leaving his muscles. He walks over to the table and starts unpacking the bags, stacking a variety of Tupperware containers that are filled with a bunch of different pastas.

"You like me?" I ask, voice both accusatory and horrifically tender.

Rylie's smile is wry, and he keeps his attention on his task. "Yes. Very much."

"And you were worried about me?" The concept is so foreign, I can't wrap my head around it. Has anyone ever done this for me before? Ever went out of their way to check on me like this?

Rylie stops at that, dropping a packet of cheese. He gives me a disbelieving look. "Of course I was, Kitten. How could I not be?"

"And you . . . you brought me food?" I say, somehow managing to drag my gaze from his earnest expression to the massive amount of containers. Tears prick at my eyes as they helplessly return to Rylie.

His look melts like hot honey, smile unabashedly decadent as he studies me. Then he shrugs. "You did say mac 'n' cheese is your love language. I was going to make you some, I just didn't know which noodles were your favorite so I—"

Before I can think better of it, I'm launching myself at him, my arms wrapping around his neck and my lips crashing against his. I distantly register the sound of my kitchen chair tipping over as Rylie stumbles into it, but he steadies us, his hands at my hips.

The need that swells through me is terrifying, and I cling to him harder. One of his palms lands between my shoulder blades, the other at the curve of my lower back, gathering me to him like he needs me too. His kiss is sunlight, dazzling me, warming me, sending brightness through my veins. His hand slides up, cradling the back of my neck, fingers gently kneading until I let out a gasp of relief at how fucking good it feels to be touched like this. I do realize that it's a bit pathetic that I'm undone this thoroughly by a bunch of pasta, but I've never claimed to have high standards.

"I'm not done talking to you," he says against my mouth, dragging his lips to my throat, tracing down to my collarbone. I thread my fingers in his hair, holding him to me.

"Can we do the talking later? Maybe tomorrow? We kind of talk a lot as is." I press my mouth to his temple, nibble at his earlobe. He lets out a hungry moan, burrowing his face against my chest. His hands curl around my hips, fingertips digging in. I hope he leaves a mark.

But with an anguished noise, he's pushing me away, arms outstretched and holding me upright as I sway toward him.

"This is important," he says, mouth swollen and hair wrecked. He reflexively pulls me toward him again, but he drops his hands and takes a few steps back. "Last night, before you fled the scene like chicken with its head cut off—"

"I think I had a bit more tact and poise than that."

"You didn't. You said this didn't mean anything to either of us. That neither of us care." His steel eyes hold mine, locking me in, holding me hostage.

I try to swallow past my dry throat, then shrug. "Yeah? So?"

"*I* fucking care," he says, slamming a hand to his chest. "I care more than I can even put into words. I care about *you*. I care about how you're feeling. What you're thinking. What you like. What you hate. How your day was. How you'll find new and absurd ways to torture me. I *care*."

I stare at him, slack-jawed, my heart pounding so hard against my rib cage I know he can probably see it, feel it, the vibrations traveling the space between our bodies like ripples in a pond.

"This means something to me," he continues. "*You* mean something to me. You did back then, and you do now. I was too cowardly before to tell you that simple truth, but I'm not going to let you go another day believing anything but the facts. I like you. I care about you. I've lost my goddamn mind over you, Eva, and I'll repeat it over and over again until you are able to trust it. Trust me."

I blink hard, breath coming in tight little gasps. His expression is so open, need rolling off him like thunder, heat crackling between us. His attention curls around me, cradles me into terrifying vulnerability. There's tension in his shoulders, a bracing like he's preparing for me to turn him away again and it will hit him like a physical blow.

The confession is glued to my tongue. I want to say it, step out onto that tightrope with him, be vulnerable, even if for a moment. But it's so terrifying, the fall from such an extreme height. But what good will hiding do me? I'm already a wreck, I might as well tell him the truth about it. This bizarre man slipped past my walls and burrowed under my skin, taking up a permanent residence in my heart. I'd be furious if I didn't adore him so damn much.

I let every emotion play out across my usually placid face. I watch Rylie see it all, every piece of me, and his lips part as he takes a step toward me. He reaches out, tucking my hair behind my ear before settling his cool palm on my flushed cheek. I let out a shaky sigh at the pure relief of it.

"I . . . I care about you too," I whisper, voice a rasp across the charged air between us.

He stares at me, devastated like I've ripped the heart right from his chest, elated like he couldn't be happier for me to hold it.

"I care about you a lot, actually," I say, finding momentum even as my voice cracks. "I think that's the problem: I always have."

His eyes are quicksilver, melting at the edges. His other hand moves to my jaw, and he frames my face.

"I'm scared, though," I admit, more breath than voice. "I'm scared of being hurt again. I'm scared of screwing this up. I'm not sure I even like myself half the time; how could I expect someone else to like me enough to stick around?"

"I like you more than enough to stick around," Rylie says. "Just let me in, Eva. Let me prove it to you."

"We argue a lot," I say, trying to pop holes in every bubble that's lifting me higher and higher to the clouds. "You said it yourself, I'm headstrong and contrarian and I'm not sure I can change much of that."

Rylie's smile is so bright it makes my eyes water. Tears slip down my cheeks, and he lets out a soft chuckle as he brushes them away with his thumbs. "Kitten, I'd rather spend every day getting in a pointless argument with you for sport than be bored and complacent with anyone else."

"I'm also pretty mean," I say, more adamant this time. I need him to see it all, every flaw. I need him to not let me feel this much for him, then leave me when he realizes I won't change. "I don't bring much to the table besides a bad attitude and incredible style."

"Don't sell yourself short," he says, his smile growing wider. "Your tits are easily in my top five favorite things."

My chin wobbles, and I make a sound somewhere between a laugh and a scoff of outrage. I try to pull back, but Rylie holds me tighter, teasing the pad of his thumb across my bottom lip. I open to him on a sigh. "Your bite is one of my favorite things about you; I'd never want you to go easy on me."

Okay, now he's just being absurd. "Well, actually, I'm—"

Rylie cuts me off with a searing kiss, stealing the air from my lungs as he loves on my mouth. His tongue tangles with mine between light nibbles at my lips, like he's trying to soothe me to the point where I can't talk . . . It might work.

When breathing becomes an alarming necessity, we both pull back. Rylie's glasses are crooked, but he doesn't let go of me, instead fixing me with that boyish smile. "Eva, I'm an idiot with an alarmingly extensive ironic crewneck collection and a denim comforter. There is literally nothing you could say that would drop you down to my league. I want you contrarian and difficult and keeping me on my toes. I want your sour moods just as much as I want your sunny ones. I'm not asking you to change. You can call me any name you want, as long as I can call you mine."

I'm crying in earnest now, shoulders shaking with my sobs and sniffling like it can do my nose any good. I'm an absolute mess.

Rylie looks at me like I'm the most beautiful thing he's ever seen.

"Okay," I whisper.

"Okay?" Rylie says back, voice lifting.

I nod, his hands still at my splotchy cheeks. "You made a pretty compelling point with the jomforter situation."

My gasp harmonizes with Rylie's laugh as he presses his smile to my lips and kisses me again.

We're slow and reverent at first, a hesitant tenderness like we're testing the reality of everything we just said. Every brush of his lips against mine feels like a promise, a declaration of adoration. I return each vow, my walls being laid to waste as we pull each other closer, kiss each other harder, a growing franticness that shifts the energy to something rawer.

"I need you," I whisper in his ear before tracing the shell of it with my tongue. Rylie's groan is low and thick, igniting a hot flame in my stomach.

I'm still in my pajamas, a silky black set with a button shirt and flouncy shorts. He fumbles with the tiny pearl buttons, but I'm too impatient for his care, and I swat his hands away, giving a quick tug at the edges of the top. The buttons clattering to the floor punctuate the pop of his dimple as he looks at me, eyes fixed on my bare chest.

He shakes his head slowly, dragging his knuckles across his lips. "God, you're unreal. So absurdly beautiful."

My smile is obscene, entire body flushing at his praise. I pounce on him again, kissing him like my life depends on it.

I back us up, his palms cupping my breasts, my fingers twisted in his shirt. "Bed," I moan against his lips, then bite the lower. We only make it as far as the couch, the world tipping and my heart swooping as he follows me down onto the cushions. I claw at his clothes, transforming into a wild, needy animal whose only focus is to feel his skin against mine. Rylie props himself up on one palm, grabbing both my wrists in his other hand and pinning them above my head. He wraps my fingers around the cool metal bar of my end table. "Hold on to this for me, sweetheart," he whispers into my ear, voice like velvet. I grip the bar with everything I have.

Rylie tries to hide his chuckle, and I glare at him but his smile doesn't flicker. He reaches behind himself, dragging his shirt over his head and tossing it to the floor. My arms flinch with the need to touch him, but he shoots me a warning glance, eyes dragging from my flushed face to the grip of my hands. "Good girl."

With a lazy assuredness, he repositions himself on his knees between my legs, my body prone beneath him, and he flicks the buttons of his jeans free. He pushes them down his thighs, his cock springing out, and he grips the shaft, giving himself a few slow strokes as his gaze drags over me. Rylie's never been a person I would describe as self-possessed, but right now, he's a man undone, hair a mess, glasses crooked, my bites marks on his neck, his expression delightfully ruined.

Seeing him like this sends a surge of need through me, and I clench against the painful emptiness between my legs, hips jerking up toward his. Rylie catches my thigh, then grips the silk of my shorts, pulling them tightly between the lips of my pussy. It creates just a hint of friction, and I groan, pelvis working even harder to find relief.

He lets out a low growl, fist moving faster as he strokes himself. I can't stop watching him touch himself, my mouth watering with a want to taste him, my body throbbing with the need for him to fill me.

"Look at what you've done to me," he says, dragging my

attention to his face. "Look at the mess you've made of me, Eva."

I let out a broken whimper, squirming as I try to squeeze my thighs together, desperate for some type of relief.

His smile is ruthless. In a flash, he grips my waist, positioning me further up the couch, my hands still clinging to the end table. He lifts my legs and tears my shorts down, tossing them to the side before shouldering his way between my thighs, head dipping to my stomach. He traces my navel with the tip of his tongue, then drags the flat of it lower.

"It only seems fair I make a mess of you too," he whispers between my thighs before pressing his mouth to my aching flesh.

I scream, writhing up into the hot, wet suction of his mouth, eyes squeezing shut as the pleasure violently rushes through me. He shows no mercy, spreading my legs wider, centering on my clit as he alternates between pulsing suction and quick flicks of his tongue. I'm wound so tight it feels like every muscle will snap. I say his name, over and over.

"I'm close, so close," I pant, torso curving up, watching his head work between my thighs. Rylie makes a humming noise against my sensitive clit, and I moan, the first flicker of my orgasm igniting. With a suddenness that has me shouting out a string of curses, he pulls back, nuzzling my inner thigh, kissing the crease of my pelvis.

"What the fuck are you doing?" I garble out, sweating and panting and trying to remember how to use my hands so I can release this bar and strangle him.

His smile is pure innocence, mildly questioning. "Something wrong, Kitten?"

I stare at him with so much fury my eyes nearly cross. He buries his smile against my leg, but I feel the vibration of his laugh.

"Keep. Going," I say through clenched teeth, twitching and trembling from the need he's built in me. My skin is hot, feverish, my teeth chattering and muscles aching. Rylie takes his time to lift his head, giving my body a leisurely perusal until his eyes meet mine.

"If you want to come," he says, pausing to drag his teeth over my hip bone and making me groan. "You need to show me how bad."

He drops his head back to my clit, and I'm torn between choking him with my thighs and outright begging him to finish what he's started. He teases me relentlessly, building me up, backing me down, every muscle in my body taut like a bowstring. I try not to let him win, try to put up a fight, but it's a losing battle.

Rylie pushes a finger in me, then a second, his lips and tongue working on my clit, his entire body moving as he fucks me with that mouth. Something in the glint of his eyes, the easy confidence he has as he drives me wild, feels like a challenge.

I suck in a tight breath as he finds an unhurried rhythm that has me grinding against his tongue for more. Fighting for steadiness, I clear my throat. "I didn't get the chance to say this last night—"

Rylie stops, lifting his head to give me a patronizing look. "Because you were running away like you're deathly allergic to feelings?"

I urge his head back down with my legs, giving his mouth something else to do other than annoy me. "But it pisses me off that you're actually pretty good at this," I say, trying to sound bored, but another sharp gasp in my voice gives me away.

Rylie's eyes were momentarily closed, those long lashes sweeping his cheeks, but they open, skimming up my body. With another lick with the flat of his tongue, he pulls back, lifting his head and smirking like the devil.

"That so?" His voice is soft and mocking, his fingers still pumping and curling into me.

I nod, opening my mouth to say something smart back, but he presses against a spot that makes my entire body buck, my cunt squeezing around him as I whimper.

Rylie pulls out his fingers and moves them straight to his mouth, tongue working as he sucks them clean. His smirk turns into a grin as he watches me pant. "Cuz something tells me you actually fucking love it, Kitten."

I want to argue. I want to say something cutting. Anything to regain some control here, but he's inside me again, stars blinding my vision, oxygen getting trapped in my throat as I desperately try to breathe.

"And I fucking love it too," he growls. Then gets back to work.

Finally, when I'm begging and crying and squeezing my thighs so tightly around his head he doesn't have much of a choice, Rylie lets me come, spasms racking my body for what feels like minutes.

He doesn't give me a moment to catch my breath, vaulting up my body and kissing me instead, his tongue swirling against mine as I taste myself on him. I'm boneless and useless, finally dropping my hands from the end table and scrabbling to hold on to his back. They fall limply at my sides.

"Give me more, gorgeous," Rylie coaxes against my mouth. I try to shake my head but I lack the energy for even that. He looks down at me. "I know you can fucking take it."

I manage to arch up into him, breathing a *yes* against his mouth, the need for him to fill me outweighing post-orgasm peace. Rylie moves back on his knees, rustling around for his jeans that were long kicked off. He fishes a condom from his wallet, rolling it on with shaky hands and just enough speed that I know he isn't as calm as he's pretending.

"Presumptuous," I say, arching an eyebrow at his cock.

"Hopeful," he corrects, showing me just how much with the way he kisses me. No teasing, no finesse, only need.

Reaching between us but never breaking the kiss, he positions himself against my entrance. He drags the head of his cock up and down, luxuriating in the wetness between my thighs. I start wiggling, needing more, needing to feel all of him.

"Stay still for me, sweetheart," he commands against my mouth.

My body tenses as I try, the violent strike of my heartbeat making me flinch and twitch.

"I love seeing you try so hard to be so good," he praises in a low rumble, rewarding me with a deep surge of his hips.

I throw my head back, nails clawing at his chest, swearing as he hits that perfect spot. With a labored grunt, Rylie retreats, only to fill me up again with a demanding thrust. My body inches across the couch as he fucks me, and without breaking his unsparing rhythm, he cradles the top of my head with his hand right before it jams against the armrest. Taking half a second to reposition, he lifts my shoulders so I'm slightly propped up. I'm overwhelmed by the sight of his body over me, in me. The tension in his arms as he holds himself up, the clench of his jaw, the brush of his chest against mine as he drags himself out of me again.

Rylie's breath is ragged, lips wet and parted, color high on his cheeks. His eyes lock with mine for a beat, and the intensity, the need, has me clenching tightly around him. His pupils eclipse his irises, nostrils flaring. He reaches for me, fingers dragging down my cheek and then gently gripping my chin. He carefully tilts my head down so my gaze lands at the spot where we're joined. "Watch, baby," he says. "Watch how perfectly you take me."

I'm gone after that, seeing the way his body moves, the desperate, coiled need in his muscles as he works himself into me, the terrifying closeness I feel for this man as he breaks me down to nothing but raw pleasure.

I come around him, crying out his name before I bite his shoulder, nails scoring down his back. Rylie lasts only a second longer, panting against my neck as he twitches inside me, both of us shaking and sweating. All his strength disappears in a blink, and his head is against my chest, limbs tangled with mine. My heart is going so fast, I can see its rhythm at my chest, Cooper's cheek absorbing every beat. With a great show of effort, he shifts slightly, placing a kiss to my sternum then smiling up at me.

We take turns in the bathroom, then finally make it to the bed. Rylie scoops me up and cuddles me close, my head resting between his shoulder and chest as his fingers trace soothing patterns across my skin.

I feel so unreasonably satisfied, so deeply safe being held

like this. I release a shaky breath, rationing out all of my courage. "Will you stay?" I whisper against his skin.

Rylie chuckles, and the vibrations of it against my cheek fill
me with warmth. "Kitten," he says, cradling my jaw and using
his thumb to tilt my face up. He smiles at me, beautiful and
adorned with that damn dimple. "You'll only ever have to ask
me to leave."

Chapter 16

TRUE TO HIS WORD, RYLIE DOESN'T LEAVE MY SIDE FOR THE next week unless I push him away with brute force—often off the side of the bed when he says something out of pocket and absurdly ridiculous—and I miss him so acutely and instantaneously, I reach for him with the grabby hands of a toddler within seconds.

We take turns between our places, enjoying the cozy privacy of my sardine-tin-sized apartment and the electric energy of his shared brownstone as we lay low, trying to avoid catching the eye of anyone else on the street.

I can't seem to get close enough to the man—wrapping my arms around his middle and hugging his back as he cooks me endless varieties of mac 'n' cheese, crawling into his lap and ripping off his shirt in a frenzy to get him inside me when he sits at his desk to work, absentmindedly playing with his fingers as we watch TV, his arm wrapped around my shoulders as we ride the subway, staring at our reflections in the dirty window with giddy smugness at how damn happy we look.

I keep waiting for the other shoe to drop, for me to say something too honest and him to run away screaming, for that subtle glaze of boredom to creep into his eyes when we talk, but he hasn't stopped staring at me like I'm a comet he's been chasing.

It helps fuel our infatuated haze that we've been ignoring social media, pretending a cell signal doesn't reach our little bubble. We agreed that being dancing monkeys on the internet wouldn't be the best way to move forward. After spending the last six years scrutinizing ourselves and each other to near destruction, we don't need the opinions of strangers adding to that. Rylie's also been focusing all his efforts on promoting Lilith's fundraiser next weekend, having her and some of her staff members on as guests of his podcast.

Besides, *Sausage Talk* has always operated on a hurry-up-and-wait schedule, back-to-back recordings followed by extended lulls while we edit and wait for celebrities and public figures to get desperate enough and publicists to confirm details. I've been focusing on admin bullshit and pursuing leads the past week, opting to work from home despite how regularly Soundbites discourages us from doing a hybrid model . . . I have no doubt they'll get rid of the option soon enough, all the easier to control us if we're physically there.

Being out of the office makes it that much easier to avoid William too. His emails are getting progressively more agitated, every subject line marked as urgent, the text essentially asking when Rylie and I will be getting our asses back on the set and creating more content to fan the viewer flames. The pictures of me leaving Rylie's place the first time we hooked up breathed new life into the social media frenzy, and William's emails clued me in that more advertisers and sponsors have signed on.

While I am getting my job done and putting more effort into finding something shiny to draw viewer attention and win me some fresh brownie points at work, I'm certainly not doing anything to prolong the spotlight staying on us, and William has made it very clear he isn't happy about that.

Rylie's feigning sick, similarly dodging William's emails by saying he can't record anything because he's down with a stomach bug. That last detail was my idea. He had me look over one of his initial emails to William, making sure he wasn't setting me up for any corporate backlash, and I added a super-subtle line about Rylie's profound diarrhea and frequent gas attacks before hitting send.

It was also in that moment that I learned I actually *can* push Rylie a little too far, but wrapping myself around him and kissing him until he sighs in surrender, smiling against my mouth, is the fastest way to bring him back to adoring me.

"Did you hear that Ray is doing the catering for Lilith's fundraiser?" Rylie asks, brightening the gloomy Saturday morning by bringing me coffee in bed. I could weep and/or gobble his dick like Kirby right here and now. "It's shaping up to be a huge event. Black tie and all that bullshit."

"He is? That's amazing!" I hide my quick flinch of emotion behind a huge gulp of coffee. I haven't been a particularly good friend the past week, so wrapped up in this bubblegum-pink brain fog. In my defense, Aida's messages to me have been a hair too passive-aggressive for my liking, centering around William's ever-simmering frustration at the lack of content Rylie and I are putting out. It seemed easier to take a breather from both her and Ray than address that can of worms, knowing anything I share with Ray would be reported back to Aida.

I've nearly finished my coffee before I realize how unsettlingly quiet Rylie's gone, and I glance at him. He's stare into his mug, a mild blush kissing his cheeks.

"What are you thinking about?" I squeeze the sensitive spot above his knee, making him giggle. He bats my hand away, working to keep his coffee from spilling. I put my mug down and settle against the pillows with an expectant look.

He opens his mouth to say something, then slams it shut, shaking his head. "None of your business."

I use my toe to tickle his side this time, and he grabs my ankle, haphazardly dropping his coffee to the bedside table before pulling me to him, making me shriek, nails scrabbling against the sheets.

He pins my thrashing body down, hovering over me with a sheepish grin. "Fine. You win."

"I always do."

He nips at my collarbone before continuing, "I was trying to think of a cute way to ask you to be my date to the fundraiser, you surly menace. You ruined the surprise. Are you happy?"

"Kind of," I croon before sliding my arms around his neck and leaning up to kiss him.

"You're an enemy of the state," he says against my mouth.

"What state?"

"The state of my mental health."

"Aw, baby girl, that was fucked long before I came around."

Rylie laughs, ducking his head to kiss me some more. Everything heats, my skin glowing as his kisses become deeper, his hand slipping under my shirt. I feel him harden against my belly, his hips sliding lazily against mine. I drag my hands through his hair, giving him another deep kiss, before pulling back. His lips are parted, eyes hazed like he's half in a dream. He dips down to kiss me again.

"I need more coffee before we continue," I say with a smile against his mouth.

Rylie groans, lips dragging away from mine as he hangs his head. "And I'm assuming I'm going to be the one to rectify this problem?"

I make a show of looking around, my nose brushing his forehead. "Don't see anyone else we can outsource this to."

Rylie groans again but sits up, fixing me with a smile like he can't deny me anything and he wouldn't want to if he could. "I'll be right back," he says, unable to help himself and leaning in for one more kiss before hopping up and heading out of the room.

I sink further into the mattress, grinning up at the ceiling. I grab one of the pillows, biting into it as I squeal, kicking my feet for good measure.

My phone buzzes, and I reach for it, half expecting it to be Rylie sending me something ridiculous from the kitchen. My heart sinks when I see it's an email from Landry with the subject line: Urgent. Please read.

Every instinct in my body tells me to throw my phone out the window instead of looking at that message, but I already feel guilty for not being as productive as I theoretically could be, and I can't do anything else to risk my job. I open it, squinting until it's slightly blurred as I try to tame the swell of anxiety rushing through me. Taking a deep breath, I sit up and start to read.

Dear Eva,

It is with great disappointment that I find myself writing this email. As you know, I've been the leader of Soundbites for over twenty years now, and I've always prided myself on hiring self-motivated professionals who rarely require micromanagement, let alone my intervention. Unfortunately, reports of your behavior of late have led me to doubt your professionalism and dedication to this organization. I am doing you the courtesy of reaching out to you first, before involving human resources and other disciplinary members of the company, including our new incoming leadership, to try and come to an understanding. To speak frankly, I am trying to talk some sense into you.

I see potential in you, Eva. A great deal of it. I see a woman who has the gumption to do what needs to be done to carve out a career for herself. I see a woman who would grab an opportunity for advancement with both hands, not let it idly slip by. Yet, your avoidance of responsibilities regarding the Rylie Cooper collaboration has me questioning what I thought I knew of your character.

You are a representative of the Soundbites brand

in this partnership with Mr. Cooper, and your negligence to do your job is reflecting poorly not only on the organization, but on me as your boss. A company cannot function on whims and flights of fancy, especially when it comes to revenue generation from ads on new content. You have failed to deliver anything new with Mr. Cooper for over a week.

I want to ask you plainly: Do you care about your career? Do you want to be a journalist? Do you have the drive to dig deep to make something of yourself?

As I said above, I see parts of my younger self in you, Eva. But I can promise you I would never risk my career for a man, nor would any woman I choose to associate with and elevate in this competitive industry. I need you to look closely at the choices you're making, and see if they reflect the values you want to uphold in your promising career. Prove to me you're the woman I think you are. I don't want to see this issue of unsatisfactory performance escalate any further.

Regards,
Landry

I read the email over and over, Landry's voice starting as a shrill buzz in my ear and growing to a roar. I return to the start again but can't get the words to focus, and I realize how badly my hands are shaking, tears welling in my eyes. I toss my phone to the side, covering my face and trying to breathe past the hornets' nest in my throat.

Fuck, fuck, *fuck*.

I'm such an idiot. What was I thinking? What did I expect, playing this hide-and-seek game with my eagle-eyed boss? Hearing I'm as grossly a fuck-up as I've always feared I am makes me want to shrivel up and die.

"You're okay," I whisper into my palms, not believing it for a second. "Everything will be okay."

I need to fix this. I can't lose this chance at a promotion, at actually making something of this stupid dream of mine. I fish my laptop out of my bag on the ground, then let out a growl of frustration when I realize it's dead. I have the sudden and irrational instinct to blame this all on Rylie and his frivolous crewnecks and ridiculous car and dick so good it's made me prioritize sex over my literal job, but the thought snuffs out before it can fully spark.

This is no one's fault but my own. Stupid me and my stupid job and my stupid desire to actually try to make it into something meaningful when it's obvious I'm not up to the challenge.

I bring my knees to my chest and try to think of how to respond, how to get back in her good graces, but my thoughts dip into self-pity instead. I either have to keep parading my interactions with Rylie around for public consumption or say goodbye to the promotion that will get me the job I've always wanted. There's no winning here.

Rylie walks in, coffees in hand, and I work to rearrange my features into something other than panic and defeat. His smile drops. The bastard can read me like a book.

"You okay, Kitten?" he asks, setting down the mugs and then climbing into bed. I hate that question. Nothing makes me panic more than that question. No, I'm not okay and admitting as much will only make me even more not okay.

"Fine," I squeak out.

"You sure? You look—"

I spring on him, throwing my leg over his hips and wrapping my arms around his neck while I kiss him—messy and deep and desperate to escape the anxiety clawing through me, the questions I don't want to have to ask myself. Rylie pulls back for a second, giving me a bemused frown, but I force my sexiest smile, letting him see it for only a second before sliding his glasses down his nose and setting them on the bedside table. I kiss him again.

Rylie melts under my touch, his hands slipping under my shirt and gliding to my ribs, thumbs grazing the sensitive skin at the sides of my breasts. I let out an exaggerated groan against his mouth, pressing myself closer to him, closer to the man who can make me feel so good I almost forget feeling terrible is possible.

It isn't long until Rylie is hard, our hips and chests rubbing together in tight movements, the friction from our pajamas maddening. He shifts us, rolling me beneath him, his hands making quick work removing my shirt then his own.

"Stunning," he whispers, expression dazed as he soaks me in like it's the first time he's seeing me. A pang of affection slices through my chest, and I pull him down to me again.

I want to escape from it all.

Rylie kisses my neck, traces my collarbones with his tongue. He touches me in all the ways he knows I like while whispering words of encouragement into my ear. And I work to lose myself in it. But emotions are tight in my chest, sealing up my throat, making it feel impossible to breathe. My skull fills with a heavy tension, a cloud of gas that has the room spinning in a way that's far from enjoyable. I cover my face with my arm, moaning into the crux of my elbow in a way I hope fools him.

Rylie's fingers play between my legs, and he feels the growing wetness, bringing it to his lips with a luxurious pull. He positions himself at my entrance, forgoing the condom like we have since we confirmed recent tests were negative.

He presses into me with a smooth glide, and I wrap my legs around his hips like I can keep him there forever. Rylie sets a slow, lazy rhythm, savoring the drag of every inch against me.

I'm whimpering, nearly crying from the combination of how good he feels, how tenderly he's loving me, and how terrified I am that I've ruined everything I've worked for. My movements are sharp and jerky, every nerve too on edge to fully enjoy the thrill of his touch and instead flinching with each caress.

Rylie clocks the tension in my muscles, and it makes him pause, lifting himself above me. He stares at me for a moment, cheeks stained with a blush and breath coming in short bursts. The fog of desire starts to clear from his eyes, his slack jaw tightening into a worried frown.

"Sweetheart, what's wrong?" he whispers, cupping my face. He's so gentle, so caring, it makes me want to bawl like a baby. Which in turn makes me want to run away. I bury my head in his chest.

"Just fuck me, Cooper," I urge, fingernails scoring down his back. I feel him shiver, his body grinding involuntarily against me before he regains control. I try to take matters into my own hands, thrusting up into him in frantic movements like I can screw my problems away.

"No," he says with force, unwrapping my arms from his body and pinning my wrists to the mattress. My breath catches in my throat at the intensity of his stare, and I try to look away. Try to stop myself from crying as tears slip from the corners of my eyes and drag across my temples.

"Tell me what's wrong," he coaxes softly, brushing away my tears.

"I'm *fine*," I say through gritted teeth, jerking out of his touch. "Would you stop fucking worrying and just have sex with me? Because this conversation is getting tedious and I'm easily bored."

Rylie stills, his expression shifting in surprise and then settling into something close to anger. In a deliberately slow movement, he grips my jaw, forcing my gaze up until I'm staring into the dark wild of his blown pupils. His touch is firm but not harsh, just enough pressure to let me know he's not interested in playing games.

"Listen here, you little demon," he says, voice threaded with tenderness. "You can be as tough and guarded as you need out there, but in here"—he emphasizes the bed with a brutal pump of his hips—"you'll show me the real you. What happens between us isn't a distraction, Eva. It's too important for that."

I look at him, blinking rapidly, trying to keep my expression from cracking. It's no use, every part of me releases the tension I've been holding, body sinking into the mattress, lips parting on a sob, tears flowing freely.

"I'm sorry," I whisper, trying to roll away from him. Rylie catches my movement, then counters it, turning us both so we're on our sides facing each other. He slips out of me, his hard cock pressed against my hip, and I want to be close to him, hold him inside my body, but he slides a hand under the curve of my ass and pulls me higher up on the bed so we're eye to eye and slightly out of alignment everywhere else.

"What's wrong?" he says again, brushing his fingers through my hair, then resting his palm on my cheek. "Talk to me, Eva."

Through blubbering sobs, I tell him everything—Landry's dangling-carrot promotion, my foolish belief that I might actually be worthy of a job like that, her email affirming I am definitely not. Rylie cradles me the whole time, making soothing sounds when I choke on the words.

The man is ruthlessly sweet, unreasonably tender, sheltering my body as I confess the insecurities that eat at me. Eventually, I wear myself out until I lay spent and boneless against his chest, my snivels the only sign of life.

"Can I offer my perspective on this, Kitten?" he whispers into the shell of my ear. I nod against his chest, another shuddering inhale racking my frame. He snuggles me closer. "If it isn't painfully obvious, I'd gladly kiss the ground you walk on if it made you smile, I think you're that wonderful." I move to push him away, making a scoffing sound, but he holds me tighter. "Fucking try me. I mean it."

My heart thumps up to my throat, every part of me wanting to fight him. *I'm not worth it. I'm not special. There's something wrong with you if you think otherwise.* But Rylie kisses me, stealing my ability to protest.

"Regardless of how enamored I am of you," he continues, nuzzling his cheek against my hair, "you're objectively brilliant."

Now I'm really annoyed. But he possesses some freakish strength in his wiry frame, so I opt to turn my face away at an awkward angle, burying it in a pillow.

"Shyness doesn't suit you, Kitten," he whispers against my neck. "Hide all you want but you know it's true. You're smart. You're witty. You have beautiful things to say that so many people are dying to hear. You're a goddamn asset to any organization that hires you, and if Landry or William want to test that, you can go ahead and prove them losers."

I let out a groan of incredulity.

"You're brilliant," he repeats with a gentle laugh in his voice. "And, not to split hairs, but you do still have a job. She didn't fire you, and from what I can tell, you've been doing your work, trying to find new avenues to keep up the segment's attention—it's just not on the topic they'd prefer. I'm the one with profuse diarrhea, apparently. This is just an empty threat."

"Profound," I correct. "Profound diarrhea."

I can feel him roll his eyes. "Right. Profound. Of course."

Slowly, like a creepy doll in a horror movie, I swivel my head to look at him. "You think I'm smart?" I whisper, voice a timid husk.

Rylie tilts his head, giving me a teasing smile. "Easily top five smartest people I've ever met."

"Who are the other four?"

Rylie laughs so hard the bed shakes, sending a delicious shiver down my spine.

"Mean you. Sarcastic you. Sweet you. Vulnerable you," he says, dipping his head to brush his nose against mine. "Sexy you is number six because she's often rendered speechless by my superb lovemaking."

"I just threw up in my mouth."

"Our pillow talk always does wonders for my self-esteem."

I laugh, pressing my teeth to his shoulder in a shallow love bite. "You think I'm witty?" I ask, feeling silly and shy for needing his compliments, but hungry for them all the same.

Rylie threads his fingers through my hair, then grabs it in a light grip to tilt my face to his. "I'll indulge you endlessly but that one is so obvious it feels redundant." I look at him, not hiding the glimmer of emotion in my eyes. Rylie's smile softens but grows. "Kitten, you're so quick, I can't keep up. I lose my breath trying to go at it with you."

A starburst of warmth erupts in my chest, and I press even closer to Rylie, placing a light, lingering kiss at the base of his throat. He hums in satisfaction. I work my way up his neck and across his jaw with intimate kisses, then across his face until I hover over his mouth.

"I'm a bit enamored with you myself," I whisper against his lips. He parts them for me, and I kiss him deeply, sipping at his lips, my tongue caressing his. Rylie kisses with his full body, his legs twisting with mine, pelvis and stomach pressed close, one hand in my hair, the other at my cheek.

"And I think you're brilliant too," I say on the quick gulp of air we part for.

I feel his smile against my temple. "Might try to get a recording of you saying that later."

"There's a lot of work you'd need to do to make that happen," I tease, nudging my hips against his.

"Oh, what a labor," he deadpans, instantly responding to the spark I've created, gently grinding against me. Tender emotions dig through me as he touches my body, one hand tracing down my spine in a torturously delicious path until he's cupping my ass and holding me close and I'm panting against his mouth, hips rocking in time with his.

Rylie's hard again between my legs, and I want him so badly my teeth ache. I push at his shoulder so he'll get on his back with me on top of him, but he resists, framing my face with his hands until I look at him. He stares at me, those gunpowder eyes destroying me all over. "You're so fucking lovely, Eva," he says, before sealing his mouth over mine.

And I feel that word, *lovely*, through every moment of his deep, sensual kiss. I feel it in the way he holds me, the way he caresses me, the hungry moan he makes as I grab at him, desperate for whatever pieces I can have. He unravels me, seam by seam, until I'm nothing but a mess of loose ends and frayed edges and he cherishes me like I'm sacred.

I whimper against his mouth, hips moving harder against his, and Rylie takes mercy. He hooks his hand under my knee and drags my leg higher over his hip, opening me to him as he works his way into my body with shallow, unhurried strokes. His steady movements create just the right amount of friction that I find myself biting into his shoulder again, harder this time, silently begging for all that he'll give me.

My thigh muscles tighten around him, bringing him even closer and he slides all the way in, filling me deeply as he lets out a rough sound of pleasure. His palm skims up my thigh, curving over the swell of my hip, then traces up my back, before reversing the motion. He soothes me. Electrifies me. Makes me want to weave myself into him and see what his gentle hands can create of us.

I'm crying as he makes love to me—the gentle possession of his movements, the praise grunted against my skin as our thrusts become frenzied, the way his fingers twine with mine and he looks into my eyes as we both reach that excruciatingly wonderful peak.

We hold each other closely after, sweaty and sated with his body still in mine, our hearts keeping time to the small wonder of being together.

When we can't avoid it any longer, we finally untangle and use the bathroom. A dreamy playfulness fizzes through me, and I race Rylie back to bed, pushing him out of the way and launching myself into the nest of sheets and pillows. Laughing, Rylie pounces on me, tossing me around like a rag doll despite our similar heights. He pins me down, blowing a raspberry into my chest, dragging his weekend stubble against my throat, making me shriek and giggle like a little kid.

The burst of energy is short-lived, and it isn't long before we're cuddling together again—Rylie propped up on the pillows, my head against his chest as he plays with my hair, threading the strands around his fingers—watching a campy horror movie as we smile like infatuated idiots.

Anxiety and worry about work periodically jump out from unguarded corners of my mind, but the warmth of Rylie's skin, the simple reverence in his touch, keeps me tethered.

"How should I respond to Landry?" I ask, trying to keep my voice even and calm.

I feel Rylie's deep breath beneath my cheek as he thinks. Tenderly, he smooths my hair back before kissing the crown of my head. "I'd be honest with her. I'd tell her how much you do care about your career, but what you actually want it to look like. I'd tell her you're doing the work, but you're so much more than reading mean comments for viewer pleasure."

I toy with the hair on his chest, mulling that over as he sinks back into the lull of the movie. It's a nice sentiment but I'm not sure I'm brave enough to be that honest with Landry, too afraid of ruffling any more feathers. I lock up the worry for good for the rest of the day. It's not going to disrupt the peace I have in Rylie's arms.

I can't stop noticing things about him, cataloging every minute detail—how the hair on his legs is a shade lighter than the chestnut waves on his head, the cluster of six freckles near the crook of his left elbow, the tiny white scar on his chin that disappears with the stretch of his dazzling grin. I feel like I could spend a lifetime looking at him and still not discover every wonderful facet. Rylie yawns then snuggles me closer, his breathing turning deep and steady as another movie starts streaming.

"Aww," I say, disrupting his drowsy quietness. I want to keep him with me, make him laugh, coax him into teasing me in that special way of his.

Rylie tilts his head to look at me. "This slasher film tickling your tenderhearted side?" he asks, eyes flicking to a particularly gory scene playing out on the TV.

I laugh. "No. Not that."

"What?"

"Oh, nothing . . ." I say wistfully, giving him a coy smile.

"Tell me," he says, ducking his head and nibbling at my throat. When I hum in approval, he drags his stubble against the area, tearing a gasp from me. My nipples harden at the next rasp.

"They're just cute," I say, squirming against him. I can't decide if I want more of the rough friction or to run away from it.

Rylie pulls back with a confused look but his mouth is still curled with amusement. "What's cute?"

"Your feet," I reply matter-of-factly.

Rylie's smile slowly falls, his face scrunched up like I just asked him to solve a calculus problem. "My . . . feet?"

"They're so small and dainty. They're precious," I coo, leaning into him and pressing my smile against his frown, letting my feet drag against his. He sits up straighter, and I slide down his torso, my head landing in his lap as I silently start to laugh.

"Precious?" he squawks. "*Precious!* My feet aren't . . ."

"Precious?" I supply.

Rylie catches the giggle in my voice. He growls, gripping my hips in a tight hold. With a fluid movement, he shifts us so my back is pressed to the mattress, his hips cradled between my spread thighs as his weight pins me down. "You are such a little shit, Eva."

"What's wrong with calling you precious?" I say through a cackle as he glares down at me, the corner of his mouth twitching up despite his efforts to frown. "What happened to all that detoxification of masculinity?"

"Stop it," he growls. "My smile is precious, maybe." He shows off a wolfish version of it, dimple and all. "My personality? Definitely precious. Hell, I have ears that are literally perfectly shaped and you've never noticed and even that would be okay to call precious. But my *feet*?"

I laugh even harder. "Let me get this straight, Barbie-foot, you're mad that I complimented the wrong part of you?"

"Of all the things I work on to get a compliment from you, my feet are not on the list," he says primly. Rylie slides one hand under my knee, hitching my leg up higher so my ankle is near his hip, my thigh pressed against my stomach. Butterflies erupt through me, each beat of their wings fanning the sudden fire in my belly. His eyes skim up my body and hold at my smile. He leans closer until his lips hover over mine, one hand still pinning my hips to the bed, the other tracing the curve of my calf . . .

And then he starts tickling my foot. I scream and flail as I try to twist away, but he holds me tight.

"I'm sorry to have to resort to brute force," Rylie says, not sounding sorry at all as he continues the onslaught. "But reasoning with you has done me no good."

I start screaming and cursing and flopping about like a fish on land, and Rylie's deep laugh echoes mine. I finally manage to unhook my leg from his grip, and "accidentally" clip his shoulder in a swinging kick. Rylie takes the blow with as much drama as possible, latching me to him as he rolls us off the side of the bed into the fallen pillows and sheets. Giddiness floods through me, and I scramble for the upper hand, returning the torture tenfold as my fingers dance down his chin, in his armpits, across his stomach.

Then one of Rylie's hands is cradling the back of my skull, pulling me toward him, the other at my heartbeat, and he's kissing me in a way that makes all laughter stop and I'm no longer tickling him but gripping him closer, palms skimming across the warm expanse of skin at his chest.

"You're the one who's precious, Eva," Rylie says, voice rough and quick as a matchstick against a striker. His hands tangle in my hair, my vision blurring as a sharp, aching want builds in me.

"You didn't answer my question from earlier," he whispers in my ear before biting the lobe. I give him a dopey series of blinks. He clears his throat, pink creeping across his cheeks. "Will you go to the fundraiser with me? As my, um, date?"

The question makes me pause, the blatant vulnerability in his voice over such an unserious question cinching like a lasso around my rapidly beating heart. He asked me like he needs me to say yes. I don't think anyone's ever acted like they needed me before.

"If you say yes, I'll make it worth your while in the morning," he coaxes, mistaking my shock for hesitation. I catch the thread of insecurity in his voice.

"How's that?" I burrow against his neck, trying to keep from floating away from all the feelings bubbling through me.

"I call it bottomless brunch, but it's actually where we lie in bed naked all morning and sip champagne straight from the bottle."

I laugh, then release a weary sigh. "I suppose I can pencil it in."

I feel Rylie's heart skip against my cheek, and he hugs me tightly. "I appreciate the sacrifice."

Anything for you, I whisper imperceptibly against his skin, not quite brave enough to let him know how deeply I mean it.

Chapter 17

"I WAS REALLY DREADING THIS, BUT IT WASN'T NEARLY AS bad as I expected. I actually had some fun," Rhys Stillwell, a fallen-from-grace childhood actor, says to me as we film with our room-temperature hot dogs. He's apparently launching a redemption arc on his ruined image, so, naturally, eating dogs with me was the best place to start.

"So much fun you'll be leaving with your own footlong?" I ask in the bland voice for the *Sausage Talk* schtick. Rhys chokes on the innuendo.

"You're quite the little perv," he says through a laugh, as if this man doesn't have a reputation for sleeping through all of Hollywood and most of Broadway.

We wrap up from there, Rhys being whisked off by his handlers and saving me any sleazy post-filming flirting.

I collapse into my chair and scroll through my phone, smiling at a text from Rylie.

Have a great day, kitten <3

I snort as I type back: Don't tell me what to do <3

He sends a wall of eye-rolling emojis then one blowing me a kiss. I'm not sure how I managed to get so lucky.

"Excellent interview, Eva." William's voice over my shoulder startles me so badly, I jump out of my chair, sending my phone flying into my makeup kit.

"William. Hi," I say, clutching my chest and trying to ignore the surge of panic that follows the tail-end of the shock. "What are you doing here?"

He gives me a cool, appraising look, then sweeps it around the room. "That's what happens when you run things, Eva," he says, fixing his stare back on me. "You keep a close eye on everything."

I nod, fighting the urge to squirm. "Of course. Yeah. And clearly you're very good at that," I say, trying to kiss as much ass as humanly possible.

His expression doesn't change. "Yes, I am."

We stand there in silence for a moment, and I pray he doesn't notice the growing rings of sweat under my arms.

I tried to implement some of Rylie's advice in my response to Landry, letting her know how seriously I take my job and listing out new initiatives and ideas I'd been pursuing, putting my efforts there to stay ahead of the curve. She never responded but I also wasn't fired on Monday so I've been cautiously optimistic I played it right.

"I got your email," William says at last, swooping into my

space to take my vacated seat. That was the second part of my good graces plan—reaching out to William directly, cc'ing Landry and Aida of course, to blame the lack of content on Rylie.

William hooks an ankle over his opposite knee, then straightens his expensive-looking watch, waiting for me to respond.

I clear my throat, shifting from foot to foot. "Oh, good. Yeah, like I said, I'm just as frustrated as you are by all of this. But I swear, I'm doing everything I can."

It's a lie and I'm sure he knows it, and I hate maligning Rylie like this, but it was his idea. He even suggested I tell William he has once again ghosted me. I fought Rylie on it at first—I already did enough work to assassinate his character at the start of all this—but he cut my endless stream of protests off with a tender kiss.

"I'd rather you lie to your boss about me blowing you off than us both have to record things for the internet lying about how we feel for each other," Rylie told me. "I can promise you, Soundbites isn't looking for content that highlights how much we like each other."

I had trouble arguing with that. So, with his blessing, I sent an email back to William saying I hadn't heard from Rylie since our last recording and was furious about it, but doing all I could to get through. I then reiterated to William how dedicated I am to my career and my dreams of branching out in the topics I cover, even pitching a few story ideas. He didn't bother to respond.

Like mother, like son, I suppose.

Aida hasn't been much better, taking my confrontation

avoidance with her after the Zoom call and playing a reverse Uno, so now I'm the one being ignored. She's also been swamped with new projects to produce, so I'm trying not to take her silence too personally.

William's coal-black eyes study me intently. "Yes, the photos of you circulating on the internet certainly prove just how hard you're working." He pauses long enough to sneer. "Hasn't anyone ever taught you the cardinal rule of this business, Eva?"

My stomach twists as acid rises up my throat. Like a fool, I shake my head.

He leans in, giving me a smile that's simultaneously conspiratorial and threatening. "Don't screw the talent." There's a beat. "Or at least don't be so obvious about it."

My pulse saws through my veins, humiliation flooding my system as I splutter. He stares at me with taut patience like I'm an ill-behaved child.

"Those photos aren't me," I finally get out, entire body hot and prickly. He arches an eyebrow. "I mean . . . yes, those photos are of *me* but I wasn't . . . that wasn't . . . Rylie and I didn't . . . It was a random hookup. Terrible time. Had to make a quick exit. You know how it is."

William looks at me like he has absolutely no idea how it is.

"He used a sheet as a curtain," I say weakly, not sure why I feel the overwhelming compulsion to give him all the gory (and false) details.

"I see," William says after a terrible stretch of silence. He plucks invisible lint off his impeccably tailored suit pants. "Such a shame about Mr. Cooper. We really could have made something of you if he'd continued participating."

I can't decide if I want to melt into the floor or blow up in his face. I force a smile. "I hate to think making something of myself is reliant on a man," I say, shocked I'm able to keep my voice even and pleasant. "And I think with new opportunities, I can really find my stride."

He gives a shallow shrug, attention drifting. "Opportunities come with the data to back up their likelihood for success." He sighs. "Such a metric-driven world we live in now. Makes you wonder if things were actually better in the old days when you could simply sleep your way to the top."

My face must express my horror, because William takes one look at me and laughs. "I'm joking, Eva. Jesus, what kind of person do you take me for? Where's your sense of humor?"

I let out a forced laugh that sounds like a vinyl needle scratching against a record. "Sorry," I say, not exactly sure what I'm apologizing for, but feeling like it's necessary nonetheless.

William stares at me, lips curving into a pitying smile. With a glance at his watch, he stands, smoothing the clean lines of his crisp suit. "I'm sure you'll figure out how to make things work. I better head out, though. Have a meeting with investors soon."

"Good luck," I say meekly, fighting the urge to cry.

"Luck has nothing to do with it." Those cold eyes stare straight into me. He turns and strides to the door, then, over his shoulder adds, "If you see Mr. Cooper, let him know our legal team will be in touch."

"Legal team," I screech for the fiftieth time as I pace Rylie's bedroom floor. He's sitting on the edge of his mattress, tracking my movements, a dreamy smile on his face. "What is wrong

with you?" I say, turning on him. "Why are you *smiling*, you knob?"

Rylie grabs my wrist, tugging me to him until I tumble into his lap. "It's really sweet to see you so concerned about me," he says, placing a messy kiss to my cheek. I thrash about like an angry cat. He holds me tighter, nuzzling against my neck.

"Are you even listening to me? William is making legal threats over all of this! It's serious, and you're moved by my *concern*?" I squirm even harder.

Rylie wrestles me to the bed, pinning my hips between his thighs as I flail my head back and forth across his awful denim duvet. "Eva, stop." Rylie cups my cheeks in his palms, his steel eyes chaining our gazes. "Don't. Worry."

"Don't worry? Don't *worry*? Tell me, Cooper, in the history of humankind, has saying that ever actually stopped someone from worrying? Especially around you? Your energy could put a monk in a spiral."

"Says the woman who would give bull riders a run for their money," he says with a laugh as I buck against him again, that boyish smile of his popping out. "But if you'd listen to me for half a second instead of working yourself into a panic, you'd realize that I am not worried about his flimsy legal threat because, believe it or not, I know a little bit about what I'm doing when it comes to my work."

I still, breathing hard as I glare up at him. "Say more."

He laughs again, bobbing his head down to kiss my forehead. "I've signed agreements for partnerships with companies before." He adjusts his weight so he's resting on his knees, hips hovering over mine. He picks up one of my fisted hands, slowly massaging the joints until I release my grip. "I learned a long time ago the importance of having a good lawyer review everything and I always, *always* make sure I have a right-to-termination clause at any point if I stop agreeing with the messaging of the collaboration."

He kisses my palm, then lays it gently on my chest, picking up my other hand and repeating the process, lulling me into some kind of trance.

"I agreed to our initial interview on *Sausage Talk* and cross-promotion between my podcast and the show for profit sharing on sponsors and advertisers. I didn't agree to a set amount of deliverable content, which is why I'm not worried about what William said. My lawyer isn't worried about what William said. Which means *you* should not be worried about what William said. He's grasping at straws here, which is why he made the threat to you in the first place. It's very transparent."

"I don't have to worry?" The idea seems like a trap. If I don't solve all his problems, what am I good for?

"You don't have to worry," Rylie repeats, sliding off my hips and stretching out next to me. He gathers me to him. "I have it all handled, sweetheart."

I open my mouth to argue, scrambling for some way I can prove myself useful here, but he cuts me off with a kiss.

"But I appreciate that you care this much," he whispers against my lips. "That means more to me than you could ever know."

The tension ebbs like a lazily retreating tide, and I let Rylie kiss me some more, luring me into a sense of calm. Could . . . could that be enough? The simple fact that I care and he knows it is enough to make me worth it?

Rylie pulls back, fixing me with a startlingly intense look. "You'll always be worth it," he says, threading his hands in my hair. I realize I whispered my thought out loud. *"Always,"* he repeats. Then shows me how much he means it.

Chapter 18

"LIFT WITH YOUR BACK," I ADVISE RYLIE FROM WHERE I lean against my apartment building, raising my face to the autumn sun while I sip my coffee. Rylie slings a series of curse words at me as he struggles with one of my giant suitcases.

"What did you pack in here? The bodies of your enemies?"

"It's shoes," I reply in a way that lets him know that should be obvious.

Rylie drops my suitcase to the curb, face twisting with incredulity. "Shoes? As in plural?"

"I'm not going to wear a single shoe, Rylie. No free feet, not even for charity."

He drags a hand down his face, slowly shaking his head. "I mean you brought multiple *pairs* of shoes?"

"Uh, yeah?"

"We're going for one night! You have three suitcases and one of them is solely for *shoes*?"

I smile at him, but narrow my eyes. "You seem to be having a lot of feelings right now, but please note that I'm not in charge of managing them."

"I'm not having a lot of feelings!" he says in a pitch that leads me to believe he's having a tremendous amount of feelings. "I'm having one feeling and it's that you exist just to torture me."

I make a show of looking around. "What rock have you been living under, bud?"

"Just help me lift this."

"I would, but I just got a fresh mani. I can't . . ." I gesture vaguely at all my shit plus the items Lilith recruited Rylie to transport to the venue uptown. She might be the first person to ever discover a practical use for a PT Cruiser.

Rylie surprised me by booking us a room at the hotel where the fundraiser is being held and I expressed my excitement by packing enough to stay for two weeks. Manipulate for the stay you want, not the stay you get, as they say.

When he's close to finishing loading my ludicrously capacious bags into his trunk, I saunter over, giving him a smack on the ass in support. He pretends to scowl over his shoulder but it quickly rises to a grin.

"Oh, shoot," I say, when he's looking away, ducking to the ground and pretending like I dropped my lipstick from my purse. Acting fast, I tear off the backing of a large bumper sticker and slap it on the fat rear of the PT Cruiser, then brush myself off nonchalantly as I return to standing.

It's all done so quickly and efficiently—Rylie fixing me

with a buoyant smile as he closes the trunk, taking a moment to cup my face between his hands as he gently brushes his lips against mine—that I think I've gotten away with it. With one last kiss, he lets me go, moving toward the driver's side door.

"Shoe's untied," he mumbles, stopping in his tracks and propping his foot on the back of the car. The way he leans over to tie his laces brings him eye level with the bright-pink holographic bumper sticker declaring in giant red letters: PLEASE BE PATIENT, BABY GIRL ON BOARD.

His foot slips, and he catches himself with his hands, bringing his face even closer to the glorious moniker. He stares at it for a second. Then another. With a deep growl he picks at the corner of it, but that sucker is sealed tight and all he manages to do is make an awful nails-on-a-chalkboard sound.

"You are a pain in the fucking ass," Rylie says, straightening. He loops an arm around my waist, hitching me against him. Glaring at me, he threads his hand into my hair with a tight grip, tilting my head to give me a deep, searing kiss. I hum in satisfaction, my hands pressed to his chest. "I'm not sure why I put up with you," he whispers against my lips.

"Oh, really?"

"Really."

"I'll remind you of that later when you're panting into my mouth and telling me how good I feel."

Rylie's grunt is somewhere between a laugh and a moan. "Never mind, you've jogged my memory. Get in the car."

Strapped in and excited like pioneers headed west, we begin our drive uptown. While our trip is only around eight miles, the instant gridlock makes our ETA no less than eighty-two minutes. With legs carelessly propped on the dash and

Rylie's warm palm on my thigh, I start to wonder if traffic might actually be a beautiful gift we take for granted.

"Music?" Rylie asks, thumbing through his phone with his free hand as we enter the fifth minute of standstill traffic.

"No. Let's sit in silence and ruminate on our most embarrassing moments."

He gives my thigh a squeeze that's supposed to be a warning, but only sends a delicious shiver through my body. I pluck his phone from his hands and hit shuffle, leaning in to give him a kiss on the cheek. I nearly headbutt him when "Monster Mash" starts blaring from the speakers as we finally start to move. I glance at him out of the corner of my eye for the first thirty seconds of the song, waiting for any signal that he realizes this is not a normal tune to have favorited.

"Is this your lovemaking playlist?" I ask casually.

Rylie's face wrinkles in disgust as he looks at me, then back to the road. "Eva, be serious for once, please." There's a thoughtful pause as he switches lanes. "Everyone knows this is a peak raunchy foreplay song. It's the perfect opener for my 'Down and Dirty Fucking' playlist."

I really shouldn't encourage him, but I let out a booming laugh. Rylie's lips twitch but he keeps his expression serious. "Obviously, I keep 'This Is Halloween' on my lovemaking playlist."

I reach over, raking my hand through the waves of his hair, then give his earlobe a gentle tug. This man is a ghoul and I like him so much my chest hurts.

"Can I ask you a question?" I say when a reasonable amount of normal songs have played and we're bumper to bumper again.

"Is it going to subtly destroy my self-confidence?" Rylie asks, flashing me a winning smile.

"Okay, so now's *not* the time to ask how you feel about the nickname Short King? Got it."

"I'm six foot!"

"Sure you are, sweetie."

Rylie pokes a spot beneath my ribs, making me yelp. "What's your question, demon spawn?"

"What led to the Rylie Cooper renaissance?"

"The *what*?" For the first time since I've met him, he looks genuinely horrified. And this is coming from the man wearing a mustard-yellow crewneck featuring Tweety Bird smoking a cigarette saying I GOT OUT OF BED, WHAT MORE DO YOU WANT?

"Your whole, I don't know"—I gesture at him—"fuckboy reformation. I know in therapy you talked about hitting rock bottom, but I guess . . . I guess I was wondering what that was. Or what made you start to climb up from it?"

Rylie's hands tighten on the steering wheel, a muscle in his cheek twitching. He stays quiet for so long—a frown notched between his eyebrows—that it seems like he's going to ignore my question entirely. Sudden panic blooms through me as I wonder if I made him mad, pushed him too far with my prying. I just want to know him so badly, so deeply. I want to collect every piece of him from over the years like I can put them in a box of keepsakes and memorize all the details.

"I'm sorry. I shouldn't have . . . We don't—"

Rylie silences me by cupping the back of my neck, gently massaging the taut muscles. His smile is strained but genuine as he looks at me. "Don't apologize, Kitten. You didn't upset me. It's just a hard question to come up with a succinct answer to."

I nod, leaning into his touch, wanting to melt at the sweet relief of his voice. This is all so new to me, this mutual vulnerability. It's like learning a foreign language, and sometimes it feels too mortifying to attempt a sentence. I'm worried I'll be tripping over the vocabulary and grammar for years. But something in Rylie's relentless patience gives me the confidence to keep trying.

"I guess it was about a year after I graduated," Rylie says, and I turn down the music so I don't miss a word. "Honestly, I wasn't a star student before I lost my sister, but my grades tanked senior year. They gave me a pity degree for sure."

"I'm sure that's not true," I grumble, feeling oddly defensive of him. "You're very smart."

Rylie's grin is so radiant, it steals the breath from my chest. "That might be the nicest thing you've ever said to me."

"Don't get used to it."

"I wouldn't dare." Rylie's quiet for a few more moments, glancing at the directions on his phone. He lets out a deep breath. "And while I appreciate your belief in me, my college self definitely didn't deserve it. I didn't even pretend to look for a job after graduation. I moved back home and took advantage of the grace people give you when someone you love dies. I slept all day, ate all the food my mom would buy, and left the kitchen trashed. I worked a few shifts at my town's Wendy's just to have some cash to buy weed and booze. I was a lowlife with no interest in doing anything different."

"That doesn't sound super unreasonable after losing a sibling," I whisper, placing my hand on his thigh.

Rylie chews on his lower lip again as he thinks, then shrugs. "Maybe it's not. But I know Hailey would have hated who I'd become in her memory." He picks up my hand, lifting it and brushing my knuckles against his mouth. "I probably would have kept going that way if it weren't for Katie. She was still so young and trapped in the rubble of our family's crumbling. I came home from a late shift one night and found her curled on the couch, bawling her eyes out. She was only thirteen or fourteen at the time, but when she looked up at me—fuck, she looked so old. So weary and lonely and broken, like life had already beaten her to a pulp. It sort of shattered me out of my fog, if that makes any sense."

I nod, encouraging him to keep going.

"She opened up to me that night; I think she'd been trying to for a long time but I wasn't in a place to listen. She talked about how alone she felt, how afraid. How she thought losing Hailey would be the worst thing to ever happen to her but over the past year she'd felt like she'd lost me and our parents too, how their marriage was falling apart. That last part was probably the most jarring. I was so numb to everything, I had no idea my parents were struggling with their marriage. I kind of . . . Well, it sounds super naive, but I kind of assumed that something like that would glue them together. Make them unbreakable.

"But after Katie talked to me, and I started paying attention, I realized how horrible things had gotten. I saw how badly my dad was failing to step up and be the partner my mom needed. It was heartbreaking to watch, to see this woman reach day in and day out for something as simple as a hug or a word of reassurance or even just acknowledgment from her husband, and not get it." Rylie's voice cracks, and he takes a moment to clear his throat.

"I didn't know how to process it," he continues. "Realizing your parents are human is a devastating thing. And I always looked up to my dad as the model man, the kind of person I wanted to be. But he checked out, and it fucked with my head. I didn't know what it meant to be a man, let alone a partner."

We stop at a red light, and Rylie tilts his head up, rolling out his neck as he thinks about his next words. "I cleaned up my act after that. Slowly, but I did. I started helping my mom around the house, talking with my sister every day, taking her out and trying to bring some enjoyment back into her life. Before the second anniversary of Hailey's death, my mom filed for divorce and it was probably one of the best things she's ever done.

"I know this will sound weird," Rylie says, glancing at me, then away. "But through all of that I found a sort of . . . *beauty* in our grief. In the way my mom, sister, and I came together. How we hurt in a way that was the same but also vastly unique for each of us. I became sort of fascinated with that, with feelings, for lack of better phrasing." He lets out a rough laugh, giving me a sardonic smile. "Probably because I was feeling so many of them for once."

I smile back, cupping his cheek as emotions knot through me.

"And I needed to find some sort of purpose. Katie was blossoming in high school, my mom was starting to carve out a new life for herself. I realized I wanted to do the same. So I took all those feelings and my fascination with them and applied for master's programs in counseling. And I loved it. I loved studying human nature and trying to understand how all of these awful, wonderful things that happen to us shape us. Then I started sharing what I was learning online in funny bits or whatever. And it resonated with people, I guess. I'm able to make a living off my stupid videos and my podcast and continually learn more about people. It's a pretty amazing thing, I think."

Rylie pulls into the driveway of our hotel and a bellman heads in our direction. The second he puts the car in park, I dive across the center console, gripping his face between my palms and kissing him with everything I have.

"It's very amazing," I say against his lips, feeling his smile. I kiss his nose. His eyelids. His forehead. Then his mouth again. "Thank you for sharing that part of your story with me."

Rylie drops his forehead to mine, our shallow breaths mingling. "Kitten," he says, dragging a palm from my throat down my back. "Every part of me is yours if you want it."

Chapter 19

"DOES MY HAIR LOOK CUTE OR DO I LOOK LIKE A YAPPY little Shih Tzu?" I ask, emerging from the hotel bathroom in a cloud of expensive perfume and setting spray.

Rylie's lying on the bed, and his eyes slowly lift from the book I loaned him to the fountain of messy hair on the top of my head. "Both things can be true, no?"

I grimace, flipping him off while fluffing my hair. His laugh is a warm amber, slipping through me and crystalizing in my veins with a delicate glow. He stretches his lanky limbs, then moves off the bed, making an unhurried appraisal of me from head to toe. His smile notches on one side when he stops in front of me, fingers toying lazily with a loose strand of my hair before ghosting down my neck to the thin silk strap of my top. I shiver slightly at the barely-there scratch of his nails on my skin, and his smile grows, touch turning bolder as his palm skims down my side until it's at my hip and he's drawing me closer.

"You look," he says, dipping his head so his lips graze my temple, breath tickling my ear, "absolutely stunning."

A shaky sigh slips out of me, my knees going wobbly, and I feel both silly and outrageously pleased at how earnestly he means it.

How does he do it? How does he make me feel like this, over and over again? Like he's spent a lifetime looking at art but I'm the most beautiful thing he's ever seen?

"And your hair looks lovely. More Yorkie than booger-eyed Shih Tzu for sure." He pulls back to smile at me. The romantic bubble is popped, but glitter sprinkles around us, making the feelings even brighter.

I love playing with him, I love our endless, ferocious need to make the other laugh or gasp or scramble to guess what comes next. I love—

I wriggle out of his grip. "Let's see how you compare."

I make a slow circle around his suit-clad body like a surveyor sizing up property. Rylie squares his shoulders and splays his palms to the sides, chin tilted toward the ceiling.

He looks so fucking good, I can't even find something to pretend to poke fun at.

His suit pants are impeccably tailored, hugging his ass and thighs in a way that makes me want to start barking, the shade a burnt sienna that could look ridiculous on a man with less confidence, but he wears it like the color was invented for him. He's paired them with a crisp, hunter-green button-down, the top two buttons open, drawing my eyes up the column of his throat and the bob of his Adam's apple as he smiles. I stop in front of him, hands on my hips.

"And this is your final decision for what you're wearing?" I ask in a falsely delicate voice.

Rylie's eyes narrow, smile growing. "Yeah. Why?"

"You know the Duolingo owl?"

". . . Yes?"

I give him a pointed look up and down, then shrug. "Just saying." I'm drowning in lust but I'd never go easy on him.

Rylie stares at me, then shakes his head, a suppressed laugh chopping up his voice. "You're such a little pill."

"It's just an observation!" I whine, wrapping my arms around his trim waist. He pretends to push me away, but I hold on tighter, the low roughness of his chuckles vibrating against my cheek. He gives up and hugs me back.

"Maybe I should download the app," he says, smacking my ass. "Learn how to say *Eva Kitt needs an exorcism*, in multiple languages."

I pull away, biting my lip as I shrug. "You already stole his look. Might as well steal his lines."

"Or *I feel like my girlfriend lacks a healthy fear of God, please help me*." Rylie laughs hard at his own joke, hands slipping from my body as he holds his middle.

My stomach yo-yos up to my throat and then bottoms out, a rush of warmth shooting sparks across my skin. My lips part, but I can't breathe, my ribs feeling like they'll crack under the pressure filling my chest.

Rylie catches my quiet, his laughter dimming as he takes in my stunned expression. "What's wrong, Kitten?"

"Did you . . . did you just call me your girlfriend?"

His expression shifts, smile softening as his hungry eyes rove over me. "I did. How . . . how do you feel about that?"

How do I feel? How do I *feel*? I feel like he just snatched out my linchpin and I'm slipping off my axis. I feel like Earth just turned upside down and my head is up in the clouds and my heart is in his hands. I feel like shooting stars are fizzing through my blood and my pockets are full of goddamn sunshine because Rylie fucking Cooper just called me his girlfriend and it might just be the best feeling in the world.

I launch myself at him, wobbling on my stilettos as I loop my arms around his neck. But he's there. He's got me. His hands at my waist, one sliding up my back, the other down my hips. His lips meet mine, opening to me, our tongues touching and my body heating and I don't think I'll ever want oxygen again for how deeply this kiss satisfies my every need.

"Words, please," he says against my mouth. I ignore him for half a second and kiss him more.

"I like being your girlfriend," I whisper when it becomes a necessity to come up for air. "Almost as much as I like having you as my boyfriend."

Rylie's smile is devastating, and he grips my head between his hands, taking a moment to look at me, eyes scouring every inch of my face. With a disbelieving shake of his head, he leans in, placing a gentle kiss to my forehead. I nuzzle against him, arms wrapping around him again in a hug. I've never been a particularly touchy person, but something about Rylie has me constantly reaching for him like I'm a plant and he's the sun.

"We better get downstairs," I say, catching a glimpse of the time.

Rylie lets out a reluctant sigh, releasing me after one last kiss to the top of my head. I touch up my makeup, then gather my purse as Rylie slings on his suit jacket. With his hand pressed to my lower back, he guides me out the door.

"Should I be worried about being seen with you?" I ask as we make our way down the hallway.

"Damn, you are *relentless*."

I giggle. "I mean, since we're doing the whole laying-low thing and you've ghosted Soundbites on behalf of both of us, I don't know how cool we have to keep it tonight in public."

He gives the question serious thought as we get to the elevator banks and he hits the call button.

"How do you feel about it?" He leans his shoulder against the wall and gives me an assessing look. "I get the concern but I also feel like the people in attendance tonight will be more focused on the actual fundraiser and not if I have my arm around you."

I bobble my head from side to side. "Yeah, stuffy rich people with enough status to get an invite to a swanky event like this probably don't have a ton of overlap with our more parasocial viewers." The golden doors open and I lead us in.

"Plus, selfishly, I *want* people to see me with my arm around you," Rylie whispers in my ear, gripping my hip and spinning me to face him as the elevator doors slip shut. He crowds me to the corner, lifting me up an inch so my ass is supported by the railing, his hand moving to my thigh and hitching my leg against his hip. "I want to show you off and grin at everyone's glare of jealousy."

I get dizzy from the statement, at the unholy excitement he seems to have for being with me. I let out a breathy giggle against Rylie's hovering lips, and he closes the distance, kissing me the entire ride down until I'm worked up and panting and gripping him to me.

Ding.

The doors slide open and Rylie steps back, smiling at the way I sway toward him. He takes my hand, guiding me out of the elevator to a secluded corner of the lobby shielded with large potted plants.

With a low, proud laugh he reaches out, using his thumb to clean up the edge of my smeared lipstick. He then frames my hips with his hands, taking a second to straighten my skirt. I try to shake off the languid, drunk feeling he's suffused through my limbs.

"You can put your arm around me," I say primly, hoping to regain even an ounce of control as I straighten his clothes too. "But that's all." I slide my hand against the slight bulge in his pants as I smooth his shirt, making him hiss out a breath. His jaw tightens as I smile sweetly up at him.

"Or we forget this entire thing and go back up to our room and you put your thighs around my ears for the rest of the night," he offers smoothly.

My entire body flushes hot, pinpricks of pleasure radiating through me. I somehow keep my expression neutral. "But we must think about the youths," I say, gesturing toward the noise of the event.

Rylie scrunches his nose. "Must we?"

I nod solemnly, smoothing the silk of my top. "But I'll make you a deal," I whisper. "Be a good boy tonight and I'll let you beg your way between my legs later." Patting his cheek, I try to step around him toward the banquet hall.

Rylie catches my wrist, spinning me back to him. "That's cute, Kitten, but we both know who will be the one begging tonight."

He places a chaste kiss on my temple, fixes his flushed face in a winning smile, and leads me, dazed and blushing, into the party.

Chapter 20

I ASSUMED THE FUNDRAISER WOULD BE UPSCALE BASED ON the address, but I wasn't prepared for this level of fancy. The large room sparkles under crystal chandeliers, the gleam of the pristine place settings and intricate centerpieces creating a magical quality to the air, like everything is sprinkled with gold. A slideshow of queer youth and young adults Euphoric Identity has helped and supported plays on the mainstage, photos and stills of Lilith and the team in action propped around the room. There's a buoyancy to the energy, an event that could so easily feel stuck-up and stuffy somehow buzzing and effervescent with the excitement of everyone in attendance.

"Lilith, this is *amazing*," I say when we finally locate the hostess. "I can't even wrap my head around it."

WELL, ACTUALLY 307

"So proud of you, Lil." Rylie gives her a big hug.

"Thank you," she says, a glint in her eyes and pink on her cheeks. She sways from side to side, her pale blue beaded skirt catching the light and making her glimmer. "I mean, it certainly wouldn't be this caliber of an event if it weren't for a collection of elder, old-money gays doing their damndest to spend their millions for good and choosing to be our bene-factors, but whatever helps the kids." We clink our glasses at that.

"And Ray's food is god-tier," Lilith adds, plucking a slice of crusty bread topped with cheese and chimichurri sauce from a passing waiter. "How did he know provoleta is my favorite?"

I share a private smile with Rylie as we shrug. Ray wanted to pay homage to Lilith's Argentinian roots in his menu de-sign, and Rylie was overwhelmingly helpful in knowing her most-loved dishes.

"Everyone is raving about it," she says with a contented moan as she finishes her bite.

"He's this city's greatest secret," I say, beaming in pride for my friend. "I swear in a few years he's going to have one of the biggest restaurants in the world."

"Based on the feral response of these rich folks asking me for his info, I'd bet it'll be a matter of months, not years." Lilith's name is called, and her attention flicks to a group of people by the bar, waving her over. "I better do a round," she says, indicating to them that she'll be right there. "Actually, Rylie, there's a few people I wanted you to meet. Eva, would you mind . . . ?"

I wave them on. "Oh my god, of course. I just spotted Aida anyway," I say, bobbing my head in the opposite direction. "You two do your thing."

I walk toward Aida, smiling and waving when she notices me. She looks amazing in a hunter-green cocktail dress that hugs her curves. Her long, curly hair rests over one shoulder, accenting her perfectly applied makeup. We haven't had a real conversation since the mean-comments thing, but I've been deluding myself that the animosity is something I've built up in my head. Neither of us would miss Ray's big debut, and I'm hoping tonight will give us a chance to clear the air.

"Hey, stunner," I say, sidling up to her and wrapping her in a big hug. I feel a current of tension in her muscles. "Can you believe this?"

"I can't think of a setting we fit in less," she says, giving the room a wide-eyed sweep. "These are the type of people who blow their noses with dollar bills."

There's a long, taut silence that feels unnatural between us, and I shift on my feet, clearing my throat a few times.

"You okay?" I ask.

She ignores my question. "Have you seen Ray yet?"

As if summoned, Ray bursts through the kitchen doors directly across the room from us, glowing in his pristine chef's jacket. A few patrons swarm him, and he shakes hands and accepts business cards. He maneuvers it all with the grace and confidence of a renowned chef, giving no hint that tonight may be the very start of a tirelessly worked-for career. Eventually, he waltzes up to us, and we nearly tackle him in a group hug, giddy with pride.

"Look at you," I croon.

"Everyone is obsessed," Aida adds.

"As was always my destiny," Ray says with a subdued shrug. "Have you two talked yet?" he asks, his tone lifting to one I recognize when there is even a whiff of drama.

My eyebrows furrow as I glance at Aida, but she avoids my gaze, eyes fixed on the ground and color rushing up her cheeks. Okay, so maybe I didn't create the tension in my head.

"Oh Jesus," Ray huffs. "Can we get this over with, please?"

"I didn't want to distract from your night," Aida snaps back, the pair staring at each other in a silent but heated conversation.

"What's going on?"

Ray nudges Aida's shoulder, and she glares at him. With an achy sense of dread, I reach out, grabbing Aida's hand with a reassuring pressure. Hers stays limp.

"I've felt really frustrated with you lately," she mumbles, gaze still on the ground.

I flinch. "You have?"

She finally looks at me, eyes slitted in annoyance. "You've been making me look pretty bad at work. William's been furious since that stupid mean-comments video, and I've been on damage control trying to deflect and save both our jobs. He wanted to fire you after your show of attitude and then you going MIA on any Rylie Cooper stuff after that hasn't made this any easier. It's exhausting."

"It wasn't a show of attitude, Aida," I say, indignation flaring. "That whole thing crossed so many lines and he knows it. The guy is a prick."

"I know," Aida says, shoulders slumping. "But he's the prick that now signs our paychecks."

"I just don't think I was the bad guy in how I reacted."

"You weren't!" A few heads turn at the earnest rise in her voice, and she clears her throat, tilting her head toward me. "You weren't. You were one hundred percent justified in being upset, and I felt awful being your segment producer and letting that happen, and I'm sorry. But I also didn't love not hearing anything from you afterward and being left to fix things on my own . . . Especially when I don't know what's actually going on with the whole Rylie thing." Her expression is bare-boned, flooding my system with guilt. "You're my best friend, Eva. I'm trying to defend you and protect you, but it's hard to do when you don't let me in enough to know what's happening."

I look down, nose and eyes stinging with the sudden urge to cry. Jesus, when did I get so damn emotional?

Aida squeezes my hand, ducking her head to meet my gaze. "I miss you, dickhead. I just want you to text me back."

"Ditto," Ray says, but there's a gentle curve to his mouth. "I hate finding out news about you from social media. I prefer the details firsthand and with as much graphic detail as possible."

Aida and I both giggle, and I have to tilt my head back, blinking carefully so no tears fall and smear my makeup. "I'm sorry," I whisper. "I . . . My life has been kind of messy lately."

"No shit."

I frown at Aida. "That's kind of the whole thing, though. It's always felt messy. I'm either in a failing relationship or dealing with roommate drama or complaining about my stupid-ass job. It's . . . I don't know. Embarrassing, I guess. I feel like you two have blossomed and I'm a weed that needs pulling. You have plans and goals and you're actively achieving them while I eat hot dogs for a living while bitching about wanting to be taken seriously."

"Babe." Ray grips my shoulders, forcing me to look at him. "I hate to ruin your pity party, but none of what you just said is special." He delivers the line so gently, I laugh. "Seriously, though. Feeling useless and directionless and like you aren't keeping up is kind of the entire point of your twenties. Everything is ass all the time and all we can do is lean on each other through it, not compare ourselves moment to moment."

"That was very live, love, laugh of you," I say through a thick throat. Ray smiles.

"None of us have shit figured out," Aida says, rubbing a soothing circle along my back. "And that's okay. But don't cut us out and make it all that much harder."

"I didn't pull away intentionally," I say, looking between them. "Things got . . . complicated with Rylie and I know that affects your work, Aida, and William was hounding me and it ultimately felt easier to kind of shut down than have to tap-dance my way through the details of everything."

"Don't get me started on fucking William," Aida groans, rolling her eyes. "That man is going to give me an ulcer. He's so obsessed it's unhinged."

"*Why* is he so obsessed, though? He must have other things to worry about."

Aida gives me a gently patronizing glance. "I think you

underestimate just how much traffic and money this whole stunt has brought in. Our views spike every time something new about you two comes out; the ad revenue has it on track to be one of our best quarters yet. He's stepping into power at a time when he'll greatly profit off the attention you two generate and it'll make him look like some sort of corporate god. Only something with more earning potential could distract him at this point."

My stomach twists, bile running up my throat. "I can't keep doing it. Things with Rylie . . . It doesn't feel good or right to keep up the whole bit."

"Yeah, okay, sorry, but I'm assuming you two are fucking now, right?" Ray, so delicately, asks. Aida pinches him and he gives her a disbelieving look. "Oh, I'm sorry. Did I offend your delicate constitution? How would you suggest I get to the heart of the matter?"

"With a bit more tact, perhaps?" Aida snaps back. There's a pause, and they both slant me a questioning glance.

My cheeks heat, a smile tugging at my lips as I try to be cool. "Um. Well. While we are, in fact—" I wave my hand.

"Fucking," Ray supplies.

I snort. "Yeah. That. But we're also kind of, um, dating?" The last word comes out as such a high-pitched squeak it'd be a miracle if anyone besides dogs can hear it.

"*You're what?*" Aida shrieks, her stunned expression matching Ray's. "It's like, legitimately a thing?"

"Good god, are we fifteen?"

"Answer the question."

"Yes. We're legitimately a *thing*," I say with a scowl. "And that's why I've been avoiding Soundbites stuff so hard. If we were just hooking up it would be different but I . . . I really like him. And I want to see what that's like without other people getting a front-row seat."

"Ray, I'm sorry to interrupt, but there's a small issue with the pastry chef," a woman in a catering uniform says, materializing at his side. "We need you."

Ray's gaze whips between me and the staff member, and he lets out a groan of frustration. "Dammit. Okay, this conversation is not done," he says, pointing at me as he walks backward toward the kitchen. "I need more information. In fact, you both are forbidden from speaking to each other until I'm back and we're in a safe place with a cold bottle of pink wine because I *refuse* to be the last to know the details."

"Whatever you say." I salute his frown.

"Tell me everything," Aida demands as soon as his back is to us.

I giggle like a schoolgirl, trying to figure out the best way to condense all of these feelings for Rylie into something that makes sense. I open my mouth, but Aida's face falls, her eyes going wide like a prey animal being cornered. "What's wrong?"

"William," Aida hisses.

"William?" There's a tap on my shoulder, and I spin around, mind doing somersaults as I come face-to-face with my boss. "William," I croak. "What are you doing here?"

He arches a thick, black brow at my less-than-couth greeting but otherwise doesn't react, taking a moment to watch me squirm.

"Soundbites is a substantial donor to the organization," he says as if this should be obvious. "Keeps the zillenials off our backs about less-savory channels of funding we have. It's good to put a face forward at events like this. My mother is here too." He takes a sip of blood-colored wine, then nods over the rim to an approaching Landry. He waits until she has joined us to ask, "And what are *you* doing here, Miss Kitt?" His tone makes it obvious he knows exactly what I'm doing here.

"I . . . I . . ."

"Our best friend is catering," Aida supplies. "Ray Williams. This is his first big solo event, so we purchased tickets to support him. Isn't the food wonderful?"

"Quite," Landry says, pursing her lips as she looks at a passing tray of hors d'oeuvres. "A bit heavy for my liking, but I'm sure there's an audience for every dish."

I'm still too surprised by their presence to speak, and Aida swoops in to save me again. "Plus, mastermind Eva here thought it might be a good chance to pin Rylie down. He's good friends with EI's founder, Lilith Flores. Had her on his podcast recently."

Aida subtly steps on my toes with her heels, and I straighten, nodding rapidly. "Yes. Exactly. Just trying to scope him out. So many people here."

William makes a low sound before taking another sip of wine. "Isn't that him approaching with two glasses of champagne?"

"My, my, what a choice of suit that is," Landry murmurs, letting distaste play across her features.

My hackles raise, and I want to snap my jaws at her for

even hinting that he looks anything but handsome. I spin
around, gut sinking as I clock Rylie approaching us. His smile
is broad, a lasso right around my heart, and my body can't
decide if it wants to panic or swoon. Reading something in my
expression, his grin sinks and eyebrows furrow. A second too
late, he registers Landry and William over my shoulder, too
close to make a beeline to safer ground.

I can see his mind working, trying to determine how to
play this, what's already been said. I give him a hopeless, desperate look that conveys my only thought: *I think we're fucked.*

Rylie's reached my side now, and I'm so attuned to his
face—spent so many of my recent nights studying every flicker
of muscle and emotion—that I don't miss the protective edge
to his posture, the lines of his dazzling smile poised to drop to
a scowl, the quick way his silver eyes assess William like he's
sizing up an enemy general, ready to go to battle at a moment's
notice.

"Mr. Cooper," Landry says, giving him a beatific smile
that doesn't reach her eyes. "I see your profound digestive issues have subsided."

"A medical miracle," William mutters.

"Who doesn't love an impromptu gut cleanse?" Rylie
counters jovially. "It's great to see you two again. Eva, Aida."
He nods at us. "You both look lovely this evening."

William rolls his eyes, taking another sip of wine as we
mumble our thanks. "Oh, good, we're keeping up the ruse. Do
you need a moment to compose a reason you're over here? A
good explanation for the extra drink?"

Rylie's mouth firms into a straight line. "Didn't think these two should be without a drink when the wine is so good and the evening's purpose is so worthy." He hands us each a flute. Mine almost slips through my shaking fingers.

"Of course," William says in a clipped voice. "Now's the part where you try to convince me of your good reasons for violating your contract. Feel free to add yours too, Eva. Wouldn't want to silence our bleeding-heart feminist risking her career for a C-level internet personality."

"Stop it." I'm startled to realize I'm the one who said that so loudly. It's hard to hear much over the pounding of my heartbeat in my ears.

William gives me a look of mild surprise, cold eyes narrowing. "Excuse me?"

"I . . . I . . ."

Holy shit. This is my *boss*. This is my *career*. I can't be snapping at the man who holds my future in his palm, especially not when his mother, my other damn boss, is right there to witness.

I look wildly at Rylie, expecting his panic to match mine. But he's calm, a soothing, steady force that tells me he's not moving from my side no matter what I say next. He's in this. And dammit, I'm in it too.

"I'm sorry for raising my voice," I say, looking at William, then to Landry. Her expression is softer, so I focus there. "And I'm sorry for lying, but you're right, Rylie and I have had contact since our last recording, and we don't want to move forward with the remaining dates and recordings."

"*See, Mom*," William whines. "I told you she was playing games. You need to—"

"Shush." Landry's eyes spark, her expression stony as she glares at her son. She turns the look on me, the softness from moments ago gone. "Care to share any details, or am I to fill in the blanks myself?"

My skin prickles with sweat under her stare. I'm a deer in the headlights, my tongue feeling too big for my mouth, like I'll choke on it before I can muster up the spine to tell her the truth.

"Don't turn prudish and coy on me, Eva," Landry says, her voice light but a thread of discipline poking through. "It's boring."

"I'm . . . I'm not," I say, shrugging like a dumbass. "It's just . . ."

"*Just* is a lazy word, dear. You should know that."

Rylie opens his mouth to speak, but I tug the sleeve of his suit jacket, stepping forward, and swallowing my trepidation like a hot coal. "Things are starting to become real. Between me and Rylie. And I ju— We no longer plan to go forward with the recordings because we're seeing each other and would both like to protect the early stages of our relationship from the stress of public observation and opinion."

I can't believe the steadiness in my voice, the cool command that somehow threads through every word while my knees feel like they're about to give out. Landry and William could ruin me right here and now, and I've given them an arsenal of tools to carry it out.

But they surprise me with silence, William seething while Landry's expression shifts from cutting to curious.

I clear my throat, having nothing to lose. "It's been harder than I anticipated, managing this level of attention. I'm sure you know how hard it can be to feel like you're under a microscope, everyone analyzing your every move, critiquing everything you do."

"We don't want your excuses," William snaps. "You—"

Landry silences her son with a touch to his arm, sharing a speaking glance with him. After a moment, she inclines her head toward me.

"Experiencing that in the context of a relationship isn't something I was prepared for," I say, voice fragile. "And to protect my mental health and the delicacy of my—our—relationship, I need to take a step back from having any of it online." I feel raw, extremely exposed, in this beautiful room filled with beautiful people admitting that I'm not tough enough to hack it and I'm not sure I really care.

Rylie's hand slips into mine, the warmth of his skin swirling through me, climbing like a vine up my arm, across my chest, shooting roots into my stomach and all the way down to my toes, something in my chest aching and expanding like a flower opening its petals to the sun.

Landry stares at me for so long, I wonder if I missed a key moment and I'm supposed to walk away with my tail tucked and head down.

"You've given me a lot to think about, Eva," Landry says at last, careful consideration in her eyes. Her voice lacks the cruelty I was bracing for, and even William gives her a double-take. I bite the inside of my cheek against a tiny gasp, not willing to risk spooking away this soft side of my boss.

"R-really?"

She nods, lips curling up in what I think is supposed to be a reassuring smile. "Let's plan to meet on Monday morning, the three of us." She gestures at me and William. "See what we can make of this tangled web. I'll have my assistant send you a calendar invite."

"Okay," I choke out. Landry spares the briefest of glances for Rylie and nods at Aida, sauntering away with her head held high and posture impeccable. William shakes his head in disgust, his look lingering much longer than his mother's on both me and Aida. He clunks down his empty wineglass and stalks after his mother.

"Holy shit," I whisper, more breath than voice. "Did that go . . . well?"

I share dumbfounded expressions with Rylie and Aida before Rylie lets out a tiny *whoop*, swooping me into a hug.

"That was so fucking hot," he mumbles against my lips before capturing them in a deep kiss. I laugh, feeling giddy and exhausted and more than a little drunk on the taste of him.

"I can't believe William didn't explode," Aida says, a rigid wariness still in her expression, eyebrows furrowed as she stares in the direction he exited. "Landry too, if I'm being honest. She's more even-keeled than her son but she's notoriously not warm and fuzzy. I thought for sure we were about to get fired."

"Maybe the tin woman had a heart all along," I say, smacking away Rylie's roving hands. He gives me a boyish smile, stealing one more sloppy kiss before I push him off for good.

Rylie looks at me with a wildfire spark in those eyes of his, catching fire in my chest and making my cheeks burn. He looks like he wants to touch me some more, like he wants to pin me against the wall and kiss me until I can't think straight, like he wants to steal me from this party and take me up to our room and not let me out until every part of me is incinerated. And, god, I hope my look tells him how much I want him to do just that.

"Rylie, there you are." Lilith materializes again at his side, making us jump. "Aida, so good to see you," Lilith adds, registering my friend.

The two hug, Aida offering a string of congratulations that Lilith graciously waves away.

"Thank you, thank you. It's been the effort of a lot of people—"

"Take a damn compliment, Lil," Rylie scolds.

She pinches his arm, making him laugh. "I'm so sick of playing nice hostess, that's for sure," she says to Aida. "Which is why—and I'm so sorry to do this to you again, Eva—but I need to steal Rylie and have him charm people into giving me lots of money."

"Please don't apologize, I'm just glad someone's found a use for him. Capitalize on it. Go, go." I shoo them, Rylie sending me an apologetic but promising smile over his shoulder as Lilith pulls him into the crowd.

Aida and I turn to each other, both still dazed over the confrontation that didn't ruin us.

"Want to get drunk and hunt for sugar daddies?" she asks, tracing the movement of a handsome, salt-and-pepper-haired man in a three-piece suit and a watch that costs more than a year's worth of rent.

"I'll wingwoman," I say with a wink.

Aida shakes her head. "Not Rylie Cooper making an honest woman out of you."

"I'm horrified too," I say with a grin, lifting my champagne flute in a cheers.

Chapter 21

THE NEXT COUPLE HOURS GO BY IN A BLUR. AIDA AND I make a few loops of the room, creating intricate backstories of people in attendance while taking diligent advantage of Ray's amazing food and the open bar.

Rylie keeps returning to me like a magnet, his hand at the small of my back, lips at my ear as he whispers an endearment or a dirty joke. He dragged me into a few small-talk sessions Lilith orchestrated, but when he realized how much more I'd rather be bullshitting with Aida than feigning interest in palm greasing, he sent me to her with a smile and a promise to find me as soon as Lilith was a little less high-strung.

Feet aching from my unforgivingly gorgeous heels, I'm parked at a table in the back of the banquet hall, alternating between people-watching and spying as Aida hits it off with some guy who works for EI a few tables over.

"Excuse me, everyone." Lilith's voice echoes through a microphone, the live band gracefully quieting. She smiles, a radiant, proud smile that I hope she wears every day from here on out. "On behalf of Euphoric Identity, I want to thank you all so much for being here. Your support and advocacy for queer youth is making a generation of difference for the young people of this city, particularly for minorities who have so often been overlooked and underserved at a disproportionate rate. We would not be making the impact we are if it weren't for your continued generosity and philanthropy. With that being said, it's about time for the grand event of the evening. The auction will be starting shortly, and entrees will be served, so if you'd all take your seats, we can begin momentarily." She makes a gracious exit from the stage as we all cheer for her.

I crane my neck as I clap, trying to catch sight of Rylie so I can sit with him for dinner. My phone vibrates with a text.

Care for a graveyard smash tonight, my queen?

I slap a hand over my mouth to hide my scream as a link comes through for a playlist titled "M0n$teR FuqKing." The only song is "Monster Mash" . . . added sixty-nine times.

I have to bite down hard on my tongue so I don't alarm anyone with the quiet laughter making my entire body shake. I do a quick Google search of the song's lyrics—because I am a normal person and don't have them all committed to memory—then fire back with: you can come to the master bedroom where the vampires feast [on this pussy]

Rylie's reply is obnoxiously fast: Eva, please. We're at a charity event for children. That's so inappropriate.

Another text pops up a few seconds later: meet me at the elevators in thirty seconds or face *monster* consequences

I'm giggling like a fool, already darting toward the exit as I respond: for the love of god this joke needs to DIE

I pass by Aida's seat, giving her a quick excuse and a kiss on the head. She's so invested in the guy she's talking to she essentially shoves me away.

I slip off my heels, feet slapping the glossy marble floor as I sprint toward the elevators, recklessness fizzing through my veins.

I come to a halt at the meeting spot, realizing I beat him there. In a futile attempt to collect myself, I fuss with my hair, trying to get my breathing under control. It's no use, I don't think I've breathed right since this ridiculous man entered my life.

A few seconds later, Rylie rounds the corner. He stops a few feet away from me, his cheeks flushed and eyes already hooded as he appraises me for half a beat. I register the quickest twitch of his lips into his signature smile before he's on me in three long strides, pressing his mouth to mine, hands cradling my jaw and fingers diving into my hair. My back makes contact with the wall, and I fumble for the elevator call button with one hand, whacking him in the back with my shoes with the other as I throw my arm around his neck and kiss him even harder.

There's a momentary delay, and then the elevator doors slide open, Rylie's hands slipping to my waist as he walks me in. A raw mix of amusement and longing flood my sensitive system as I watch Rylie impatiently fuss with his room key and our floor button, his hands shaking and gaze returning to me every half a second like it's killing him to not be touching me right now.

We finally shoot up, my stomach swooping low as his hands are back on me. It could be two seconds or twenty minutes, and we're tripping out the doors and down our hallway, a punch-drunk tangle of need. With a growl of frustration over our slow progress to our room, Rylie picks me up, hitching my long skirt up my thighs and wrapping my legs around his waist, his nose pressed to the base of my neck as he breathes me in, carries me home. With more deftness using the keycard than in the elevator, he gets us inside the room, kicking the door closed behind him.

We make it as far as the bathroom, Rylie sliding my body down his until I'm leaning against the doorframe, one of his thighs wedging tightly between mine, my hips instantly nudging for friction.

And I don't know why but we're giggling. Then panting and touching in such a blur my head spins. Everything with Rylie is a blur, a glimmer of golden energy that creates an unbearable warmth in my chest.

"I'm furious that 'Monster Mash' line worked," I gasp as his head drops to my breasts, the wet heat of his tongue working against the white silk of my top until it's soaked and I'm whimpering for more.

"Really?" he says, pulling back with his eyes fixed on my tight, aching nipples he can see the outline of through the fabric. He ghosts a touch over them with his thumbs, and a small shiver rushes through me. His eyes snap to mine as he pinches the tight peak, making me gasp. He gives me a lazy smile. "Because I couldn't be happier."

He ducks his head again, devouring my breasts, biting and

sucking and murmuring how *fucking good* I am as I continue to writhe against his thigh, fisting his hair, pulling him closer, needing every molecule of space to be obliterated.

With a groan, Rylie pulls his mouth away, glasses askew as he looks at me. Gently, reverently, I reach out and slide them from his face, and his smile carves a tattoo of happiness across my heart. Moving us again, Rylie grips my hips, stepping us fully into the bathroom as he lifts me a few inches, seating me on the edge of the counter.

"This dress has been driving me wild all fucking night," he mutters, eyes staring murderously at the sheer material draped over my legs. He drags his hands through the gossamer fabric as he kisses my neck, placing a bite at my collarbone, then licking the spot.

"Well, actually it's not a dress. It's matching separates," I explain through a gasp. "Bustier and a skirt."

Rylie pauses, forcing his lust-hazed eyes into a bland look, muscles coiled with tension and his lips wet and swollen from kissing me.

"Eva," he says evenly, but there's a warning charge to his voice, his patience a fraying thread. "I adore you, but I cannot tell you how little I give a shit about the specifics of this outfit right now."

I laugh at the deep frustration in his voice. Rylie catches my amusement, and there's a hunger so desperate and wild in his expression, the laughter dies in my throat, all air leaving me on a fractured sigh.

Rylie fists the skirt, dragging it up my thighs. "Hold whatever this is," he says gruffly, taking one of my hands and curling my fingers around the balled-up fabric.

"It's chiffon, it'll wrinkle," I protest weakly out of habit. Because I know he loves it.

"Shut up, Eva," he growls, pinning my hand holding the fabric against my stomach. He drops to his knees, ripping my thong down my legs and leaving it tangled at my ankles. I hear a seam rip as he jerks open my thighs, and I honestly couldn't care less because Rylie's fingers tighten into the skin of my hips, his breathing jagged and lips parted as he stares at the center of me.

Pink crests his cheeks and across the bridge of his nose, his hair wrecked from my relentless grip moments ago, and I feel my pulse in every inch of my body. After what feels like a lifetime, he drags his gaze up my body like he wants to memorize every piece of me, until his eyes finally lock with mine. The only sound in the room is our ragged breathing.

Then, with a smile that destroys me, he whispers, "God, you're fucking pretty," and presses that wicked mouth against my aching pussy.

I arch, the back of my head hitting the mirror, fingers clawing for purchase on the marble countertop, anything that can anchor me so I can press closer against that perfect mouth. Without lifting his head, he hooks my legs and drapes them over his shoulders, my feet resting on his back.

With two sure, clever fingers, Rylie presses into me, rubbing and caressing against a spot that makes me see stars, forget my own name, scream out his.

It doesn't take long until I'm crying and begging and being way too loud but I don't fucking care because Rylie has me. Rylie wants me. He wants me messy and lost and needy and telling him exactly what I want.

He tells me in the grunts against my aching clit, the grip of his free hand around my thigh, the rough, elated sound from low in his chest when he feels me clench around his fingers. Desire is like the turn of a screw, burrowing deeper and deeper into every cell of my body until I'm bucking against his mouth, wave after wave of pleasure capsizing my body.

With something almost like worship, Rylie kisses my throbbing, pulsing center through the aftershocks, nuzzling his cheek against my thigh as I slump against the bathroom mirror, boneless and satisfied to an unholy degree. He kisses his way up my leg, then arm, neck, jaw, until he's sipping at my lips with gently coaxing kisses.

"Let me take care of you," I say, somehow finding the strength in my woozy state to reach for him.

I don't miss the fresh flush of pink across Rylie's cheeks. "That's okay, Kitten," he whispers, intercepting my hand and lacing our fingers together. He lifts my arm so it's wrapped around the back of his neck.

I frown at him, old insecurities of past relationships dying hard. Does he . . . Did he just give me one of the best orgasms of my life and not want me enough to get off himself? Rylie must read some of the panic in my face, because his eyes flash wide, his mouth crashing against mine in a messy, dirty kiss like he wants to embed his need on my skin.

"Believe me, I always fucking want you," he rasps against my lips.

"So have me," I say, voice wobbly.

He pulls back an inch, dropping his forehead to mine and closing his eyes. He lets out a rough, sheepish chuckle. "I, uh, wanted you a little too much during all that."

I blink at him for a moment, our eyes so close together mine cross as I try to process what he said. With a start, I rear back, focus bouncing with delight to his crotch, the outline of his softening erection still visible in his fitted slacks, a dark stain confirming his statement.

Sweet Jesus. Rylie Cooper gets off just from eating pussy.

I grab his face, kissing him hard, and we both start giggling into it. With infinite care, Rylie slides me from the counter, taking his time to undress me, kissing every inch of newly exposed skin. I turn in his arms, doing the same for him. He reaches around me, turning on the shower and letting it warm up, a thick fog hugging around us as we step in.

We hold each other under the hot water, his hands coasting over me in gentle circuits as he murmurs soft, lovely words into my ear, my cheek pressed to his chest as I memorize his heartbeat. We wash like we're one being, never getting further apart than necessary. Only when the water starts to get cold do we reluctantly get out and dry off. We're in sweatpants in no time, and I covertly steal one of Rylie's crewneck sweatshirts.

He stares at me for a moment in his clothes, lips parted, eyes glinting. I can't read everything in his expression because he turns coy, dragging his knuckles across his mouth, hiding a delighted smile.

"Get over yourself," I say, pushing him toward the bed. He falls into the sheets without a fight, pulling me down with him. Settling me so I'm leaning against the headboard, he lays his head on my lap, and I luxuriate in the simple pleasure of playing with the thick locks of his hair, the drag of them through the sensitive skin between my fingers.

Without having to ask, Rylie turns on the TV and pulls up where we left off on my favorite true-crime show.

It's all so simple. So easy. So perfect.

Part of me wants to cry with a sudden, jolting fear that I'll lose this undemanding sense of peace I've found with Rylie like I've lost it with everyone else. Then again, I've never actually had it with anyone else . . .

I refuse to let that fear win. Rylie came back to me. I can't live in fear I'll lose him a second time and miss these perfect moments in that worry. So I hold him closer, pick up his hand and kiss the tip of each finger, then the center of his palm, then place it over my heart, and let the quiet comfort of the TV lull me to sleep with his arms wrapped around me.

Chapter 22

LANDRY'S OFFICE ON THE FORTY-SECOND FLOOR DOESN'T necessarily rank as a safe space for me. I mean, granted, I've never actually been invited this high up in the Soundbites office before—they like to keep me in the basement in the damp, hot-dog-generated humidity—but I still have a rising level of apprehension as the elevator climbs the floors.

Which is ridiculous. Landry got it, she understood where I was coming from when we talked at the fundraiser, even if William wasn't on the same page. If nothing else, this is a strategic planning meeting on how to pivot our refreshed engagement toward other avenues. I shouldn't be stressed, I should be relieved she's actually willing to talk things out further and come to an even firmer understanding. But dread still trickles through me as I step off the elevator and give Landry's assistant my name. There's something about the twitch of his lips, the flash of recognition in his eyes as he types on his computer—alerting Landry of my arrival—that sets my teeth on edge.

I sit in one of the straight-back chairs outside of the executive suites, leg jiggling as the seconds tick by.

"Can I get you any water or coffee?" the assistant asks without looking at me, making it very apparent that saying yes isn't actually an option.

"I'm fine, thanks." Another stretch of silence.

"You've become quite the Soundbites celebrity, huh?" he says, still not bothering to look away from his computer screen. His voice is as smooth and cutting as a razor.

"Um, that's definitely overstating things, but I've had a few recent hits on my segment." I can't tell if he's a loud breather or if he just laughed at me.

He finally looks at me, eyes flicking down my body in lengthy appraisal. His smile makes me think he's tasted human flesh and didn't hate it. "I mean, after this morning's big reveal, I don't think I am overstating things."

I stare at him blankly. "This morning's what?"

He tilts his head, smile growing. The computer dings, and he doesn't bother to look at the screen. "Landry will see you now."

"What did you mean by that?" I say, standing up on shaky legs. He ignores me, slipping in AirPods and turning back to his work. I have the urgent desire to dart to the bathroom, scour my phone for whatever the hell he's alluding to. But I can't. I'm on such thin ice with Landry and William, I can't start chipping at it by making them wait.

With an unsteady hand, I knock gently on the door then

let myself into her office. Landry doesn't say anything when I step inside or bother to look up as I take the seat in front of her. I wonder if her assistant learned the trick from her or vice versa. William leans against the bookshelves behind her desk, suit jacket slung on one of the chairs, the sleeves of his crisp, white button-down rolled up to his elbows. He sweeps an unimpressed glance up my body, toying with the end of his black tie.

"Good morning," I say, trying to make my voice pleasant. It cracks like I swallowed a hot pepper.

Landry's gaze finally flicks up to mine. She stares at me, expression as impassive as her son's. With a slow, assured movement, she leans back in her chair, steepling her fingers in front of her. The only sound in the room is the ticking of her expensive-looking wall clock as the Doughrights pin me with their dark eyes.

When it becomes so tense my skin starts to crawl, I clear my throat. "Is now still a good time to talk?"

William scoffs, adjusting his fancy watch, and my heart rabbits in my chest.

Landry's nod is slow and self-possessed. "I was giving you an opportunity to explain yourself first."

"I'm sorry?"

Her eyebrows rise mockingly, and she shares a look with William. "That's a start, I suppose. Although I would have delivered it with a bit more conviction and less of a question if I were in your position."

"My position?" I'm sweating now, palms damp and sticky as I grip the edges of the chair.

"Are you going to repeat everything I say?"

I stare at her with wide, terrified eyes, trying to formulate a sentence while my throat feels too tight and tongue too swollen to get words out. "I'm . . . I'm a bit confused on what's happening here."

Landry's look is a combination of bored and surly, and she rubs her fingers along her forehead with a sigh.

"Allow me to clarify things for you, Miss Kitt," William says, pushing away from the shelves and planting his palms on the large desk, leaning toward me. "You have this thing called a job. I have one too. And my job is to be your boss. Are you keeping up with me so far?"

I'm horrified to feel myself nodding.

"Good. I was worried even that would be too complex for you." His smile is cold. "Your job is, in essence, to make money for this company. And the best way you can do that is dress in your trendy little clothes and make your sarcastic little comments and shove hot dogs in your mouth to attract male viewers. Your job is also to do as I tell you. And I told you to see this thing through with Rylie Cooper. Why? To make this company money. Still with me?"

The force of his calm anger sucks the air from the room, and I feel lightheaded with how tight my breaths are.

"But you have apparently decided that you are too good to do the job we pay you for," he continues softly. "You flouted our directions in favor of your precious feelings. Not only that, but you *lied*, Eva. You made a fool of me, and in a public place, no less. Do you have any concept of how unflattering it is to have an employee talk back to me at a charity event I've donated tremendous money to on behalf of the company I'm in charge of?"

Heat floods my cheeks, my heart pounding so hard against

my sternum I'm scared I'm going to pass out. "I'm sorry," I choke. "I'm so, so sorry. That wasn't my intention at all. I didn't mean to be disrespectful. I didn't—"

"But you *were* disrespectful," Landry chimes in. Her voice isn't raised or even harsh, just dripping with disappointment. "Everything about this, from your lies to your gall at the fundraiser to initiating a tawdry affair with someone you were engaged in business with and letting it interfere with your work, was disrespectful."

"I'm sorry," I repeat, tears pricking my eyes. Landry acknowledges them with a pitying purse of her lips, but a flash of satisfaction alights on William's face. "I see where you're coming from and I'm sorry. I never intended for anything to happen with Rylie. I swear. But things have started to become real, and I—"

"Things are *real*, are they?" William doesn't use air quotes, but I sense them. "How Pollyanna and adorable. So glad you're going steady and sporting his letterman jacket. But I'd also like to remind you this is the *real* world. You signed up for transparency around this and that's what you were expected to give us. If you had any journalistic integrity and hope of making a name for yourself, that is."

"I do have journalistic integrity," I sob, feeling close to getting to my knees to beg for mercy. I know I'm the smallest fish in the vastest ocean, I know how insignificant I am, but I can't lose this job, I can't lose this chance to actually make something of myself. I'm too attached to the only dream I've ever had to see it shatter to pieces like this.

"I want nothing more than to build a long, meaningful career in journalism," I say, turning to Landry. "But this pop culture beat isn't for me. I'm sorry I messed things up the way I did, but I promise, if given the chance to apply my passion to something I'm interested in, something I really care about, I can do so much more. I'll make it up to you, I swear."

"Oh, Eva, don't you get it?" William's voice is scalding, his smile a hot knife that slices through me when my eyes slide to him. "You're fired."

My blank stare makes him laugh.

"Oh my god, did you not know that? Did you actually think this was a legitimate conversation about you lying to us that you could bargain your way out of?" His laugh is cold and empty. "Stop pretending to be some puppet master when you are, in fact, the strings we pull."

"W-why are you doing this?" My lips tingle, a high-pitched buzzing growing in my ears as I struggle to process everything. "Why did you make me think this would be civil?"

His look of disgust makes me flinch. "It's solely your own naivety that made you think this would be anything other than a well-deserved termination. You lied. You proved yourself financially useless. You are dismissed."

"You can't let him do this," I beg, splaying my palms to Landry in surrender. "Please. Woman to woman here, you have to understand where I'm coming from, right?"

Landry's expression shifts from pitying to patent disbelief. She shakes her head, letting out a cool laugh that matches her son's. "Please don't make this more embarrassing than it needs to be."

"Landry, *please*. You said you saw potential in me. Saw some of yourself in me. I can prove it to you. Please, please, just don't fire me."

"My god, what do you expect me to say?" she says, face twisting. William snorts. "Are you expecting me to chant *girl power* while throwing my fist in the air? This is a *business*, Miss Kitt. Does that not compute? It doesn't have feelings or qualms or guilt about whether you're up to the task of doing what it takes to get ahead. You have proven you are not. We have proven that we are. And that is why we are leading and you are about to file for unemployment. But don't worry, HR will be sending you a severance agreement with a reminder not to share private company information. I'm sure that will ease any difficulties as you look for a new position. Perhaps TMZ is hiring."

I stare at them, tears streaming down my face. William's focus back on his watch, Landry's eyes slipping to her computer.

"Are you—"

"You are *dismissed*," Landry snaps, leaving no room for argument. I scramble to the exit.

"Been a real treat working with you, Eva," William says dryly right before the office door closes behind me.

I stand there for a moment, world spinning, vision swimming. I'm going to be sick, pass out, dissolve right into the floor. It travels to me from a distance, but I register a laugh disguised as a cough from Landry's assistant.

Somehow—as my insides crumble and the scaffolding of my identity crashes down—I manage to walk to the elevators and get in without collapsing to my knees and crying.

I'm frozen as the elevator glides down to the bottom floor. How am I supposed to get off it? Where am I supposed to go? Home? And do what? What am I supposed to do with

the endless, empty vastness of my life that now stretches before me?

My phone vibrates in my purse as I step out of the building's beautiful, grand doors for the last time. In a daze, I fish
my phone out, not processing the sheer number of notifications popping up.

A ton of missed calls from Rylie. And Ray. And Aida.
Texts from them too.

Where are you?

Are you okay?

Please don't panic

We'll figure this out.

Seriously, let me know you're okay.

How do they know? Embarrassment hooks in my chest,
threatening to crack me open rib by rib. Was I truly the only
one who didn't realize I was being fired this morning?

Another text buzzes through. This ones from Rylie.

Eva, honey, please let me know where you are and that you're
okay? I have my team looking into things, but we need to talk. Let
me come to you.

His team? What would his team have to do with my firing?

In a horrible burst of memory, I remember what Landry's
assistant said to me before I went in. With trembling fingers
and hands so slick with sweat that I drop my phone to the sidewalk twice, I search my name and Rylie's. A series of recently
released posts and stories pop up, each thumbnail showing the
same image.

Despite knowing what will happen when I click on the
linked video, the way it will destroy me, I tap it.

It's me. It's Rylie. It's the elevators of the beautiful hotel.

It's his body caging mine against the wall, the arch of my back and desperate thrust of my hips as I press into him. The way he kisses me like he'll consume me. The whimper of need like I hope he will. The way he maneuvers me into the elevator and the greedy way I can't stop touching him.

It's our private moment caught on camera.

And it's trending on the internet.

Chapter 23

MY PLAN IS TO HOLE UP IN MY APARTMENT, DELETE EVERY app, and put my phone in airplane mode for at least a week. I'll curl up in bed and cry about what a fucking idiot I am and how I've ruined my career. I'll scream into my pillow in rage and embarrassment that something so private and personal is circulating in group chats and DMs and, from the limited scrolling I allowed myself on my pitiful walk home, branding me as a slut that sleeps her way to any sort of recognition.

My plan is to ignore everything and everyone, including Rylie, until I can look at my reflection and not want to break the glass.

But Rylie fucking Cooper has a keen knack of disrupting all of my plans, and he only grants me a few hours of solitary confinement before he's knocking on my door.

"I know you're home, Eva," Rylie's muffled voice calls from

the hallway. I gave him a key last week that lets him into the building, and while I appreciate the fact that he didn't use it to come into my apartment, I'd appreciate him a lot more if he left me alone to my misery.

"Go away," I croak back, staring at the peephole from a few feet away. I can't bring myself to look at him. Loneliness curls around me, arms cradling me to its chest as distance stretches between me and him.

"Let me in."

"Don't think I will, thanks."

"Goddammit, Eva. Don't do this. Don't push me away."

An uninvited tear rolls down my cheek. How else will I stay whole unless I push him as far away as possible? How am I supposed to drown in my shame, if not in isolation? Am I expected to let him bear witness to something like that?

But there's a disconnect between my reasoning and my body, and my wobbly legs drag me to the door. I stop in front of it, reaching out a shaking hand, fingertips glancing over the wood before my arm falls to my side. There's a leaden silence. It stretches and bends for so long, I wonder if he's walked away. Part of me hopes he has. Part of me will break if he has. I lean my forehead against the door, a sharp, quick sob breaking out of me before I can bite it back.

"Please, Eva," comes Rylie's fractured beg. "Let me in, sweetheart."

I shouldn't. I'm a mess. This is a mess. I've never felt so succinctly wrecked. I shouldn't let him see me like this.

I internally scream as I watch my hand move to the dead-bolt. I flick it to the left, the snick of the undone lock echoing around me. I stumble back a few paces. I can't do more than that. I can't open that door. I can't willingly give him a clear view of my inadequacies.

My heartbeat stutters, pulse pounding in every joint. With a definitive turn of the knob, the door swings open. Rylie stands there for a moment, only a step inside, his face lined with stress, eyes heavy with weariness. He's drained of his usual spark; I've sucked all the energy from him.

"You're dressed like a bruise," I whisper, eyes flicking up and down his maroon pants and indigo crewneck that says PHILADELPHIA WOMEN'S ROWING SCHUYLKILLS IT.

"Thanks." A smile ghosts across his face. He shuts the door. "It matches how I feel, I suppose."

The silence is back, heavy and weighted, pulling me under. "I'm sorry," I say at last, needing to break up the quiet, a final kick toward the surface before I fully sink under. I stare at the taut lines of his throat, the clench of his jaw, unable to meet his eyes.

"You're sorry?"

I nod, a bone-deep exhaustion carving through me. "Yeah. I'm sorry."

"Sorry for what?"

I let out a surly snort, flicking through my files of self-loathing at a rapid pace. "I'm sorry for all of it. The original stupid video I posted calling you out. Showing up at your place when I knew it was a terrible idea. Talking to Landry and William in the most unprofessional way possible during your friend's beautiful evening. The leaked video of us . . . I'm sorry."

Rylie stays silent, absorbing the reality of the mess I've gotten us into.

"I lost my job," I say, eyes dropping to the floor in embarrassment. "As if all of this couldn't get worse, there's that."

"I wish you would've quit first."

My gaze flashes up to Rylie's and it's a mistake. His gunmetal eyes hook me, holding me. There's so much frustration in his expression. So much disdain.

"Not like I'm a particularly desirable job candidate," I say, voice monotone but laced with self-deprecation. "All I'm good for is eating hot dogs and acting bitchy."

"Stop it." The flare of anger in Rylie's voice makes me flinch, my face falling into a frown. I take a step back. He follows me.

"You stop it," I say, old habits dying hard and a decent response not at the ready.

"No, *you* stop it," he repeats, taking another step. I square my shoulders, meeting him halfway.

"Everything's a mess and it's my fault. Don't tell me to stop when I'm telling it like it is."

"You are delusional," he says, color high on his cheeks, nostrils flaring with the labor of his breathing.

"No, you are," I snap with the petulance of a child. "This will only look bad for you—some lowlife social media wannabe clinging to you and your success and the goddamn kindness of you."

I'll be branded a whore, a fame fucker. The internet has already proven itself relentless and this is candy for the comments section. He'll see what they say about me, he'll get tired of defending my name. I can't ask him to weather this storm when it will undoubtably tear our house to the ground.

Rylie's lip curls in disbelief. "The last thing I care about right now is how this will look for me."

"I think we should break up."

"I know you do."

The calmness of his voice slices me to ribbons, making me blink repeatedly so tears won't fall. I scramble to compose my face, a placid mask so he can't see the hurt. "Cool. Glad you agree. It will all be easier for you to do damage control that way."

Rylie shakes his head, deep lines etched between his eyebrows and around his mouth. "That's not what I said."

"It's what you meant."

"No. It's not."

I go to fight, but he cuts me off, gripping my shoulders with a grounding pressure.

"I meant exactly what I said, Eva." His gives me a gentle shake, and it loosens the knot of tears growing behind my eyes.

"I know you think we should break up," he continues. "I know you think things just got exceptionally messy and the easy thing to do would be to part ways and lick our wounds in private, you adding another layer, another wall, around that heart of yours. Tough shit. I'm saying no."

I gape at him. "You're saying *no*?"

Rylie shrugs, a flicker of a smile passing over his face. "Yup. I'm saying no. You might say you think we should break up, but that's the decision of two people, as far as I'm concerned, and my answer is no. I'll give you space. I'll give you time. I'll give you anything you need as long as you actually need it and you aren't doing it as some self-fulfilling prophecy of disappointment. But I won't agree to breaking up. Sorry."

I squirm out of his grip, scrambling back until I'm on the other side of the living room, my couch a barrier between us. I glare at him with a mix of astonishment and irritation. "Well, that's a really fucking annoying thing to say."

Rylie's face shifts through various unreadable emotions, then settles on soft amusement. "Well, Eva, I hate to break it to you, but right now your hardheadedness is really fucking annoying. So I guess we're even. Doesn't change my decision, though. We aren't breaking up."

I splutter, scraping at the bottom of the barrel for something, anything, that will bring this man to his senses. "Be serious, I'm begging you. The honeymoon phase lasted less than two weeks for us and now we're already back to arguing. This was a social experiment that was doomed from the start. So stop being so obstinate and let it go."

"I love you, you little demon." Rylie storms toward me, eyes lightning bolts. My pulse pounds, panic squeezing a tight fist around my heart and coiling my muscles with the instinct to run. He skirts around the couch. I take a frantic look around the room, but I've backed myself into a corner.

"Do you hear me?" he says, stopping only when his toes are touching mine. Both of his hands come up to face, cradling my head in a gentle but firm grip. "I love you."

"Stop it," I demand, fingers knotting in the fabric of his sweatshirt. I can't tell if I want to push him away or pull him closer.

"No." His voice is a growl. "I love you, and there's nothing you can do to stop me, so you might as well accept it."

"I refuse." Tears slip down my cheeks. I'm horrified to realize my hands have landed on his hips.

Rylie's laugh is a soft puff against my cheek, electrifying and soothing all at once. "I don't care."

He brushes his lips against mine in the gentlest of caresses, and sweetness floods through me. Nonsensical protests tumble from my lips, but he silences them with a firmer kiss, and I open to him, my body trembling as he anchors himself to me, steadying me.

"I love you," he says again.

"You shouldn't."

Rylie pulls back to look at me, and I'm mortified at the way I cling to him. And then I realize that he's still holding me too, just as tightly, one hand pressed against the curve of my spine, the other stroking away the tears from my cheek.

"You are the sharpest, fiercest person I know. I have never been more off-kilter than when you let me into your life. I can't even begin to predict what godless thing you'll say or do next, and I have a very healthy fear of your bad side. And, fuck, I love you. I want to spend every day listening to you be an absolute shithead to me. If at the end of my life someone asked me what I'd do with one more hour, one more minute, I would fight with you. Argue with you. Kiss you and hug you and hold you. Anything for one more second with you. I'd choose this every single time. Because I know you love me too."

I suck in a stuttering breath through my sobs, resting my head against his chest. Rylie tucks me to him, swaying us gently.

"I'm scared to love you," I choke. "I'm scared to feel this much and risk losing you. Risk you realizing I'm not worth it."

"Eva, my love. I've had six years to let you go and decide you're not worth it. Give me six hundred more and it still wouldn't matter. I'm yours. It's okay to be afraid. I'll be brave for us both until you learn to trust it. Trust me." He places a kiss to my temple. "Let me prove it to you." Another on the tip of my sniffling nose. "Let me take care of you." A hot, gentle brush across my lips. "Let me love you."

I'm wrung out from emotions, every cell depleted. But slowly, like a gentle mist swirling through my veins, a new sensation fills me. It's luminous and warm and creates a weightless sensation in my chest. It takes me a moment to realize it's hope.

With a shaky sigh, I seek out Rylie's lips, kissing him, tasting him, luxuriating in the electric spark created with each new press of my mouth to his. A soft hum vibrates low in his throat, and he moves us until our bodies are flush, my back to the wall. With reluctance, I break the kiss, both of us breathing hard.

"While it goes against my nature to give you what you want," I whisper, "your insistence has worn me down."

I feel Rylie's smile against my own, his hands threading through my hair. His rough laugh is equal parts relief and amusement. "I feel like the crewnecks also helped me win you over a bit."

I laugh, then start to cry again. This time in release, deep waves of comfort rippling through my muscles as I hold him tighter. "You never left me any choice but to fall in love with you, huh?"

Rylie nods, forehead brushing mine, and he catches my mouth in a tender kiss.

"I love you so much," I murmur against his skin as his lips create a hot trail along my throat and collarbone. "I have no idea how to do this, but I'm going to try with everything I have."

He retraces his path up, his glasses askew and our noses clashing as we dive in for more. It's such a luxury to love him like this, slow and unhurried, like we have nothing but time.

His words are a promise against my skin: "And that will always be enough."

Chapter 24

"WHAT DO I DO NOW?" I ASK THE NEXT MORNING, SNUGGLED in bed with Rylie. I play idly with the hairs on his chest, and it isn't until he gently flattens my palm against his heartbeat that I realize I was starting to pluck at them in my anxiety.

"With work?" he murmurs, tucking me closer into his side and placing a soft kiss to my hair.

"Work. My identity. My livelihood . . . The simple stuff that people rarely stress about."

"I don't know that your work being tied to your identity is a super-healthy thing."

"Okay. Sure. But you also can't even raw-dog vision so I'm not particularly eager to take life advice from you."

Rylie lets out an indulgent chuckle, the vibrations caressing my cheek. "If journalism doesn't work out, maybe give life coaching a try. You're so gentle and uplifting."

I smile, pressing a kiss to his pec before lightly biting the spot.

"You could do freelance for a while," Rylie offers after a few moments. He traces random patterns along my arm, lulling me into a happy drowsiness where I actually consider the idea. "You've even said yourself that your Babble account has been getting more attention. Maybe figure out how to monetize it or use popular pieces as pitches for different outlets?"

I let out a long breath through my nose, wanting to argue, wanting to point out every idealistic flaw in his plan. But maybe . . . maybe he's right? Maybe I could figure out a way to do that. I'd be pinching every penny and would have to dip into the meager savings I have, but at least it's an immediate plan that doesn't make me want to scream myself into oblivion.

I try to scrounge up the courage to admit I'm considering it, when my buzzer cuts through our golden bubble.

I jolt up, chest tight as my brain trips over itself with who that might be. What kind of heathen shows up unannounced at someone's doorstep . . . besides Rylie. And . . . um . . . me, on occasion.

"Want me to get it?" Rylie asks, voice still groggy with sleep as I'm already scrambling out of bed.

"Hello?" I ask hesitantly, finger on my intercom.

"It's me. Why is your phone turned off?" Aida's voice sends a flood of relief through me, and my weight collapses into the unlock button as I let her in. A few moments later, she's traipsing through my door.

"Oh, hey," she says casually, shucking off her coat. "What's up? Anything new?"

I can't even muster up a good-natured scowl, folding into her outstretched arms as fresh tears start to pour.

"Tell me everything," Aida coos, dragging her hand up and down my back. "Then I have a few things to tell you."

She guides me to the couch, and I fill her in on my firing, the subsequent discovery of the video of me and Rylie. It's all so fresh, so raw, that each word is salt in the gaping wound. For the first time in a long time, I find myself curled up in a ball, my head on Aida's lap, pouring out my heart as she willingly and lovingly comforts me.

"I'm so sorry," she whispers, pushing a tear-dampened strand of hair from my cheek. "That's awful. You don't deserve this."

I cry harder.

"What did you have to tell me?" I finally manage, when my breath is ragged and my tears are all but dried up behind my swollen eyes. With gentle hands, Aida guides me to sitting, repositioning us so we're facing each other cross-legged on the sofa. At the same moment, we become aware of Rylie standing in my bedroom doorway wearing one of my baggy T-shirts and a pair of my pajama bottoms that show off quite a bit of ankle.

"Hey," Aida says, leaning over to pat the seat of the open chair. "You'll probably want to hear this too."

Rylie situates himself, pulling the chair closer so his hand rests on the back of my neck, massaging until I marginally relax.

Aida clears her throat as she decides where to start. "Things seemed weird, at least timing-wise, with all of this," she says, eyes narrowed as she looks up at me. "I guess you could call it a hunch, but I felt something was off with how everything unfolded with Landry being so calm at the fundraiser and then the video being leaked."

Out of the corner of my eye, I see Rylie nod, and Aida keeps going.

"I couldn't shake the feeling that something wasn't right, so I had one of the tech guys at Soundbites do some digging on his off time—"

"A tech bro did you a favor?" I ask, mouth twisting with incredulity. A laugh catches in Rylie's throat.

Aida frowns. "Of course not. I promised him a three-month subscription to Instacart if he helped me. Regardless, I had Brett look into the original video posted on social media and then some of the outlets that first reported on it. He went into all kinds of details that made my eyes glaze over but the important piece is, he traced the IP address of whoever originally leaked the video back to Soundbites."

I stare at her blankly. I am a woman in STEM only in the sexy, tenacious, emotionally malicious sense.

Aida waves my confusion away. "Essentially someone at Soundbites posted the original video and sent it around to media outlets to make sure it was seen."

"Wait, I'm sorry . . . Are you implying William took the video and leaked it?" Rylie asks, dropping his hand from my neck, disgust and rage etching lines on his face I've never seen before.

"Or Landry," Aida says. "Who else at Soundbites would, you know?"

"Um, I don't have a full list but it also wasn't like I was some cherished member of the team there," I remind her.

Aida rolls her eyes. "Okay. Sure. Fair. But look at the time-stamp, dude. It was posted at five fifteen in the morning. Do you know how few people are at Soundbites at that time?"

As someone who drags their feet well past a nine o'clock arrival, I can't tell if this is rhetorical.

"Not many, bitch," Aida says, tiptoeing toward frustration that I can't keep up. "So I had my boy Randy from security—"

"Who the *fuck* is Randy from security?" I ask, getting annoyed that not a single part of this story is explanatory to me.

Aida's resulting frown could reduce most to tears. "Big Randy? You know Big Randy. He works the graveyard shift."

I nod, remembering the jolly, kind man whom I've seen at the check-in desk on evenings I work late. He always dresses up as Santa at the company holiday party.

"Anyway," Aida continues, pace picking up. "I asked him to do me a solid and check the swipe-in logs—"

"He'd do that for you?"

"Big Randy would do anything for anybody. But guess who was one of the few people who had used their badge to swipe in for work before the video was posted? William."

"Holy shit," Rylie whispers, voice scraping from his throat. "Do you really think . . ."

"I'm sorry, but time-out." I straighten holding up my palms. "This is a big accusation first thing in the morning. When did you become some sort of super-tech spy girl, Aida?"

She gives me a dull look. "I try to give things a few hours' worth of thought and fact-finding before sinking into the useless depths of self-pity."

"That might be the most unrelatable thing you've ever said to me."

"It makes sense, Eva," she says, eyes wide and face animated.

"The bar's in hell, but do you really think he'd go this low?" Aida's look speaks for itself. "Okay, sure, maybe *he* would, but surely Landry wouldn't let him?" She treated me like dog shit yesterday, but I have a hard time believing my idol, this woman who's a living legend for breaking barriers in a male-dominated field, would do this to me.

"You need to stop believing she has any goodwill or kind intentions toward anyone but herself and her son. She had a major stake in the success of you two being public with your whole schtick. She's fueling the nepotism pipeline with William, and his success is a reflection of her. She championed the idea, promised big numbers with engagement and dollars, actually saw those projections being met and then some. She and her son had a lot to lose when you said you weren't going to play the game anymore, both financially and their professional credibility with other executives and board members. She probably gave him a gold star and pat on the back for releasing it."

I chew on the inside of my cheek, shaking my head.

"Do you know who immediately reported on the video of you two?" she asks. "Soundbites. The first outlet to pick it up and start circulating. And guess what, the backlist of your other videos has seen an uptick from all this publicity too."

The silence is a heavy weight, grinding into my shoulders as I try to connect all these pieces. I rub my fingers to my temples, the pulse of a headache starting. "She wouldn't do that . . . " The woman I admired so much would have enough decency to spare me this kind of humiliation . . . right? "She wouldn't put me through this just for a corporate pat on the back and continued profits that would dry up eventually, would she?"

The resulting looks from Aida and Rylie answer that.

"I'm turning in my resignation tomorrow," Aida says as I continue to process, my mind a scribble I can't untangle. "I was thinking about waiting it out until she or William inevitably fires me so I could apply for unemployment, but even the fact that this is potentially true is enough. Plus, William and Landry's fucking mind games are too much, all these cryptic and passive-aggressive emails about my performance when we all know I'm damn good at what I do. I can't keep living like this. I'm so stressed I can barely see straight most days."

I nod, my teeth grinding together as visceral memories ping through me. While I hadn't worked with Landry this closely before the incident, I know that Soundbites leadership in general takes a chronic hazing approach. The late-night calls, the cutting remarks, the looks of disappointment—it's all chipped away at me piece by piece until Landry decided to turn me to dust.

"It isn't just us," Aida says in a way that's supposed to be comforting.

In some ways it is. It's not like Landry or any of the other higher-ups handpicked us out of a lineup, deemed us the special ones to torment. But in other ways, it makes it so much worse that we're interchangeable playthings to poke and prod and stretch until we lose our shape and they decide to discard us.

"It's like we're dirt. Someone in the fashion beat even started a chat where everyone shares screenshots of the bullshit sent in emails and chats. Whoever receives the meanest comment gets a free drink at the end of the week."

I jerk back, affronted. "I feel like I missed out on a lot of free drinks by not being included in that."

Aida gives me a warm, loving smile. "You aren't exactly the most approachable when it comes to a camaraderie attempt, babe."

Fair enough. "I mean, I'm glad we're all collectively licking the same festering wound here, but what do we actually *do* about it?"

"You could sue," Rylie offers, as if the idea of even googling how to do that isn't the most time-consuming and overwhelming thing I could ever think of, let alone pursue. "For wrongful termination or something like that."

"This is America. I feel like you can pretty much be fired at any time for anything if your boss has enough power."

"Not if you're being bullied and harassed leading up to it," Rylie says with a sad shrug. "Sorry, just trying to be helpful."

"You think that's what this was?" I ask, blinking as my brain whirrs. "Bullying?"

Rylie stares at me like I have three heads. "I witnessed William forcing you to read horrible things said about you online and record it. And we have pretty decent evidence that he leaked a private video you did not consent to having taken. What part of that doesn't scream *bullying* to you?"

"While the small, awful things add up to a bigger picture of harassment, I could still see so many people calling it hearsay," Aida says in a pragmatic but defeated tone.

Rylie turns fully toward me, his hands coming to my

shoulders. "We know it's not hearsay, Eva. So make people fucking hear it."

"You mean . . . ?"

Rylie's nod is slow. Sure. A support beam in my crumbling life. "If anyone could do it, it's you."

I stare at him, my heart beating in an uneven rhythm, blood stinging as it pumps through my veins to every muscle. What he's saying is ridiculous. Outlandish. A huge risk to the few threads of dignity I have left and my actively deteriorating self-esteem.

Rylie's eyes scour over my face, reading everything there. "I support you no matter what, but I also know you're the best, maybe the only, person to bring justice to all of this."

He believes in me.

Holy hell, *I* believe in me. The thought seems so audacious, so radical, so much bigger than I've ever allowed myself to feel. Rylie doesn't move, doesn't even breathe as I stare at him, gathering my thoughts in rapid, fragmented pieces as I map out a plan. An attack.

Without looking away from his quicksilver eyes, I say, "Aida, think you could add me to that group chat?"

Chapter 25

One month later

Former Soundbites Media employee Eva Kitt has
collected the harrowing stories from various
whistleblowers at the company who suffered from
workplace bullying and harassment by executives, particularly founder Landry Doughright
and her son, William. Furthermore, Soundbites
has released an official statement that they are
utilizing a third party to investigate the
accusations, including the allegation that
William Doughright leaked private photos and
videos of one of the employees to generate media
buzz and traffic to the site . . .

My exposé came out in the *Times* two days ago. It was
quickly picked up by *The Washington Post*, CNN, *USA Today*, and

local news stations. I got an email that the *Today* show might run a segment about the ongoing investigation.

Goddamn, does revenge taste so fucking sweet.

"Were you scared to write the article?" Rylie asks as we finish up our podcast recording. I gave him an exclusive interview because sometimes (rarely) I can be a really good girlfriend. We're live-streaming the episode, the engagement through the roof.

I chew on my lip, giving serious thought to the question. "I wasn't scared to tell the truth, but I was scared about the personal repercussions I'd face."

"What do you mean?"

I give him a mildly sardonic glance. "A video of us making out started circulating at a rapid rate and the vast majority of comments were essentially slut-shaming me for kissing my boyfriend and asserting that any career success I have is because I fucked my way there. A piece looking at a hostile work environment rooted in misogyny and my own experiences with it didn't exactly seem like a safe topic to explore."

Rylie nods, eyes glittering with pride as he looks at me. "I agree, so many of the responses to that video were either congratulatory toward me for being with someone like you, or tearing you down for sharing an intimate moment with someone."

I snort. "It wasn't congratulatory for being with someone *like me*, it was pure and simple locker-room talk asking how I stacked up."

"Fair," Rylie says, expression dipping into a frown. "It was disgusting."

"No shit."

"So why did you do it? Why did you take the risk and write the exposé that you did?"

My heart squeezes as I reflect on the past few weeks, the brutal rush to find out everything I could, the gut-twisting horror at how widely and deeply Landry and other execs had sliced their way through the office for years, belittling people to crumbs in some sick power trip. The crazed anxiety that I wouldn't help anyone in time, wouldn't get their story in front of people fast enough for anything to actually be done.

And then I think of Rylie—his soft, exuberant presence through every second of it. The brush of his thumbs at my cheeks when I'd cry in frustration. The gentle kneading of his fingers along my shoulders and neck as I worked well into the early morning, typing and researching in a desperate hunt to find my own purpose in the pain of it all.

"I did it because I wanted to support other people experiencing the soul-sucking demoralization of working for someone who treats them like less than a person. We've become far too comfortable as a society disregarding the humanity of people and using them as output machines we can abuse until they break." I take a deep breath, eyes locked on Rylie's. I see the glint of affection in his as he gives me the space to keep going. "I felt what it was like to finally be unconditionally supported, and encouraged to demand better for myself, and I wanted to carve out a space for other people to get there too."

Rylie's smile is wide and adoring, sending butterflies through my stomach. "So what comes next for the indomitable Eva Kitt?"

I laugh, a soft, breathy sound that I would have felt embarrassed about two months ago, but now feels as indulgent as chocolate cake, and Rylie's resulting smile is even sweeter.

"I don't know," I answer honestly, glancing at my silenced phone on the table. The screen hasn't stopped lighting up since the article released. Talk show invites and legal threats and painfully honest notes from people who resonate with the story. There were some job offers, even a literary agent inquiring if I had interest in representation for a book of essays based on my Babble posts. "Maybe I'll start a podcast."

Rylie's grin is electric, flooding me with currents of joy. "Hell, you could come on and cohost this one. God knows I could use the help."

"I'm sure I'd add a level of likeability that you're missing."

He laughs so loudly, he has to cover the mic. He keeps his palm cupped over the microphone, using his free hand to guard his mouth from the camera as he whispers, "I like you so damn much, it's impossible to me that anyone wouldn't."

I love you, I mouth, not bothering to hide it from anyone viewing. Everyone should know how lucky I am to love a man like him.

Both of us catch the charge between us, and we wrap up the interview with little style and a lot of stolen smiles. With a definitive click, Rylie shuts off the camera and powers down his phone. I do the same, breezily swiping away the hundreds of notifications before the screen goes black. That's for tomorrow, for future Eva with a career path that isn't nearly as bleak as I thought, but just as scary. The fear doesn't seem to matter as much, not when I have Rylie marching with me.

He crosses the room to me, crooked smile glowing on his

face moments before he swoops me up in a kiss. He holds me, both of us vibrating with the magnitude of what we just did, all that I've said in such a public way.

"I'm so fucking proud of you," Rylie whispers against my neck, tracing his lips up and down. "So fucking amazed to know you."

"Jesus, Rylie, try not to be so stingy with the praise."

He laughs, making an arduous circuit along my jaw, then across my forehead.

"I'm so lucky to know *you*," I say on a sigh, feeling swamped with pleasure. It's cheesy and I'm infatuated and I couldn't care less about anything or anyone but the man layering words and sensations of adoration onto me.

We eventually break for air, giggling like we're teenagers touching each other for the first time. Somehow, I know the feeling will never fade.

"So . . ." Rylie starts, smile shy and cheeks pink. "Want to go on that sixth date?"

My eyebrows furrow, lips still buzzing from his kisses as I fix them into a frown. "And skip over four and five? *Wow*."

Rylie cups my cheeks, laughing as he brushes his nose against mine, filling me with warmth and light and a want so sharp, only a promise of forever can dull the edge. "Easy, Kitten. I'll give you as many dates as you need. You just have to ask nicely."

"Nice isn't really my style."

Rylie looks at me, eyes bright and hopeful and a mirror to every feeling flooding through me as I stare at the man I love.

He kisses me again, slowly at first, then with a bite of hunger, a franticness neither of us are ever able to curb. Need and comfort and hope and desire swirl around us, bringing us closer. He pulls back, indulging my whine of protest with a few quick pecks along my cheeks.

"I wouldn't have you any other way," he whispers, then kisses me some more.

The fucking end

Acknowledgments

I've never had more fun working on a story than this one, and I'm so incredibly thankful for the continued opportunity to write books. Thank you to my editor, Eileen Rothschild, for believing in my work and trusting my process regardless of how many unhinged and incoherent emails I send you. Thank you to my SMPG pub team—Char, Alyssa, Kejana, and Brant—for cheering this book on to the finish line. Huge thank-you to Layla Yuro for being so patient with my many grammar mistakes. I promise not to make them again (but I'm glad you'll be around to catch them when I slip). Endless thank-yous to my agents, Claire Friedman and Jess Mileo. You took me on when I was at my lowest and have breathed new life into my creative process. I, quite simply, appreciate the shit out of you.

Jenifer Prince, you have once again given me the best

cover in the entire history of the world. Your art inspires me endlessly. Kerri Resnick, thank you so much for your keen eye for design and for bringing all this beauty into a book-shaped final product.

Mom, thank you for always laughing at my jokes even when they aren't funny and being ready to talk shit at a moment's notice. I'm the menace I am thanks to you. <3

Tremendous thank-you to my sensitivity readers. Your insight and care were invaluable in crafting these characters. Thank you to Megan Stillwell and Serena Kaylor for saying no every time I asked if a joke went too far. Thank you to Elizabeth Everett, Ali Hazelwood, and Libby Hubscher for backing up Megan and Serena when I ultimately took the question to the larger group chat, then somehow convincing me to push the envelope further. I will direct any complaints about the book to you. Thank you to Jessica Joyce and Ava Wilder for beta reading and holding my hand through many emotional breakdowns over this book. Thank you to Saniya and Emily for being there when the first spark of this idea came to be and for brainstorming so much with me. Your excitement and humor were incredible motivators.

I want to acknowledge and emphasize that I would be nowhere near the author I am today if it weren't for you, my incredible readers. Whether you're a bookseller, a librarian, or an enthusiastic book pusher, your support and sharing of my stories with others is what has made this career sustainable, which is the greatest gift I have (and will) ever receive. My primary goal has always been to write books that make people feel seen, and the outpouring of love you've shown my characters makes that dream feel realized a thousand times over. I'm not sure there's anything else I could ever want for.

And, finally, thank you to my sweet husband. The very first time we met, I was a pink-haired punk who distracted you without mercy in our freshman seminar, then asked you at the end if you wanted to be best friends, to which you responded, "No, you're very weird." It only took me a month to wear you down. Twelve years later, I'm still struck by how special it is that I get to spend my life with someone who loves me exactly as I am, crewnecks and all.

About the Author

Ben Eisdorfer

Mazey Eddings is a *USA Today* bestselling author, dentist, and (most importantly) stage mom to her cats, Yaya and Zadie. She can most often be found reading romance novels under her weighted blanket and asking her husband to bring her snacks. She's made it her personal mission in life to destigmatize mental health issues and write love stories for every brain. With roots in Cleveland and Philadelphia, she now calls North Carolina home.